DALE BROWN

A NOVEL
AIR BATTLE FORCE

HARPER

An Imprint of HarperCollinsPublishers

This is a work of fiction. Names, characters, places, and incidents are products of the author's imagination or are used fictitiously and are not to be construed as real. Any resemblance to actual events, locales, organizations, or persons, living or dead, is entirely coincidental.

HARPER

An Imprint of HarperCollins*Publishers*
10 East 53rd Street
New York, New York 10022-5299

Copyright © 2003 by Air Battle Force Inc.
Excerpt from *Shadow Command* copyright © 2008 by Air Battle Force Inc.
ISBN: 978-0-06-009410-2

First Harper paperback printing: April 2008
First Avon Books paperback printing: May 2004
First William Morrow hardcover printing: June 2003

HarperCollins® and Harper® are registered trademarks of HarperCollins Publishers.

Printed in the United States of America

Visit Harper paperbacks on the World Wide Web
at www.harpercollins.com

10 9 8 7 6

This story is dedicated to the victims of the terrorist attacks on America on September 11, 2001 . . .

. . . and to the courageous men and women around the world who will relentlessly avenge their deaths

ACKNOWLEDGMENTS

Special thanks to Brigadier General Stanley Gorenc, commander of the Ninth Reconnaissance Wing, Beale AFB, for a great tour of his Wing and for setting up the orientation of the future Global Hawk and Predator unmanned reconnaissance aircraft units soon to be located at Beale. Born in Yugoslavia, Stan Gorenc is, I believe, at the top of the new generation of air warriors with the vision, determination, energy, and style to lead the United States Air Force boldly into the twenty-first century.

Special thanks as well to Colonel David Fobian, commander of the 940th Air Refueling Squadron, Air Force Reserve, at Beale AFB. When I served in the Air Force many years ago, I pulled strategic alert at Mather AFB with the 940th, and to be perfectly honest, we active-duty guys resented the laid-back style of the Reservists. In stark contrast, on this recent research trip I found every member of the 940th at Beale to be sharp, professional, and dedicated.

I especially want to salute the crew of the 314th Air Refueling Squadron's "Petro Pony," the most beautiful forty-two-year-old KC-135 aerial-refueling tanker I have ever seen, which flew us to Air Force Plant 42, Nellis AFB, and Indian Springs Air Force Auxiliary Field on this incredible research trip. It was a perfect example of the vital and professional way the Reserves fly and fight these days.

Thanks to Major Bob Couse-Baker, chief of the 940th Air Refueling Wing public affairs; and especially to Captain Mike Strickler, Second Lieutenant Tawny Halvorson, and Second Lieutenant Brady Smith of Ninth Reconnaissance Wing public affairs.

Thanks to Lieutenant Colonel Celeo Wright, commander, and Master Sergeant Jim Koharik, public affairs chief, Air Force Plant 42, Palmdale, California, for leading the tour of the U-2 Dragon Lady spy plane and B-2A Spirit stealth bomber depot maintenance facilities and the Global Hawk assembly facility.

Thanks to fellow B-52 crewdog Colonel Bill Percival, commander of the Ninety-eighth Range Wing, Nellis AFB, Nevada, for inviting us to view the incredible CAPSTONE airpower live-fire demonstration; and to Ms. Martine Ramos, public affairs officer for the Air Warfare Center, Nellis AFB, for her attention and support.

Thanks to Lieutenant Colonel Paul Geier, commander, and Lieutenant Colonel Michael Hake, deputy commander for operations, Eleventh Reconnaissance Squadron, Indian Springs, Nevada, for the orientation and tour of the Predator unmanned reconnaissance aircraft formal training unit.

Thanks to Chief Master Sergeant Bill Wayment, 555th RED HORSE Squadron, Nellis AFB, Nevada, for his pride and professionalism. Definitely a topic for a future novel!

Thanks to Dean and Meredith Meiling for their friendship and generosity.

AUTHOR'S NOTE

Your comments are welcome! Send them to readermail @airbattleforce.com. Individual replies may not always be possible, but I read every message. Thank you!

CAST OF CHARACTERS

Major General Patrick McLanahan, commander,
First Air Battle Force (1 ABF)

Brigadier General David Luger, deputy commander,
First Air Battle Force

Brigadier General Rebecca Furness, commander,
111th Attack Wing; commander, 1 ABF/Air Operations

Colonel Hal Briggs, commander,
1 ABF/Ground Operations

Sergeant Major Chris Wohl, NCOIC, 1 ABF/GO

First Lieutenant Mark Bastian, Ground Ops squad leader

Gunnery Sergeant Matthew Wilde, ABF
Ground Operations

Colonel John Long, 111 AW Operations
Group commander

Colonel Daren Mace, commander, Fifty-first Bomb
Squadron (QB-1A)

Captain William "Wonka" Weathers, munitions chief

Major Samuel "Flamer" Pogue, AC

First Lieutenant Dean "Zane" Grey, AC

Staff Sergeant Marty Banyan, munitions

Senior Airman Todd Meadows, munitions tech

Colonel Nancy Cheshire, commander,
Fifty-second Bomb Squadron (EB-52 and AL-52)

Colonel Kelvin Carter, operations officer,
Fifty-second Bomb Squadron, AL-52 AC

Major Frankie "Zipper" Tarantino, AL-52 MC

Thomas Nathaniel Thorn, president of the United States

Robert Goff, secretary of defense

Richard W. Venti, USAF general, chairman of
the Joint Chiefs of Staff

Douglas R. Morgan, director of Central Intelligence

Edward Kercheval, secretary of state

Darrow Horton, attorney general

Franklin Sellers, secretary of the treasury

Maureen Hershel, deputy secretary of state (Operations), acting secretary of state after Kercheval's resignation

Isadora Meiling, assistant deputy secretary of state, Hershel's assistant

AFGHANS

General (originally Captain) Wakil Mohammad Zarazi, member of the Hezbollah sect of the Taliban, warlord of eastern Turkmenistan

Colonel (originally Lieutenant) Jalaluddin Turabi, Zarazi's second in co-mmand

Abdul Dendara, his aide

Captain (originally Lieutenant) Aman Orazov, Turkmen army and Zarazi's henchman

TURKMEN

Kurban Gurizev, president of Turkmenistan, former chairman of Supreme Council (Majlis, or legislative branch)

Saparmurad Niyazov, former president of Turkmenistan

Lieutenant General Boris Kasimov, Russian liaison to the Turkmen government

RUSSIANS

Valentin Gennadievich Sen'kov, president
of the Russian Federation

Ivan Ivanovich Filippov, minister of foreign affairs

Sergey Yejsk, national security adviser and secretary
of the Security Council

Army General Nikolai Stepashin, commander,
Ministry of State Security
(chief of all intelligence bureaus)

Vladimir Rafikovich, minister of federation
and internal affairs

Alexander Bukayev, minister of defense

General Anatoliy Gryzlov, chief of staff of the
armed forces

Major Boris Bolkeim, Tu-22M-3 bombardier

Captain Mikhail Osipov, Tu-22 DSO

Colonel General Yuri Kudrin, commander, Second
Heavy Bomber Division, Engels Air Base

Colonel General Boris Kasimov, the Russian liaison to
the Turkmen general staff

WEAPONS

AGM-211 "mini-Maverick," small
TV-guided attack missile,
28-pound thermium nitrate (TN) warhead,
glide- and rocket-boosted, 6-mile range

AGM-165 Longhorn TV- and IIR-guided attack missile,
200-pound TN warhead, MMW radar guidance,
60-mile max range, 2,000 pounds each

AIM-120 Scorpion AMRAAM air-to-air missile,
50-pound warhead, 35-mile max range, triple-mode
active radar, passive radar, or infrared,
max speed Mach 3

AIM-154 Anaconda long-range radar-guided air-to-air
missile, 50-pound TN warhead, 150-mile max range,
ramjet engine, active-passive radar/IR guidance,
max speed Mach 5

AGM-177 Wolverine cruise missile, turbojet-powered,
50-mile max range, 3 weapon bays, IIR or MMW radar
terminal guidance

ABM-3 Lancelot air-launched anti-ballistic-missile
weapon, 200-mile max range, plasma-yield or
conventional warheads

REAL-WORLD NEWS EXCERPTS

CAMPAIGN PROVES THE LENGTH OF U.S. MILITARY ARM—*INTERNATIONAL HERALD TRIBUNE,* November 19, 2001—The first phase of the Afghan War so far proves that American military might, including its devastating firepower, can be delivered against targets thousands of miles from the nearest friendly military base. This U.S. military capability is the main lesson being delivered by analysts after last week's campaign destroyed the Taliban's hold on power. . . .

FIGHTING BACK WITH SCIENCE AND TECHNOLOGY— Evan Thomas, *WASHINGTON POST,* November 21, 2001—America faces a new kind of arms race. We must marshal all our scientific and technological expertise to combat those forces that seek America's destruction. . . .

TURKMENISTAN—*DEFENSE & FOREIGN AFFAIRS HANDBOOK* (ISSA, ALEXANDRIA, VA., 2001)— . . . The U.S. Trade and Development Agency on April 23, 1998, agreed to finance a feasibility study of a natural gas pipeline that would run beneath the Caspian Sea, giving Turkmenistan access to the Turkish natural gas market without transiting either Russia or Iran. President Niyazov was guest of honor at the White House in Washington during the signing. . . .

   . . . Defense Minister Khikmatulla Tursunov on September 22, 1998, echoed statements by President Karimov warning of a threat from Afghanistan caused by increased terrorism, religious extremism and worldwide drug trafficking which could spill over into neighboring states. . . .

HIGH-TECH WEAPONS CHANGE THE DYNAMICS AND THE SCOPE OF BATTLE — *INTERNATIONAL HERALD TRIBUNE,* December 28, 2001

The main battlefield lesson learned from the Afghan War is that small U.S. combat teams on the ground and high-performance aircraft with precision-guided weapons can be coordinated under almost any circumstance. The devastating aerial attacks on Taliban and al Qaeda targets give testimony to the effectiveness of high-tech warfare practiced by U.S. forces. . . .

THE POSITION OF TURKMENISTAN IN THE LIGHT OF AN INTERNATIONAL COALITION AGAINST TERRORISM — MAYSA MAMEDOVA — www.gundogar.com, 1/26/2002

. . . The U.S. Department of State admitted that a high level U.S. delegation led by the Under Secretary of State John Bolton traveled to Central Asia, while the U.S. Secretary of State Colin Powell met Kazakhstan's Foreign Minister and communicated via telephone with the Presidents of Turkmenistan and Uzbekistan. These efforts resulted in the following agreement: all of the concerned states, except Turkmenistan, would provide assistance to the U.S., from the use of their ground bases for humanitarian operations only to the use of their airspace and additional facilities on the ground. . . .

JAMES ROCHE, SECRETARY OF THE U.S. AIR FORCE — *BUSINESSWEEK,* February 11, 2002

USAF Secretary James Roche has shown flashes of inspiration during the war on terrorism. He electronically linked AC-130 gunships with unmanned Predator drones and created an even more devastating weapon. His ultimate goals include creating an Air Force capable of locating and tracking a single moving target, such as a tank, and instantly destroying it with precision bombing. That would help keep down the number of civilian casualties that occur during war. . . .

U.S. UNDERTAKING GENERATIONAL WEAPONS SHIFT—STRATFOR, WWW.STRATFOR.COM, 3 MAY 2002—A recent Defense Department decision to kill a costly artillery system program represents the start of a generational shift in weapons systems. . . .

. . . The key representatives of this new breed of system are cruise missiles and other reusable unmanned aircraft. As the range and speed of these systems increase, it will be possible to carry out the mission of delivering munitions without a massive forward deployment of men and matériel. . . .

REPORTED CRASH OF SPY PLANE BODES BADLY FOR U.S.—STRATFOR, WWW.STRATFOR.COM, 12 JUNE 2002—A U.S. unmanned aerial vehicle (UAV) crashed near Qorveh in the Iranian northwestern province of Kordestan in late May, according to Iranian media sources June 12. . . .

. . . If the United States is supplementing its satellite surveillance on these facilities by committing unmanned vehicles to conduct real-time, low-level reconnaissance, this may be a sign that the administration is preparing to evoke its emerging "preemption" and "defensive intervention" strategic doctrine and may be preparing to strike Iranian WMD facilities. . . .

U.S. USING TURKMEN OPPOSITION TO PRESSURE PRESIDENT—STRATFOR, WWW.STRATFOR.COM, 25 JUNE 2002—U.S. officials appear to be giving cautioned support to opposition leaders seeking Turkmen President Saparmurad Niyazov's ousting. Washington is likely trying to send a message to Turkmenistan's authoritarian ruler to let U.S. military forces and businesses into the country. Niyazov is likely to follow his survival instincts and accede to some U.S. demands to preserve his regime.

. . . But the U.S. interest in the opposition reflects a deeper American interest in Turkmenistan's gas and oil. This interest is unlikely to die, meaning some changes in the regime are likely. Niyazov knows what to do to ensure his survival, and when American pressure intensifies he will likely make a deal with Washington. Introducing democracy would not be in the cards, but some U.S. military presence and concessions to Western investors would.

"HEAVYWEIGHT CONTENDER," BY JOHN A. TIRPAK, *AIR FORCE MAGAZINE,* JULY 2002— . . . Air Force Secretary James G. Roche has suggested that a very large UCAV [Unmanned Combat Air Vehicle]—bomber-size—might be a good idea, since bombers typically go after fixed targets, which can easily be programmed into a UCAV's flight plan. Moreover, bombers in Afghanistan orbited the battlefield waiting to be called on to precisely deliver ordnance. Such a mission might be well-suited to an air refuelable, large-scale unmanned vehicle, Roche suggested. . . .

RUMSFELD WEIGHS NEW COVERT ACTS BY MILITARY UNITS—THOMAS SHANKER AND JAMES RISEN, *NEW YORK TIMES,* 12 AUGUST 2002—Defense Secretary Donald H. Rumsfeld is considering ways to expand broadly the role of American Special Operations forces in the global campaign against terrorism.

. . . Proposals now being discussed by Mr. Rumsfeld and senior military officers could ultimately lead Special Operations units to get more deeply involved in long-term covert operations in countries where the United States is not at open war and, in some cases, where the local government is not informed of their presence. . . .

PROLOGUE

GHOWRMACH BORDER CROSSING, NEAR ANDKHVOY, FARYAB PROVINCE, NORTHERN AFGHANISTAN
January 2003

Captain Wakil Mohammad Zarazi deployed two of his youngest, most inexperienced—and therefore most expendable—troops right beside the road for the ambush, promising them promotions and high honors if they survived—and a place at the right hand of God if they were killed. Yes, they still believed they would get both.

The boys hid behind piles of snow and rocks until the lead armored personnel carrier, an old Russian-made BMP, cruised by, and then they threw RKG-3 antitank hand grenades under the chassis. When the grenades were rolled under the BMPs, they righted themselves, then fired copper-sheathed, high-explosive, hollow-charge warheads up into the crew compartment. The molten copper blew through the ten-millimeter armor underneath and spattered molten copper throughout the crew compartment, instantly killing any soldiers inside. The BMP died quickly and messily—and, Zarazi hoped, all on board did, too.

His men, emboldened by the success of this first attack, streamed out of their hiding places and went on the attack, hitting the other vehicles in the convoy with small-arms fire. To Zarazi, the company commander of the guerrilla forces that surprised this small United Nations detachment, the apparent success of the hastily planned ambush was unexpected. His men had been on the move for months in some of northern Afghanistan's worst weather; they were cold, tired, starving, and low on ammunition, morale, and courage, continually hounded by American and United Nations air forces.

Maybe they had such clear success because starving men made fiercer fighters—if they didn't succeed, they were dead.

Their intelligence said this detachment, moving west from Andkhvoy since just yesterday to set up a communications relay site somewhere along the border, would have better security. Zarazi's unit was well below full company strength, but they hurried to be in position to make this ambush anyway because of the chance to capture some superior weapons and vehicles to use in their guerrilla war against the Northern Alliance. Zarazi was disappointed at the small size of the detachment—he was hoping for more weapons and more captives. He might get only fifty captives and a few weeks' worth of food and supplies out of this convoy. Still, it was better than nothing.

Zarazi was suspicious, too—a quality that had kept him alive for most of his thirty-eight years, twenty-two of them as a Taliban freedom fighter. Zarazi was born in northwest Afghanistan near Sheberghan. Originally members of the Mujahidin guerrilla fighters that battled the Russians, Zarazi's tribe refused to join the so-called Northern Alliance, composed mostly of ethnic Uzbeks, Tajiks, and Pakistanis, and instead took large numbers of Russian weapons and vehicles and moved back to the tribe's historic provinces in the northwest. Zarazi became a provincial commander of the Hezbollah, or "Army of God," a radical and fundamentalist sect of the Taliban regime, and continued to harass the Northern Alliance forces at every opportunity.

This substantial and apparently important detachment, moving thirty kilometers west of Andkhvoy toward the northeastern edge of the Bedentlik wastelands on the Turkmenistan-Afghanistan border, presented the perfect opportunity to make a major strike against the Northern Alliance and its Western puppet masters. Still, it was strange they had no heavy armor or helicopter support anywhere nearby. The closest helicopter base camp was twenty minutes away; the closest large military base was over an hour away by helicopter. And with some bad weather closing in—a sandstorm, most likely—help would take even longer to arrive.

The intelligence data was remarkably detailed and timely as well—maybe too detailed and timely. Although the Northern Alliance forces, aided by the United States, had effectively wiped out the Taliban militias in this area, Zarazi thought it strange that the United Nations would dare send such an important detail so far away from their strongholds without support. The Taliban still had a large and for the most part well-equipped and viable guerrilla force, especially near the Uzbekistan and Tajikistan frontiers, where friendly forces were more plentiful and the terrain more hospitable. The Turkmenistan-Afghan frontier was nothing but desert for a thousand kilometers— obviously the United Nations forces never thought they would encounter any resistance out here in the wastelands.

The infidels' overconfidence would be their downfall.

The scout vehicles deployed in front of the column were Russian BTR-40 and larger BTR-60 wheeled reconnaissance vehicles, fast and nimble and very well armed.

They turned and scattered as soon as the first BMP exploded. Zarazi's men started lobbing smoke grenades from all over the area—it took dozens of the things to create enough of a screen in the ever-increasing, swirling winds, but within moments visibility had been cut to just a few yards. The gunports were already open, the soldiers inside looking for targets.

That was exactly what Zarazi was waiting for. His men dashed out from their hiding places under cover of the smoke, jumped aboard the BTRs, and stuffed tear-gas grenades into the open gunports. Within moments the drivers were forced to stop their vehicles to evacuate the soldiers inside before they were asphyxiated by the noxious gas. Soon all of the vehicles in the convoy were stopped, billowing with tear gas. The hatches and doors opened, and terrified and nearly suffocating United Nations soldiers and workers dashed out, their eyes swollen and burning. The battle took less than five minutes. Zarazi's men had destroyed one BMP and one BTR and captured one BMP, four BTR scouts, and four five-ton trucks loaded with supplies. No casualties. Perfect.

"We hit the mother lode, Captain," Zarazi's lieutenant, Jalaluddin Turabi, said a few moments later as the crews and workers were being herded together. "Looks like they were going to set up a semipermanent outpost. They have two weeks' worth of food for about fifty men, plus boxes labeled 'Communications Equipment.' I see power generators, fuel tanks, cold-weather tents and clothing, and fencing material. This stuff will sell for millions on the black market!"

"Stop gawking and start unloading those supply trucks, Jala," Zarazi snapped. "If this detail has air support nearby, they'll be on us any minute. We need to be out of here as soon as possible."

The United Nations soldiers were lined up kneeling in

the snow, hands on their heads. Captain Zarazi paced back and forth in front of them, studying each man and woman carefully. Many nations were represented, mostly from the Northern Hemisphere: Canada, Northern Ireland, Norway, South Korea. Zarazi allowed his men to strip off the peacekeepers' gloves, scarves, and parkas—many of his men had perished in the Turkestan and Selseleh'ye Mountains due to exposure, and keeping warm was more important than eating to most of them.

"I am Captain Wakil Mohammad Zarazi, servant of God and commander of the Balkh Armed Resistance Regiment," Zarazi said in Pashtun. He noticed the uncomprehending stares, then said in halting English, "Who is interpreter?" There was no reply. Zarazi continued to examine the captives, finally coming across one soldier in the robin's-egg blue helmet, but with a beard, who appeared to be Afghan. Zarazi dragged him to his feet. "Do you understand me?" The man nodded. "Who is the commanding officer?" He did not respond. Zarazi pulled a long knife from his belt, turned the interpreter, and raised the blade to his throat.

"Stop," a voice said. Zarazi looked around as one of the officers kneeling right beside the interpreter got to his feet, his bare hands still on top of his helmet. "I am Major Dermot O'Rourke, Republic of Ireland, commander of this detachment. We are on a peaceful mission on behalf of the United Nations Afghan Relief and Rehabilitation Council."

After the interpreter translated, Zarazi said, "You are spies for the Northern Alliance and their wild dogs from the United States of America, invading territory claimed by his holiness Mullah Mohammad Omar and his sword of vengeance, General Takhir Yoldashev."

"We are not spies," O'Rourke said. "We are here to set up a cellular phone and radio-relay site, that's all."

"You are spies, and you will all be executed according to the laws of Islam and under the orders of General Yoldashev," Zarazi said. "You—"

Just then Zarazi's lieutenant came running up to him. "Wakil, there's trouble," Turabi said. He ran past Zarazi and over to O'Rourke, yanked his beret from his head and stripped off his jacket, searching him. Moments later he pulled a small black box on a wire out of the back of the man's battle-dress uniform jacket.

"What is it, Jala?" Zarazi asked.

"Our communications officer picked up some kind of high-frequency transponder that was just activated," Turabi said. "It looks like a sort of radio beacon. He must've set it off when the convoy was attacked."

"A trouble signal?" Zarazi asked. "We've detected no other forces in this area. And a helicopter patrol would take hours to come from Andkhvoy or Mazar-e-Sharif. What good would it do . . . ?"

"An air attack—with a jet already in the area, covering the convoy," Turabi said. "That's why our intelligence was so detailed and why this convoy was so poorly protected—it's being covered from the air. It might even be one of those American Predators, the unmanned little aircraft that can fire Maverick missiles. They could be starting their attack *right now*."

Zarazi looked at the officer in puzzlement—and then his eyes grew wide and his mouth dropped open. "Get the men ready to get out of this area and take cover." He stepped over to O'Rourke. "Who is watching us? What is happening?"

"I'd advise you to surrender, Captain," O'Rourke said. "Just lay down your weapons, put your hands in the air, and kneel down. They won't attack if you surrender."

"Who are 'they'? *What* are they?"

"There's no time for questions, Captain. Surrender right now."

"Bastard! Unholy bastard!" Zarazi pulled his sidearm and shot O'Rourke in the forehead, killing him instantly.

Several of his men had started unloading crates and removing tarps from pallets in the back of the supply trucks. "*Run for your lives!* Get away from those trucks! *Run!*"

Four hundred miles away, orbiting at twenty-eight thousand feet fifty miles south of the Pakistani coastline over the Arabian Sea, an EB-1C Vampire orbited lazily, watching and listening. The EB-1C was a U.S. Air Force B-1B Lancer long-range bomber, built in the mid-eighties, but it had been upgraded and modified so much since then that its builders would probably never recognize it now. But as incredible as the Vampire was, the aircraft it controlled were even more amazing—in fact, they represented Patrick McLanahan's future of aerial combat.

"Oh, my God, they killed Major O'Rourke," U.S. Air Force Major General Patrick McLanahan said in disbelief. He studied the high-resolution digital video display on a large, multifunction "supercockpit" monitor before him. "That bastard! He was unarmed! He surrendered. . . ." He closed his eyes for a moment, hoping the image he saw would go away. When it didn't, his hate bubbled up past the boiling point. "I count about a hundred men, about two dozen Toyota pickups off away from the road. Stand by to attack."

His aircraft commander, U.S. Air National Guard Brigadier General Rebecca Furness, squirmed restlessly in her seat. "Let's get busy and nail those suckers, sir," she spat.

The images Patrick and Rebecca were watching were

coming from a StealthHawk Unmanned Combat Air Vehicle, or UCAV. It had been launched several hours earlier from the EB-1C Vampire's forward bomb bay and had been scanning the area around the United Nations truck convoy with its infrared sensors and high-resolution digital cameras. The StealthHawk resembled a big, wide, fat surfboard, its lifting-body fuselage slightly triangular in profile. There was a large air inlet, mounted atop the fuselage to lower its radar cross-section, for the aircraft's single turbofan engine. It had no wings—the StealthHawk had a special flight-control system called a "mission-adaptive lifting-body skin" that actually used computers and tiny microhydraulic actuators to change the outer skin on the fuselage to increase or decrease lift as necessary. The EB-1C could carry three StealthHawks in its bomb bays, one in the forward bomb bay and two in the center. Each StealthHawk could carry a payload of five hundred pounds, along with enough fuel for several hours of flight.

Patrick touched a control button and spoke, "Stealth-Hawk, commit attack," and the fight was under way. Orbiting at ten thousand feet over the truck convoy was a second StealthHawk, launched from the EB-1C's center bomb bay. Instead of sensors this one carried weapons— six AGM-211 "mini-Mavericks," hundred-pound, short-range, precision-guided attack missiles.

"Commit StealthHawk attack, stop attack," the computer responded. When Patrick did not countermand the order, the computer added, *"StealthHawk engaging."*

"Excellent," Patrick said. "StealthHawk reporting code one so far."

"Then that would be a first for one of Masters's gadgets," Furness said dryly. Rebecca Furness was the wing commander of the one and only EB-1 Vampire squadron in the world, the 111th Bombardment Wing of the Nevada Air National Guard based at Battle Mountain Air National

Guard Base. Although the Vampire bomber had been used in several conflicts and skirmishes around the world in recent years, from Korea to Russia to Libya, it was still considered experimental, and therefore the aircraft's designer, Dr. Jon Masters, worked closely with Furness's unit to make improvements and fixes to the state-of-the-art weapon system to get it ready for initial operational capability.

But Jon Masters, a Ph.D. since the age of thirteen and a world-class aeronautical and space engineer, was also a world-class pain in the ass—not exactly a people-friendly person. Rebecca's job was hard enough—standing up a new unit with an experimental high-tech bomber at a newly constructed air base in the middle of nowhere in north-central Nevada—without the nerdy and conceited Dr. Masters disrupting her life.

Although Patrick received the sensor data from the StealthHawk on the supercockpit display in the Vampire bomber, the StealthHawk had already identified most of the vehicles in the target area and had presented its target priority list to Patrick continuously during its surveillance. "The StealthHawk detected a twenty-three-millimeter antiaircraft gun on one of the Toyota pickups," Patrick said. "That's the first target."

Even Rebecca had to be impressed with the StealthHawk system's target-detection and classification capabilities—she was accustomed to dropping bombs on a group of vehicles or an entire area, not selecting just one vehicle out of many similar vehicles for attack.

"I count ten vehicles total in the target area—no, make that twelve. Two have already bugged out."

"What's it waiting for? Get it in there, and let's make some scrap metal."

"It's already on the job," Patrick said. At that moment the StealthHawk released a single mini-Mav missile from its internal bomb bay. The missile fell away from the StealthHawk, gliding toward its target while it adjusted its track with lead-computing cues and wind-drift-correction information datalinked from the Vampire's attack computer. When about a mile from its quarry, the missile's small rocket motor fired, and the missile covered the last seven thousand feet of its attack run in less than two seconds. The mini-Mav's warhead was twenty-eight pounds of thermium-nitrate-energized high explosive, which had the power of ten times its weight in TNT. The truck and its six occupants disappeared in a cloud of dust, smoke, and yellow-red explosions.

The StealthHawk's laser radar remained locked on to the target for postattack analysis, but from the large secondary explosions and size of the smoke and fire clouds surrounding the target, it became clear only seconds later that the truck was toast. "Target appears to be destroyed," Patrick said.

"Damn, I'll say," Rebecca breathed as she watched the last moments of the StealthHawk's bomb-damage assessment on Patrick's multifunction display. She had a lot of experience with the thermium-nitrate explosives and knew that that same mini-Mav missile could take out a main battle tank—"overkill" was a gross understatement when describing a thermium-nitrate warhead hitting a little Toyota pickup. "Pretty awesome weapon."

"StealthHawk engaging the second pickup," Patrick said. "Missile two away. . . ."

The StealthHawk leveled off two thousand feet above the ground and headed for its second target, a column of two Toyota pickups filled with guerrilla soldiers. This time the occupants saw it coming. *"Split up! Split up!"* Zarazi screamed. He raised his AK-74 rifle and opened fire, and the other five men in the back of the pickup opened fire as well.

It was like looking down the barrel of a gun just before the trigger was pulled—and then realizing the barrel was pulled away right at the very last second. Moments after Zarazi's truck veered away, the first truck disappeared under a tremendous explosion. Zarazi and the guerrillas in the second pickup saw the other pickup emerge from the cloud of flame and smoke looking as if the truck had been blasted apart by a giant shotgun, set afire, and then tossed across the ground. "Allah, have mercy," Zarazi muttered. "Allah, get us out of this, and I promise I will avenge myself on the infidels that send these demon robot planes to kill your faithful servants—I swear it!"

"Oh, *baby!*" Patrick exclaimed. The mini-Mav's infrared sensor clearly showed the second pickup truck and its terrified occupants as the missile homed in. At least six automatic rifles were firing at both the mini-Mav and the second StealthHawk, but it was too late. He switched to the first StealthHawk's imaging-infrared camera as the mini-Mav missile hit, and its picture disappeared. Tires, engine, fuel tank, ammunition, and bodies exploded in perfect unison, and the truck cartwheeled in a cloud of fire across the wasteland. "Got the sucker!"

"Got one more truck trying to get away!" Furness exclaimed. "He knows we're on his tail, and he's hauling ass."

"Don't worry, the StealthHawk has lots of ammo and fuel," Patrick said. "That third truck is toast." Patrick entered commands to launch a third mini-Maverick . . .

But instead of the missile's releasing and gliding to its target, the StealthHawk UCAV itself started to descend.

"Check altitude . . . altitude two thousand . . . check altitude, altitude two thousand . . . Shit, I think I lost contact with the UCAV."

"Well, at least we get a ringside seat for the impact," Rebecca said. But the unmanned air vehicle didn't make impact—instead it leveled out at two hundred feet above-ground, clearly in view of the Taliban fighters below, and began flying westward. "Okay, General, where in hell is it going?" Rebecca asked.

"Damned if I know," Patrick replied. "But it'll run out of fuel in forty minutes."

"Another one bites the dust."

"But it might *not* bite the dust. It might make a nice soft landing in the desert," Patrick said worriedly. "And if it does . . ."

"Then those Taliban goons or anyone else who gets their hands on it will have themselves the latest in American UCAV technology," Rebecca said. "In forty minutes it'll be halfway to the Persian Gulf. Can't you self-destruct it?"

"I have no control over it at all," Patrick said. He thought for a moment; then: "Follow it."

"What?"

"Maybe if we can get closer to it, it'll respond to our direct datalink signals." He spoke commands into the computer, and the heading bug on Rebecca's multifunction display swung westward. "There's your heading bug. Center up."

"No way, General," Rebecca said. "That'll take us over . . . hell, General, that heading takes us over Iran!"

"We'll stay in the mountains—fly some terrain-avoidance altitudes," Patrick said. "We've got to cut off that UCAV before we lose it."

"We're not authorized to fly over Pakistan, and we're sure as hell not going to overfly Iran," Furness repeated.

Because the United States had had to take the "war on terror" into its former ally, Pakistan, to hunt down the last remaining Taliban and Al Qaeda terrorist cells, a rift had developed between the two nations. Pakistan now prohibited overflights by any military aircraft, and it regarded any military combat aircraft flying over Afghanistan as hostile.

Despite this ban, President Thomas Thorn had authorized McLanahan to launch a StealthHawk unmanned aircraft to patrol Afghanistan, even though it obviously had to overfly Pakistan to reach its patrol area. One or two unmanned aircraft flying over a remote part of Pakistan were not a threat—at least that would be the Americans' argument, if the stealthy UCAVs were ever discovered.

But a high-tech B-1 bomber was a completely different story.

"General, we can't remain hidden long enough," Rebecca argued. "We stay in the mountains a short time, but eventually we get over the desert, and there's nowhere to hide. . . ."

"Rebecca, it's now or never," Patrick insisted. "If we fly over the Mach above the unpopulated areas and slow down near the populated areas, we'll catch up to the StealthHawk in about twenty minutes. We'll have just enough time to get it turned around before we have to bingo and refuel."

"Get approval from the Pentagon first."

"There's no time," Patrick said. "Center up on the bug, push it up to Mach zero point nine, and descend to COLA to penetrate the coastline. I'll get a new intel satellite dump, and we'll pick the best course."

"Oh, God, here we go again," Rebecca muttered as she commanded the bomber to accelerate and descend to COLA, or Computer-generated Lowest Altitude. The flight-control system commanded a twenty-degree nose-down pitch, automatically sweeping the EB-1's wings all the way back and altering the curvature of the fuselage to gain as much speed as possible.

As soon as they headed northward, the threat-warning receiver blared, *"Caution, SA-10 search mode, ten o'clock, one hundred ten miles, not in detection threshold."*

"The Iranian coastal-defense site at Char Bahar," Patrick said. "No factor."

" 'No factor,' huh?" Rebecca retorted. "Aren't those things capable of shooting down a bomber-size aircraft at treetop level?"

"Not *this* bomber, it won't." They were headed for the Pakistani coastline between the towns of Kapper and Gwadar, just fifty miles east of the Iranian border—well within range of the high-performance SA-10 antiaircraft missile system—but the threat-warning computers measured the signal strength of the search radar and determined that it was not strong enough to get a good reflection from the stealthy EB-1C Vampire. "Keep going." He keyed his secure command satellite net's mike button. "Control, Puppeteer."

"We see it," Patrick's friend and deputy, Brigadier-General David Luger, replied. Luger, a fellow navigator and aeronautical engineer who had been partnered with Patrick since their early days in B-52 bombers, was watching the mission from the "virtual cockpit," a system that displayed all of the EB-1C Vampire's flight information on computer screens back home and allowed crews and technicians there to monitor and even partially control the actual flight mission. "I've issued recall instructions to the surveillance StealthHawk—it'll ditch itself in the Arabian Sea, and the Navy will retrieve it for us. Still no contact with the strike StealthHawk—it's still operating normally, still looking for targets but not responding to satellite steering commands.

"I've got a call in to the State Department," Luger went on. "I *strongly* recommend not crossing the Pakistani border until you get permission. Do I need to remind you about your Russia mission?"

"You do not," Patrick said. The last time he'd been in a bomber, an EB-52 Megafortress over southwestern Russia, he made a decision to violate orders to help a special-ops mission in trouble—and that decision had almost cost him his life. "Put in a call to Hal and Chris, too," he said.

"They're monitoring everything and are briefing up an insertion mission," Luger said. Stationed in the Gulf of Oman on board a large civilian freighter was Patrick's backup rescue team: Hal Briggs, Chris Wohl, and ten highly trained commandos, outfitted in Tin Man electronic battle armor. Hidden in the freighter's cargo hold was an MV-32 Pave Dasher tilt-jet aircraft, an MV-22 Osprey tilt-rotor aircraft modified with jet engines to give it more range, speed, and load-carrying capability. With a range of over two thousand miles, air-refuelable, and with the capability of flying below radar, the Pave Dasher was the ideal way to insert rescue or attack troops deep inside hostile territory. "They're working several problems: They'll be right at the extreme range of the Pave Dasher— the farther the StealthHawk flies into Turkmenistan, the more problematic the situation becomes, and there's some pretty bad weather closing in."

"Let me know what they say," Patrick said. "If there's any way they can try it, I want it done."

"Stand by," Luger said.

Rebecca Furness rolled her eyes in exasperation. "We can't 'stand by,' " she said. "We'll be feet-dry in"—she glanced at her navigation display and muttered—"now. We're in violation of I don't know how many international laws."

"The SA-10 is down," Patrick told her. "They lost us.

No other threats detected, just search radars, all below detection levels."

"Bad news, Muck," Luger radioed a few minutes later. "The weather is getting worse down there in eastern Turkmenistan. Hal says it's your call."

"What do you think, Texas?"

"If it was to pick up any of our guys, no question," Luger replied. "But to pick up a two-thousand-pound UCAV from across a hostile border in Turkmenistan, with the Pakistanis, Iranians, and maybe the Russians looking on? Sorry, Muck. I don't think it's worth the risk."

"General?" Rebecca Furness asked. "You lost it. Let's get back over the Arabian Sea, get our gas, and go home."

"Just keep going," Patrick said. "We're clear of the Pakistani coastal-defense sites—take it up to Mach one point one, five-thousand-foot clearance plane."

"This is not a good idea," Rebecca said—but she found herself pushing up the throttles anyway.

"I'm running your range numbers," Luger radioed, studying the fuel-flow data being transmitted to him via satellite from the Vampire. "At your current fuel consumption, and assuming you don't take extra time retrieving the StealthHawks or dodging air defenses, you'll be almost at emergency fuel state at the scheduled refueling control point. If you couldn't tank, you might not have enough fuel to make it to Diego Garcia."

"Copy," Patrick responded.

They skirted along the Iran-Pakistan border and descended to three hundred feet terrain-following, giving an extremely wide berth to the Iranian border city of Zahedan, which had the largest fighter-interceptor wing in all of Central Asia. They detected more SA-10 surface-to-air units and several short-range, radar-guided antiaircraft artillery units situated along the border—they all had their search-and-acquisition radars on full power. Soon they also detected Iranian fighters—more than a dozen of them, a mixture of French, Russian, and even former American jets. "Damn, we've got the entire Iranian air force looking for us," Rebecca said.

"The closest one is forty miles away," Patrick said, "and he doesn't have us. The Iranian jets aren't crossing the border either."

Just then one Iranian MiG-29 surprised them—he suddenly turned directly toward them, illuminating them with his radar, and headed quickly east, crossing the Pakistani border near the town of Saindak. *"Caution, MiG-29 search mode, nine o'clock, thirty-three miles, high, below detection threshold,"* the threat-warning computer reported.

"General . . ." But the Vampire bomber had already responded—it activated its radar trackbreakers and unreeled the ALE-55 fiber-optic towed decoy from a fairing in the tail. The ALE-55 was a small, bullet-shaped device that transmitted jamming and deception signals to hide the bomber and deflect any incoming threats away from it. It was a very effective but definitely last-ditch device to help the bomber escape if it was under direct attack. "We will *never* launch on a mission ever again without having defensive weapons on board, I promise you that," Rebecca went on. The Vampire could carry a wide array of defensive air-to-air missiles, from short-range Stingers to extremely long-range Anaconda missiles—but this wasn't supposed to be an attack mission.

"Pakistani search radar, three o'clock, forty miles," Patrick reported. "Well below detection levels."

"Warning, MiG-29 tracking mode, nine o'clock, twenty-five miles."

"Trackbreakers active," Patrick reported, punctuating the report with a curse. The trackbreakers could spoof and interfere with the fighter's tracking radar but would also tell anyone around them that a warplane was in the area—and enemy fighters might be able to track the origin of the jamming signal or fire a missile with the ability to home in on the signal.

"Puppeteer, this is Control," Luger radioed. "Step it on down to COLA and head northeast. He doesn't have a solid lock on you yet."

Patrick studied the large supercockpit display on his forward instrument panel. The terrain to the northeast near the Pakistan-Afghan border was completely flat, with several dry lake beds farther north. A bomber the size of a B-1, even as stealthy as it was, would be easy to track against a flat desert from a MiG-29 chasing it from above. The MiG-29 also had an advanced infrared sensor that could spot the B-1's red-hot engines over twenty miles away—it wouldn't need its radar to attack.

"Hard left ninety-degree turn," Patrick said.

"What? You want me to turn toward Iran?"

"If we get caught in the open, we'll be a sitting duck," Patrick said. "We'll stay in the higher terrain to the west." Rebecca did not argue further but turned sharply left. The tactic worked. Once they turned ninety degrees from the MiG-29's course, the MiG's pulse-Doppler radar detected no relative speed difference and squelched out the radar return. "The MiG broke lock," Patrick reported. "He's moving to seven o'clock, twenty-five miles. We're out of his radar cone."

They weren't out of the woods yet, but soon they left the fighters from Zahedan behind them. There were still several short- and long-range surface-to-air missile sites along the border, but as they flew along the Mighand Highlands northbound, they were actually flying *behind* them. As soon as they were clear of the dry lake beds, Patrick steered the EB-1C back across the Afghan border.

They were able to climb up to fifteen thousand feet, high enough to escape visual detection and stay away from any antiaircraft artillery units that might pop up unexpectedly.

"Puppeteer, this is Control," David Luger radioed. "I show you going across the Turkmen border. The Turkmen army uses lots of Russian antiaircraft systems, and a lot of that stuff is right in front of you."

"I'm going to make one try at linking up with the StealthHawk, and then I'll bug out," Patrick responded.

Minutes later Patrick had locked the StealthHawk's encrypted beacon up with his laser radar, and they began a tail chase with the StealthHawk drone, which had already crossed the border into Turkmenistan. Rebecca turned the bomber to the northeast, closing the distance rapidly on full military power. "We're sucking gas like crazy," she mused. "How much longer before you're in direct datalink range?"

"About five minutes," Patrick said, "if our range calculations are . . ." As soon as they did close to within ten miles, Patrick was able to reestablish the uplink to the StealthHawk. "Got it!" Patrick crowed. "It's responding!"

At the same instant their threat-warning receiver came to life. *"Caution, SA-4 surveillance radar, twelve o'clock, thirty-eight miles, well below detection threshold,"* the threat-warning computer announced. The SA-4 was a high-performance mobile antiaircraft missile—even launched from so far away, it could reach them in less than two minutes.

"For Christ's sake, General, we're flying right for that SA-4 . . . !"

"Keep going, Rebecca. We've almost got it."

"Warning, SA-4 target-acquisition mode, twelve o'clock, twenty miles." The system activated their countermeasures system, including the towed countermeasures array—they

were an item of interest again. But there was nothing they could do until they got the StealthHawk turned around.

"Damn . . . the Turkmen might be picking up our datalink signals," Patrick said. Although the signals between the bomber and the StealthHawk drone were encrypted, the transmissions themselves could be detected. Soon, the Turkmen could pinpoint their location, no matter how stealthy they were.

"Let's get out of here, McLanahan!"

"Almost got it. . . ." He quickly entered in instructions for the StealthHawk to turn around, and it responded. "StealthHawk responding!" Patrick said. Rebecca immediately started a hard left turn. "*Wings level,* pilot . . ."

"I can't—we're going to get shot right in the face by that SA-4!"

"Closer, Rebecca," Patrick urged. "It's turning away from that SA-4. We'll be okay. Head back toward it and at least give me a chance of nudging it back."

"No way."

"Then descend," Patrick said. "It'll keep us clear of that SA-4. If we go below two thousand feet, it'll lose us."

"Two thousand feet! You expect me to descend *below* two thousand feet?"

"If we lose that StealthHawk, it'll be the military and diplomatic embarrassment of the decade," Patrick said. "A few more minutes, that's all, Rebecca."

Furness looked at Patrick with an expression of fear and anger—but she made the turn and pushed on the control stick. "Damn it, General, this better work—and *fast.*"

It did. As soon as they cruised back within the ten-mile arc of the StealthHawk, they were able to get it turned back toward them. They were fifteen miles inside the Turkmen border, but at least they were headed away from the long-range SA-4 missile site. The warning of the SA-4's "Long Track" surveillance radar still blared in their ears—they were still being detected, possibly tracked. Patrick entered commands into the UCAV's control computer, and the StealthHawk performed a rejoin on the EB-1C Vampire bomber.

Suddenly they heard a fast, high-pitched *deedledeedle-deedle!* warning, followed by a computerized female voice that calmly said, *"Warning, SA-4 missile launch, four o'clock, twenty-eight miles. Time to impact, fifty seconds. . . . Warning, second SA-4 missile launch, four o'clock, twenty-eight miles, time to impact, fifty-eight seconds."* The voice was so calm and pleasant that one almost expected it to sign off with "Have a nice day."

"Damn you, General . . . !"

"We've got time," Patrick said. "Once we get the StealthHawk turned around, we'll be okay."

"Puppeteer, *what is going on up there?*" David Luger radioed. "You just got fired on by an SA-4!"

"Thirty seconds and we're out of here."

"You don't *have* thirty seconds!"

"We've got the 'Hawk, Dave. Twenty-five seconds and we'll be cleaned up."

"You're crazy, man," Luger said seriously. "You won't have enough time to accelerate out of there in time."

"Countermeasures ready . . . trackbreakers active . . . towed array deployed," Patrick said.

"Forty seconds to impact."

"We're going to get nailed if we don't get out of here, General!"

"We'll make it. Fifteen seconds."

"Thirty seconds to impact."

Suddenly Patrick said into the computer, "Let's get out of here, Rebecca! I'm setting COLA. Go to zone five, *now!*"

"General . . . ?"

"The SA-4s are speeding up—they're diving on us,"

Patrick said. "We ran out of time. Zone-five afterburners, *now!* Flight-control system to terrain-following, set clearance-plane COLA, ninety left!" Rebecca responded instantly—she shoved all the throttles forward to the stops as the EB-1C nosed over into a steep twenty-degree nose-low dive for the flat, moonlike desert floor below. Patrick's order set their altitude for COLA—and with very little high terrain below them, they were heading to less than a wingspan's distance above the earth. Patrick ordered the StealthHawk to activate all its radar sensors and open all its weapons bays—anything he could think of to increase the UCAV's radar cross-section and make it look larger than the Vampire's to the SA-4 missile-guidance radar tracking them. . . .

Seconds later Patrick reported, "Lost contact with the StealthHawk! The SA-4 got it. Ninety left again, up and down jinks! *Hurry!*" Rebecca hauled the bomber into a steep bank, turning the EB-1C so they were directly nose-on to the SA-4's radar, presenting the smallest possible radar cross-section, then furiously started yanking the control stick forward and back in sharp, fast cycles. They hoped the SA-4 would try to match their fast altitude changes and eventually crank itself off a smooth intercept track. "Trackbreakers on . . . chaff . . . chaff . . . Oh, shit, *hang on!*"

The SA-4 missile missed—but when it was only a few hundred feet away from the left side of the Vampire bomber's nose, the missile's three-hundred-pound war-head detonated. The cockpit was filled with a blinding yellow-red burst of light from the fireball. Patrick closed his eyes in time, but Rebecca was looking directly at it when the warhead went off. She screamed just as a giant invisible fist slammed into the bomber's nose. It felt as if they were tumbling upside down out of control. . . .

But when Patrick was able to get his bearings again, he discovered with surprise that they were still upright. One multifunction display on the pilot's side was out, and two generators on the left side were offline, but everything else seemed all right.

All except Rebecca. *"Shit!"* she cried. "I can't fucking see! You got the aircraft, MC!"

"I've got the aircraft," Patrick responded. He issued voice commands to the autopilot and got the plane leveled off at five hundred feet above the ground, turned away from the SA-4 site, and heading for the Afghan border—in three minutes they were across. Between the city of Andkhvoy and the Turkmen border, Patrick started a climb, and in ten minutes they were at a safe cruising altitude, heading south across Afghanistan for a perilous Pakistani frontier crossing.

"Patrick, I've got the generators back online," David Luger reported as he and several technicians studied the real-time reports datalinked from the stricken Vampire bomber. "Engines, hydraulics, pneumatics, and electrical are all in the green. We've got the aircraft. How's Rebecca?"

"I'll be all right," she muttered. Patrick examined her eyes carefully and found no apparent damage. "I'm just flash-blinded, that's all. It's coming back. Give me a couple aspirins out of the medical kit and see if there's any eyewash or salve in there." She stared out her windscreen. "Hey, there's something wrong here. I can't see out my windscreen. Is it me or something else?"

Patrick looked, too. "The windscreen is all blackened and crazed—the blast from the SA-4 might have instantly delaminated it." He shone his flashlight outside toward the nose. "I think we might have some problems out there. Do a check of the refueling system, Dave."

"Stand by." It took only a few seconds. "Yep, looks like we got a problem—self-test of the refueling system failed. Looks like your slipway doors are damaged."

Patrick got out the high-power floodlight and looked. "I see all kinds of sheet metal loose out there," he reported. "Looks like the slipway doors might have been blown loose and are jammed or hanging halfway inside the slipway."

"We're in deep shit if we can't refuel, guys," Rebecca said.

With the help of the technicians back at Battle Mountain, Patrick began reading the flight-manual checklist for the refueling system. The checklist eventually directed him to pull the circuit breaker that actuated the slipway doors. "Last item—manual slipway door-retract handle, pull," he read.

"Give it a try, Muck," Luger said. "You got nothing else you can do."

Patrick firmly and positively pulled the small T-handle on the upper instrument console, then shone the big spotlight outside again. "Well?" Rebecca asked.

"Still looks the same. Looks like the slipway door ripped off its supports and is jammed inside the slipway. Dave . . ."

"We're running the best range numbers now," Luger responded.

Patrick switched seats with Rebecca—she couldn't see quite clearly yet, so it was better for her not to be in the pilot's seat—then immediately set the Vampire's flight-control system to max-range profile. The Vampire used mission-adaptive technology, tiny actuators in the fuselage that subtly changed almost the entire surface of the bomber's fuselage and wings to optimize the aerodynamics. The system could be set to increase airspeed, improve slow-flight characteristics, help land in crosswinds, or re-duce the effects of turbulence.

Patrick told the flight-control system to conserve as much fuel as possible. When he did so, the airspeed dropped off considerably, and they started a very slow climb. The mission-adaptive technology flattened out the flight controls as much as possible, reducing drag—they could barely maneuver, but they would be saving as much fuel as possible. As they climbed, their airspeed increased in the thinner air, so they traveled farther on the same amount of fuel. But their four-hour return flight became five, then soon settled into a five-and-a-half-hour endurance run.

And they still had the gauntlet of the Pakistani air defenses, now on full alert, to run.

"We've worked the numbers as best we could, Muck," David Luger said, "and the best we can figure is, it'll be close. The winds aren't helping you—you have a twenty-minute deficit. But if you can make it up to at least thirty-nine thousand feet and then do a very shallow idle-power descent, we think you'll make up the deficit. How's that slipway looking? Anything fly off yet?"

"Still looks like someone left a wad of scrap metal in there. Seems like we might lose part of the left side of the radome, too."

"Roger. If the slipway still looks blocked, we'll have to send the tanker home. He doesn't have enough fuel to wait for you."

"Send him home," Patrick said. "Have him gas up and then launch after us. Maybe we'll move into precontact in the descent and have the boom operator take a close look."

The Iran-Afghanistan-Pakistan frontier was a jumble of search radars and frantic radio messages in several different languages. "We may have lucked out," Patrick said.

"Sounds to me like everyone's running out of fuel and heading home. The Iranian SA-10s are still active, but they're intermittent. They might be afraid of shooting down their own aircraft or firing on a Pakistani jet over the border."

"Great," Rebecca said, putting more saline drops in her stinging eyes. "Maybe we'll avoid getting caught in the crossfire long enough to splash down in the Indian Ocean."

"Wait, they're not going home—they're chasing another target!" Patrick exclaimed, studying the datalinked composite tactical display. He switched to his own laser-radar display and took a two-second snapshot. "There's a big target at our one o'clock position, eighty-three miles, low. It's huge—it looks as big as a 747, and it's radiating on several VHF, UHF, and some navigation search frequencies." He switched radio frequencies. "Tin Man, this is Puppeteer."

"Hi, boss," Hal Briggs responded. Air Force Colonel Hal Briggs was an Army- and Air Force–trained commando and security expert, a longtime partner of Patrick's, and a close friend. He was now assigned as the commander of a secret unit at Battle Mountain Air Reserve Base called the Battle Force, comprising highly trained and heavily armed commandos that supported special-operations missions all over the world.

"What do you guys think you're doing?" Patrick asked.

"Just trying to clear a path for you," Hal replied. He had launched in the MV-32 Pave Dasher tilt-jet aircraft off the deck of their covert-operations freighter as soon as he saw Patrick's turn inland to pursue the errant StealthHawk. Loaded with extra fuel as well as electronic warfare jammers, Hal and his crew sped inland and established an orbit right along the Pakistan-Iran frontier, then activated their jammers and decoy transmitters. The decoy transmitters made the MV-32 appear a hundred times larger than its actual size on the Iranian and Pakistani radarscopes—too inviting a target to be ignored.

"We appreciate it, Tin Man," Patrick said, "but we see at least a half dozen Iranian and Pakistani fighters within thirty miles of your location and one less than twenty miles that might have detected you. Get as low as you can and bug out to the southeast."

"We're outta here, Puppeteer, but not to the southeast," Hal responded. "You head southeast. We'll draw the bad guys away until you're clear. Save your fuel."

"Are you armed?"

"Negative," Hal replied. Normally the MV-32 carried two retractable pods that held laser-guided Hellfire missiles, Maverick TV-guided attack missiles, Stinger heat-seeking antiaircraft missiles, Sidearm antiradar missiles, or twenty-millimeter gun pods—but they also held three-hundred-gallon fuel tanks, and that's what this mission required. The MV-32 had a chin-mounted twenty-millimeter Gatling gun—that was its only defensive armament, almost completely ineffective against high-speed aircraft. "I need you to give us a heads-up on where the bad guys are, Puppeteer—and remember the third dimension."

"I hear you, Tin Man," Patrick replied. He switched his display to one that accentuated terrain even more—the laser-radar view was so detailed and precise that it looked like a daylight photograph. "Head south and stay as low as you can. Nearest bandit is at your four o'clock, moving in to fifteen miles, high. He's painting you with his radar. You have your jammers on?"

"Roger that."

"There's a pretty deep crevasse at your one o'clock, eight miles. See it yet?"

"Negative."

"He's counterjamming you—looks like he's got a solid

lock on you," Patrick said. "Turn right twenty degrees, *hard*." Patrick knew that the MV-32 was fitted with infrared suppressors on the exhaust end of its fanjet engines, but they would still create very hot dots against the night sky that made easy targets for heat-seeking missiles. The first important task was to turn those hot exhausts away from the Iranian fighter's infrared sensors. "He's descending and slowing. He's trying to line up a shot."

"Terrific."

"He's too far away for us to reach you in time, Tin Man," Patrick said. "Turn ten more right. He's closing to max IR missile range. Get ready to—"

"He fired!" Briggs shouted. "He fired again! Two incoming!" The MV-32 carried a tail-warning receiver that tracked the heat of enemy aircraft behind it—when the system detected a flash of heat from the same target, it assumed that the target fired a missile and issued a MISSILE LAUNCH warning. "We're   maneuvering . . . popping flares." Patrick could hear the tension in Hal's voice, hear him grunt as the MV-32's pilot maneuvered hard into the missile. Once the Pave Dasher turned toward the missiles, the decoy flares would be the hottest dots in the sky, and the enemy missiles would go after them instead—he hoped.

"Translate positive Z!" Patrick shouted. "Now!"

The Pave Dasher had one feature the Iranian fighters lacked—the ability to fly vertically. As Patrick watched the pursuit unfold on his multifunction display, the MV-32 Pave Dasher suddenly stopped in midair, turned directly toward the incoming missiles, then flew straight up at five hundred feet per minute. Now there were two objects in the sky even brighter than the decoy flares—two fat, red-hot, yet invisible columns of jet-engine exhaust. It was too irresistible a target. Both missiles headed right for the tubes of heat and exploded harmlessly more than a hundred feet underneath the MV-32.

Patrick didn't see that. What he saw was the Iranian fighter still barreling directly at the MV-32. Either the Iranian was "target fixated"—so intent on watching his quarry die that he ignored his primary job of flying the airplane—or he was closing in for another missile attack or a gun kill. "Bandit's at your twelve o'clock, five miles, slightly high, closing fast!" Patrick radioed. "Lock him up and nail him!"

The MV-32's pilot immediately activated his own infrared targeting sensor and aimed it where Patrick told him. At less than six miles, the fighter was a huge green dot on the pilot's targeting scope. He immediately locked up the fighter into the targeting computer, slaved the twenty-millimeter Gatling gun to the target, and at three miles opened fire.

The Iranian pilot decided to fire his own thirty-millimeter cannon at two miles—that was the last mistake he'd ever make. The MV-32's shells sliced into the fighter's canopy and engines a fraction of a second before the Iranian pilot squeezed his trigger. The jet exploded into a fireball and traced a flaming streak across the night sky until it plowed into the mountains below, less than a mile in front of the Pave Dasher.

"Good shooting, guys," Patrick said when the fighter disappeared from his tactical display. "Now start heading southwest. Your tail's clear. Nearest bandit is at your five o'clock, thirty-seven miles, not locked on."

"Thanks for the help, boss," Hal Briggs radioed. "See you back at home plate."

"Don't hold breakfast. We're going to be up here awhile," Patrick said. Rebecca Furness groaned but said nothing.

Five hours later, with the bomber still over three hundred miles from home, the Sky Masters support aircraft—

a privately owned DC-10 airliner converted as a launch and support aircraft by the StealthHawk's designer, Jon Masters of Sky Masters Inc.—maneuvered slightly above and ahead of the Vampire. The DC-10's pilot, flight engineer, and boom operator, sitting in the boom operator's pod in the rear looking out through the large "picture window" underneath the boom, all came to the same conclusion: "Sorry, Puppeteer," the boom operator reported. "The whole left side of the slipway is pushed in, and the slipway door is crumpled up inside there."

"Any way you can use the boom to pry the door away from the slipway?" Patrick asked.

"It's worth a try," the boomer said. Slowly, carefully, he used the refueling boom as a pick, trying to push and pull pieces of metal away from the receptacle at the bottom of the slipway. Twenty minutes later a large piece of metal bounced off the windscreen—thankfully, not cracking it. "Let's give it a try, Puppeteer."

Patrick had to do the flying—Rebecca's eyesight was still too marginal for her to perform this delicate task. Patrick switched the flight-control computers to air-refueling mode and maneuvered the Vampire bomber up into contact position. The boom operator extended the probe. They saw the probe bounce and skid around the broken slipway, then finally ram against the receptacle. "No contact light," the boomer said. "Toggles aren't engaging. But I'm right in there."

"Start the transfer," Patrick said.

The boomer started the transfer pumps—and immediately the windscreen iced completely over as hundreds of gallons of jet fuel gushed out of the receptacle, streamed back across the windscreen, and froze. "I lost contact with you," Patrick said, activating the windshield de-ice system. "But I think we took some gas. I'll keep it as steady as I can—you just keep plugging me."

It was the weirdest, scariest, and most violent aerial refueling Patrick had ever done. Time after time the refueling nozzle slammed into the damaged slipway; every time
the probe reached the receptacle, the boom operator
forced the nozzle tight against it, then turned the pumps on
low. More fuel streamed out—but some *was* going into the
Vampire's tanks.

One hundred miles away from Diego Garcia, the small
island in the Indian Ocean leased by the United States
Navy from Great Britain as a forward operating air base,
the DC-10 unplugged for the last time. "We transferred
two hundred thousand pounds, guys—but I have no clue
how much actually went into your tanks."

"At least you stopped the needles from moving to 'E'
for a while," Patrick said ruefully. "Thanks. See you on
the ground."

"Good luck, Puppeteer."

After putting the flight-control system back on its max
endurance program, Patrick and Rebecca discussed the
approach and landing. There was only one choice: a
straight-in approach to the downwind runway. The winds
near Diego Garcia would be pushing them toward the island, but the Vampire wouldn't have the fuel to try to turn
into the wind for landing. Patrick would have to do the flying—and he would get only one shot at it.

Patrick tuned the number-one radio to the Navy's approach frequency. "Rainbow, this is Puppeteer."

"Puppeteer, this is Charlie," the U.S. Navy captain in
charge of air operations at Diego Garcia Naval Air Station
responded. "We've been monitoring your flight progress.
State your intentions."

"Straight-in approach to runway one-four, full-stop
landing."

"Will this landing be under full control?"

"Unknown, Charlie."

"Stand by." Patrick didn't have to stand by long: "Request denied, Puppeteer," the captain said. "Sorry, Puppeteer, but we can't risk you shutting down the airfield with a crash landing—too many other flights rely on us for a dry strip of concrete. We can vector you to a ditching or bail-out zone and have rescue and recovery units standing by. Advise your intentions."

"Charlie, we can make it," Patrick replied. "If it looks like we won't come in under control, we'll divert away from the island. But I think we can make it. Requesting permission to land."

"Request denied, Puppeteer," the captain responded. "I'm sorry, but that answer comes from Hemingway." "Hemingway" was the four-star commander of U.S. Central Command, who had overall operational authority over this mission.

"Sir, Puppeteer is declaring an emergency," Patrick announced. "We have fifteen minutes of fuel and two souls on board. Our intentions are to attempt a full-stop landing on the downwind runway. Please have men and equipment standing by."

Charlie was already talking—no, *shouting*—on the frequency when Patrick let go of the mike button: ". . . repeat, you *will not* attempt a landing on Diego Garcia, Puppeteer, do you understand me? Your aircraft represents an extreme hazard to this base. Accept vectors to the ditching zone. Acknowledge!"

"I copy, Rainbow," Patrick said. He knew that the ops officer at Diego Garcia knew that Patrick was going to go over all their heads. He didn't care. The Vampire was in trouble, big trouble, and they weren't going to make it unless they got permission to land at Diego Garcia.

But a few minutes later Patrick got his answer from the secretary of defense himself—permission to land at

Diego Garcia denied. It was too risky closing down that important Indian Ocean runway.

"What do we do now, General?" Rebecca said, remarkably calm for an aircraft commander who was going to lose her plane in just a few minutes. "We brief these contingencies for days before these missions. I can't believe we actually have to do it."

A pair of U.S. Navy F/A-18 Hornet fighter-bombers rendezvoused with the Vampire bomber to look it over and take pictures. Patrick thought the fighter pilots would try to crowd the bomber off its final approach path—they were tucked in tight, but they weren't going to try to bully the bigger jet away. "Puppeteer, don't do it," one of the Navy pilots radioed. "If you shut down that runway, *I* might have to punch out. I won't take kindly to that—neither will my wife and kids." Patrick did not reply.

"General, think of your family," someone else said. "Don't risk your life with this. It's just a machine. It's not worth it."

Patrick still did not reply. In fact, for most of the five-hour-plus flight out of Central Asia, that's all Patrick had thought about—his son, Bradley, waiting for him back in Nevada. Bradley's mother, Wendy, had been brutally murdered during a mission in Libya, along with Patrick's younger brother, Paul. Patrick came home to see his son and bury his brother and then left again to try to rescue his wife when the exiled Libyan king located her in a Libyan prison.

The rescue mission was a failure: Wendy was killed, and Patrick barely made it out alive. He was finally able to bring her body home after the Libyan king set up a new constitutional government in Libya, and they cremated her remains and scattered her ashes in the Pacific Ocean. After that, Patrick vowed he would never leave Bradley's side. . . .

But he broke that promise shortly afterward, when President Thomas Thorn gave him Air Force major general's stars and command of the Air Battle Force wing at Battle Mountain. At first it was short trips away from home only, to the Tonopah Test Range or Dreamland, maybe to Washington. Bradley was being watched by Patrick's sisters either at his home in Battle Mountain or at their home in Sacramento; many times Patrick took his son with him. Bradley was making friends, playing T-ball, and he seemed happy to see his father when he finally came home, not traumatized or clingy. Bradley was a tough kid, Patrick thought. He had gone through a lot during his short life.

But now Patrick was on a weeklong mission, flying out of Diego Garcia in the Indian Ocean. He rationalized it by saying it was only a UCAV control-and-monitor mission—there were no plans whatsoever to fly over hostile territory, so he would be as safe as he could be in a 470,000-pound combat aircraft. Now even that flimsy rationalization was exploded. At the very worst there was an extremely good chance that he would leave his son an orphan—at best he was probably going to lose his commission. Again.

Finally the Hornets went away, glad to be out of midair-collision range with the bomber, and the Vampire was all by itself.

The bomber was several miles north of the island of Diego Garcia when the first engine flamed out from fuel starvation. "Shut down the opposite engine before you get two flaming out on the same side," Rebecca told him, but Patrick was already ensuring that the computers were doing just that. Rebecca stared hard out her windscreen, but all she could see were blurs. "How are we doing?" No reply. "Patrick? You okay?"

"I . . . I was thinking about my son," Patrick said. "I barely made it home after the Libyan ordeal and his mother's death, and now I might just orphan him with this stunt."

"It's not too late to get out. I'm ready to go. All you have to do is say the word."

Patrick paused—but only for a few moments. "No. We'll make it."

"Puppeteer, you are too low," the tower controller called. "Start a slow turn now, away from the final approach path, or you won't make it."

"It's now or never, Patrick," Rebecca said, firmly but evenly. "If you wait and try to turn too tight later, you'll stall and crash. If we lose another engine, we won't make it. And if we lose an engine while in the turn, we'll spin in so fast they'll need a dredger to dig us out of the ocean bottom. Turn now."

"No. We can make it."

"General, don't be stupid—"

"If we ditch, Rebecca, we'll lose a three-hundred-million-dollar plane," Patrick said. "If we land and we end up crashing it on the runway, maybe even shutting the place down, so what? I doubt if we'd do more than three hundred million worth of damage."

"You're nuts," Furness said. "You have much more than just a problem with authority—you have some sort of sick death wish. Need I remind you, sir, what happened to you the last time you violated a direct order from the National Command Authority?"

"I was forced to retire from the Air Force within forty-eight hours."

"That's right, sir," Rebecca said. "And you nearly took me down with you."

"We'll make it," Patrick said. He keyed the microphone. "Diego Tower, Vampire Three-one on final for full-stop landing runway one-four." He used his unclassified call sign on the open channel.

"Vampire Three-one, this is Diego Tower," the voice of the British tower controller replied. "You do not have proper authority to land."

"Diego Tower, Vampire Three-one is declaring an emergency for a flight-control malfunction, five minutes of fuel on board, requesting fire equipment standing by."

"Vampire Three-one, you *do not* have permission to land!" the controller shouted, his British accent getting thicker as he grew more and more agitated. "Discontinue approach, depart the pattern to the east, and remain clear of this airspace."

"Puppeteer, this is Rainbow," the American naval air operations officer cut in on the secure channel. "I order you to break off your approach and leave this airspace, or I will bust you so hard that you'll be lucky to get an assignment changing tires at the motor pool back at your home base rather than commanding it."

Patrick ignored him. Yes, he was taking an awful risk, not just to his career—which was probably over at this point—but to everyone on the ground. This was loco. Why risk it? Why . . . ?

"Puppeteer, I order you to break off this approach, *now!*"

At that moment the computer said, *"Configuration warning."*

"Override," Patrick ordered. "I'm leaving the gear up."

"General . . . ?"

"I'm committed," Patrick said to Rebecca's unasked question. They weren't going to make it. They were so low that Patrick couldn't see the runway anymore.

Just before he hit the water, Patrick pulled both throttles to IDLE, lifted them, and pulled them into CUTOFF. He then turned all the switches—ignition, power, and battery—off. They were passengers now, along for the ride.

The big bomber sank out of the sky like a stone. It smacked into the ocean less than a half mile from the approach end of the runway. The bomber skipped off the surface of the ocean, sailed into the air, and started to roll to its left—but just as it did, it skittered up onto the beach, crashed through the approach-end runway lighting, through the security fence, rolled right, and careened up onto the large mass aircraft-parking ramp on the north side of the runway. The bomber skidded to a halt on its belly just a few dozen yards away from several parked military aircraft.

The fire trucks were on the bomber within moments, dousing it with firefighting foam and water, but there was no fuel on the plane anyway, it didn't break apart, and it had been shut down long before landing. It looked like a wounded duck shot out of the air by a hunter, but it was intact.

"Oh, God—we made it!" Rebecca said breathlessly. "I don't believe it."

"We made it," Patrick breathed. "My God . . ." He made sure everything was switched off, then safed his and Rebecca's ejection seats, unlatched the upper escape hatch, and climbed up on top of the fuselage. They were helped down by rescue personnel and taken to the base hospital. A huge crowd of sailors and airmen had come out to watch the bomber belly flop onto their little island.

As they were being wheeled into the hospital, Patrick could see several naval officers striding toward him, all wearing the angriest, most chew-ass expressions he'd ever seen. Sailors and spectators quickly peeled out of their way as if they were radioactive. Patrick completely ignored them. Instead he looked up and spoke, "Patrick to Luger."

"Go ahead, Muck," David Luger said. Their subcutaneous microtransceiver system gave them global communications and datalink capability anywhere in the world, even on a tiny island in the middle of the Indian Ocean. "Good to see you made it okay. Is Rebecca all right?"

"Yes, she's fine."

"Good. The commander there wants to have a word with you. I'm sure CINCENT and SECDEF will be on the line soon, too."

"I copy," Patrick said. "But put me through to home first."

"*Home?* Patrick, the admiral wants—"

"Dave, put me through to my son, *right now,* and that's an order," Patrick said. "I've got to say hello to Bradley."

NEAR THE VILLAGE OF TABADKAN, TWENTY KILOMETERS WEST OF ANDKHVOY, ON THE TURKMENISTAN-AFGHANISTAN BORDER
That night

Even with a new government in place in Afghanistan, the border-crossing points were not very well manned on the Afghan side—even on the larger highways there was usually only a small inspection and customs building, with a swinging counterweighted metal pole to delineate the border itself. Infiltrators never used the border crossings anyway; no one ever wanted to visit Afghanistan, and the country was certainly not going to keep anyone from *leaving*—why did Afghanistan need an armed border crossing?

On the other side, however, it was a different matter. None of Afghanistan's neighbors wanted any refugees or accused terrorists to cross the borders freely, so the border checkpoints were usually well manned and well armed. Thus it was with the Republic of Turkmenistan.

Tabadkan was typical of almost all of the Turkmen border checkpoints—a small but heavily fortified Turkmen border-guard base with a few support buildings, a large tent barracks for enlisted men and a towable building for the officers, a supply yard with portable fuel and water tanks—and a detainment camp. The Republic of Turkmenistan routinely turned away anyone—refugees or rich folks, it didn't matter—who did not have a visa and a letter of introduction or a travel itinerary drawn up by a Turkmen state travel bureau; but any people without proper identification papers or passports were placed in the detainment camp until their identities could be verified. The Afghan government usually sent officials to the border crossing to help in identifying its citizens and getting them released from Turkmen custody at least once a week, but in bad weather—or for a number of other reasons—it could sometimes take a month or more for anyone to come to this remote outpost.

So it was now—the detainment camp had almost a hundred detainees, substantially over its capacity. Women and children under age ten were in a separate sheltered area of the facility and were generally well treated; older boys and the men were in another section, exposed to the elements. Each man was given two carpets and a metal cup; four buckets of porridge made with mung beans and rice and four buckets of water had to serve about sixty men for the day. To keep warm, the men took turns around a single large peat brazier set in a lean-to made from hides—if a man was lucky, he might make a snack of a captured and roasted sand rat, jerboa, snake, or sand crocodile.

Zarazi examined all this with his binoculars from the relative safety of a sand dune about a kilometer east of the border crossing. The wind was howling now, at least forty kilometers an hour, blowing sand that stung like sandpaper rubbed across bare cheeks and foreheads. "Those bastards," he spat. "They've got several dozen of our people caged up like animals." He let his deputy commander, Jalaluddin Turabi, check through the binoculars. Sure enough, they looked like Taliban fighters, although from this range and with the winds kicking up, it was hard to be positive.

"No patrols out tonight," Zarazi went on to Turabi, who was prone in the sand beside him, two scarves covering all but a tiny slit for his eyes. "We might actually pull this off, Jala."

"We can just as easily go around this post, Wakil," Turabi said worriedly. "We have enough supplies to last us another two or three days, long enough to make it to Yusof Mirzo'i or back to Andkhvoy. Once we get more weapons and ammo, we can come back for those men."

"But they'll be waiting for us to head back toward the city," Zarazi said. "They won't expect us to go across the border to Turkmenistan."

"For good reason—there's nothing but unmanned oil wells, scorpions, and sandstorms for a hundred kilometers," Turabi retorted. "If we make it to the Kara Kum River, we may survive, but there's nothing but Turkmen border guards until we reach Holach. What's the plan, Wakil?"

"The plan is to stay alive long enough to strike back at the blue-helmets and the Americans who drove us from our homes," Zarazi replied bitterly. "Revenge is the reason we must survive."

"There's no one to take out our revenge on in the Kara Kum wastelands, Wakil," Turabi said. "Sure as hell not the Americans. They are nice and safe up in their supersonic stealth bombers, or sitting back at home flying their robot attack planes via satellite."

"They are all cowards, and they must die like cowards," Zarazi said. "I prayed to Allah while we were under attack, and I made a bargain with the Almighty—if He let me live, I would be His sword of vengeance. He answered my prayers, Jala. He is pointing the way, and the way is

out there, in the desert—through this place, not around it."
He turned to his friend and fellow freedom fighter. "We
will hoist the United Nations flags on our captured vehicles and turn on all the lights. We must act nice and
friendly. Then we shall see what Allah has in store for us
tonight." Zarazi patted Turabi's face. "Time to get rid of
the beards, my friend."

"Military vehicles approaching!" a sentry shouted. "Someone coming in!"

The commander in charge had just settled in for a cat-
nap when the cry was relayed to him. Swearing, he got to
his feet and joined his senior sergeant at the observation
window facing the checkpoint. The sergeant was trying to
see who it was through a pair of binoculars. "Well,
Sergeant?"

"Hard to tell through the sandstorm, sir," the sergeant
said. "It looks like a BTR towing a pickup truck—wait,
sir, I see a flag now. A United Nations patrol. They look
like they're towing a captured Taliban truck."

"Why didn't they announce first?" the commander
mused. "This looks pretty damned suspicious. Why in hell
are they bringing it to us?"

"I see the commander up in the cupola. He's wearing a
blue helmet," the sergeant said. As the trucks got closer to
the spotlight along the checkpoint, he could make out
more details. "Looks like they might have gotten into a
firefight, sir. I see damage to their radio antenna. That
could be why they didn't radio ahead. There could be casualties in the back of the pickup truck. They might be lost
in the sandstorm, too."

"Incompetent imbeciles! All those blue-helmets think
if they have their precious little GPS receivers, they'll be

fine. This is what happens when you rely on them too much and they crap out on you."

"All their lights are on, sir. They're certainly not trying to sneak in." A moment later he said, "The commander and one other man are dismounting, sir. Looks like United Nations troops to me. Can't tell his nationality."

"Bring the T-72 up. I want the gun right in their nose," the commander ordered. "I want to teach those blue-helmets a lesson. They just can't drive up to a border post in an armored vehicle. Somebody might think they're terrorists and blow their shit away for them."

"But, sir . . ."

"I know, I know. We don't have any ammo for the main gun," the commander said. "*They* don't have to know that." No one at headquarters expected a tank battle out here in the middle of nowhere, especially with Northern Alliance progovernment forces in charge again in Afghanistan, so rations of critical ammunition supplies such as rounds for the main tank guns were reserved only for the army units in the cities and Caspian Sea ports, not the border outposts. They were lucky to have any ammo at all. "Get to it, Sergeant. I want to see the commander of that detachment right away. I'll chew on him for a few minutes while you find some bunk space and rations for them." As angry as the commander was for being roused late at night, no Turkmen would ever consider being inhospitable to anyone traveling across the desert. Even a professional military officer in the twenty-first-century Turkmen army was only a couple generations removed from his nomadic roots. Every real Turkman knew the etiquette and rules of survival in the desert, and the prime rule was that any unarmed man riding into an oasis, even an artificial one such as this border outpost, was to be made welcome.

* * *

"Wakil, they're moving a tank up to the gate!" Turabi radioed. "We've been discovered!"

"Relax, Jala," Zarazi said. "I'm not worried about the tank just yet. I'm worried about the barracks. If we start to see troops running out of those tents, we may be in for a fight."

Troops soon did start emerging from the tents, but only a half dozen or so. Zarazi could soon see that they were rushing toward one of the supply buildings and emerging moments later with their arms full of carpets. He realized with amused surprise that they were preparing to bunk down the newcomers. "Steady. I think they want to make us feel welcome."

Several minutes later the gates opened and a soldier walked out and greeted Zarazi. He spoke in Turkmen first, which Zarazi understood, but he thought it best to pretend he did not. *"Zdrastvooy,"* he said in Russian, raising his right hand. The soldier smiled and made a short bow—Turkmenistan had been heavily Russified over the years of Soviet occupation, and only recently was Russian replaced by Turkmen as the national language. Zarazi quickly searched for the soldier's rank, saw he was a major in the border guards, and went on, "I am Colonel Petrovich of the Republic of Ukraine, representing the United Nations High Commission on Refugees. Our column was ambushed by marauders outside of Andkhvoy, and we have several wounded. Can you help us?"

"Da. Ya paneemayoo," the soldier replied. He removed a glove and extended a hand.

Zarazi shook it, then gave him a curt embrace and patted his shoulder.

"We picked up some transmissions of some sort of skirmish east of here, but we couldn't make out what happened." The soldier motioned to the Toyota pickup. "Were they Taliban?"

"Bzduns!" Zarazi said, turning to spit on the sand. "They hit us before we knew they were in the area. Luckily for us, we insisted on going on patrol armed. We suffered a few casualties before the cowards ran off." Zarazi motioned to the detainment facility, where a number of the men inside had gotten up and moved toward the fence to get a look at what was going on. "Did you capture anyone in the past few hours?"

"Not since this morning," the soldier said. "But you are welcome to look them over and interrogate them if you wish. Speak any Pashtun?"

"Nyet," Zarazi lied. "But I have men who do."

"The base commander wishes to meet with you. You are welcome. You'll have to keep your vehicles outside the compound until we have our ordnance men look them over, but we can help you with your dead and wounded right away. Come."

"Spaseeba bal'shoye. I am grateful," Zarazi said. He turned toward the BTR and stepped out of earshot of the Turkmen officer—which wasn't too far in this weather—and said into his radio in Pashtun, "Come on in as we planned. Don't destroy the tank. Neutralize the guards around that detainment facility and see if there's anyone inside from our tribe. Then get them ready to move."

A few moments later Zarazi was brought before the base commander, an older man who seemed to be struggling to stay awake. His Russian was even better than his deputy's. The pleasantries were short and strained. Then: "You are fortunate, sir, that my culture and my conscience prohibit me from turning you away in the desert. Don't they teach you blue-helmets anything about approaching a border crossing in military vehicles? We could have destroyed you at any time."

"Ezveeneetye," Zarazi said. He did not remove his helmet or his sand goggles, a move that obviously irritated his host. "It's been a long day, sir. It won't happen again."

The commander narrowed his eyes even further when Zarazi spoke. The Afghan terrorist knew that his time was running out quickly. He had made the mistake of telling the major he was a Ukrainian, but surely the Turkmen had heard from and dealt with plenty of Ukrainians in the past—and Zarazi definitely didn't sound like one. The commander tried to erase the alarmed expression on his face and even managed to give Zarazi a slight smile and nod. "Well, in this weather, with what you went through, it was an honest mistake. You and your men are welcome." He picked up the telephone. "I'll make sure we have suitable quarters for—"

Zarazi drew his sidearm. "I'm sure your quarters will be more than suitable for me," he said. "Put the phone down, turn around, and get your hands up on the wall—*now.*"

The old officer did not look surprised as he replaced the receiver on the cradle, then did as he was told.

"You stupid old man. Law of the desert or not, you never open your gates to an unidentified military force. Didn't the Russians teach you anything?"

"The Russians taught me to hate the Mujahidin. I had no reason to do so, until now," the old officer said bitterly.

As if to punctuate his statement, the sound of gunfire was heard outside. The old man turned toward the telephone on his desk, hoping he would get a report saying that his men had captured or executed some terrorists—but his shoulders slumped and the corners of his eyes drooped when the gunfire subsided and the phone did not ring.

"What is it you want? Weapons? Fuel? Food? We are in short supply of all these things."

"Then the fewer men we have here on this base, the better," Zarazi said calmly—and he put a bullet into the old officer's forehead. Zarazi then stationed a Turkmen-speaking man inside the office to cover the phones and went outside with gun in hand to see how Turabi was progressing.

"It went smoother than I ever expected," Turabi reported. "The border guards here are all conscripts, none more than twenty-five years old. We found one career officer and one career NCO and executed them. The conscripts practically kissed our boots in return. We shouldn't have any trouble with them. They are refueling our vehicles now."

"Very good." Zarazi motioned to the detainment facilities. "What do we have there?"

"Women and children in there, men over here, existing just a little bit better than a herd of cattle," Turabi said disgustedly. "Damned Turkmen—they think their country is so special. What do you want to do with them?"

"Release the women and children with enough rations to last them a couple days. By then they'll either be discovered by relief troops or they'll decide to walk to Andkhvoy." Turabi nodded. "As for the men—if there's anyone willing to join us, they may."

"They'll *all* want to join us, Wakil. Either that or starve."

"Then weed out any who are from hostile tribes, foreigners, unbelievers, or anyone who doesn't wish to join us, and execute them," Zarazi said. "Keep one or two of the older men here to supervise the rescue of the women and children. Make sure they all understand that if they tell anyone what happened here, I will return and execute them and their entire families. Put the others to work burying our dead and collecting weapons, ammunition, food, and water. The sooner we get out of here, the better."

"Where are we headed"—Turabi paused, then added with a smile—"Colonel?"

" 'Colonel' will be fine—Major," Zarazi said with a smile. "North, to Kerki."

"We're going to stay in Turkmenistan? Why not head east back toward home?"

"Because the Northern Alliance, the United Nations, and the Americans will pursue us and hound us until we are destroyed," Zarazi said. "The Turkmen garrison at Kerki will have more ammunition, weapons, and supplies, and we'll be safe from our pursuers."

"What about the Turkmen army? They'll pursue us even more relentlessly than the Americans."

"If the state of this border guard detachment is any indication of the state of the Turkmen army, I'm not concerned," Zarazi said. "The Turkmen government is weak and corrupt. Taking what we want shouldn't be too difficult for us. Even if we had to assault this border post, we would have had no trouble."

Zarazi stared out into the darkness to the north and fell silent for several long moments. Turabi thought his superior officer was entering some kind of trance. Just before he was about to ask if anything was wrong, Zarazi went on, "And I have been chosen by God to be His instrument of revenge against the nonbelievers," he said. "God saved me from the American robot planes. He wants something of me, Jala, I know it. Something great. Something important. I will not stop fighting until I have accomplished it."

ONE

I apologize for holding this press conference in this kind of weather, with no shelter," former president of the United States Kevin Martindale began. As he did, the early-morning downpour seemed to intensify. "Out of respect for this place, I chose not to set up any tents or shelters and add any more to the circuslike atmosphere I'm already creating here. It's also why we're out here in the visitors' parking lot instead of on the grounds themselves, and why I requested that no cameras be aimed toward the cemetery itself. But I did come to Arlington for a reason."

Despite the weather, Kevin Martindale, standing on the running board of his armored Suburban, looked as groomed and polished as if he were in a television studio. In his early fifties, tall and handsome, a former two-time vice president and one-term chief executive, Martindale still looked every inch the political pro and commander in chief. He kept himself in good shape; he still dressed impeccably; he had shaved his beard and cut his hair for this appearance. The famous "photographer's dream" was still there, even in the rain—the two locks of silver hair that automatically mirrored his mood. If he was angry, they curled menacingly across his forehead, as they did right now; when he was contented, they swept gracefully back across his salt-and-pepper mane.

"I asked you to meet me out here today so I might make an observation and an announcement," Martindale said. "The weather happens to match my mood pretty well.

"Today is a very solemn anniversary: the twelfth anniversary of the last postwar combat deaths of Operation Desert Storm. Two weeks after the Iraqi army was decimated and a cease-fire was declared, a U.S. Army Blackhawk helicopter went down in bad weather over Kuwait, and six brave soldiers were lost. Some of those heroes are interred here in Section H at Arlington National Cemetery. That these losses happened at all is a huge tragedy, but to suffer such a loss after such a great victory against the Iraqi army makes the loss even more grievous.

"Yet it *was* a great victory for freedom. The mission to release Kuwait from the clutches of Saddam Hussein took only six weeks to accomplish; Iraq surrendered just one hundred *hours* after the ground war began, after being pummeled into submission by forty days of continuous aerial bombardment. Coalition forces lost just five hundred brave soldiers, against nearly one hundred thousand Iraqi casualties. It was clearly one of the most lopsided wars in history. Those soldiers' deaths were tragic, but it was a mission I feel the United States needed to accomplish. They did not die in vain.

"I bring all this to your attention today to point out an alarming fact: that the United States does not now have the capability to perform that same fight for freedom," Martindale went on. "The United States mobilized two hundred and fifty thousand soldiers, sailors, Marines, and airmen in six months to fight that last battle. Today it would take us *years* to mobilize and move the same number of troops and send them halfway across the world to fight. We have no ground forces stationed overseas— *none*. We have a total of fifty thousand Marines deployed aboard ships around the world with aircraft-carrier battle groups. Those are the only ground forces that can respond to an emergency. We also happen to have two fewer aircraft-carrier battle groups operational, which in essence leaves one-fifth of the world unpatrolled at any given time.

"In addition, the forty-first president managed to commit, organize, mobilize, and direct another two hundred and fifty thousand troops from fifty-seven nations in the war against Saddam Hussein, including those from six Arabic-speaking nations and another seventeen Islamic nations," Martindale continued. "The current administration has managed to ignore, cancel, violate, and abrogate dozens of treaties; it has alienated most of our allies, created distrust among the nonaligned world, and angered our enemies.

"Thomas Thorn continues to cut the size of the United States military at a ridiculous rate, especially our Army," Martindale said, his voice rising in anger. "The Army is now one-half the size it was just two years ago, and it continues to shrink. The size of the Reserves and National Guard has increased, but the overall force is still one-third smaller. We have abrogated numerous mutual-defense and cooperation treaties with dozens of nations, most important among them the North Atlantic Treaty Organization, which in my opinion has ensured the safety and security of the entire world for almost half a century. Thanks to Thomas Thorn's shortsightedness, the United States is a friendless, futureless desert island hopelessly lost and forgotten in the sea of global geopolitical affairs. We are not adrift—we are being purposely and maliciously steered around every tragedy, every responsibility, and every crisis, all in the name of splendid isolationism. It is time for that policy to end.

"Now for my announcement: I am hereby announcing the formation of an exploratory committee to become the Republican Party nominee for president of the United States."

Even from this group of Washington reporters, who had been hearing rumors about such an announcement for weeks, there was a loud murmur of surprise. Martindale's aide stepped toward the former president, whispering in his ear that several networks wanted to go live with this press conference. Martindale turned from the podium for several moments as if adjusting his trench coat, but he didn't need to do so—everyone in attendance knew what was happening. Less than ten seconds later the networks gave the sign that they were ready.

"I realize that the phenomenon of a former president who was in office, was defeated, and then successfully ran for office again hasn't happened since Grover Cleveland did it in the 1880s," Martindale went on after repeating his announcement. "Former U.S. presidents, especially in the postwar era, are expected to retire gracefully, refrain from active politics, go on the lecture circuit at a million dollars a pop, build their libraries and write their memoirs, and quietly accept the tributes and criticisms aimed at them, until they die.

"Well, that's not my style. Since I left Sixteen Hundred Pennsylvania Avenue, I have been speaking out in Republican forums around the country and in many venues around the world, blasting the unorthodox and, frankly, rather bizarre policies of Thomas Thorn. But I've begun to realize that retired presidents who criticize seated presidents, especially those defeated by the ones they're criticizing, are at best labeled sore losers. The public politely listens, then promptly ignores them. I realized that if I want my voice to be heard, I have to get out of retirement and get back in the game.

"My qualifications and background speak for themselves. As a former state attorney general and U.S. senator from the great state of Texas, I stood on a policy of engagement and open dialogue in all aspects of life and politics in America. As secretary of defense I advocated a strong national defense and engagement with all our enemies and potential adversaries, whether they be a few dozen terrorists or an international superpower. As vice president, I advocated the use of America's military might in support of many national and foreign-policy issues, from border security to drug control to nuclear proliferation to counterterrorism. As the former president, despite a shrinking defense budget, I fought to build the most high-tech, cutting-edge military force possible.

"I stand before you now committed to rebuild the American military into the greatest peacetime force in the world. Under my leadership America will not retreat from its obligations. America will not disengage. We will use our technological superiority, our diversity, our values, and our spirit to once again take our rightful place as the leader and defender of the free world. With the blessing of God and the support of the American people, if I am nominated and elected, I promise to fight to restore America's greatness."

Martindale motioned toward the cemetery before him. The rains had stopped, and, as he concluded his remarks, the sun actually appeared through breaks in the clouds. His handlers could not have hoped for a better outcome to this press conference. "The shades of the heroes who lie in Arlington expect nothing less than strength, leadership, courage, and honor from the commander in chief," he said. "I ask for your help to begin the campaign to bring leadership and honor back to the White House. Thank you, and God bless America."

Unbidden and completely out of character, the reporters started to applaud. Martindale's silver locks were back—the former president was on the warpath once again.

THE PENTAGON, WASHINGTON, D.C.
That same time

"I seriously think you need to have your head examined, General," Secretary of Defense Robert Goff said. He was busy packing a briefcase, stuffing it with papers with short, angry stabs. Short, white-haired, what some might call puckish, Robert Goff was one of the United States' leading military and international-affairs experts. If he had not already been a close friend, campaign manager, and adviser to President Thomas Thorn, his name would still have been at the top of Thorn's or any president's short list of candidates for secretary of defense. "Just a few months on the job, and now I've got to go to the White House and explain what in hell you were doing over Turkmenistan and why you found it necessary to crash a B-1 bomber on Diego Garcia after you were specifically ordered to ditch it."

Standing at attention in the middle of Goff's office were Major General Patrick McLanahan and Brigadier General Rebecca Furness. Both were still in sweat-stained flight suits. There had not even been time to get fresh uniforms. They'd been on the ground less than thirty minutes in Diego Garcia before being whisked out of there on a military jet transport, and in less than eighteen hours they were back in Washington. Standing at parade rest off to Goff's right was the chairman of the Joint Chiefs of Staff, Air Force General Richard Venti, with a passive and completely unreadable expression on his young fighter-pilot face.

"I went to bat for you over this, Patrick," Goff continued disgustedly. "The president gives you the newest combat wing in the U.S. military, weeks after you almost start a nuclear war in Libya. . . ." He didn't press the events during that period of time—because Patrick had lost both his brother and his wife during those battles in North Africa. "With no forward bases in Central Asia, we trusted you to take your unmanned aircraft over Afghanistan— avoiding overflying any populated areas or doing anything that could draw attention—and hunt down the Taliban raiders that have been stirring up trouble. You assured me that none of your manned combat aircraft would violate sovereign airspace.

"Instead, not only do you violate Pakistani airspace, but you throw in Iran, Afghanistan, and Turkmenistan as well for good measure! Then, to make matters worse, you ignore a direct order from superior officers and *me* and crash-land your plane on an important active runway instead of ditching it. So tell me, McLanahan—what in hell do I say to the president?"

"Sir, tell him that our mission was accomplished, we brought all of our aircraft home or had them destroyed beyond traceability, and all crew members returned home with only minor damage and injuries," McLanahan replied.

"Are you trying to be funny?" Goff retorted. "Are you trying to make me look like a fool? You really expect me to go in front of the National Security Council and tell that to the president of the United States? Do you think he'll find the humor in my statement after he reads the entire report that the director of Central Intelligence will undoubtedly give him and finds out what *really* happened?"

Goff stared at McLanahan, who had his eyes caged straight ahead. "Well? I've got two minutes before I go. You'd better start talking—and *fast.*"

"Sir, the mission *was* a success," McLanahan said. "Our mission was to locate, identify, track, and if necessary interdict that group of Taliban raiders that has been killing United Nations aid workers and Afghan government security forces. We were successful, and the systems we employed worked perfectly, until we were hit by ground fire, went out of control, and were in danger of crash-landing almost intact in Turkmenistan. The only way to retrieve the aircraft was to switch to line-of-sight radio control." He didn't need to explain what that was— Robert Goff was an industrialist and engineer and knew almost as much as any aerospace scientist.

"It was supposed to recall itself if there was a problem," Goff said. "It was supposed to come back if it sustained any damage or lost contact with you."

"I have no excuse for that, sir—I haven't had time to analyze the data we were able to retrieve from the UCAV's flight-control computers," Patrick responded. "We couldn't recall it or self-destruct it, and I knew we couldn't just let it crash-land in Turkmenistan—our most sophisticated unmanned combat aircraft would be in the hands of the Russians or sold on the black market. No special-ops forces were available to retrieve it. The only choice I had was to dash across Pakistan and Afghanistan, reach it before it ran out of fuel, and hope it responded to direct line-of-sight commands instead of satellite-relay commands. Flying over Iran was unavoidable as well. We were able to reach it and get it turned around, but at the same time we were attacked by Turkmen air defenses. The drone was shot down, and we sustained damage to our aerial-refueling system. I thought we had enough gas to safely reach the runway." He paused, then added, "I was right."

"Don't smart-mouth me, mister," Goff said. "You were ordered *by me* to ditch that plane. Why did you ignore that order?"

"Sir, I felt an ejection and ditching under those circumstances would be hazardous to my crew, pose a danger to vessels and aircraft in the area, subject the United States to unnecessary security and negative publicity exposure, and result in unnecessary loss of a valuable military asset," Patrick McLanahan replied. "I made a decision as senior officer on board the aircraft to attempt a landing. I felt the risk was minimal compared to an uncontrolled crash-landing at sea."

"I don't care what you felt or what you decided—you violated a direct order from several superior officers," Goff said. "You could have caused unmentionable damage to that airfield and the aircraft parked there. Both of you could have been killed." Goff looked at Venti, who had remained silent during this entire meeting. "Well, General Venti? What do you think we ought to do to these two?"

"Sir, I recommend the Air Medal be awarded to both Generals McLanahan and Furness for successfully completing a dangerous mission over hostile airspace, for bringing their crippled aircraft home, and for preserving and protecting the secrecy of their mission, even at considerable risk to their own lives," Venti responded, a broad smile spreading across his face.

"Make it the Airman's Medal. We can award that in peacetime, can't we, General?"

"We can indeed, sir," Venti replied happily.

"Good," Goff said. "I'd make it the Distinguished Flying Cross, but I know that *can't* be awarded in peacetime." He enthusiastically shook hands with McLanahan and Furness. "Stand at ease. Damn fine job, you two. If either that drone or your B-1 went down anywhere in Central Asia, even Afghanistan, the president would've been embarrassed enough to make him consider resigning. Not that he ever would, of course, but he'd consider it for the good of the country. That means *I'd* be the one forced to resign. The situation is so screwed up over there, who knows what would have happened? Good job."

"Thank you, sir."

"General Venti says you want to send in a team to look at the wreckage of the drone, recover the critical components, and destroy the rest?"

"Yes, sir. The team is already in place aboard a salvage vessel in the Arabian Sea—"

"The ones that went in over Pakistan to divert attention away from you so you could escape?"

"Yes, sir. We've got the location of the wreckage pinpointed fairly accurately by satellite—about fifty-five miles southwest of Kerki, about twenty miles south of the Kara Kum Canal. It's uninhabited, but close enough for a patrol to go out searching for the wreckage. We need to get there first."

"How soon can you have the team in?"

"The recovery team is standing by, sir. We're ready to go in immediately if our satellites spot any activity near the crash site," Patrick replied. "The rest of the team will be in place within twenty-four hours."

"You want to go back there in twenty-four hours? That's impossible. From what the CIA tells me, the Iranians and Pakistanis are still on full air-defense alert—hell, even CNN still has reporters in the area. It's too hot to try a recovery effort now. You'll have to wait until things calm down."

"Our plan has taken that into account, sir," Patrick explained. "Our plan calls for three aircraft plus Air Force tanker support. Two aircraft will be CV-32 Pave Dasher tilt-jets, based off our salvage ship in the Arabian Sea. One of them will be used as an aerial-refueling tanker—it'll go three hundred miles inland with the leader, refuel him, and return to the ship. The lead aircraft will carry the recovery team—Sergeant Major Chris Wohl and three commandos."

"*Four* commandos? That's *all?*"

"Four Tin Men, sir," Venti pointed out.

Goff nodded—he knew what just *one* of the Tin Men was capable of. "Almost sounds like overkill now," he quipped. "I'm afraid to ask, but . . . what's the third aircraft?"

"An EB-1C Vampire missile-attack aircraft," Patrick responded.

"A Vampire bomber? The same one that you almost got shot down in over Turkmenistan?" Goff asked incredulously.

"The Vampire can attack air, ground, and even surface targets with the right mix of weapons," Patrick said. "It'll stay at high altitude and keep watch over the entire recovery team from launch to landing. It's stealthy enough to stay out of sight by search radars, and it can defend itself if any fighters manage to get a lock-on and approach it."

"For Pete's sake . . . ," Goff muttered. He looked at Patrick and said, "I suppose you already have this Vampire in the theater?"

"Not quite, sir," Patrick replied. "I've launched one EB-52 Megafortress attack plane, which will go on alert on Diego Garcia in about twelve hours, ready to respond in case the salvage vessel is threatened. I want to launch the EB-1C Vampire attack aircraft within forty-eight hours to be ready to go into the recovery area in case someone goes looking for the wreckage."

Goff looked at General Venti. "Any other assets we can use in the region, General?"

"The Twenty-sixth Marine Expeditionary Unit can be

within range in forty-eight hours," Venti replied. "But flying nine hundred miles across four hostile countries is a long haul for them, and their support is all nonstealthy fixed-wing planes. They would be able to execute the plan within forty-eight hours, but I wouldn't give them the same chance for success as General McLanahan's troops."

Goff shook his head—but soon relented. "All right, the mission is authorized. But let me be perfectly clear, General McLanahan: That drone is not worth a scratch on one man or woman's little finger. If it looks too hot, I want your troops out. No downed aircraft, no captured troops, no screw-ups for the president to admit to on the evening news. It gets done perfectly or you don't do it. Understood?"

"Yes, sir."

"General Venti also says you have a project you want me to consider—some new force concept you want to establish out there at Battle Mountain," Goff said. "Well, first things first. You pull this one off, General, and you'll have your chance to make your pitch to me and the White House. We're up against an enormous budget crunch, as you know, but you know what the president and I like: state-of-the-art, cutting-edge stuff. Stretch the limits. Build in lots of redundancy, make it reliable and powerful, make it a definite force multiplier, and—most important—dazzle us. If you can do that, you've got a chance."

"Thank you, sir."

Goff looked at his watch. "Catch up with me, General. Congratulations for bringing your cripple home, you two." He headed toward the door, then stopped and turned. "I don't need to tell you both that you have lots of enemies in the administration and on Capitol Hill," he said. "Unfortunately, your crash-landing on Diego Garcia will be considered a major screw-up, not a success. Blowing this recovery mission will probably put an end to everything you want to accomplish and everything you're being considered for. Can you handle that, Patrick?"

"Yes, sir," McLanahan replied with a smile.

The secretary of defense was definitely *not* smiling. "Try *real* hard not to screw this up, General," Goff said seriously, and he hurried off.

"I've got your Air Battle Force proposal," Richard Venti said, tapping a folder under the crook of an arm. "I want my staff to look it over first—might take a few days. We'll have to do it by video teleconference when you get back."

"I'd like to show you what we've done, sir," Patrick said. "Instead of a videoconference, come on out to Battle Mountain and see for yourself."

"How much time do you need?"

"One month, sir."

Venti raised Patrick's briefing folder. "One month—for all *this?*"

"I've hit the ground running, sir," Patrick said. "We'll put on a show for you that you won't believe. All I need is a few people, and we'll dazzle you."

"Where's your money coming from?"

"Most of it will come from HAWC, sir," Patrick replied. HAWC was the High Technology Aerospace Weapons Center, Elliott Air Force Base, Nevada, which tested high-tech weapons prior to their becoming operational. "Most of the aircraft and weapons still belong to HAWC. Once I get a real budget, I'd like to find funding for my own unit."

"Where's the rest of it coming from?"

"I thought it would come from the One-eleventh Wing," Patrick said, turning and looking at Rebecca Furness. "Her unit owns the EB-1C Vampires, and their base up in Battle Mountain has the space to accommodate us."

"General Furness? Are you in on this plan, too?"

Rebecca looked at Patrick but managed to reply without too much hesitation, "Absolutely, sir. We're ready to help any way we can."

"O-kay, if you say so," Venti said, shaking his head. "I'll brief SECDEF later on in the week—assuming there won't be a hue and cry for our scalps from the NSC. The vice president has some kind of big trip planned to the West Coast in a few weeks. I'll see if he wants us to work your demo into his itinerary. I'm sure SECDEF won't want to miss it. If you can convince the VP, you're in." Venti grabbed his briefcase; McLanahan and Furness snapped to attention as he departed the room, hot on the secretary of defense's heels.

Rebecca Furness looked completely deflated. "Oh, shit, I thought we were goners—again," she breathed. "Christ, McLanahan, how in the hell do you get me into shit storms like this? And what in hell is this new Air Battle Force thing all about? I'm the wing commander out there, re-member? Those are my planes, my troops, my budget, and my ass on the line, and I don't even know what this is about!"

"Do you want me to get you involved in another 'shit storm,' Rebecca," Patrick asked, "or don't you?"

"Maybe if you'd let me in on your plans *before* the shooting starts or before the brass calls us on the carpet, I could help you keep things from degrading into deep, dark shit storms."

"Rebecca, if I bring you in on this, my objective will be to *upgrade* our situation into a major deep, dark shit storm," Patrick said. "At least it'll be a major one for the bad guys."

"Well, if you put it that way," Rebecca said, rolling her eyes in disbelief—and maybe a little apprehension, "how can I possibly refuse?"

THE WHITE HOUSE, WASHINGTON, D.C.

A short time later

Since its formation in 1947, every U.S. president had treated the National Security Council in a different way. Some presidents, like Kennedy and Johnson, largely ignored the NSC except in the direst emergencies; others, like Eisenhower, treated it as an extension of the military; other presidents used the NSC as a clearinghouse for data from all the different departments; still others used it as a leash to try to keep the executive departments in line. Many times the NSC ran the foreign-affairs show; other times it was seen as just another bureaucratic hunk of sludge, slowing down the government machinery.

In 1961 President Kennedy appointed the first national security adviser, McGeorge Bundy, and set him up in the Situation Room in the basement of the White House to monitor the abortive Bay of Pigs invasion. Although the National Security Council met only forty-nine times in Kennedy's administration and was soon obviated by Kennedy's "whiz kids" and Johnson's "Kitchen Cabinet," at that point the position of national security adviser was crafted and remained fairly similar. . . .

Until the turn of the twenty-first century and President Thomas Nathaniel Thorn. This president never appointed a national security adviser; the National Security Council staff was reduced from over two hundred staffers to just four dozen. The other statutory members of the NSC—the president, vice president, secretary of state, secretary of the treasury, secretary of defense, chairman of the Joint Chiefs of Staff, and the director of Central Intelligence—used their own staffs to collect, distill, and analyze the mountains of information that poured into the White House every hour.

The national security adviser was not the only cabinet-level position never filled by Thomas Thorn—not by a long shot. The vice president, Lester Busick, acted as the president's chief of staff and press officer; the secretary of defense, Robert Goff, was director of Homeland Security and was considered the de facto national security adviser and the president's closest counsel. Several cabinet departments had been combined: the Department of Health and Human Services now included the Departments of Education, Veterans Affairs, Labor, and the Office of National Drug Control Policy; the Treasury Department now included the Commerce Department, the Office of Management and Budget, and the U.S. Trade Representative; the Department of the Interior now included the Departments of Agriculture, Energy, Transportation, and Housing and Urban Development, plus the Environmental Protection Agency. Because of this organization and the extreme degree of cabinet-level involvement with day-to-day government operations, the president kept in very close contact with all his cabinet officers each and every day.

President Thomas Thorn was a young man, in his late forties, quiet and unassuming. Married, with five children, Thorn was a former governor of Vermont and, before that, an ex–U.S. Army Green Beret who had served during Desert Storm, leading platoons of troops deep into Iraq to laser-mark targets for the F-117 stealth bombers that struck the first blows against Baghdad. Thorn was the founder and leader of the Jeffersonian Party and the first third-party candidate to be elected to the White House since Abraham Lincoln—and that was only the beginning of what had to be the most unusual administration anyone could remember.

Thomas Thorn was a true "techie" who made great use of computers, e-mail, and wireless devices to gather, analyze, and disseminate information. His usual style was to gather daily briefs from the cabinet secretaries and the military via secure e-mail, fire back questions and requests, and then get follow-ups. The cabinet officials had access to the president at any time, but the administration was now greatly decentralized—the secretaries were expected to handle situations and make decisions on their own, with only general thematic guidance from the president himself. The president's chief of staff was not nearly as powerful as past holders of that office—he was little more than an assistant, trying to manage the president's busy schedule and his voracious appetite for information.

Thomas Thorn treated the office of president of the United States as a sacred trust, putting his duties only a millimeter under his devotion to his family. He never took vacations, played no sports, had no hobbies, and only rarely used the Camp David retreat. Since the Jeffersonian Party was little more than a philosophy, a way of thinking devised, managed, and practiced only by Thomas Thorn himself, he had virtually no political apparatus behind him, so he rarely made campaign speeches and never went on fund-raising trips.

The National Security Council members met every Thursday morning at 7:00 A.M., usually in the Oval Office for routine matters, in the Cabinet Room for larger briefings, or in the Situation Room for crisis-management meetings; today the meeting was in the Oval Office. The outer-office secretary admitted the cabinet members all at once, and Thorn greeted them with a smile as he made final notes on his wireless PDA. "Seats, everyone, please," he said. "Welcome." The NSC members took their usual places at the chairs and sofas in front of the president's desk, and a butler brought in each person's preferred beverage. Thorn usually paced the office while the meeting was under way—although he virtually carried his life in the personal digital assistant, he rarely referred to it during meetings.

"You see Martindale's press conference today?" Secretary of State Edward Kercheval asked no one in particular. "They did a 'breaking news' thing—I thought we'd dropped a nuke on China or something."

"Brutal," Vice President Lester Busick said. "The guy's a nut. He'll be the laughingstock of Washington in no time."

"I didn't think you were allowed to use Arlington National Cemetery for political events," Darrow Horton, the attorney general, said. "Maybe I should check into that."

Robert Goff, the secretary of defense and the president's de facto chief political adviser, nodded in agreement. "Good idea," he said. "But I wouldn't be too concerned about Martindale. When word about some of the things he's been doing over the past couple years starts leaking, he'll have no choice but to pull out. The American people won't stand for an ex-president who uses his office to carry out secret mercenary missions."

"Let's get started, shall we?" the president began as he put away his PDA. "I saw the item in this morning's news on the fighting in Chechnya. What's the latest?"

"A bit more aggressive Russian response to what they view as escalating extremism in that region, sir," Director of Central Intelligence Douglas Morgan responded. He knew enough to get his coffee with three sugars fast, sit down, and be ready to go right away, because he was usually the first to be called on. "We've been watching that for many weeks now, since the shake-up in Moscow following the imprisonment of General Zhurbenko and the implication of President Sen'kov in dealing with Russian mobsters. Bottom line: Sen'kov is cracking down on any kind of dissent in the Russian Federation, using more strong-arm tactics to gain maximum advantage for Russia."

"Sen'kov has an election scheduled for 2005—it's as if he's already on the campaign trail," Kercheval added.

"I just wish he'd be a little less bloodthirsty about it," the vice president added. "The press said twenty-seven killed. . . ."

"We believe the number is much higher—and that's just in the past week," Morgan said. "The death toll could be as high as fifty. The Chechens have an equally high body count—perhaps as many as forty Russian soldiers killed, as many as a hundred wounded in attacks. We can expect the Russian military to continue to crack down."

"The question is where," Busick said.

"Wherever and whenever they can," Morgan surmised. "They have a vast, fractured empire that I think they would dearly like to take back."

"I agree," President Thorn said. He noticed the secretary of state make a quiet sigh and start examining his fingertips. "Comment, Edward?" Thorn asked.

"You know the question, Mr. President: What would we do about it even if we knew what the Russians were going to do?" he asked. It was no secret or surprise to anyone that Edward Kercheval was not a big fan of the president and his policies. What *was* the big surprise was that Thorn kept Kercheval around—or that Kercheval deigned to be around. Brash, opinionated, and considered one of the most knowledgeable secretaries of state in the past fifty years, Kercheval knew his stuff. Many speculated that Thorn had him in his cabinet simply to keep Kercheval from having enough time to mount a campaign against him come election time. "You didn't intervene in the Libya-Egypt conflict, and your role in the Russia-Balkan conflict was barely noticed. Chechnya seems way outside your attention zone, sir."

"You're right—I wouldn't intervene in Chechnya," Thorn said. "I wouldn't intervene in any conflict involving Russia's trying to quell any sort of uprising or revolution within its federation."

"That's certainly your prerogative, sir." It was obvious from Kercheval's tone of voice both that he expected the president to say as much and that he did not approve of that position. "However, sir, if you're concerned that Russian aggression against its ethnic minorities might spill over to other countries, a course of action might be advisable."

"I know you don't think I'm showing much of a leadership role in world affairs, Edward," the president said. "But I think it doesn't make much sense to attempt to support the Chechen rebels when we've been uncovering some of those very rebels hitting United Nations peacekeeping convoys in Central Asia. Those are exactly the kinds of cross-efforts that I wish to avoid if at all possible." Thorn turned to Morgan and asked, "Speaking of Central Asia, Douglas, what's the latest there? We still have a few surveillance and counterterrorist operations running there, don't we?"

"We currently don't have any military or intelligence operations running in Central Asia, sir," Director Morgan replied. "The last was Operation Hilltop, which was a recon-and-interdiction operation using unmanned combat aircraft to counter some Taliban raiders operating in northern Afghanistan."

"That was run by Air Force General McLanahan and General Rebecca Furness from her new unit at Battle Mountain, Nevada," Joint Chiefs of Staff chairman General Richard Venti interjected. "His force successfully uncovered and attacked a force of approximately two hundred Taliban fighters that attacked the convoy. It was an operation conducted solely from the air, with assets operated by a single unit."

"So McLanahan finally decided to join the right team?" Busick asked. He glanced at the president, who did not react to the comment. Busick knew that the president had given McLanahan and many of his men their military rank and privileges back after a series of privately run and financed military missions. In the president's eyes McLanahan was a leader—but in Busick's eyes he was nothing but a loose cannon.

"General McLanahan has built a unit comprised mostly of long-range aircraft and unmanned armed drones," General Venti went on. "Cutting-edge stuff."

"I feel a 'but' coming, General Venti," Busick said.

"McLanahan's mission was a success, but the Taliban fighters weren't completely out of the fight," CIA Director Morgan said. "Apparently it was survivors from that attack that raided a border-crossing base in Turkmenistan, killed the base commander and a number of Turkmen soldiers, and captured weapons and vehicles.

"After that those fighters moved north, first taking on a Turkmen army patrol and then raiding a helicopter cavalry unit near the town of Kerki. Almost two thousand Turkmen soldiers deserted their posts and joined with the Taliban. The raiders then moved east, capturing another military post at Gaurdak, where they obtained large quantities of weapons, including heavy armor, artillery, armored personnel carriers, and more light weapons, plus as many as three to five thousand more recruits and deserters. They have captured several oil-pumping stations, power plants, and water-control facilities, all of which are vital to that region. The force is now moving west along the river, consolidating their gains and creating very effective supply lines. Their route of march primarily follows the TransCal oil and gas pipelines along the river."

"That's smart. Not only can they easily find supplies

along the river, but they protect themselves from attack," General Venti interjected. "Anyone attacking them risks blowing up the lines."

"Maybe it's time to lend our support to the Republic of Turkmenistan to help wipe out these Taliban fighters," Vice President Busick suggested. "After all, we're partly to blame for what this group of fighters is doing."

"I don't think we can rely on any cooperation from Turkmenistan," Secretary of State Kercheval said. "I've received complaints from several nations—Pakistan, Iran, Turkmenistan, even Afghanistan—claiming illegal over-flight by American warplanes. All of those nations are demanding an explanation."

Busick turned to Robert Goff. "We were assured this mission was going to be completely stealthy and foolproof, Robert. What went wrong?"

"According to his report," Defense Secretary Goff responded, "McLanahan lost control of one of his unmanned combat aircraft for unexplained reasons. He could regain control of it only by flying in close proximity to it—unfortunately, that happened to be several miles inside Turkmenistan. He was fired upon by Turkmen air defenses and sustained some damage to his aircraft but managed to bring it back to Diego Garcia. Minor injuries, minor damage."

"So why is Iran squawking?"

"In order to catch up to his drone, he had to overfly eastern Iran," Goff replied. "He was briefly highlighted by Iranian and Pakistani air defenses but was not discovered or attacked."

"Good God," Busick moaned. "All that for a lousy drone?"

"That drone was a multimillion-dollar unmanned attack vehicle representing the absolute state-of-the-art in sensors, secure satellite communications, and weapons," General Venti said. "General McLanahan felt that it might crash-land intact when it ran out of fuel, so he took the chance and tried to retrieve it."

" 'Tried'?"

"The drone was shot down by Turkmen air defenses," Venti said. "Apparently it was not completely destroyed."

"McLanahan wants to insert a special-ops team to retrieve any surviving critical components, and blow up the rest," Goff added. "I authorized the mission. It'll get under way in the next few days."

"Keep me advised, Robert," the president said.

"This is *insane*," Secretary of State Kercheval said angrily. "None of this was approved by us at all. Something needs to be done about this McLanahan. What do you intend to do with him, Robert?"

"I intend to give him a commendation, Edward," Goff said. Kercheval's eyes bugged out in disbelief, so Goff hurried on. "That crew risked their lives to retrieve an important piece of military hardware and keep it from falling into the wrong hands. They sustained battle damage but still managed to bring their crippled aircraft back with no casualties. The citation to accompany the award writes itself."

"*You will not* reward that maniac with a medal for violating international law!" Kercheval retorted.

The president raised both hands. "Enough, enough," he said. "The decision to give out commendations will be made at a later time. As far as the incident involving unapproved overflight of certain nations—I intend to admit everything."

"My God, Mr. President," Kercheval said. "You . . . you can't do that . . . !"

"I can and I will," Thorn said. "I will say that in an effort to prevent Taliban raiders from attacking and destroying United Nations peacekeeping units in northern

Afghanistan, the United States launched unmanned aerial patrol-and-attack aircraft from the Arabian Sea. When one of the drones sustained damage, to avoid endangering innocent lives on the ground and to avoid losing a valuable piece of military hardware, the on-scene commander elected to violate sovereign airspace in order to retrieve the drone. He flew his unarmed control aircraft across Pakistan, Iran, Afghanistan, and Turkmenistan in an effort to retrieve it." He turned to Goff. "The control aircraft *was* unarmed, wasn't it, Robert?"

"Yes, sir. Defensive electronic transmitters only."

"No lasers, subatomic weapons, plasma bombs, any of that other cosmic stuff McLanahan plays with on a regular basis?"

"I believe it uses lasers to blind incoming antiaircraft missiles," Venti said, "but no offensive weapons of any kind."

"What kind of aircraft was it?" Kercheval asked.

"A modified B-1 Lancer bomber called a Vampire."

"Oh, God," Kercheval muttered. "The same aircraft we lost in Russia?" He closed his eyes in horror when Goff nodded in the affirmative, then turned to Thorn and said, "Surely you can't admit *that*—"

"Yes, I will," Thorn said evenly. "I'll prepare a statement for the ambassadors or foreign ministries that want an explanation, and we'll prepare talking points for the staff when the press starts to ask about the incident—but only *after* McLanahan's retrieval mission is completed." Kercheval shook his head in confusion but decided there was nothing he could say to change the president's mind. "Let's move on." Thorn again turned to his director of Central Intelligence. "Douglas, you wrote in a message this past week about some factors that might warrant increased involvement in Central Asia, especially Turkmenistan. Give us a rundown."

"Yes, sir," Morgan responded, withdrawing a thin briefing file from an attaché case. "Turkmenistan can potentially be a big powder keg. Turkmenistan is very much like Saudi Arabia, Kuwait, Iraq, and Libya were shortly after the discovery of oil—Turkmenistan's true wealth and strategic importance are only now beginning to be realized, and it could potentially become a battleground because of its location in the crossroads of several different religious, political, and ethnic factions. Turkmenistan's mineral wealth is probably on a par with that of any Persian Gulf nation, and it could possibly be the richest oil-producing nation on earth in a few years."

"*Say again,* Douglas?" Vice President Busick interjected. "More oil than Saudi? I didn't think that was possible."

"That's the consensus from our analysts," Morgan confirmed. "It is believed that Turkmenistan's oil and gas wealth equals Saudi Arabia's, but Saudi's currently producing wells will be depleted in less than ten years—Turkmenistan's haven't even begun to be exploited. They could be producing petro products fifty years after Saudi Arabia runs out of oil. At least four-fifths of that nation's oil and gas reserves are *unexplored,* let alone untapped."

"The Russians *must* realize what they lost when the Soviet Union broke apart and Turkmenistan became independent."

"I'd agree," Morgan said. "The Russians still have a few fighter bases in Turkmenistan, and the Turkmen still use Russian officers on contract for their own military. But living and working in Turkmenistan was considered a hardship tour for the Russians—never more than ten percent of the population was Russian, and we know that the climate in Turkmenistan is so inhospitable that even the Russians had a hard time extracting oil and natural gas from there—and the Russians have developed oil fields in nasty places like Siberia."

"But oil has a funny way of bringing out the worst in governments," the president mused. "Go on, Douglas."

"From 1985 to 2002, Saparmurad Niyazov was in charge of the country, initially as the Soviet first secretary and then as its president," Morgan went on. "He played all sides and swung with the winds more than a weather vane in a tornado. He was a staunch Russian supporter when the Russians controlled the government; when the Soviet Union broke apart and nationalist forces started to gain in strength, Niyazov became a nationalist—replacing Russian with Turkmen as the official language, setting up Muslim religious schools, and so on. When the Taliban took over Afghanistan and threatened to take over some fundamentalist provinces in the east, Niyazov brought some pro-Taliban mullahs into his government. He ruled with an iron fist. Every member of the Turkmen parliament had to be approved by the president; the president appointed his own censors and editors in every media outlet in the country—the list goes on and on. It was Niyazov who inked the big TransCal oil deal, the first large-scale production deal in Turkmenistan and potentially one of the wealthiest oil deals in history.

"Niyazov finally retired in 2001 and held elections, but there was only one candidate: Kurban Gurizev, the leader of their parliament and deputy chairman of the Democratic Party, what used to be the Communist Party. Like Niyazov, he ruled with absolute authority. He continued to outlaw opposition parties, had to approve all candidates for public office, and created a virtual police state. He is strongly antiforeigner, anti-Muslim, and staunchly pro-Russian."

"The military must hate Gurizev," Goff observed.

"The Turkmen military is practically nonexistent," Morgan said. "Maybe forty thousand troops in all, including paramilitary and reserves; four-fifths conscripts, lots of ex-Soviet equipment in very poor condition. Most of the officer corps is Russian—the officers who wanted to stay simply kept their posts and are being paid by the Turkmen government. Naturally, they have the best equipment."

"I wonder who they take their orders from once the shit starts hitting the fan?" Busick asked.

"My bet would be with Russia," Morgan said. "Kurban Gurizev was born and educated in Russia, not Turkmenistan—we think Kurban is not his real first name, but an adopted Turkmen name, part of Niyazov's nationalist movement. He speaks no Turkmen. He had been known to butt heads with Niyazov on occasion in matters dealing with oil and gas development. Gurizev thought it best to maintain close ties between Russia's oil infrastructure and Turkmenistan; Niyazov signed agreements with several different developers at the same time. Turkmenistan has deals with several Western companies to transport oil and gas across Afghanistan to Pakistan, with Azerbaijan to transport oil to the Black Sea, with Russia to transport oil to Russia, and even with Iran to transport oil to the Arabian Sea. On the face of it, it's pretty smart. They get money from several sources and can supply oil to markets around the world regardless of geopolitical concerns. Although there are several development projects ongoing in Turkmenistan, in various states of progress, right now the country exports oil only to Russia, at cut-rate prices."

"I think it would be a good idea to start monitoring events in Turkmenistan—perhaps put some intelligence assets on the ground," Kercheval said. "My concern is the ongoing oil projects by Western, primarily American, companies—we don't want them in the way if the Russians decide to move back in or, worse, if they storm on in, like they tried to do in the Balkans." He turned to Franklin Sellers, the secretary of the treasury who served also as the secretary of commerce and the U.S. trade representative in the Thorn administration. "Can I get a briefing on the status of any approved projects in Central Asia, Franklin?"

"Sure, Edward." Sellers, a former vice chairman of Nasdaq, was one of the youngest ever to hold that position; he was also, along with Secretary of Defense Robert Goff, one of the few members of Thorn's Jeffersonian Party serving in the cabinet. "Just off the top of my head, the current project that I'm most familiar with is TransCal Petroleum's proposed three-billion-dollar oil and natural-gas line that would pump and ship oil and gas from Turkmenistan through Afghanistan to ports in Pakistan. With the elimination of the Taliban from Afghanistan, their project is back on. They also have a one-billion-dollar project to transport natural gas from Turkmenistan to Uzbekistan for the Central Asian and Indian markets— this one was designed to placate India, who was upset with the idea of the U.S. involved in a project that could make Pakistan rich." He paused, then added, "From a political aspect, it certainly wouldn't hurt to back TransCal's projects either, sir. I think they could be very valuable financial supporters for the upcoming reelection campaign."

"I'm not concerned about the reelection campaign, Franklin," Thorn snapped. "My job is to do what's best for the nation, not for TransCal."

Sellers nodded and fell quiet, then glanced over at Robert Goff with an unspoken question. Robert Goff nodded that he understood Sellers's query but indicated that he wanted to wait. "However," Goff interjected, "I think the United States government has a duty to get involved if a foreign government reneges or interferes with the performance of a contract, or if that government is unable to protect the U.S. company from outside interference or from danger to American citizens working overseas. I think that's what I'm hearing from State and Intelligence—that the Taliban's actions and Russia's possible reaction could threaten U.S. citizens and interests in Turkmenistan."

"That's a pretty long stretch, in my estimation," Thorn said. "Companies like TransCal take a risk by investing in countries like Turkmenistan. I won't automatically commit troops to action in Turkmenistan simply to protect an American company's risky overseas investment. If Gurizev cancels the contract or Russian troops move into Turkmenistan on Gurizev's invitation and shut down work on TransCal's pipelines, I'm not going to send in the Marines to take it back. Let's move on. Next I want to hear—"

"Excuse me, Mr. President, but is *that* going to be your official public position—that the U.S. won't protect American interests in Turkmenistan or anywhere else in the world?" Secretary of State Kercheval asked incredulously. "With all due respect, sir—what kind of policy is that?"

"It's a realistic one," Thorn said. "It's a responsible one. I'm not going to force any country to sell oil to the United States, and I'm not going to send American fighting men and women to protect a company's right to make money overseas. If it's too dangerous to be in the business of drilling and shipping oil in Turkmenistan, then perhaps we shouldn't be over there doing it."

"Sir, it's dangerous only because terrorists or authoritarian governments are interfering," Kercheval argued. "American companies spend billions of dollars developing business opportunities in countries like Turkmenistan—they expect and deserve a return on their investment, and they expect and deserve some protection from their government. It's in the Constitution you so love to quote, Mr. President: 'life, liberty, and the pursuit of happiness . . . ' "

"That's in the Declaration of Independence, Mr. Kercheval, not the Constitution," Thorn corrected him.

"Whatever," Kercheval said. Thorn blinked in surprise at the "whatever" thrown out so flippantly at him by his secretary of state—to Thorn, confusing the Declaration of Independence and the Constitution was a very big deal—but he did not interrupt. Kercheval knew that arguing the contents of American historical documents with Thomas Nathaniel Thorn was a losing battle. "The point, sir, is that the U.S. government has an obligation to protect its citizens and ensure stability and free enterprise."

"We have had this discussion many times in the past, Edward," the president said with a hint of exasperation. This surprised Robert Goff, the man who knew Thomas Thorn the best. Normally, Thorn was the most patient man he had ever known. He could debate any issue in any venue, day or night, and be assured of winning almost every point. Now, in a forum where discussion and consensus were most important, he seemed impatient and unwilling to talk. "As the commander in chief, I am not interested in sending U.S. troops overseas to force any leader or regime to do business with the United States. If Turkmenistan fails to live up to its obligations, TransCal should pull out—"

" 'Pull out'? Mr. President, TransCal has invested billions in building those oil and gas lines in Turkmenistan," Kercheval argued. "They'd lose it all if the government there suddenly decides to renege—"

"Edward, let's table this discussion for the time being," the president said. "I'm ordering no action in Turkmenistan for now. If contracts between American companies and the Turkmen government are violated, I'll have the attorney general's office expedite handling of lawsuits and trade sanctions. Otherwise we do nothing. I would like position papers on this topic submitted to the vice president as soon as possible. End of discussion."

"My objections are on the record, sir?" Kercheval asked.

"Yes. Next matter: Chinese intentions in the South China Sea. What do we have on this?"

The meeting lasted another hour, with the same pattern: the latest intelligence information, the usual lively, sometimes heated discussions, followed by a general policy statement from the president. Edward Kercheval grew quieter and quieter as the meeting went on.

And the president, vice president, and secretary of defense found out why, moments after everyone else had departed.

"Mr. President, I regret to inform you that I cannot any longer support your administration and your policies, and I intend to submit my resignation to you immediately," Kercheval said formally, standing almost at attention in front of the president's desk.

Busick and Goff wore completely stunned expressions. Finally Busick spluttered, "For Christ's sake, Edward, what in hell do you want to do that for?"

"Edward, there's no need to resign," President Thorn said, holding up a hand to silence Busick. "I fully intend to do something to protect our interests in Central Asia— as soon as we reach a consensus about where our interests lie. For now my decision is to do nothing. I expect everyone to contribute to the discussion. Lester will put it all together for me, and I'll make a decision. But I'm not going to act without careful deliberation."

"Mr. President, I don't expect you to act precipitously," Kercheval said. "But I do expect you to issue some sort of statement declaring your support for American interests in Turkmenistan."

"The president *does* support American interests, in Turkmenistan and everywhere in the world," Robert Goff interjected. "Why issue such a statement just for Turkmenistan?"

"Goff's right, Ed. There's nothing going on in Turkmenistan yet," Vice President Busick emphasized. "You heard Morgan—a few Taliban runnin' around doesn't mean all of TransCal's investments go up in smoke. Relax, for Christ's sake. Don't get flustered here."

Kercheval ignored them all. "Mr. President, I find I simply can't support your foreign-policy decisions. It's not just Turkmenistan; it's your policy regarding our alliances, our treaty commitments, our military, and our overall guardianship of peace in the world. I was happy for the first few years to mouth your words in place of my own. I feel I can no longer do that."

Thomas Thorn looked at Kercheval for a long moment, then nodded. "I understand, Edward," he said.

"How do you wish me to depart, sir?"

"Nominate your replacement. Give us time to talk to him, check him out, and let him meet and greet the folks in Congress," the president said. "Once we have a good solid core group of senators warming up to him, you can depart."

"Yeah, you can tell the press you have some unexplained brain disorder," Busick muttered.

"Mr. Busick—"

"It's all right, Mr. President. I suppose I deserve that," Kercheval said. He glared at Busick and added, "I expected nothing else." Busick scowled at him but said nothing. "And I expected nothing less from you, sir. Even under adversity you are a gentleman. I intend to nominate Deputy Secretary of State Maureen Hershel as my replacement, and I will prepare a perfectly plausible and palatable explanation for my departure." He shook hands with Thorn, nodded to Goff and Busick, and departed.

"Snake," Busick said under his breath.

"Lester, have Miss Hershel come see me right away." Busick nodded. He was familiar with her. Maureen Hershel was a career State Department official and an expert on many different facets of running the department, from administration to operations.

"What a damned prick," Busick exclaimed as he picked up the telephone beside him.

"Those comments will cease immediately," Thorn ordered. "Keep them to yourself. Edward Kercheval was a valuable and trusted member of this administration and is still a good friend and a great American. He follows his heart and his conscience, as we all do, but that doesn't diminish his loyalty to his country or his service and dedication to this administration."

"Mr. President, no one who takes an oath to serve the administration resigns except under extreme personal crisis," Busick said as he waited to be put through to Hershel's office. "In other words, he had better be on his deathbed or a convicted ax murderer if he wants to bail before the end of a term. He serves at the pleasure of the president, not at his own personal pleasure. He resigns only to save the administration the embarrassment of kicking him out or prosecuting him. Edward is an experienced Washington player—he knows what he's doing. This will look bad for him, but it will look very, very bad for us."

"Hershel is a good choice," Goff said. "Former FBI, very good credentials, good background, lots of international experience."

"She's a babe, I know that," Busick remarked. Goff nodded agreement, even though he knew that the president would not approve of such locker-room talk. "Well, at least Kercheval did *something* right. But Jesus—a year before the election, and Kercheval punches out. The only thing that's going to save our political butts now is if he develops a brain tumor or rectal cancer or something."

"Lester, let's move on," Thorn said. "Edward resigned. We've got a good and experienced replacement for him. I'm not concerned about the political fallout right now. Tonight, after the paperwork is cleared up and the phone stops ringing, I'll start worrying about the politics."

Robert Goff stayed behind after the vice president departed. He walked with the president to his study, adjacent to the Oval Office. "Mr. President, I think we need to sit down and have a talk with Kercheval," Goff said. "Invite him to dinner in the residence. Feel him out, find out what he wants."

"I think I know what he wants, Robert," Thorn said. "He wants me to act more like a traditional president. He wants me to be engaged in world affairs, not passive. I respect that. But I can't do it his way. He has every right to quit."

"No, he doesn't have a right to quit," Goff insisted. "The vice president said it: Accepting a cabinet post is a position of trust and responsibility, not only to you but to the government. There are times and ways to leave the post—in case of illness or between terms. Resigning just because you disagree with a particular policy is *not* right."

"I'm sorry he resigned, and I know it'll be hard on us, especially with an election coming up," Thorn said, "but it can't be helped. Let's get his replacement up to speed as soon as possible, and I'd like to speak with the leadership so we can get through the confirmation hearings quickly."

"They'll be waiting for you, that's for sure," Goff said. "Thomas, let me make a suggestion—"

"All right, Robert, I'll call Edward and find out if he wants to meet and talk," the president said resignedly. "But I don't think it'll do any good."

"I was going to suggest something else," Goff said.

"Morgan seems pretty sure of something stirring over in Central Asia. I know you said you don't feel that events in Turkmenistan warrant sending American troops. . . ."

"That's right. I don't." The president looked at Goff. "But you're not talking about troops—you're talking about something else. Robot planes, perhaps?"

It was scary, Robert Goff thought, to consider how intelligent Thomas Thorn was. A guy with a mind and a body as sharp as his would make a very, very dangerous adversary. "We've scheduled a campaign swing out west anyway for next week—that Lake Tahoe environmental forum speech, followed by appearances in Reno, San Francisco, Monterey, Santa Barbara, Las Vegas, and L.A. I suggest we make a stop prior to arriving in Reno."

"Battle Mountain?"

Goff nodded. "General McLanahan did a great job standing up that unit so fast," he said. "His first mission over Afghanistan was a success, despite what Morgan suggested. I authorized a mission to recover the drone shot down out there, and I predict that'll be a success, too."

"I agree, and I'm proud of McLanahan. He's suffered a tremendous loss recently, he's suddenly become a single parent, yet he's worked hard and done well," the president said.

"I know we've already got the travel schedule built," Goff said, "but McLanahan might be able to give you some options in case we do need to conduct operations over there."

"I don't foresee conducting any military operations in any of the 'Stans, Robert," the president said. "But . . . you are considering McLanahan's facility as an alternate national command center, correct? Battle Mountain is the underground air base, right?"

"It certainly is," Goff replied, smiling. "And it does have a very sophisticated communications system—extensive satellite earth stations, microwave, extremely low frequency—for communications with their robot aircraft. It's also far from any other major target complexes or population centers, and it has a twelve-thousand-foot-long runway—the facilities to handle the Airborne National Command Post as well as Air Force One. It would make an ideal alternate command center."

"Then get together with Lester and build in a visit," the president said. "I imagine you'll get a briefing from him beforehand on his Afghanistan operation and his take on the situation in Central Asia. If you think I'll need to hear his report, build that into the schedule, too."

"Yes, sir," Goff replied. He paused and then looked carefully at his friend. "You don't need an excuse to go talk to your troops, Thomas."

"I know."

"You also don't have to come up with excuses to visit a military base just so you don't appear as if you're placating Edward Kercheval."

"Do you think that's what I'm doing?"

"I think you're more disappointed than you let on about losing him," Goff observed. "It's important to you to give your cabinet a lot of responsibility, but it's also important to show you're in charge."

"Do you think I rein Kercheval in too much?"

"Kercheval is a type A, action-oriented guy, Thomas," Goff replied. "He's also accustomed to being in charge. Secretaries of state in recent years have been very powerful individuals. Kercheval probably wishes he were as powerful and influential as Madeleine Albright, James Baker—"

"Or Robert Goff."

"Or Robert Goff," he echoed. "I encourage you to talk with Kercheval, sir, even though I know you won't. There are plenty of folks just as well qualified as he. I only wish we didn't have to take the flak I think we're going to get."

OVER VEDENO, CECENO-INGURSSKAJA PROVINCE, RUSSIAN FEDERATION

That same time

Damn, it was good to be alive, Anatoliy Gryzlov thought happily. He clasped his copilot on the shoulder and headed aft to stretch, have a cigarette, and enjoy life a bit before things got busy again.

Air Force General Anatoliy Gryzlov liked to get out of the office at least once a month and fly. With training hours in short supply, it was a luxury even most Russian general officers could not manage. But Gryzlov was different: Because he was the deputy minister of defense for the Russian government and the chief of the general staff of the military forces of the Russian Federation, he got everything he wanted. The troops loved seeing the former bomber pilot, test pilot, and cosmonaut at their base, and they were absolutely thrilled to see the fifty-nine-year-old chief of the general staff take command of a mission.

Unlike many Russian military men, Gryzlov was slight of stature, slender, and quick, with light brown hair cut short—he actually looked good in a flight suit, even a bulky winter-weight one. He found it easy to maneuver inside his favorite aircraft, the famed Tupolev-160 long-range strategic bomber, the one the West called the "Blackjack" bomber. Originally designed to attack the United States of America with nuclear weapons, the Tu-160 was still by far the world's largest attack aircraft. Capable of supersonic dash speeds in excess of two thousand kilometers per hour at midaltitude and near-supersonic speeds at terrain-following altitude, the Tupolev-160 could deliver as many as twelve cruise missiles or a total of more than forty thousand kilograms of weapons at unrefueled ranges of well over fourteen thousand kilometers. Only forty were built, but the little wing at Engels Air Base near Saratov, six hundred kilometers southeast of Moscow, was the pride of the Russian air force.

Gryzlov made his way back from the cockpit and sat in the instructor's seat between the navigator/bombardier and defensive-systems officers, who sat side by side in their ejection seats behind the two pilots. Although the Tu-160 was a dream to fly, and the best seat in the house was definitely the cockpit—except during landing, when the long nose and very high approach and landing speeds made landing the Blackjack very, very hairy—all the action was back here. He stopped at the "honey bucket" in the rest area between the pilots' and systems officers' compartments and took a pee, glancing wryly at the toilet-paper holder hanging on a wire next to the bucket—the only piece of wood, it was said, carried aloft on a Russian attack plane.

The systems operators' compartment was dark but spacious—there was even enough room for beach chairs and ice chests back here for very long flights, although they were not needed on this one. "How is it going, Major?" Gryzlov asked cross-cockpit.

"Very well, sir," Major Boris Bolkeim, the navigator/bombardier, replied. He gave the DSO, or defensive systems officer, a swat on the shoulder, and the other man hurriedly safed his ejection seat and started to unstrap so Gryzlov could sit there. But Gryzlov shook his hand at the DSO to tell him to stay put and instead took the jump seat. "Twenty minutes to initial point. The system's doing well."

"Any warning broadcasts, Captain?"

"None, sir," responded Captain Mikhail Osipov, the defensive systems officer. "All known frequencies are silent. I'm a little surprised."

"Hopefully it means everyone's done his job," Gryzlov said. Bolkeim offered Gryzlov a Russian cigarette, but the chief of staff took out a pack of Marlboros, and both he and the DSO accepted hungrily. As they smoked, they chatted about the mission, the military, their families at home. It was just like old times, Gryzlov thought—taking a break before the action started, talking about everything and nothing in particular. This was the part of the job he really enjoyed, getting out into the field with the troops, having a little fun, and doing some serious business at the same time. Sure, he was showing his stars, too, but that wasn't the main reason he did it.

It was not a particularly good time to be chief of the general staff. Anatoliy Gryzlov was unlucky enough to take over the position from the disgraced and imprisoned Valeriy Zhurbenko, who had tried to make a deal with a Russian mobster to force a number of Balkan states to agree to allow the mobster, Pavel Kazakov, to build a pipeline through their country. Gryzlov was nothing more than a politically expedient choice—he was a highly decorated and capable but profoundly unpolitical air force officer—just the way the Russian parliament wanted it.

Unfortunately, that also meant he was no friend of anyone in the Kremlin, especially the president, Valentin Gennadievich Sen'kov. So far that didn't seem to make too much difference. Sen'kov was lying low, reluctant to poke his nose out of the Kremlin too far for fear of its getting bitten off by some zealous—or jealous—politician. Things were just plain stagnant in Moscow these days. There was no money to do anything—which was fine with most folks, since no one really wanted to do much of anything anyway.

But Gryzlov wanted something more. Gryzlov was a former Russian air force interceptor pilot, flight test pilot, and astronaut. With his gymnast's physique, he exuded energy—and he saw most of his energy going to waste in the eyes of his troops, everyone from generals to the lowliest clerks and cooks.

A perfect example of the lack of Russian determination: Chechnya. The little Russian enclave in southern Russia, between the Black Sea and the Caspian Sea, had already been granted limited autonomy by the Russian government, yet the Muslim separatists there still held considerable power and still performed acts of terrorism throughout Russia, especially in neighboring Dagestan province. The separatists were being openly supported by the pro-Muslim governments of nearby Azerbaijan, who in turn were funded and supported by the Islamic Republic of Iran and the Republic of Turkey.

The place was still a Russian province, for God's sake. And with just a few hundred thousand people in all of the province of Chechnya, most of whom lived in the major cities of Grozny and Gudermes, and very few resources except for the fertile farmlands in the east. It should be simple, Gryzlov thought, to crush the Chechen rebels no matter how much support they were getting from overseas. But the terrain was very rugged in the south, which made it easy for guerrillas and terrorists to covertly move out of the country into Dagestan and the former Soviet republic of Georgia.

That's why, when reliable intelligence information came in about rebel movements, it was important to react quickly. Sending in ground forces was almost always a waste of time—the rebels knew the mountains better than the military did. Helicopter gunships were effective, but the rebels had every known or suspected full- or part-time helicopter base within five hundred kilometers under constant surveillance. If a single helicopter moved, the rebels knew about it instantly.

The best way to deal with the rebels was by air from well outside the region. Anatoliy Gryzlov preferred the long-range bombers. Not because he was a former bomber pilot, but because they were the most effective weapon system for the job—as long as the political will to use them still existed. He was determined to spark that political will. He wanted nothing more than to begin an era of Russian military dominance in all of Central Asia and Europe—starting with the breakaway province of Chechnya.

"Ten minutes to initial point," the bombardier announced.

"General?" the pilot called back on intercom.

"I'll stay back here," Gryzlov said. The spare pilot took the copilot's seat, and Gryzlov tightened his shoulder straps in the jump seat and got ready for the action.

Large numbers of rebel forces had been detected moving north from the Republic of Georgia along the Caucasus Mountains between Dagestan and Chechnya. They had been untouchable and virtually untrackable until they were most likely forced to leave the protection of the mountains—driven out, no doubt, by the freezing temperatures and unbearable living conditions of the mountains—and moved into the small mining town of Vedeno, just sixteen kilometers north of the provincial border. The force was estimated at about two to three thousand—a very large force to be traveling together. Not all were fighters, perhaps four or five hundred; the rest were family members and support personnel.

"Initial point in one minute," the navigator/bombardier announced. He checked his inertial navigation system's drift rate—less than two miles per hour, pretty good for this system. He made the final radar update and zeroed out all of the system's velocity errors, then dumped the latest alignment, heading, position, and velocity information to the twenty-four Kh-15 short-range attack missiles they carried in the bomber's two huge bomb bays.

The plan was simple: first cut it off, then kill it.

At the initial point the bombardier began launching the

missiles. One by one, each 1,200-kilogram missile dropped from its rotary launcher, ignited its solid-rocket motor, and shot off into space. A protective coating kept the missile safe as it flew at over twice the speed of sound up to fifteen thousand meters altitude, then started its terminal dive on its targets.

The first twelve missiles, carrying 150-kilogram high-explosive warheads, hit bridges and major intersections of the roads leading in and out of the rebels' sanctuary at Vedeno. Since the missiles had a range of almost ninety kilometers, no one on the ground had any warning of the attack. Five other Tu-160 Blackjack bombers also launched their missiles around the outskirts of Vedeno from long range, blasting away at known vehicle-marshaling areas, storage facilities, hideouts, and encampments outside the town.

The second phase of the attack didn't commence for ten minutes. The reason was simple: The rebels' typical pattern when under attack was to leave their families behind in town and try to escape into the mountains. In ten minutes they should just be discovering that their escape routes had been cut off—leaving them out in the open. At that moment the Tu-160s opened up their aft bomb bays.

And the real carnage began.

All the aft bomb bays carried twelve more Kh-15 missiles on rotary launchers, but the warheads on these contained fuel-air explosive devices. Explosive fuel was dispensed in a large cloud about two hundred meters aboveground and then ignited, creating a massive fireball over three hundred meters in diameter that instantly incinerated anything it touched. And each missile was targeted not just for the outskirts of Vedeno but for the town itself.

Within moments the place that was once the city of Vedeno was completely engulfed in fire. Over four square kilometers were leveled and burned instantly, and the overpressure caused by the multiple fuel-air explosions destroyed anything within seven square kilometers. The only thing left standing was the Caucasus Mountains, completely denuded of all vegetation and wiped clean of snow, with immense blankets of smoke and steam rising into the night sky.

"Good job, everyone," Gryzlov said. He shook hands with the systems officers, then returned to the copilot's seat. The pilot was just checking in the rest of the formation—all aircraft in the green, all aircraft released live weapons, all aircraft returning to base. "Excellent job, everyone," Gryzlov radioed on the secure command frequency to the other bombers in the formation. "I'm buying the first round back home."

BATTLE MOUNTAIN, NEVADA
That evening

Air Force Colonel Daren Mace decided to drive his beat-up Ford pickup into town to look around before heading out to the base. The town of Battle Mountain was hardly more than a dusty bump in the road off Interstate 80 in northern Nevada. With the construction of the Air Reserve base, several civilian construction projects were also under way—a large chain hotel and casino, a sizable truck stop, several apartment buildings, and a small single-family-home subdivision—but even after three years since construction began on the base, the town had changed very little. It still had its old, isolated, mining-town rough edge.

Closing in on the big five-oh, Daren Mace had recently turned into the world's biggest health freak, which for him was a complete one-eighty from his previous lifestyle.

Not long before, his favorite hangout for everything from mission planning to dating to doing his taxes was in a tavern somewhere—he was such a fixture in some of his favorite places that he could often be seen serving drinks or repairing equipment in his spare time. But then he found himself needing glasses for reading, found his flight suits getting a little tight around the middle, so he started an exercise regime. Now every day started off with a run. His consumption of beer, cigarettes, and pizza also declined, as did his blood pressure and cholesterol count, so he was able to maintain the same lean, trim figure he'd had most of his adult life, even though he was getting more and more deskbound in his military career.

Sure, the hair was turning grayer, and he was popping aspirins almost every morning to counteract the unexpected little aches he'd encounter. But those were all signs of maturity—weren't they?

Maturity was never one of his strong suits in the past. Born and raised in Jackpot, Nevada, several hours' drive northeast of Battle Mountain, the younger Mace found that his main concerns usually involved staying one step ahead of his strict parents, the game wardens during his many illegal hunting trips in the high desert, the fathers of his various love interests, and—first on the list—getting the hell out of back-country Nevada. The Air Force was his ticket out.

His twenty-three-year Air Force career wasn't all aches and pains. Because of his exceptional knowledge, his skills, and his ability to think, plan, and execute quickly and effectively, Mace was one of the youngest aviators ever chosen to fly the FB-111A "Aardvark" supersonic strategic bomber, at a time when there were only forty of the long-range nuclear-armed bombers in the Air Force inventory and only six navigators per year chosen from the entire force to serve on them. He didn't disappoint. He was not only a knowledgeable and hardworking bombardier and crew member, but he took the time to study the aircraft, all its systems, and its incredible capabilities. Mace soon became known as the primary expert in all facets of the "Go-Fast" supersonic strike aircraft.

So in 1990, during Operation Desert Shield, Daren Mace was the natural choice for one of the most important and dangerous missions conceived as a result of the Iraqi invasion of Kuwait and the tensions created in the Middle East—the American response to an all-out nuclear, chemical, or biological attack by Iraq or one of the other hostile nations against U.S. forces in the region. Should such an attack take place, Mace's mission was to take off in his FB-111A bomber from a secret air base in eastern Turkey and launch thermonuclear-tipped missiles at four of Iraq's most important underground command-and-control centers, all in one mission.

On January 17, 1991, the Iraqis attacked Israel with a SCUD rocket armed with what was thought to be a chemical-weapon warhead, and several more SCUDs hit areas of Saudi Arabia, close to where American troops were garrisoned. Mace and his squadron commander took off from Batman Air Base in Turkey on their deadly mission to stop the Iraqi war machine from launching any more weapons of mass destruction. Loaded with four three-thousand-gallon fuel tanks and four AGM-69A short-range attack missiles tipped with three-hundred-kiloton thermonuclear warheads, they zoomed in at treetop level under cover of darkness, at full military power or greater the whole way. They received the execution order: It would be America's first nuclear attack since World War II.

Except it hadn't been a chemical-weapon attack. It was determined that the Iraqi warhead did not contain chemical or biological weapons—the rocket had hit a dry-cleaning facility, and the chemicals released from inside the building mimicked chemical weapons. Within minutes an abort code was sent to the strike aircraft.

Moments before launch, the crew received a coded message. There was no time to decode it before launch, and they already had a valid strike order authorizing them to launch their missiles—but Mace canceled the attack anyway. Legally, procedurally, he should have fired his nuclear missiles. Instead Mace used his common sense and his gut feeling and aborted.

Now deep inside enemy territory, flying right over Iraq's most sensitive military areas, the crew had relied on the nuclear strike to help them escape. Without it they were in the fight of their lives. With no fighter protection, low on fuel, and heavily loaded with dangerous weapons, they were attacked mercilessly with every weapon in the Iraqi air-defense arsenal. Mace's aircraft commander was badly injured and his plane shot up and flying on one engine. Mace managed to do an emergency refueling with a KC-10 aerial refueling tanker that had crossed the Iraqi border to do the rendezvous before the FB-111 flamed out, then crash-landed his plane on a highway in northern Saudi Arabia.

In anyone's book, in any other situation, Mace would've been a hero. Instead he was ostracized as the bombardier who couldn't follow orders and had lost his nerve. He was bounced from assignment to assignment, squirreled away in remote operational locations, and then finally offered a Reserve commission. His fitness reports were always "firewalled"—meaning he always got the highest marks on job performance—but he was never considered for any command assignments, never believed to have the right stuff to command a tactical unit. His last assignment was as a protocol officer in the secretary of defense's office, where he'd been relegated to escorting VIPs and running errands for the honchos in the Pentagon.

Battle Mountain seemed to be the newest "squirrel's nest" for him.

Daren always seemed to gravitate toward bars and taverns located on the wrong side of town, and he did so again that night. There were four very small casinos in Battle Mountain, one open-all-day restaurant and eight that were open part-time, eight motels, four gas stations, and one truck stop. The truck stop had billiard tables, friendly waitresses, good burgers . . . and, next door, a brothel.

Donatella's looked nothing like the hundreds of antique stores, rock shops, or tourist traps that lined the highways. A flashing sign with a slinky black cat was the only visible advertisement. A long, wide ramp—the place was fully wheelchair-accessible—was enclosed and brilliantly lit, with a valet-parking attendant and buzzer-operated iron gate at the bottom and a doorman/bouncer and another buzzer-operated gate at the top of the ramp. It reminded Daren of entering an alert facility when he pulled nuclear duty in the FB-111s. There was even covered parking for motorcycles. Daren was impressed. He'd never been in a brothel before, so he decided to check it out.

Once buzzed inside, Daren found himself in a large, comfortable room, with two living-room areas to the right, a long mahogany bar in front, and a space to the right with several dining tables. His view of the bar, however, was blocked—by six lovely women in evening gowns standing before him. When the buzzer button at the bottom of the ramp was pressed, Daren assumed, it gave the otherwise unengaged ladies time to assemble at the front door for the "introductions."

"Good evening, sir," said the madam, who introduced

herself as Miss Lacey. She extended a hand in a courtly, almost old southern manner. "How nice to see you."

"Good evening, Miss Lacey," Daren responded. He took a moment to make eye contact with each of the ladies arrayed before him. "How is everyone tonight?" They all murmured responses while maintaining their seductive poses and inviting smiles. He'd never seen anything like this before, not even growing up in Nevada. Brothels were strictly off-limits to kids under eighteen—his parents strictly enforced that rule, and Jackpot was too small to get away with much—and he was out of Nevada before he turned eighteen.

"I'd like to introduce you to the ladies." Miss Lacey named them, one by one, using their "stage" names. "Please make yourself comfortable. If you'd like a tour, please feel free to ask at any time. Enjoy yourself tonight." The ladies slowly departed, making eye contact again—the last sales pitch before working the room again.

Daren went to the bar. He automatically picked up a menu, just as he did at the truck stop, but was shocked to find it was a menu of sex selections, not food selections. A big guy behind the bar in a Hawaiian-print shirt stepped over to him. "Good evening, sir," the bartender said. "I'm Tommy. What'll you have?"

Daren put a ten on the bar. "Sparkling water. How's it going tonight?"

"Not bad, not bad." The bartender served him a bottle of Pellegrino and a chilled glass. "Are you military?" he asked as he poured.

"Yep."

"Can I ask you a question?"

"You a spy or something?" Daren asked, grinning over the rim of his glass as he drank.

"No. I just wanted to know if you knew how long

they keep recruits incommunicado after they start basic training?"

"You have a kid in boot camp?"

"My oldest son. I only just heard he was going into the service. Me and his mother split up—she didn't approve of me workin' here at Donatella's, even though the money's good—and she moved off to Reno with the kids. I found out he's in San Antonio."

"The only phone recruits can normally use is in the orderly room," Daren explained. "They can't hang out in the orderly room until the weekends, and only if they've finished all their other duties, which they can rarely do. Most of the time, even if they're all caught up, they're too exhausted after the first week to do anything else but sleep and eat."

"So what do I do?"

"Wait till next weekend. The drill sergeants are good about reminding recruits to call home often. In fact, most DIs withhold money from recruits' pay for phone calls, postage, stationery, haircuts—that sort of thing."

"Is that right? Thanks," Tommy said. "He's my oldest boy, and I hardly seen him at all since the old lady moved to Reno. I should've taken the time and gone to his high-school graduation—I didn't know he enlisted and had to report right after graduation."

"I can help you find out when basic training is over. You get the time off and go," Daren suggested. "You won't recognize him. He'll have lost a bunch of weight, he'll call you 'sir' until you're sick of it, and he'll be as hard as a rock."

Tommy looked amazed, since he himself was six feet four and weighed more than three hundred pounds—no doubt his son was more than a chip off the old block. "No shit? That I gotta see. Thanks again." He went about his business.

A few moments later one of the courtesans came up to Daren. "Hi there," she said. "I'm Amber."

"How are you tonight, Amber?"

"I'm fine, really fine." Amber looked as if she was in her mid-twenties. Her blond hair was real, but the life had gone out of it, and she obviously overdosed on mousse to fluff it up. She was thin, verging on gaunt, but she was adorned with a fabulous set of breast implants that could have easily weighed more than the rest of her entire body.

"Would you like a drink?"

"Yes, thanks. Same as you is just fine." While her drink was being served, she stepped around him, letting her fingertips trace a line across his chest, and started kneading his shoulders. She certainly had *very* strong hands—she might even have been a masseuse at one time, but Daren thought she'd probably earned those strong hands in a number of other pursuits. "Hard day at work, handsome?"

"Just got into town."

"New job?"

"Yep."

"New boss, new town—lots of tension, huh?"

"You know it."

She waved her hand and snapped her fingers. "I can take away all that tension for you, just like *that*."

"How?"

"How about a dip in the hot tub and a massage. Care to join me?"

"A hot tub, huh? That sounds like fun." He'd never done anything like this before, and he had no idea what was in store—but he knew it involved copious amounts of money. "What does a dip in the hot tub and a massage with you go for?"

"Follow me and I'll show you around first." Daren believed that she had practically pushed him away from the bar and down a long hallway, but in fact he'd moved perfectly well on his own.

Amber led Daren into a room with a king-size bed, a pillow-backed couch, a bathroom with a large double-headed shower, and a TV with a VCR bolted to the ceiling, tuned to CNN. Somehow Tommy the bartender had already placed a large bottle of ice-cold Pellegrino with two chilled glasses on a coffee table in front of the couch, where Amber now led Daren.

Exactly when Amber poured him a glass of Pellegrino, Daren couldn't tell, because she did it so seductively and so tantalizingly that he wasn't watching the glass. "I want you to just sit back, relax, and unwind," Amber said. She took a sip and sat next to him. "I'm here for whatever you'd like to do." She gazed at him as she drank.

"First time in a brothel?"

"Definitely."

"It's simple: We're here to make you feel good and make sure you have a good time," Amber said.

"I saw the sex menu—nearly fell out of my chair."

"Oh, that's for the tourists mainly," she said with a smile. She got up, walked behind him, and continued massaging his shoulders. "But don't go by that. It's whatever you want tonight. If it's just a back rub, I'm pretty good at that. If you think you might want to try the hot tub or the shower or a full-body massage, we can do that. If you'd like the whole round-trip ticket, we can do that, too."

"This back rub is good for starters. What do you get for a back rub?"

"I do this for tips," Amber said. "But I specialize in massages—hands-free, whole-body massages."

" 'Hands-free' massages? What's that?"

She crossed around in front of him, stepped between his knees; her hands went to the back of her gown at her neck, and she undid something. The gown fell away like a wisp of vapor.

"Ohhh . . ."

This had to be part of the sales pitch, the gab, the come-on. Okay, Daren figured, he'd let the pro do her thing.

Amber's hips were swaying, her humongous breasts seemingly tracing their own separate orbits in front of him. "What do you say, baby?"

"I say that's the best damned sales pitch I've ever seen."

"Thank you." She poured herself a glass of Pellegrino, took a sip, moved around behind him again, then continued her back rub, using her elbows on the knots she found. She brushed her bare breasts against the back of his neck while continuing with her massage. She was good, Daren thought, *very* damned good. "You're a sweet guy"— Amber let her hands roam across his chest, delicately pinching his nipples under his shirt—"and you definitely got it goin' on."

"Thanks, Amber."

"Are you in the military?"

"Yes."

"A flier?"

He nodded.

"Things are getting busy out there at the base, but it still seems like an awfully lonely place."

"Is that part of the sales pitch, too?"

"Anything I can do to keep you here a while longer, I'll do." She let her breasts touch his neck again. "Anything at all." The law of diminishing returns said get him the hell out of there before she lost too much more money on him that evening. "What do you say, flyboy? A relaxing hot tub, my deluxe full-body, hands-free massage, a nice shower—one hour, two hundred dollars. Anything else you think you'd like, just tell me, and we'll renegotiate."

Her instincts were right. "Maybe some other time," Daren said. He downed the last of the Pellegrino. "You could be a first-class masseuse in any hotel in San Francisco or Hawaii, Amber."

"Thank you," she said. Her eyes glistened with humor. "I am first class, that's for sure. You need to find out for yourself someday."

"Maybe I will."

"You don't think highly of the world's oldest profession?"

"I never thought about it before now."

"It's a job like any other—your attitude determines what you get out of it," Amber said as she put her gown on again. "The reality is, I make a lot more money than you do, I work fewer hours, I live my life the way I want, and here in Nevada no one messes with me. I'm an independent contractor. There are thirty-seven legal brothels in the great state of Nevada, and if Battle Mountain bores me, I can pick up and work in any one of them tomorrow without a problem. I have lots of boyfriends and girlfriends, and I'm never alone if I don't want to be. As long as I stay clean, off the booze and off the coke, I'll be okay. Oh, and did I mention? I make a hell of a lot more money than you do."

"Chasing the almighty dollar."

"Damned right I am," Amber said. "There will come a time when the money won't matter, and then I'll get out."

"Hopefully before you catch some STD."

"You fly military jets and drop bombs with thousands of guns, missiles, and fighters after your ass trying to blow you out of the sky—and you think *my* line of work is dangerous? Give me a break. Besides, I get more medical exams and blood tests in one month than you do in two years. And we don't mess around with the DC here—I check my clients out very carefully, each and every time, or they don't get to ride the pony. And everyone wears a raincoat—even my boyfriends, the ones I've known for years. How do you flyboys put it? 'Managed risk'? That's what I do. That's what we all do."

She gave him one more of her patented seductive looks. "Please don't be judgmental, of me or of yourself. I'm happy—you should be happy, too. Learn to enjoy life. That's why I'm here. If having sex with a pro bothers you . . . well, there's lots of things I can do with you to please and entertain you, even if you don't want the whole round trip. A nice hot tub, a massage, then . . . we'll talk about what comes up?"

Daren laughed at the old joke despite himself. He certainly never expected to meet someone like her in a place like this.

"You look worried about something."

"New job, new boss . . . old flame."

"You mean your new boss in your new job is an old flame? Jeez, no wonder you're tense, baby." She continued to massage. "So who left whom?"

"She left me. Moved onward and upward. I kinda moved . . . sideways."

"Now you work for her? Ouch."

"Yeah."

Amber moved her hands down over his shoulders and across his chest in a last-ditch effort before dumping this guy and moving on to the next prospect. "You have nothing to worry about, tiger. I have a feeling the wrong one got promoted. Now she realizes she needs you back. But she's hoping you'll drag the old luggage along with you, because then she'll have emotional control as well as pull rank on you. Don't do it. Don't go in there carrying a torch." She leaned over and nibbled on his ear. "Let Amber take some of that heat. Give it to me, tiger. Right now."

Daren felt the serpent stir, but his mind was not on the

task Amber had in mind. "You're a sweetheart, Amber. Maybe some other time." He got up and left a few twenty-dollar bills on the table.

"I hope to see more of you," Amber said, giving him a head-to-toe appraisal and one more smile. Daren smiled in return, gave her a similar once-over, nodded in approval, then left.

It was not quite dark outside yet. Daren's car was parked across the street at the truck stop. When he paused outside Donatella's on the side of the dusty chip-and-seal road to wait for traffic to pass, he thought that this had to be one of the more interesting and yet otherworldly places he had ever visited in his Air Force career. He'd certainly been in more remote places, but . . .

When he finally snapped out of his musings, he noticed that the traffic he'd been waiting for still hadn't passed by him. He looked up at the driver to see if whoever it was was waiting for him to cross.

And realized with surprise that he knew the person behind the wheel—it was none other than Rebecca Furness, his new wing commander. Oh, *shit* . . .

Nine years earlier both Mace and Furness had been assigned to the 394th Wing of the Air Force Reserve at Plattsburgh Air Force Base in upstate New York, flying the RF-111G Vampire reconnaissance-strike aircraft. At the time Rebecca was a highly decorated major. Daren Mace was a lieutenant colonel, newly assigned as the bomb wing's maintenance-group commander. As Reservists, they both had lives outside the Air Force—Rebecca ran a small air-delivery service, Daren did fix-it jobs for a biker bar in town. Somehow—perhaps because they were both loners who craved respect and recognition from their peers but could find it only in each other—the two developed a mutual attraction, and then a passion.

Just a few months after Daren joined the unit, the wing

unexpectedly deployed to Turkey. Russia had invaded the Republic of Ukraine, a fledgling member of the North Atlantic Treaty Organization. The president of the United States at the time distrusted the military and didn't want to chance starting a war, no matter what the risk to the nation, so he decided to send a single reconnaissance unit to Turkey, simply to monitor the conflict and help Turkey keep an eye on its feuding neighbors. Rebecca and her fellow fliers weren't supposed to do any fighting—they were there in Turkey simply for show, to try to prove that the United States was committed to helping its allies even though the president really didn't want to get involved.

As it turned out, Rebecca and her squadron became the heroes of the war, leading a joint Ukrainian-American-Turkish air armada that managed to temporarily blind and deafen the entire command-and-control system in southwest Russia. Russia had no option but to stop its offensive and withdraw its military forces from Ukraine and other neighboring republics.

From then on, Rebecca Furness's rising star became a shooting star that seemed unstoppable. She was given the choicest assignments available and promoted at every possible opportunity. It was Rebecca's example that designed the shape of the United States Air Force's structure for the next decade: drawing down the size of the active-duty force and giving more and more war-fighting responsibility to Reserve forces. She was quickly promoted to full colonel and became the first female wing commander of a combat strike unit, the 111th Bomb Wing of the Nevada Air National Guard, flying the B-1B Lancer supersonic bomber from Reno-Tahoe International Airport. Following successful action against Chinese and North Korean forces after the reunification of the Korean Peninsula, as well as her efforts over Russia and the Balkans, Rebecca was promoted to brigadier general.

Daren's career wasn't at all meteoric—in fact, it was virtually stagnant. Although he crewed with Rebecca in the RF-111G and was responsible for the successful planning and execution of the raid on the Domodedovo underground military command center south of Moscow, he kept his "black cloud" reputation for always being in the middle of the action when things went bad. When the RF-111G program was canceled a short time after the Russia-Ukraine conflict, Daren continued to be steered into quiet, out-of-the-way assignments. He was eventually promoted to full colonel without any fanfare. He did manage to complete all the service schools required for him to assume command of a flying unit, including the Air War College, the Joint Forces Warfighting College, and the Industrial College of the Air Force. But he still lacked operational command experience.

Now he stepped over to the passenger-side window of her GMC Yukon, and she rolled down the window. "Holy cow, Rebecca," he said. "What a surprise."

"Daren Mace. Yes, it is a surprise." She glanced over his shoulder at the flashing black-cat sign in front of Donatella's. "I see you're not hanging out at biker bars anymore. Getting the 'lay' of the land?"

Daren suddenly realized what she meant, and he couldn't stop his face from falling in shock. "I . . . no, I didn't . . . I mean, I went in, but I didn't—"

"It's okay, Colonel," she interrupted. "Paying money to have sex with strange women is perfectly legal in Lander County—pathetic and sad, but still legal." She rolled up the window and sped off.

This assignment is starting off just great, he thought ruefully. Just great.

* * *

It was not far to the base from Donatella's. Daren Mace liked to show up at a new assignment several days early and wander around anonymously to get the overall layout and a sense of the pace, the tone, and the mood of the place. But he quickly realized that this place didn't have a pace, a tone, or a mood—in fact, it didn't have very many paved roads, a front gate, or even very many human beings for that matter.

The government had been working on Battle Mountain Air National Guard Base, outside the town of Battle Mountain in north-central Nevada, for three years, and they had virtually nothing to show for it. All he could see were a few sterile-looking multistory buildings scattered across the high desert plain. There was a runway out there, of course: twelve thousand feet long, he knew, three hundred feet wide, stressed to take a million-pound aircraft, but he couldn't see it at all. He remembered reading the Internet articles about the world's biggest boondoggle—a twelve-thousand-foot-long runway in the middle of nowhere, with no air base around the monstrous strip of reinforced concrete. The control tower's location didn't give a clue as to where the runway was, because there *was* no control tower.

Further, it really didn't look like very much work was being done now—he would've thought there'd be armies of construction workers swarming all over the place. What had they been doing here all that time? Was this base going to open or not? He did see a few aircraft hangars and decided that was the only place his new unit could be.

As it turned out, Battle Mountain Air Force Base did have a security force—a few minutes after driving onto the base, he was stopped by a patrol car. "Good evening, Colonel Mace," the officer, an Air Force sergeant, greeted him, after stepping up to his car and snapping a salute.

"I'm Sergeant Rollins, One-eleventh Attack Wing Security Forces. Welcome to Battle Mountain Air Force Base."

Mace returned the salute. "How do you know who I am, Sergeant?"

"We've been monitoring your arrival, sir," Rollins replied. "I've been asked to start your in-processing."

" 'In-processing'?" Mace asked incredulously. He looked at his jogger's Timex. "It's seven P.M. Is the Support Group still open for business?"

"I just need your ID card and orders, sir," Rollins said. After Mace fished out the paperwork from his briefcase, the sergeant held out a device and asked Mace to put both his thumbprints on it, like an electronic inkpad. "Thank you. Please stand by, sir," the sergeant said, and he returned to his vehicle with Mace's ID card and orders. Mace had to wait almost ten minutes and was just on the verge of getting out of the car to complain about the delay—but he was pleasantly surprised when the officer returned with a base decal, an updated ID card, a flight-line pass, and a restricted-area pass. Mace looked at all the documents in wonder. "Where did you get this photograph?" he asked, motioning to the new ID card.

"I took it, sir."

"When?"

"The moment I walked up to your vehicle, sir," the officer replied. Sure enough, the guy's flashlight contained a tiny digital camera, because the face on the picture *was* him, sitting in his car.

"You can't use that picture on my ID cards, Sergeant," Mace protested. "I'm not in uniform. I haven't even shaved yet."

"Doesn't matter, sir," the officer responded. "We use biometric identification equipment now—you could have a month's growth and we'd still be able to ID you. We've already taken your picture a dozen times since you've been driving around the base. We've registered your vehicle and correlated the registration with your identity, we've scanned you and your vehicles, and we've even noted that you're carrying unloaded weapons in your trunk. If you'd like, I can register them for you right now." Mace opened the trunk for the officer and took the guns out of their locked cases. The officer simply scanned the weapons with his flashlight again, and minutes later he had electronically added the registration information to Mace's ID card. "You're all in-processed," he announced.

"I'm *what?*"

"Security Forces can network in with the wing's computer system from our cars, so we can initiate in-processing when the newcomers arrive on base, sir," Rollins said. "Everything's been done—housing, pay and allowances, official records, medical, pass and ID, uniforms—even predeployment. You'll be notified by e-mail if anyone needs to see you in person, such as the flight surgeon or base dentist. Orientation briefings are conducted by videoconference or by computer. Your unit duty section and the wing commander's office have also been notified that you're on base. Are there any questions I can answer for you, sir?"

"Is there a base gym?"

"Afraid not, sir. Each unit on base will probably set up its own facilities until the base builds one. Security Forces has a pretty good one, which you're welcome to use until the Fifty-first builds its own."

"The Fifty-first?"

"Your squadron, sir." The Security Forces sergeant smiled mischievously. "That happens all the time, sir— my system knows more about you than you do. The duty officer will be able to direct you to motels in the area that can accept your PCS orders as payment until you find permanent quarters."

"Already taken care of," Daren said. "Mind if I just drive around a bit?"

"Not at all, sir," the officer said. "Your duty officer will be able to direct you, and she'll keep you away from any restricted areas. Call her using this." He handed Mace a small plastic case. "This is your commlink. If you need anything, just call the duty officer. She's expecting your call. Let me be the first to welcome you." He shook Mace's hand, then snapped him a salute. "Have a nice evening, sir."

Daren Mace sat in his car and marveled at what had just happened. No one else around for what seemed like miles except him and a sky cop—and he was already in-processed into his new unit. Amazing. In-processing was normally a weeklong drudgery of meetings, briefings, and paperwork. He just completed it in ten minutes. He put the commlink away. Someone would have to explain how to use it later.

Instead of asking for directions, Daren thought he'd drive around a bit. Although there were very few buildings anywhere, the northeast side of the base seemed completely deserted, with only construction equipment and concrete-making stuff—Portland cement, gravel, sand, and stone—piled everywhere. He noticed a forty-foot steel trailer painted in desert camouflage sitting about a hundred meters off an access road, with a few cars and trucks parked nearby. He could see no evidence of the container's having been dragged or trailered off the road—it must have been airlifted in, or brought in an awful long time ago.

Daren decided to check it out for himself, so he stepped out of his pickup truck and walked up the access road toward the big trailer. There was a power generator running—he could hear it, but he couldn't yet see it. As he got closer, he could see a small satellite dish, a microwave antenna, and several smaller antennas on top. What in hell . . . ?

He heard a loud *fwooosh!* and suddenly his path was blocked—by some kind of android-looking figure dressed in black. It had appeared out of nowhere. It wore a seamless dark suit, a full-head helmet with an opaque visor over the eyes, a thin backpack, and thick boots.

"This is a restricted area, sir," the menacing figure said in an electronically synthesized voice. Daren stumbled backward in complete surprise, scrambled around, and started to run back to his car. "Hold on, Colonel Mace," the figure said.

Daren didn't stop running—in fact began running harder—until he ran headlong into what felt like a steel post. It turned out to be the android figure, again appearing right in front of him as if out of thin air.

"Relax, Colonel," the android said. Daren thought about running again, but this time the figure clamped its right hand around his left forearm, and Daren could tell right away it was not letting go. "Let's go, sir."

The android led him toward the trailer. Daren hadn't seen it from the road, but two camouflaged tents had been set up beyond the steel trailer, with two Humvees nearby. The android led him over to the smaller of the two tents, then released his arm. "He's expecting you inside, sir," the android said. It took three or four steps—then disappeared again after another loud, sharp *fwooosh!* sound stirred up a large cloud of desert dust.

Daren opened the tent flap and saw a man perhaps a few years younger than himself at a small camp table, typing on a laptop computer. Notebooks and computer printouts were scattered over the table. A small military field propane heater kept the tent reasonably warm, and on a small propane cookstove there were a pot of macaroni and cheese, half consumed, and another pot of water.

"C'mon in, Colonel," the man said. "I didn't know you'd be here on base so early. It's my good luck you happened on us tonight." He stood and extended a hand. "I'm—"

"I know who you are. Major General Patrick McLanahan," Daren said. "I recognize you from the news reports—President Thorn's first national security adviser."

"I doubt that," Patrick said tonelessly. "Nice to meet you."

"Nice to meet you too, sir," Mace said. They shook hands. "You were involved in that Korean conflict a couple years ago—you developed a squadron of B-1 bombers that launched ballistic-missile-interceptor missiles."

"That's right." What was left unsaid was the rest of the story: that McLanahan got himself kicked out of the Air Force as a result of the recent conflict with Russia over activities in the Balkans and the much-publicized crash of a B-1B Lancer bomber in Russia. Before that, his name had come up a few times: his experience with the now-defunct (but soon to be resurrected) Border Security Force and his work in defending Korea right after unification made him the front-runner in both the Martindale and now the Thorn administrations for national security adviser.

McLanahan's was a strange career, Daren thought, most of it shrouded in secrecy, rumor, and legend. Whenever there was some explosive, fast-moving international crisis that threatened to expand into a nuclear conflict, his name started popping up. "I would guess you were involved in that recent incident in Central Asia. Iran is claiming that one of our bombers illegally attacked Muslim forces inside Turkmenistan—then, the same day, that B-1 crashes in Diego Garcia. Iran claims it was the one that violated their airspace."

McLanahan shrugged. "I don't care much what Iran claims," he said dryly, taking a seat and busying himself on the laptop. Mace noticed it was not a denial, but he knew better than to quiz the guy who was probably his new boss, or at least a very high muck-a-muck. "What makes you think I had anything to do with something in Turkmenistan, Colonel?"

"Your reputation definitely precedes you, sir," Mace said. McLanahan glanced up; Daren couldn't tell if it was an irritated glare or an amused look. "If it makes any difference to you, sir, I think it's the kind of reputation *I'd* like to have," Daren added.

"If you care about working here and about your career in the military, Colonel, I wouldn't recommend it," McLanahan said. There was an uncomfortable pause. Then he went on, "I was impressed with your work with the Global Hawk wing at Beale Air Force Base. Those unmanned aerial vehicles had been in use for many years, but they still had some problems. You were able to overcome them and stood up the wing in very short time—the very first unmanned air wing. I thought you should have been given command of the wing—but their loss is my gain."

"Thank you, sir. I had a lot of good folks working for me. Actually, I ripped off a lot of the technology I used to bring the Hawks online from Zen Stockard and you guys at HAWC—specifically, your 'virtual cockpit' technology."

"Glad to be of help. We've done great improvements with the VC, and we're building a state-of-the-art facility to exploit it. What we needed was someone with both operational and engineering experience. We're going to ask you to do the same for us that you did with Beale's Global Hawks—get our aircraft and organization up to speed as quickly as possible. Your job will be to work with the wing commander and the engineering staff from the Tonopah Test Range."

Daren shook his head. "I'm confused, sir," he said. "I thought this was a tanker unit."

"We've got tankers here, yes."

"What other aircraft do you have here?"

"You haven't spoken with anyone from wing headquarters yet?"

"Well . . . I did run into General Furness in town a little while ago, but we didn't really talk."

Patrick's eyebrows raised in question at that. "I thought you two knew each other."

"It wasn't a good time to chat," Daren said, stumbling. He was thankful to see McLanahan nod, apparently willing to let it drop. "I just arrived tonight. My report date isn't until next week, but I decided to show early. I didn't imagine in-processing would only take ten minutes."

"Now I see why you're in the dark," McLanahan said with a slight smile. "You haven't had the nickel tour yet. I think I'll leave that up to General Furness or Colonel Long."

"What are you doing out here tonight, General?"

"Trying to nail down all the interface parameters between my virtual cockpit and my plane," he replied, "but we're missing something. We can't find it in the VC, I can't find it out here. It must be in the plane, but we still can't isolate it."

"What plane are you talking about, General?" Daren asked. "I haven't seen any planes here yet. And why in hell are you—"

"Shh. Not so loud—and watch your French." Patrick motioned with his head to his right, and Daren saw a small boy in a sleeping bag, lying on an inflatable mattress.

"Is . . . is that your *son*, General?" Daren whispered incredulously.

Patrick nodded. "Bradley James. I've been so busy the last several days, I haven't been with him very much. I couldn't stand being away from him any longer, so I told him we were going on a camping trip. I know it's forecast to go below freezing tonight, and he's got school, but I did it anyway. We cooked hot dogs and macaroni and cheese—his favorite comfort foods—we looked at the stars through a telescope, and he conked out."

"You took your son out to the desert while you're working on a project?"

"Couldn't think of anything else to do," Patrick said. He looked at his son and sighed. "I always wanted to take him out camping, but his mother didn't relish the idea. He has a rough night if we do something that we used to do together, so camping seemed to kill two birds"—he swallowed a bit, then corrected himself—"I mean, it seemed to fit the bill nicely."

Daren had heard something about some great tragedy in McLanahan's life, but no one had laid it out for him, out of respect for the man. It obviously had something to do with his wife, Bradley's mother. This was a very surreal scene: a young commanding general, personally monitoring a major project being conducted in his high-tech unit, but concerned—disturbed?—enough to bring his son out to the site in a sleeping bag. How weird was this?

"Anything I can help you with, sir?"

"I hope so. That's why I got you assigned here from the Pentagon," Patrick said. He ran his hands wearily over his face and his short-cropped hair. "This is not an official wing project, Daren. I've got no budget—not one dime. I'm stealing fuel and flight hours from the wing already as it is. But I promised the chief that I'd have something to show him."

"I don't get it, sir," Daren commented. "Aren't you the commanding officer here?"

"Officially, Daren, I don't exist here," McLanahan admitted. "The First Air Battle Force was stood up here, but we don't have a mission. It's my job to build one. The One-eleventh Wing is the only official unit here. My funding runs out September thirtieth of this year. I talked the chief and SECDEF into bringing them here to see if we can integrate them into a deployable force, but I don't have a staff or a budget. When the money runs out, it closes down."

"Excuse me, sir, but what exactly are you working on?" Daren asked.

McLanahan finished typing notes, got up, checked on Bradley to make sure he was warm enough, then motioned to Daren. "Come with me, Colonel."

Daren followed McLanahan out of the tent. He immediately saw the tall, android-looking figure standing nearby, now carrying a huge futuristic-looking weapon. "Excuse me, sir, but what in hell is that?"

"You mean 'who,'" Patrick corrected him. "Gunnery Sergeant Matthew Wilde, Air Battle Force ground operations," Patrick replied.

"Ground operations? You mean, *combat* ground operations?"

"That's the idea."

"What's he wearing? What's he carrying?"

"He's wearing electronic battle armor; he's carrying an electromagnetic rail gun."

"A *what* . . . ?"

"I'll explain later." They stepped quickly over to the steel trailer. McLanahan unlocked the door by pressing his thumb on a pad; the door opened with a hiss of pressurized air. Inside the tightly packed trailer were two seats facing simple consoles with two hand controllers; on either side of the seats were computer terminals; on the leftmost side, facing the front of the trailer, was a fifth console with three computer monitors, manned by a technician furiously entering commands into a computer keyboard. The inside of the trailer was so loud from the sound of the air-conditioning that the tech had to wear hearing protectors. But all this occupied only about a third of the trailer. The rest was jam-packed with electronics, circuit-board racks, power supplies, communications equipment, and air-conditioning units.

Daren recognized it all instantly: "It's a virtual-cockpit trailer," he said, surprise in his voice. "It's a lot bigger than I thought."

"How much bigger?" Patrick McLanahan asked.

"Global Hawk's entire control suite could fit in the back of a Humvee," Daren said.

"This is definitely first generation," McLanahan said. "We developed this trailer at Dreamland five years ago, and it was amazing that we fitted it all in here. I just flew the trailer out here today, but there's some snafu in the satellite link."

"The satellite link was the simplest part of the Global Hawk system," Daren said. "It's normally bulletproof. We had a simple satellite-phone hookup relaying instructions back and forth from the aircraft and control station." He went over to the middle left seat. It was obviously the pilot's seat, with a left-hand throttle control and a right-hand flight-control stick, but there were no other instruments visible—not even a computer screen. "What are you trying to control anyway?"

"Sit down and take a look," Patrick said. After Daren was seated, Patrick handed him a headset; it looked like standard aviation issue except for some strange protuberances on the crossband. When Daren tried to adjust the small, sharp probes that dug into his scalp from those arms, Patrick said, "No, don't touch those. You'll get used to them."

Daren sat with the strange-looking headset on his head and waited—and suddenly he was standing outside the tent, in the desert, in broad daylight, looking out across the runway! Superimposed on the image were all sorts of electronic data and symbology floating in space: magnetic heading, range readouts, a set of crosshairs, and flashing pointers. He whipped off the headset in complete shock, and the image instantly disappeared. *"What in hell . . . ? That was no projected image or hologram—I saw those images, just as clearly as I'm looking at you right now! How did you do that?"*

"An outgrowth of the ANTARES technology we developed about seven years ago," Patrick replied. "ANTARES stands for—"

"I know: Advanced Neural Transfer and Response System," Daren interjected. "Zen Stockard is a good friend of mine. I know he was spearheading the resurrected program a few years back. I applied for it myself." Jeff "Zen" Stockard was a flight test pilot at the High Technology Aerospace Weapons Center; along with the man standing before him, Patrick McLanahan, Stockard was one of the few people alive who had fully mastered the ANTARES thought-control system. Daren had applied for the ANTARES research program at Dreamland several times, thinking that surely the Pentagon would relish the idea of squirreling him away at that supersecret desert facility— but, like most of his requests for choice assignments, it was denied.

"Zen was big on any program at Dreamland that could help skilled pilots become better aviators," Patrick said. That was most evident in Zen's own case—he'd lost the use of his legs in a training exercise at Dreamland. "The system sends neural images to the wearer's brain, so he 'sees' all sorts of images transmitted to him—TV cameras, sensor images, text messages, computer data, any number of things—just as if the optic nerve were sending electrical signals from the eye to the brain.

"The problem we always had with ANTARES was we were trying to design a system that could control an entire aircraft by thought," Patrick went on. "Piping visual, sensory, or data images to the brain is a relatively simple task—it doesn't require any specialized theta-alpha training. So instead of using heads-up displays or fancy holograms to replicate an airplane cockpit, we just pipe datalinked images directly to the brain. The user can control which images he sees with ease—as quickly and easily as thinking about what you want to see. And everything stays simple if we eliminated the need to control the aircraft with ANTARES."

Daren donned the special headset again, and a few moments later the images returned. He could swivel his head and look all around the airfield. When he centered the crosshairs on a target such as the hangars on the other side of the runway, he got an exact range and bearing readout. When he turned his head to follow the flashing pointers, he found himself looking at a wooden box about ten feet square, exactly 425 meters away. "What am I looking at?" Daren asked.

"Some targets we set up south of the field."

"Where is the camera?"

"You're looking at what Sergeant Wilde was looking at."

"The big guy with the electronic armor and rail gun?"

McLanahan nodded. "The computer stores what he's already looked at in image files; when you tap in to his visual system, you can look at the latest stored image files that he's sent, as if you're looking at them yourself. You can look at what he's looking at in real time, too, but he can control that."

"Cool. How do I stop it?" But as soon as he thought about not looking at the image, it stopped, and he was again looking at the interior of the virtual-cockpit trailer. "Hey, I switched it! Very cool!" Daren switched the image back and forth with ease. "That works great. But what's the purpose?"

"Switch back to the virtual image." Daren did it in an instant. "Look at the target box. Got it?"

"Yep."

"Designate it as a target."

"How do I . . . ?" But again, as soon as he thought about doing it, the crosshairs blinked three times, and then a red triangle appeared superimposed on the box. "Aha! Got it."

"You've got a FlightHawk airborne with mini-Mavericks on board," Patrick told him. "Attack that target." This time it was simple: He thought about attacking the target, and a voice in his head announced, *"Attack ground target, stop attack."*

"Why did it say 'stop attack'?"

"That's the command you'd issue to stop the attack," McLanahan explained. He turned to a computer terminal beside him and verified that the original problem still existed—and sure enough, it did. "But here's where the problem comes in: The satellite datalink is messed up. The FlightHawk is either not receiving the command or receiving it but not executing it. We had the same problem with an operational test a few weeks ago. We couldn't get it to respond until we established a direct UCAV-to-aircraft link."

"Very cool—commanding a FlightHawk from guys on the ground using this virtual mind-link thing," Daren commented. "It's a pretty sophisticated routine—lots of data shooting back and forth over very long distances."

"But you did it with Global Hawk all the time, right?"

"Well . . . we don't actually *fly* a Global Hawk unmanned recon plane from the ground, sir," Daren pointed out. "It has to have a flight plan loaded in memory first. We can make lots of changes to that flight plan, but it has to have the flight plan first."

"I *want* to be able to fly the UCAV, Daren," Patrick said. "I understand what you're saying about Global Hawk, but the ability to keep the man in the loop is important to any attack mission. Besides, we still have to be able to manually control the plane for certain phases of flight."

"Which phases, sir? Certainly not flying straight and level?"

"How about a rendezvous with another aircraft?"

"As in refuel a FlightHawk from a tanker?"

"How about fly one right up inside the bomb bay of a B-1 bomber?"

"A B-1 bomber!" Daren exclaimed. His eyes widened in surprise, but then he shrugged. "Why not? I think you have the technology to do that right now. A computer the size of my wristwatch can fly a B-1 better than any pilot I've ever known." He paused for a moment, then said, "We can do it one better, sir."

"How?"

"Why don't you fly both the FlightHawk *and the B-1 bomber*—right from the VC."

"Make the carrier aircraft *and* the attack aircraft *unmanned?*"

"Why not?" Daren Mace asked. "I know you can already monitor and control most every system aboard the B-1 from the virtual cockpit. It wouldn't be too much of a stretch to make the Vampire fly *itself.*"

"But why are we interested in making the carrier aircraft unmanned?" Patrick asked. He already had some answers himself, but he wanted to hear Daren's reasoning.

"I have a feeling I'm preaching to the choir, sir, but here goes," Daren said. "First: cost savings. Conventional wisdom holds that the cost to train and keep crew members in an aircraft like the B-1 bomber exceeds the cost of the aircraft by a factor of ten over its service life. Make the planes unmanned, run by computers, and now you don't need rated officers to fly them anymore—technicians can monitor the computer systems, and technicians and intelligence experts can pick targets to attack.

"Second: Removing the human-necessary systems in the plane would really create huge savings in weight, system complexity, performance, electrical load, and dozens of other areas," Mace went on. "The weight of an ejection seat with all its associated systems and plumbing is five times the weight of the guy that sits in the seat. We wouldn't need to sap bleed air from the engines for pressurizing the cockpit—that would boost available engine power by at least twenty percent, maybe more. We'd have enough surplus electrical power on board to install newer, faster computers just by not having to illuminate the crew compartment.

"Third: Missions wouldn't be restricted by the humans," Daren concluded. "Even with backup crews on board, you can't simply keep refueling a plane and keep it aloft for days and days—eventually the crew has to land the plane and get out. You can keep a robot plane on station for days, even weeks. You do away with crew rest requirements, you don't waste flight time by doing crew-proficiency tasks, and you don't need to provide for flight crews on mobility or deployment. And obviously we're not risking any human crew members in high-risk missions."

"We just have to make it work, then sell the gear and those arguments to the Pentagon."

"I worked at SECDEF's office for over a year, sir," Daren said with exasperation in his voice. "I saw perfectly outstanding projects killed on nothing more than a whim: The contractor was from the wrong state and wouldn't relocate or open up an office in a certain congressional district. A three-hundred-page proposal was missing a few pages. Or some staffer didn't get a luxury suite when he or she visited a base or plant. You can bust your butt and develop a great program, and they may still cancel it for reasons as stupid as they don't like the color you painted it.

"Defense procurement is bullshit, sir. The best programs get killed all the time while the crummy ones get funded. Then, years later, the good program gets the green light, even though it costs twice as much as it did the first time." Daren nodded toward McLanahan's son sleeping on the ground just a few feet away. "If you pardon me for saying so, sir, there is no project I've seen in all my years in the Air Force that's worth putting a child in a sleeping bag on the ground in the middle of winter so you can keep on working on it. Do you think anyone outside this base cares if you're successful or not? I can tell you honestly, sir—no one does. It wouldn't be worth a young boy getting even one sniffle."

At that moment Daren saw something ignite in McLanahan's eyes. Whoops, he thought, I just pissed the guy off.

Then McLanahan smiled a deadly-looking smile if Daren ever saw one. "You're wrong, Colonel—and you're right," he said. "You're wrong because I believe this project is *that* important. I can't do anything about what the Pentagon thinks or if Congress will fund it or if the president will deploy it—all I can do is make it work, and that's what I'm going to do. You're right that this project is not worth having my son or any child get hurt by it. That's why *you're* going to make it work. Do you think we can get the system tweaked down enough to do complex maneuvers like air refueling?"

"Excuse me, sir, but we're both navigators," Daren pointed out. "We know damn well the Air Force can train chimpanzees to fly a B-1 bomber."

Patrick laughed—and his laughter instantly seemed to brighten the dim, stifling, noisy interior of the little trailer. "You've given me a lot more to hope for in five minutes than anything I've heard in the past week, Colonel. Can you help me with this?"

"I'll be glad to give it a try, sir."

"Good." He motioned to the fifth console, where the technician was struggling with a debugging program. "Take a look at this, Daren. We've been fighting with this routine all night."

Daren took a quick look, narrowing his eyes as he scanned the readouts. "What program is this, sir? Where did you get it?"

"My guys at Dreamland wrote it several years ago."

"With all due respect, sir, I think you've been hanging out at Dreamland too long," Daren said. "That program is not only several years old—it's a generation too old. I guess part of the problem of working at a supersecret research facility is that you never hear when a really good tool is fabricated in the field. My guys at Beale wrote a satellite datalink routine trace-and-synchronization setup program for Global Hawk that'll knock your socks off. I'm sure we can adapt it for the FlightHawks and eventually the B-1."

Patrick McLanahan clasped Daren Mace on the shoulder and said, "Outstanding, Daren. Get on it first thing in the morning." He looked at his watch and added, "I mean, *later on* this morning. I know that John Long, the ops group commander, has a pretty tight checkout schedule drawn up for you. I'll get you out of it as much as I can."

"No problem, sir. There doesn't seem to be a hell of a lot else to do around here."

"Not even at Donatella's?"

Daren smiled and felt himself blushing.

"We keep pretty close tabs on all our troops out here, Daren."

"It was an interesting visit, sir, but I don't think I'll be back anytime soon," Daren said. "I'll call the Pentagon and put in official requests for the software to be transmitted to us. It'll be refused, of course, but then I'll make a few more phone calls to my boys and girls in the computer labs at Beale, Palmdale, and Wright-Pat, and I'll have the latest version of the software up and running here by noon. We'll let the software set up a conversation between your ground station and the aircraft. It'll tell us where the glitches are and what we need to do to fix them, and soon, in a day or two, we should either be up and running or begging for more money for parts and equipment. But from what I've seen in here tonight, you have all the basic stuff already in place—we just need to sort out and correct the bugs. I'll get right on it."

"Outstanding," Patrick said. He motioned to the door and led Daren outside. "And I," he went on, "will take my boy home with me, and I think we'll both have a good night's rest for a change."

"It's gotta be tough," Daren said, "being a two-star general on active duty *and* a single dad."

"I've got plenty of support—friends, family, nanny— but I never knew it could be so tough," Patrick said. "But it's even tougher to hear your own sisters and your mother arguing that it would be in Bradley's best interest to let him stay with them. It tears me apart, and I work even harder to solve a problem to free up more time to be with him—and what I end up doing is only digging a deeper hole for myself." He looked at Daren earnestly and said, "I wish I'd brought you in on this project the moment I set foot on base, Daren. I guess I wasn't thinking straight. I knew your background with the Global Hawks—that was the reason I asked for you in the first place—but then I let Furness and Long schedule the usual wing-orientation stuff with you. I've been spinning my wheels out here for weeks."

"I'm not guaranteeing results, sir," Daren said, "but

we'll start looking at all the conversations between your systems and your aircraft, track down the breaks, and see what happens. Maybe we'll get lucky."

"I feel lucky already," Patrick said, and he held out his hand. Daren shook it. "Let's meet tomorrow afternoon, and you can bring me up to speed on your progress. And if you want anything, buzz me. You'll get whatever you need."

"Yes, sir." Daren watched as Patrick McLanahan went inside the tent and a few moments later emerged with his son clasped tightly to his chest, still snuggled down in his sleeping bag. The big armored android McLanahan named Wilde appeared with the big rifle—did McLanahan call it an "electromagnetic rail gun"?—slung on his shoulder and offered to carry the boy for the general, but Patrick waved him off with a smile on his face.

This damned Air Force had its really shitty moments, Daren thought as he headed back to his pickup truck, but right now he felt like the happiest man in the entire U.S. military. For the first time in many, many years, he finally felt like a part of something special.

He couldn't wait to get started. He seriously doubted that he was going to get much sleep that night. At first he thought he was going to be dreaming about Amber and what he once had with Rebecca Furness. Now maybe it was going to be about flying robot warplanes.

TWO

OUTSIDE THE CITY OF KERKI, WESTERN TURKMENISTAN
That same time

Well, here they were again, just like two days ago: almost out of food, water, fuel—and getting pretty desperate.

A few things had changed. Wakil Mohammad Zarazi now called himself "General," and Jalaluddin Turabi now called himself "Colonel." They had a much larger force traveling with them, well over a full company and a half, and perhaps close to a full battalion. The T-72 tank was still going strong, and they still had plenty of ammunition for its machine gun, although they still hadn't procured any rounds for the main gun—not that it mattered, since no one in the company knew exactly how to aim and fire the thing anyway. But it looked like a real fighting force now.

His force was battle-tested now as well. Zarazi's little band had been attacked yesterday morning by a Turkmen patrol about thirty-two kilometers south of Kerki. It was an ill-conceived raid—obviously the young Turkmen lieutenant in charge thought the mere sight of a few tanks and a few platoons of regular-army soldiers would be enough to frighten him off. In less than an hour, Zarazi had procured three T-55 tanks, a number of armored personnel carriers, upgraded and far more reliable infantry weapons, thousands of rounds of ammo, a few more loyal fighters, and, best of all, a victory.

But now the real challenge was about to begin. Zarazi and his regiment were on the Qarshi-Andkhvoy highway that connected Uzbekistan, Turkmenistan, and Afghanistan, a few kilometers outside the city of Kizyl-arvat and sixteen kilometers from their objective, the Turkmen army air base at Kerki. Scouts had reported a buildup of regular Turkmen army forces at the bridge across the Amu Darya River and at the port facility there. It looked as if the Turkmen army was going to make a stand at Kizyl-arvat.

Military helicopters had been flying nearby all day, probing Zarazi's forces. Zarazi had ordered his men to attack one helicopter that strayed too close, and his troops shot an SA-7 shoulder-fired missile at it but missed. Since then the Turkmen helicopters stayed just outside range. They weren't attacking, probably only taking pictures, gathering intelligence, but it was making everyone nervous. He had to do something, or else his fragile military unit might start disintegrating.

Zarazi and Turabi formulated a plan. They loaded two ZSU-23/2 [twenty-three millimeter] antiaircraft guns onto the backs of flatbed trucks, covered them with tarps braced with lumber, then covered the tarps with sand and dirt. From the air they looked—the two men hoped—like big piles of dirt or garbage. They drove them along with a couple of pickup trucks full of soldiers westbound down the Kizyl-arvat–Kerki highway on the south side of the Amu Darya River.

It wasn't long before a lone Mi-8 helicopter of the Turkmenistan army intercepted them, about seven kilometers east of Kerki. At first the helicopter stayed two kilometers away, scanning the convoy visually; Zarazi could see a door gunner with a 12.3-millimeter machine gun, but no rockets or other heavy attack weapons. Zarazi's men carried rifles, but no other weapons were visible. Still cautious, the Mi-8 touched down a bit less than four kilometers away and dropped off about a dozen infantrymen up ahead, apparently to set up a roadblock. After a few more passes, the helicopter started to move in for a closer look, the port-side-door gunner at the ready.

Zarazi could tell when they were in range, because the Turkmen door gunner cocked his own weapon and steadied up on the lead truck. "Now!" Zarazi shouted. "Attack!"

A rope connected to a pickup truck trailing behind each flatbed truck pulled the tarps off, immediately revealing the antiaircraft guns. Before the helicopter pilot could react, they opened fire. Both ZSUs jammed after just a few seconds, but firing at a rate of one hundred rounds a second per barrel, it was enough. The helicopter's engine section exploded, and it nosed over and dove straight into the desert. The crew and ten infantrymen died in the explosion and fire that followed seconds later.

Half the Turkmen soldiers on the roadblock up ahead, mostly the conscripts and officers, ran when they saw the smoke and fire rising from the desert at the crash site; the rest, mostly the young professional soldiers, stayed to fight. Zarazi parked his armored personnel carrier about a kilometer down the highway from the roadblock, stood on top of the vehicle so they could see him and also see that he wasn't afraid of snipers, and spoke into the APC's loudspeaker: "This is General Wakil Mohammad Zarazi, servant of God and commander of the eastern division of the soldiers of Hezbollah. I am addressing the brave soldiers of the Islamic Republic of Turkmenistan who did as you were ordered to do—stay at your posts and defend your homeland like soldiers and like men. The others of you who turned and ran away are cowardly dogs, and you deserve to die like dogs.

"To those of you who stayed, I tell you this: If you are true believers, if you want to serve God and protect your homes and your families above all else, I will not harm you. You have proven your valor and courage today. I give you a choice: You may withdraw now and return to your unit, and you can suffer whatever fate your cowardly superiors offer you. You may stay and fight and be destroyed. Or you may stay, swear allegiance to me and to Hezbollah, and join my army. You will be made welcome and allowed to fight the oppressors and cowards who dared to call you subordinates.

"My mission is simple: to serve God by carving a home for his dedicated soldiers out of the desert where we may train and prepare for jihad. The Crusaders, the unbelievers, the infidels, and the traitors destroyed our previous camps in Afghanistan and Pakistan. But God has ordered me to take my army and build for him a new mosque and a new training center, and this is what I will do.

"Many of you are worried about your families. I say this unto you: If you join me, I will protect your families from retribution. And if I cannot save them, I will avenge them. If the cowards touch the families of a true servant of God, the families of the righteous shall be taken into heaven, and the cowards shall be cast into the fire. I promise this will be so, as God is my witness. So choose. I will give you five minutes, and then I will remove your roadblock. May Allah protect you."

Turabi smiled at him when he sat back down in the cockpit. "You're getting good at that praise-God stuff, Wakil—"

"Shut up, Colonel," Zarazi snapped. "Do not disgrace yourself by mocking God."

Turabi wiped the smile off his face fast. He had noticed the change in his friend over the past several days. Zarazi truly believed that God had saved him from death, and he believed he'd been called upon to build this army and fight this war. He was turning into a zealot—and zealots, Turabi knew well, made fearsome leaders and sometimes powerful fighters, but rarely did they make good soldiers.

Whatever Zarazi really believed, his speech had worked. All but two men who stayed behind at the roadblock surrendered and swore loyalty to Hezbollah. The last two refused to join Zarazi and were shot on the spot. "Damn it, Wakil," Turabi said after Zarazi had executed both men. "You said you would let them go if they surrendered. Those new recruits just saw you break your word."

"I said if they withdrew, they could live," Zarazi said. "Those two were not true believers."

"They surrendered. You took their weapons. They were kneeling in front of you. They didn't want to join you, and they didn't want to fight. All they wanted was to live."

"Colonel, what they wanted was to prove to their superiors that they weren't cowards by not running, but they didn't fight because they were afraid to die," Zarazi said angrily. "What do such men believe in? Are they soldiers or are they mice?"

"Wakil—" But Turabi stopped short when he saw that warning glare. "I mean, General . . . all I'm asking is this: Do you want to lead these men by fear or by the goals of your mission and your leadership skills?"

"I don't care if they love me or hate me, Colonel," Zarazi responded. "If they follow me, I will lead them into battle. If they oppose me, they will die. It's as simple as that."

"That's fine for those of us who are members of your tribe, General," Turabi said. "You are our leader by birth and by proclamation of the elders, and that has been good enough for our people for a thousand years. But now you have recruits to your cause, men who are professional soldiers, many now from other countries. They expect certain things from their leaders, things like trust, strength, courage—"

"I have all those things."

"You don't show trust or leadership when you execute someone who surrenders to you, no matter what the reason," Turabi said. "Hold them as prisoners, release them, ransom them, try to convert them—but don't kill an unarmed man."

"Colonel, that's enough," Zarazi said. "I am leader because God wills it. There is nothing more to be said. We will return to the regiment and plan our attack against Kerki. We strike tonight."

Turabi could do nothing else but comply. Arguing wasn't doing any good.

Whatever Zarazi's style, Jalaluddin Turabi couldn't argue with his effectiveness. It was easy to blame the lax border security on Turkmenistan's eastern frontier, or the element of surprise, or Zarazi's sheer audacity, for his initial successes, but the siege of Kerki was different. The base there had plenty of time to prepare; they had already lost a helicopter and its crew to enemy action. They must have believed that the loss of the helicopter was either an accident or a fluke, because the base at Kerki was completely unprepared for an attack.

Zarazi sent out probes to the air base as soon as it was dark; they returned three hours later. "The Turkmen are obviously preparing for an offensive," the squad leader reported. "There are at least eight Mi-8 troop transport helicopters on the aircraft parking ramp, clearly being prepared for a mission. They have extra fuel tanks and target-marking rocket pods loaded."

"That's at least one hundred and ninety-two infantry-men, General," Turabi said. He cautiously chose to address Zarazi by his purloined rank whenever anyone else was around—and most times when they were alone, too. "About half the size of our own force."

"And these are not border guards or light infantry scouts—they are regular infantry, sir," the squad leader went on. "We saw heliborne fast-patrol vehicles, heavy machine guns, mortars—they are coming in force and getting ready for a major engagement."

"When do you think they'll launch?"

"Possibly dawn or shortly thereafter," the squad leader said. "Weather report talks of a small storm, possibly a sandstorm, tomorrow morning."

"What about other aircraft?"

"We could not get near the other helicopters," the squad leader went on. "But they are there, inside hangars and well guarded: four Mi-24 attack helicopters. We saw anti-tank missiles, bombs, machine guns—they are being very heavily armed."

The Mi-24 was the old Soviet Union's deadliest attack helicopter: fast, heavily armored, and extremely accurate. During the Soviet occupation of Afghanistan, the Mi-24s were called *krazhas*—"undertakers"—by the Pashtuns, because they could both kill you and then create a hole big enough to bury you in. "If they launch those choppers, General," Turabi said seriously, "we're dead. It's simple as that."

The men looked at Zarazi with genuine fear in their eyes. Eastern Turkmenistan was flat and wide open—they had no chance against an Mi-24 attack helicopter out in the open. They had survived attacks in the past because, if they could escape into mountainous terrain where the chopper couldn't chase them, the Mi-24 had to either land and dismount its infantry or go home. Out here, marching on Kerki, it would be suicide. Their twenty-three-millimeter antiaircraft weapons were no match for the Mi-24's longer-range missiles, rockets, and equally powerful machine guns.

"It appears we have only one option left to us—surrender," Zarazi said. Turabi looked at him in horror, but then he could see that his old friend's mind was racing ahead with a plan. "Colonel, disperse your men and unload the trucks. We have business to attend to in Kerki. But first there is something you need to do for me. . . ."

BATTLE MOUNTAIN AIR FORCE BASE, NEVADA
Later that morning

Daren Mace was up at dawn and on his way back to the base from the little motel room he'd found near the truck stop. It was still early, but Daren decided to find the squadron building. He opened the little plastic case and found a device that rested behind an ear—a tiny wireless, hands-free earpiece. There were no instructions on how to use it. He wasn't sure if it was working, so he said experimentally, "Duty Officer?"

"This is the duty officer, Colonel Mace," a woman's voice responded immediately. "Welcome to Battle Mountain Air Force Base."

"Thank you," he said. This entire reservation, Mace decided, must be buzzing with data flowing wirelessly in all directions—he'd never heard of a base so connected before. "How do I get to the Fifty-first Squadron building?"

"Proceed straight ahead, turn right at Powell Street, left on Ormack Street, and right again on Seaver Circle," the voice, pleasant if somewhat toneless, responded. "You will find your designated parking spot."

"Thank you. I'll be there shortly."

Seaver Circle was the main road that paralleled the aircraft-parking ramp. What he'd thought from a distance along the road were aircraft hangars were actually aircraft alert shelters—huge structures big enough for a large aircraft to taxi through, open at both ends. There were eight KC-135R Stratotanker aerial-refueling tankers lined up inside their shelters. He was a little disappointed—the Fifty-first was apparently an air-refueling squadron. Although Daren had worked on several aircraft in his career, he mostly loved the strike aircraft, especially the fast-movers. Tankers were great and a vital part of the Air Force, but it would definitely be a change of pace for him. So where were the B-1 bombers McLanahan was working on?

The only sign of life he saw was a sweeping crew, using a large truck-mounted vacuum to suck up debris—called FOD, or foreign object damage, in the military—from the taxiways and runways. FOD caused more damage to military aircraft than enemy action did, he knew, so it was important they keep up with the FOD patrols, but that was the only activity he could see anywhere. Where in hell were the maintenance crews?

Outside the tall fence surrounding the flight line was a small building, and it was there that he found his parking spot. The door to the squat brick and concrete-block building was unguarded, but the door was securely locked. Mace found a metal box and opened it, expecting a telephone, but instead he found only what appeared to be a camera lens and a small glass panel roughly two inches square. He was about to close the door to the box and try another door—or call for the duty officer again—but then he remembered the device the Security Forces sergeant used and decided to touch the glass square with his thumb. Sure enough, as soon as he touched it, he heard the lock release, and he pulled the door open. He was inside a small room, an entrapment area, big enough for only one person and some gear. As soon as the outer door closed and locked behind him, he heard a faint humming sound that reminded him of an X-ray machine, which it probably was. When the humming stopped, the inner door opened.

The place looked like any other welcome area of a squadron headquarters building, neat and orderly, except this was even more so. In fact, it looked as if it had hardly been used. There were two trophy cases on either side of the welcome area, both empty. It had the new-paint and new-carpet smell of an office freshly finished or remodeled.

As he stepped inside, the same woman's voice said in his earpiece, "Welcome, Colonel Mace. Please meet your party in your office. I will notify them that you have arrived."

Mace looked around. There was no one but himself in the lobby. "Where are you?" Mace asked aloud. "Duty Officer, what's your name? Why aren't you out here?"

"I am an electronic duty officer, sir," the voice replied. "If you need assistance at any time, please just make your request on your commlink prefaced with my name: Duty Officer."

It was a damned *machine?* he asked himself incredulously. He was being polite to a *machine?* "There's no one on duty here?" There was no response, so he rephrased his question: "Duty Officer, there's no one on duty here?"

"I am on duty at all times, Colonel Mace. You may reach me anytime, anywhere, by commlink, by using the base tactical VHF or UHF frequencies or by telephoning the squadron number."

He cruised the hallways of the squadron building, finding little. There were a few administrative offices, all locked; a briefing room that also looked unused; a TV lounge—the first room in this place, he observed, that had windows. The large plasma HDTV was tuned to an all-news channel. There were cafeteria-style tables and chairs, some sofas along the wall.

Mace felt ridiculous talking to no one but addressing it as "Duty Officer." "Where's my office?" he asked impatiently. When the system didn't respond, he shouted, "Duty Officer, where's my *fucking* office?"

"To the right, down the hallway, fourth door on the right, Colonel Mace," the voice replied.

"Bite me," he said. As he approached the door, he heard it unlock. There was an outer office, which had a desk, a computer, and shelves but appeared unoccupied, and then the door to his office; it, too, unlocked as he approached it. Pretty amazing, he thought. It appeared as if he was being continuously tracked and monitored. The computerized duty officer knew where he was, anticipated his needs, like unlocking his doors, and did it for him. He couldn't wait to try it elsewhere and see.

And then he saw that his office was not empty. Inside, sitting at his desk, was Rebecca Furness.

He watched her rise to her feet, her lips parting as if she were going to say something, but then she decided against it, so he took that moment to let his eyes roam.

She was older, of course—so was he. She was tall and still athletic-looking, with plenty of curves that no baggy flight suit—rumpled and well worn, like McLanahan's—could hide. She was cutting her brown hair shorter now—she'd always kept it long, below-shoulder length, when he knew her before—and it was darker than he remembered, with wisps of gray visible, but her almond-shaped eyes still had that sparkle, that energy.

"Hello, Colonel," she said simply. Even with such a brief sentence, her voice was still clipped, impersonal. Rebecca Furness had always been, and probably would always be, all business. "I hope you don't mind my using your office. We're not exactly set up around here."

"Hello, Rebecca. What a surprise." He held out his hand to greet her. She took his hand and shook it firmly. Yep, all business, as usual. She'd once been nicknamed "the Iron Maiden"—maybe she still was; he didn't know—because of her no-nonsense, businesslike attitude toward most everybody and everything. Still, they did know each other, and, yes, they had a history. But he remembered only one or two tender moments in the short time they'd had together.

He surprised himself by pulling her carefully toward him and turning the handshake into a friendly hug. There was a helmet bag or something on the floor between them—he had to reach out awkwardly to her. He thought it was only going to be a casual hug, one that old buddies might give to one another, so it didn't matter that they couldn't get close . . .

. . . but that thought faded fast when, before he knew it, the hug turned into an embrace, and the embrace morphed into a full-scale liplock of the kind that Daren hadn't had much of an opportunity to do in a long time.

But just as quickly as it began, it ended. Daren felt her body and her lips tense, and he knew their personal little reunion was over. He backed away and searched her face. It was back to her businesslike facade, but he looked carefully and didn't see any hint of anger—there was a little confusion, certainly no joy, but no rejection either. She seemed to accept the pure spontaneity of the act, allowed herself to enjoy it just for a moment, then pushed it out of her consciousness.

"Welcome to Battle Mountain, Daren," she said, as if she couldn't think of anything else to say—awkward silence number one. She motioned to a sofa set up against the wall in the office; he sat down and took a bottle of water from her that she retrieved from a small cooler as she took a seat in a chair across the coffee table from him. "Making yourself at home?"

"Rebecca, about Donatella's . . ."

"It's okay. You're an adult—chronologically, at least—and that place isn't off-limits."

"I've never been in a brothel before."

"Did you enjoy it?"

"I didn't do anything."

"It's okay, Daren."

"I didn't do *anything!*"

"Okay, okay," Rebecca said. She couldn't help smiling at his embarrassment, and they both felt the tension slowly dissolve. "You look great, Daren. Really great. Buff, I'd say."

"Thank you."

"Stopped hanging out in biker bars, I assume?"

"I ride into one every now and then," Daren said. "You know, midlife crisis—a guy's gotta have a Harley. But I cut out the beer and the pizzas. My cholesterol count and blood pressure were racing each other to see which could kill me first." She smiled and nodded. "You look terrific, as always. I like the short hair, too." There was the second of what it seemed would be many awkward silences. "Congratulations on getting your star," he added quickly. "You deserve it. You always did."

"Thank you."

Awkward silence number three. Thank God, he thought, for the water bottles. "And now you're the wing commander here. Congratulations again." He looked at her seriously. "I must have you to thank for getting me this assignment."

"Your record spoke for itself."

"My record is crap and we both know it, Rebecca," Mace interjected. "My last assignment as a brand-new full bird colonel was running an office that prepared audio-visual presentations at the Pentagon. I had more responsibility when I was a swing-shift manager at McDonald's in high school."

"We all have to pull our share of desk jobs."

"Which one was yours—the bomb squadron in Reno or senior combat air-strike adviser to CINCPAC?"

"What is this—bitterness? Toward the Air Force? You're not the type."

"At least you still thought of your friends on your way up the ladder—nine years later."

"Now we're sinking into sarcasm and resentment against *me,* is that it? I advise you to drop that attitude right now, Colonel." Daren fell silent and briefly lowered his eyes, his only concession to her rank and authority. "If you need a shrink to help you examine these feelings of resentment and rejection, Daren, we'll find you one. But we've got a wing to run. Do you want some time to contemplate your navel and examine your feelings about your father, or do you want to come look around?"

He stood but did not move toward the door. She stood and watched him for a few moments. "Rebecca, you know that I'm grateful for whatever you did. . . ."

"All I did was give them a name—the Air Force and General McLanahan did the rest," Rebecca said. "You may have been stuck in some less-than-thrilling jobs, but you must've done something right, because you were picked to come here anyway. General McLanahan hand-picks everyone who sets foot on this base. And all I know about you is what you say and what you do, Daren. Sometimes I wonder if I ever knew you at all."

"I guess you're right," Mace said. He gave her a sly grin. "But as I remember it, neither one of us was intent on exploring the other's feelings. I think we both had only one thing on our minds then."

Rebecca smiled, despite all her efforts not to let him take her back to that point in time. She never liked to think that she *needed* a man—men were responsible for so many of the headaches, heartaches, roadblocks, and defeats in her career. But back when her career, her sense of self-worth, and the world seemed to be flying apart all at once, she needed a man to want her without demanding anything of her. Daren was there for her, and, as he demonstrated through most of the things he did, he didn't disappoint. He was caring without being clingy and needy, strong without being macho, and sensitive without being stifling.

He also never asked for anything. Consequently, he never got anything. What would he be like, she wondered, if he started demanding respect instead of earning it—like Rinc Seaver?

Rinc was her ill-advised romantic relationship that had filled the void left in her life when she was promoted up and away beyond Daren Mace. Both men were strong, handsome, and intelligent. Unfortunately, Rinc Seaver knew it, and he never let anyone forget it. He had a chip on his shoulder the size of the Golden Gate Bridge, and it would take a nuclear bomb to knock it off.

Unfortunately, that's exactly what did him in.

"Daren, it's good to have you here," Rebecca said seriously. "And it's good to see you again. But I don't have the time to worry about your feelings toward the Air Force or me. I'm here to stand up a flying wing, and I picked you to help me. I recommended you because I know you can do the job. You were the de facto wing commander at Plattsburgh when no one else on the entire base knew a thing about generating combat aircraft for nuclear war. You pulled us through that. You did some amazing things at Beale with the Global Hawk wing. Now I need you to pull the Fifty-first through this ramp-up and initial cadre-training phase. I'm counting on you."

"Rebecca, you know I'll do it," Daren said. Again, that was a weird comment. What's so hard about ramping up a KC-135 unit? The Stratotanker had been around for almost forty years, and it would probably be around another ten or twenty at least. What's going on here? he wondered. What he said was "Seeing you . . . well, it just reopened a few old wounds, that's all. I'm over it." He nodded, smiled, and added, "The kiss didn't help—but it didn't hurt either."

"Glad to hear both of those things." She headed for the door. "I'll show you around. You're not going to believe this place."

"The objective of this place," Rebecca said, after Daren had met up with her in the TV lounge, "was to build the most modern military facility in the world: highly secure, as secret as you can make an airfield, and efficient in any kind of weather and tactical situation. Battle Mountain Air Reserve Base is the first military base with a flying mission to be built from the ground up in over fifty years."

"From what I've seen so far, it's pretty high-tech," Daren commented. Why in hell was Rebecca blathering on about this place? There were no more than a dozen buildings on the whole base, and, except for the sensors and information datalinks they obviously had set up here, there was no security that he could see. Most of the base looked like open rangeland. The aircraft hangars didn't even have doors—and Daren knew how cold and snowy it got here in the winter.

Rebecca slid Daren a sly glance, which he noticed. Why was she giving him a look like the joke was on him? "We are still technically a Nevada Air National Guard base," she went on, "so we don't have much in the way of facilities like base housing or recreation—we have to rely on the local economy for that. But we do get a lot of assistance from the active-duty force, so we expect to build more and more facilities as time goes by." She looked at her watch. "We've got a launch in a few minutes, and since we're the only ones around, we get to do the last-chance inspection. Let's go."

"Okay," he said. A last-chance inspection on a KC-135 tanker? Last-chance inspections were usually reserved for aircraft that might have things falling or shooting off them, like bombs or missiles. But it was something to do. They climbed into a Suburban that was laden with radios and had a runway braking-action accelerometer unit installed, and headed off down the taxiway. They reached the departure end of the runway and stopped at the hold line, their flashing lights on.

"When do you expect them to finish your control tower?" Daren asked.

"We don't get a control tower," Rebecca replied. "We control the airfield by using sensors in the ground and cameras and radar for the surface and sky."

"Aren't you worried that you're depending an awful lot on all these sensors and datalinks?" Daren asked. "Wouldn't you feel more secure if you had more sets of eyes out here?"

"I'll show you the security and monitoring section next—you won't believe what we can see," Rebecca said. She received a green light at the hold line, looked up and down the runway for incoming traffic, then pulled out onto the runway and headed back toward the other end. "But we still use humans for a lot of chores, such as runway inspections. We have sensors that can detect a piece of metal on the runway as small as a pea, but we still do visual inspections. Some habits die hard, I guess."

"Tell me, Rebecca, where's General McLanahan's office?" Daren asked.

"You've met the general?"

"Last night, working in a virtual-cockpit trailer out on the other side of the runway."

"Hmm. He doesn't really have offices here. He travels a lot, usually to TTR or Dreamland." TTR, or Tonopah Test Range, was the classified flight and weapon test facility administered by the ninety-ninth wing at Nellis Air Force Base near Las Vegas. High-value weapon systems underwent detailed secret test and evaluation programs at TTR before being deployed.

"Is he current and qualified in the planes assigned here?"

"He's fully qualified to fly all the planes here. In fact, he's one of the *few* who are qualified here, including me," Rebecca replied. "You know, Daren, I don't really know what the general's mission here is. I know he's trying to start up some sort of a high-tech joint-forces command center based here at Battle Mountain—"

"Based *here?* Where? You don't even have room for the tanker squadron, let alone a joint-forces command. And what 'joint forces' are you talking about? All I see are some tankers. Or is this something we're going to be standing up in the next few years?"

"You'll see."

A few minutes later one of the KC-135R Stratotankers taxied over to the end of the runway but stopped well short of the hammerhead inspection area. "C'mon, boys, taxi up here, we won't bite," Mace murmured. He noticed Rebecca stifling another smile. "Why doesn't he taxi up to the hammerhead?"

"He's okay for now," Rebecca said. Into her commlink, she spoke, "Bobcat Four-one, Alpha, clear me in for last chance."

"Roger, Alpha, radars down, brakes set, cleared in."

"Alpha's coming in." They started their slow drive around the Stratotanker, looking for open access panel, preflight streamers pulled, landing-gear downlock keys removed, serviceable tires, and to be sure the flaps were down, takeoff trim set, the refueling boom stowed, and the tail-support bar removed. The KC-135R was the reengined version of the venerable KC-135, a Boeing 707 airliner fitted with a boom operator's pod, rear observation window, director lights, and a refueling probe and pumps; it also did double duty as a medium-capacity, medium-range freight hauler. These KC-135s, Daren noticed, also had wingtip-mounted hose-and-drogue refueling pods, so they could refuel U.S. Navy, Marine Corps, NATO, and other nations' aircraft that used the same system. The fin flash letters were "BA," for Battle Mountain.

"Everything looks good to me," Daren said.

"Me, too," Rebecca acknowledged. On her commlink she said, "Bobcat Four-one, this is Alpha, safety check complete, you appear to be in takeoff configuration. Have a good one." To Daren she added, " 'Bobcat' is our unit call sign; the tankers start with 'four.' "

"Four-one copies, thanks," the pilot replied.

"You always use the commlink, even talking to aircraft?" Daren asked.

"The commlink is not just a cell phone—it can tie in to many different radio frequencies, satellite communications, computer networks, about a dozen different systems," Rebecca said. "It's secure and pretty good quality, so we use it all the time. They're working on an even smaller version."

Rebecca started to drive around the KC-135, turning to the left side so they'd be in full view of the pilot. "So do the tankers here get the usual taskings from all the services," Daren asked, "or do we just get taskings from—?"

He stopped short, his mouth gaping open in utter surprise.

Because directly in front of the KC-135R, in the hammerhead aircraft-inspection ramp, were two B-1B Lancer supersonic bombers. They had appeared completely out of nowhere! "What . . . in . . . *hell . . . ?*"

"What?"

"What do you mean, 'what'? *Where did those bombers come from?*"

"You mean to tell me you didn't notice them when we drove up here?" Rebecca asked, totally serious.

"Don't bullshit me, Rebecca!"

"All right, all right," Rebecca relented. "Let's do this last-chance, and then I'll explain everything."

Daren was absolutely speechless—but his astonishment was nowhere near complete. The first thing he noticed was that the swing-wings of the B-1s were not fully extended. "They don't look like they're in takeoff configuration," he said.

"With these planes they are," Rebecca said. "Our bombers usually keep the wings back for all phases of flight."

"But how can they do that?"

"Mission-adaptive technology," she replied. "The whole fuselage is a lift-producing surface and flight control. C'mon, let's finish this, and I'll fill you in." They did a last-chance inspection of both bombers. As soon as they were done, the bombers were airborne, followed by the tanker. In less than five minutes, the airfield was completely quiet again. Rebecca drove around to the hammerhead parking area. "Let's step outside."

"Rebecca, how did those bombers get there?" Daren asked excitedly as he followed her out of the Suburban. "And how . . . when . . . shit, Rebecca, what's going on here?"

"You're about to find out." At that moment Daren felt a slight rumble under his feet.

And the entire section of aircraft-parking ramp under their feet started to descend!

"You actually *built an underground air base?*" Mace asked incredulously. Two huge sections of the hammer-head parking area were actually aircraft elevators, like the ones on an aircraft carrier but a few times larger. He stared wide-eyed as several feet of concrete, rock, armor, dirt, and steel passed overhead, followed by banks of overhead lights. Six stories below they could see men and equipment scurrying around. "This is amazing!"

"It's an amazing engineering project," Rebecca said. "There are eight of these elevators—two on each end of the runway and four in the mass parking area. We have a solar-charged backup system that can operate the elevators and air-circulation system in case the commercial power goes out. We can seal the interior against chemical or biological attack, and it can withstand anything but a direct hit with a nuclear weapon. We have accommodations for over a thousand men and women down here, plus twenty aircraft. We have twelve assigned here now."

Once the large elevator—which Daren thought looked like a moving city block—reached the bottom, they drove off into a parking area and stepped out so he could see the complex on foot. It was truly impressive. Except for the echo, it looked and felt like any military flight line at night, illuminated only by artificial light. The complex was enormous, stretching out seemingly to infinity. "I . . . I can't believe this," Daren gasped. "It doesn't feel like we're underground at all, but when I remind myself that we are, it doesn't seem real. How in the world can the air stay fresh enough to breathe?"

"It's a completely passive air-circulation system," Rebecca said. "Air from the surface vents up from the surrounding mountains through natural crevices and tunnels in the rock. We didn't have to drill one hole to get the ventilation system running. The hot air from here is cooled and dispersed enough through the mountains that the exhaust can't be detected from a satellite, so the bad guys can't guess how many planes we're launching. The complex is naturally conditioned to a temperature of fifty-five degrees and fifty percent humidity, which is almost ideal for living and working and uses about as much power as a standard four-story office building."

"Nice—if you enjoy living like a mole," Daren said dryly.

"Get used to it. Your squadron is based down here," Rebecca said.

"Down here? I'm confused. You keep more tankers down here?"

"Yes, we can if we need to." They had stopped at one of the B-1 bombers, which looked as if it had just returned from a mission. "But you don't belong to the tanker squadron. You're the new squadron commander of the One-eleventh Attack Wing."

Daren Mace broke into a wide grin. "A B-1 squadron!" he exclaimed. "Very cool."

"Not just a B-1 wing," Rebecca said. They piled into an electric golf cart and drove down the aircraft taxiway. Even though brilliantly lit from above, the planes emerged from the vastness of the underground chamber like beasts appearing through a thick fog.

"This is incredible, simply incredible," Daren said, still shaking his head in amazement. "You know, you've just made me an extremely happy man, Rebecca."

"You weren't happy being a tanker commander?"

"No offense to the tanker toads, but I've always been a fast-mover, and I'm happy to be one now," Daren admitted. "I've always loved the Bones."

"Then you'll be really happy with the Vampires," Rebecca said.

"Vampires? You named these 'Vampire,' too, like the RF-111Gs?"

"These are what the RF-111s *aspired* to be," Rebecca said. "You won't believe what they can do."

"Then let's go have a look. I assume I'll be cleared to go in the plane?"

"You're checked in, and your security clearance has been entered. If there's a problem, the sky cops will stop you," Rebecca said.

Mace was like a kid in a toy store as he stepped toward the sleek aircraft. The Security Forces officer asked to see Daren's line badge, and Daren took a few moments to talk with the young airman.

Rebecca nodded to Daren as they reached the plane. "The security units are also part of your squadron," she pointed out. "I'm happy you stopped to talk to the young troops. Crew dogs are usually too busy to talk with the junior enlisted guys."

"I have to admit, I'm guilty of that, too," Daren said. "But I'm just sightseeing here—he's the one on duty." Daren looked over the bomber. "I see a few changes right away: a much smaller vertical stabilizer, no horizontal stabilizer, and no gust-load alleviator vanes."

"Very good, Colonel," Rebecca said. "The EB-1C uses adaptive skin technology—'smart skin'—on the forward and aft sections of the fuselage and on the wings. The composite structure is reshaped by computer-controlled microhydraulic actuators that can create lift or drag as needed without the use of rigid control surfaces. Same on the wings: These planes don't use spoilers for roll control or flaps for angle-of-attack control. We pretty much use full seventy-two-degree wing sweep for all phases of flight, because the smart skin is more effective in controlling angle of attack than anything else. If the adaptive-wing-technology computers fail, we need to go back to using wing sweep and the lift-and-drag devices, but the system is pretty reliable."

As soon as Daren stepped up inside the plane, he noticed the difference. The two systems officers' positions in the crew compartment behind the cockpit were gone, replaced by racks of solid-state black boxes. "My God, this is incredible!" he said for what seemed like the twentieth time. "It seems spacious in here now compared to before!"

"Hell, we had to put three thousand pounds of fuel tanks up here to compensate for all the crew stuff we took out," Rebecca said. "The mission-adaptive technology takes care of the rest. We've increased range and performance another twenty-five percent by taking out all the human stuff back here."

They crawled through the tunnel connecting the systems operators' compartment to the cockpit. Rebecca saw that Daren was speechless with surprise as he looked at the completely empty space on the instrument panels. Almost all of the tape instruments, gauges, knobs, and switches had been replaced by multifunction displays—only a few backup gauges remained, relegated to lower corners of the instrument panel.

"Welcome to the electronic bomber, Daren. The B-1 was always a highly automated, systems-driven aircraft, but now the humans have been taken completely out of the equation. You don't fly this thing anymore—you *manage* it." Still looking at Daren, Rebecca spoke, "Bobcat Two-zero-three, battery on, interior lights on." Immediately the lights in the cockpit snapped on.

"Don't tell me you *talk* to the planes, like you talk to the duty officer?"

"That's exactly what you do," Rebecca said. "In fact, with most missions, you don't even have to talk—the air-

craft does its preflight according to the mission timetable."
She shrugged and added, "The computers are smarter,
faster, and more reliable than human crews. Why not let
them do the fighting and dying? The plane doesn't care. In
fact, it probably enjoys not having to lug around human
beings with their need for warmth and their heavy life-
support systems. We're a slow, inefficient, wasteful redundant subsystem, totally unnecessary to the completion of
the mission."

"Jesus, Rebecca, you sound like some kind of Isaac
Asimov robot character."

"No, I'm doing an imitation of General McLanahan,
General Luger, Colonel Cheshire, Colonel Law, and most
of the brain trust here at Battle Mountain," she responded.
"Daren, just between you, me, and the fence post, the guys
who run this place are the biggest technonerds you've ever
met. They've all come from Dreamland, designing and
building these things for the past fifteen-odd years, and
their minds are in the friggin' ozone. Everything is high-
tech and computerized, from the phone system to the la-
trines. You'd think the whole bunch of them just beamed
down to earth from the Starship *Enterprise*."

"So you and me—we're the old heads, right?"

"The HAWC guys, they've done some shit," Rebecca
said. "I'm not saying they're total neophytes. They've
been in some scrapes even since I've known them, so I'm
sure there are dozens of other adventures they've been involved in that I just as soon don't want to know about.
There are some things you'll learn about this place, the
missions that we prepare for, that'll curl your toes. But
technology is the answer to everything for them. Everything has to be done by a satellite link or computer. The
days of sitting down at a table, unfolding a map and a frag
order, and building a strike mission from scratch are definitely over."

"Fine with me. I'm perfectly happy to let a computer draw up flight plans and steer the plane," Daren said. "So what do they need us for?"

"Because as brilliant and high-tech as McLanahan and his buddies from HAWC are, they don't know very much about running a flying unit," Rebecca said. "McLanahan has recruited kids—and I literally mean *kids*—to come here.

"I think it's our job to build the squadron and let McLanahan and his egghead cronies build the machines. The kids these days know computers. As soon as they can sit in a chair by themselves, they know how to use a computer. What they don't know is organization, discipline, esprit de corps, teamwork, and mutual support. It's up to us to teach them."

"God, Rebecca, you're making me feel pretty damned old right now," Daren said wryly. But he shrugged and patted the top of the instrument panel's glare shield. "I'll make them a deal: If they teach me how to talk to B-1 bombers, I'll teach them how to think like a team."

"That's what I like to hear," she said. "Listen, there's going to be a lot of brass hanging around in the next few days. Rumor is the president and secretary of defense are going to stop by sometime in the next couple days for the nickel tour."

"Cool. Well, this place will certainly water their eyes."

"The general has this big project he wants to get funded."

"He briefed me on his project," Daren said. "It's awesome, but we've got a lot of work to do. You want me to stay out of sight, Rebecca?"

Furness looked at the deck for a moment, then back at Daren and said, "Let's just say that we've used some creative accounting practices to fund a few of the general's pet projects."

"So you need me to play along—make like I know and

approve of all the 'creative accounting practices.'"

"Something like that."

Daren shrugged. "I'm a team player. You got nothing to worry about from me." He smiled at her, then nodded knowingly. "It's nice to be sharing a cockpit with you again, Rebecca," he said. "Really nice. I miss it."

She squeezed his hand. "Me, too, partner," she said, smiling back. "Me, too."

BATTLE MOUNTAIN AIR RESERVE BASE
Early the next morning

A few minutes before six-thirty in the morning, an Air Force full colonel strode quickly and purposefully over to Daren Mace in the squadron lounge—Daren's de facto office most of the time—and practically snapped to attention in front of him. "Colonel Mace?" He extended a rigid hand; Daren stood and shook it, stifling an amused smile at the guy's officiousness. "Welcome to Battle Mountain, sir. I'm Colonel John Long."

"Good to meet you," Daren said. He looked around the room. "Is that two-star here again?"

"General McLanahan? No, sir."

It was meant to be a half-joking, half-sarcastic remark, but this guy Long was all business here. "Then let's dispense with the 'sir' stuff, okay, John?" Long was—contrary to his name—short, wiry, and tough-looking, with dark brown hair, beady little eyes, and a pointed nose. He looked like a bantamweight prizefighter—mean and jittery, his eyes, hands, feet, and mouth all in constant, rapid-fire motion. "We're both full birds."

"But you *are* senior to me," Long explained with a strange expression on his face. Then he gave Daren a conspiratorial wink and added, "But we'll dispense with the formalities when the bosses aren't around, how about that?" Then he relaxed and did away with the academy routine.

Daren finally realized with faint surprise what the bastard was doing—he was reminding Daren that, although he was senior and outranked him by time in grade, Long was the boss. Daren kept his amused smile, but inwardly he was saying, Why, you little prick. We've known each other for just sixty seconds, and you've already proven what a jerk you can be.

"As you know," Long went on, dropping all pretext of friendliness, "there is no lead-in program for the EB-1C Vampire, so I built the training program for both pilots and mission commanders—we don't call you 'navigators' anymore. It's a pretty tough program. Normally it takes a well-qualified officer about four months to complete the course. I hope you've been reading the tech order, Colonel." They took a seat. "We've got you on a pretty steep learning curve."

"I'm a fast study," Daren said.

"I hope so. McLanahan cracks the whip pretty hard around here."

"He seems like a nice guy."

"That's only for the folks who don't know him," Long said. "Once you get to know him like I do, you'll find he's really the ultimate prima donna. His only saving grace is that he wears navigator's wings. If he was a pilot, he'd be the king of the assholes."

Daren thought about the phrase "the pot calling the kettle black" but decided not to verbalize it.

"So. Tell me a little about yourself," Long said. It was an idle question. He immediately began fiddling with some paperwork moments after asking it, not really listening.

"Not much to tell, John," Daren replied. "I'm just happy as hell to be here."

"What was your last assignment?"

"Office of the secretary of defense," Daren replied.

Long nodded, impressed. "Very good," he said. "Which division? Plans? Operations?"

"Protocol. I was in charge of flipping slides, making coffee, and emptying wastebaskets."

Long gave him an amused smirk and said, "Well, I guess *someone's* got to do that stuff. Where before that?"

"Beale Air Force Base, standing up the RQ-4A Global Hawk unmanned reconnaissance squadron; I did Wright-Pat with the Air Force Research Labs, on UAV projects. Before that, deputy commander of the Thirty-ninth Wing at Incirlik. Before that, Air War College."

"Not much operational experience," Long observed haughtily.

Daren had no doubt that if he *hadn't* gone to any schools, Long would've criticized him for that, and it made him wonder what Long's background was.

"Global Hawk, huh? All this talk about unmanned aircraft and weapons scares me," Long commented. "If you listened to all the brass around here, you'd think the entire force is going to be unmanned in a few years."

Sooner than you think, Daren thought.

"The Thirty-ninth was the support unit for units deploying to Turkey and the Middle East?"

"Yep."

"Any operational command experience at all?"

"Not since I was the DCM at the Three-ninety-fourth Wing at Plattsburgh—until they closed the base."

"Maintenance group commander at a *Reserve* unit?" Long exclaimed. "Did you do any flying?"

"I flew both the RF-111s and the KC-135s based there—"

"Because you had to. Your unit deployed to Turkey and got itself creamed," Long said. "I learned that unit's history from General Furness. What a goat-fuck that turned out to be. We're all lucky a nuclear war didn't break out."

All that wasn't exactly true, but Daren didn't correct him.

"What was your last flying assignment?"

"Seven-fifteenth Bomb Squadron."

"The B-2 stealth bomber squadron at Whiteman?"

"No. The FB-111A. Pease Air Force Base, New Hampshire."

"The Aardvarks? They retired the FB-111s in . . . in *1992?*" Long said, wide-eyed. "That's the last operational assignment you've had? *Over eleven years ago?*"

Daren shrugged.

"When was the last time you flew?"

"I've kept current."

"In what—Piper Cubs?"

"Anything I could get my hands on at Andrews and Maxwell—everything from C-37s to T-37s and T-38s, even a couple rides in F-15Bs."

"So you haven't flown operationally in over eleven years, and you have no operational command experience. Not exactly what I'd call the ideal candidate for command of a bomber squadron. And you're probably the oldest guy on the entire fucking base."

Prick. "Makes me wonder why they didn't give the command to you, John."

Long narrowed his gaze at Mace but let the comment slide off him. "I was the ops-group commander of the One-eleventh Bomb Wing," Long said. "I've already put my time in with the Bones. My skills are better utilized on the wing-command level."

"The One-eleventh? Sorry to hear about your last predeployment. You've obviously bounced back from being the only Air National Guard wing ever to go non-mission-effective in peacetime."

Long's nostrils flared angrily. "Where'd you hear that nonsense?"

"You're denying it, John? You're saying it didn't happen?" Long wisely decided not to say anything. "I worked at the secretary of defense's office, remember, John? I prepared weekly briefings for SECDEF on each unit's mission effectiveness. I know everything that happened out in Reno."

"What happened to my wing in that pre-D had nothing to do with my fliers and everything to do with General McLanahan," Long retorted. "The fix was in—we were programmed to fail from day one so he could act like he was going to save us, be the big hero, and then snatch us up and drag us off to Tonopah for his big, crazy ideas. We were doing fine before he showed up."

"Of course. I should know better than to listen to all the things I heard at SECDEF's office about you guys," Daren said with an evil smile. "What with all the hotdogging, the accidents, the procedure violations—you guys were in fine shape the whole time. What a relief to know that."

Long blanched. He didn't like the idea of his name's coming up in conversations at the secretary of defense's office.

"Good thing they had you, John."

Long's jaw tightened at that remark, but he didn't respond. "*This* wing will be fully mission-ready, Colonel—I'll see to that," he said. "I have my doubts about exactly what your contribution is going to be toward that effort, but I wasn't consulted on the choice of squadron COs."

"I'm sure you had other wing-command-level decisions to make."

Long quickly decided to stop the verbal sparring. He wasn't scoring any points at all. "All right. Well, let's get you started.

"The mission of the Fifty-first Bomb Squadron is to

equip and deploy the EB-1C Vampire bomber for intercontinental strike, anti-ballistic-missile defense, antisatellite operations, and long-range-reconnaissance missions," Long began. "Your squadron has twelve EB-1C Vampire bombers in the Pit." Most everyone called the underground hangar complex the "Lair," which Daren thought sounded much cooler than the "Pit"—it was no surprise to Daren that Long called it something less flattering. "Normally we're able to keep nine to ten operational and one in training status, but frankly, our maintenance guys need a swift kick in the ass sometimes to keep them up to speed."

"I used to be a maintenance-group commander," Daren reminded him. "And I know that no one responds well to 'a swift kick in the ass,' especially maintenance techs."

"You motivate your troops the way you see fit, Colonel," Long said. "You do whatever it takes to get the job done."

"Yes, sir," Daren said. "I see no reason we can't keep the training birds mission-ready at the same time. We'll figure out a way."

"One reason might be the rotary launchers," Long said. "Since rotary launchers are maintenance-intensive, we generally don't upload them in the training birds."

"I'll have RLs in every bird on the line, training or not, loaded or not," Daren said. "RLs need to be used. The bearings in those things are designed to rotate twenty thousand pounds of weapons at ten rpms at minus fifty degrees Fahrenheit at up to nine Gs. They like to be exercised frequently, or they get cranky."

"It puts the squadrons at a great disadvantage if we end up with a broken rotary launcher," Long said with growing irritation. "We run the risk of going non-mission-ready if a sortie goes down because we can't use an RL. We will not use them unless absolutely necessary."

"That's why they break down, John," Daren repeated. He noticed that Long bristled when he used his first name, but, hey, screw him—there was an unwritten code about officers of the same rank not calling each other "sir," even if one was your boss. "If you want RLs that work, you put them in the planes, hook them up to power, hydraulics, and air, fly them, and use them. Every mission. Without fail. From now on."

"Hey, Colonel, how about we do it *my* way until you're up to speed?" Long asked pointedly.

"Whatever you say, John," Daren responded.

Long gave Mace a warning glare, then, in an effort to defuse the tension between them, said, "In my opinion it's hard to motivate guys who work eighty feet underground. Why McLanahan chose to build the aircraft shelters underground, I'll never figure out. For what he spent on that complex, we could've fielded five more planes."

"I did some research on this complex, John," Daren said. "McLanahan didn't build it."

"What? Of course he did. It's been under construction for the past three years—"

"The big runway and all the high-tech gadgets, yes," Daren said. "But the underground complex was actually built about *fifty* years ago. It was first created as an underground 'doomsday' shelter, designed to house almost two thousand civilians plus an F-101 fighter-bomber squadron. It's been used in various ways since then: as a classified-weapon research center, as a nuclear-weapon storage facility, even as an emergency Strategic Petroleum Reserve storage facility. Before McLanahan got the funding to turn it into an air base, Battle Mountain was the Federal Emergency Management Agency's national civil command center for the western U.S.—"

"Whatever," Long interrupted. "It's a stupid place for an airfield. That's my bottom line. Let's move on. We've had a lot of success with the EB-1C, and we'd like to maintain our string of successes. Unfortunately, General McLanahan's recent mishap hasn't helped our mission-effectiveness record."

"The crash in Diego Garcia?" Daren asked. "I remember something about it in the news."

"The mission was a disaster, we were embarrassed, we lost two unmanned drones and nearly lost a B-1 bomber, and we still don't know exactly what happened," Long said angrily. "But instead of getting his ass chewed out, characteristically, General McLanahan is treated like the conquering hero. He nearly closed down America's most important Asian air base and disregarded orders that came from the Pentagon."

"He saved his plane and his crew," Daren observed. "Crew prerogative—do whatever it takes to save your people and your aircraft. Who cares if it caused a mess on some ramp in Diego Garcia?"

"General Furness saved the aircraft. It was probably McLanahan who pushed to keep on going with the mission."

"An operational test is still an operational mission—it just means the unit isn't mission-ready," Daren pointed out. "I'm sure the *crew* was responsible for bringing their plane back in more or less one piece."

"Apparently the Pentagon saw it the same way," Long grumbled. He handed Daren a sheet of paper.

"What's this?" Daren asked.

"What's it look like, Colonel? Bold-print malfunction-procedures test. Required before every flight. Closed-book and solo effort. It needs to be one hundred percent correct, word for word, or you don't fly. Turn it in before you step."

"I didn't know there was going to be a test first," Daren commented softly. He looked at the test—it was twice as long as any bold-print test he ever remembered having to take. "I haven't had much time to study this stuff yet, John."

Long eyed the new squadron commander with a look of disgust. "Then maybe you shouldn't be flying right away, Mace," he said. "Maybe you need to get into the books a little more."

Daren did not respond. He *knew* he needed to get back into the tech orders, especially on this new aircraft, but he badly wanted to get back into the air. He didn't want to spend three months in academics, just watching the rest of his squadron flying without him.

Long shook his head, then shrugged his shoulders. "But the boss wants you flying as soon as possible, so I guess we're going flying anyway," he said. "Get together with your instructor pilot and complete the test before you step."

"You got it."

"I've built a qualification course for you and the other newbies in your squadron. You'll start the flying phase of that course today."

"I appreciate that, John, but I think getting *me* stick time in these planes is a waste of *everyone's* time," Daren said. "It seems to me that I was hired for some other reason than to be a flying squadron commander. I need to know how they work, not how to fly them. General McLanahan has hinted about doing some special engineering mods to the fleet. I think I'd better be—"

"Colonel, again, how about we do it *my* way until you're up to speed out here?" Long asked irritably. "We've got you scheduled for several meetings with the folks from

Sky Masters Inc. and the engineers at the Tonopah Test Range. You'll get a briefing on the current project status and the completion timelines. Your job will be to ensure that they all meet the milestones—or give me a damned good reason why they missed it."

"I got a copy of the project timelines from the general. I think we can beat those deadlines," Daren said. "We should think about bringing the engineering staff from TTR up here."

"As I'm sure you've noticed, there's no place on this base for a one-hundred-person engineering staff," Long said. "It's easier for us to bring the planes to TTR than it is to bring everyone up here."

"Nah. I made visiting generals and heads of state stay in tents and trailers at Incirlik all the time—the engineers from TTR and Sky Masters can do the same. We're the customer—they can do it our way. I should be studying the mission profiles and weapon characteristics and—"

"If you're not completely checked out as a primary crew member, Mace, you can't even *look* at my aircraft," Long said sharply. "It's as simple as that. I'm not going to let any unqualified personnel near my planes. And since we're the only unit that flies the EB-1C and there's no lead-in school, I designed the training program that has been approved by the Air Force. You will follow it to the letter or you will *get out* of my wing. This wing will not go mission-ineffective because someone hasn't done the basics."

"I'll take responsibility for the mission-effectiveness of myself, my crews, and my planes," Daren said firmly. "Believe me, I know what I'm talking about."

He then handed Long a sheet of paper: the completed bold-print emergency-procedures test. He'd done it so quickly that Long didn't even notice he was filling it out as they were talking. Long checked it carefully, but he needed only a moment to realize it was perfect—every word, even every punctuation mark, exactly in place.

"I may not have any command experience, Colonel," Daren added, looking directly into Long's eyes, "but I guarantee you one thing: I know systems. I eat, sleep, and dream systems. I read tech orders in the fucking bathroom."

Long met his gaze—but only for an instant. He looked away and remarked, "Now, there's an image I'd rather not have." He crumpled up the test and threw it in the direction of a nearby wastebasket. "I've got your instructor pilot coming by soon." He looked at his watch. "Grey better not be late," he grumbled under his breath.

"Sorry I'm late, sirs," Daren heard a voice say. He turned—and saw what looked like the youngest crew member in a flight suit he'd ever seen. The guy—kid, Daren thought at first, then corrected himself—set his documents bag on the dais, then quickly extracted some paperwork.

"Make us wait again, Grey, and you'll be ramp monkey for another week," Long warned. Apparently, Daren thought, around here being ten minutes early for a briefing was considered late. Long motioned to the young officer. "Colonel, this is First Lieutenant Dean Grey. Grey, Colonel Mace, your new squadron CO."

Grey, a tall, lanky guy with a high forehead, very close-cropped spiky blond hair, and—of all things—a pinhole in his left earlobe for an earring, stepped over and enthusiastically shook Daren's hand. "Pleasure to meet you, sir," Grey said.

"Dean Grey? 'Zane' Grey—the guy that led the Air Force Academy to an NCAA championship in men's volleyball? Cover of *Sports Illustrated?* Rumors of you and Anna Kournikova, Gabrielle Reece . . . ?"

"The same, sir," Grey said. When he smiled, it made him look five years younger.

"No offense, Zane, but . . . exactly *when* did you get

your wings?" Daren asked. "Didn't all the *Sports Illustrated* and *Playboy* interviews happen just last year?"

"Yes, sir," Grey said with his boyish grin. "Got my wings last month."

"Last *month?*"

"General McLanahan likes 'em young, as you'll readily find out," Long moaned, shaking his head wearily. "Average age of the entire squadron is just a wet dream or two past puberty. Same with all the squadrons we're standing up around here. Now, if we could postpone the trip down memory lane for another time?"

"Sure, John."

"Get to it, Grey," Long ordered.

"Yes, sir." To Daren he began, "Welcome to Battle Mountain and the Fifty-first, sir. I'm your acting executive officer. Anything you need or want, just let me know, and I'll take care of it." He gave Daren a card with binder holes punched in it. "I took the liberty of writing out a list of all the squadron personnel with their ratings, schools, experience—"

"Already did it," Daren said, flipping to the pages in his personal "plastic brains" booklet. "I got the dope from General Furness. I went through the entire roster—we've got some stellar personnel here on the patch, all right. I also got a status report on all our present and future airframes and their mod status."

"Excellent, sir," Grey said. "Our mission today is a standard-flight-characteristics orientation flight for mission commanders. As you know, sir, the Vampire uses pilot-trained navigators in the right seat, so MCs need to be well familiar with all phases of flight. The standard profile for this mission is to observe, but we like to accelerate the program, so we'll give you as much as you can handle. We'll show you once, then have you try it."

"We're not going low today?" Daren asked.

"Where have you been the past five years, Colonel?" Long asked with a smile.

"We . . . we don't go low anymore, sir," Grey said.

"You don't go low-level in the B-1?" Daren asked incredulously. "Why in the world not?"

"Well, a few reasons," Grey replied. "The main reason is, the standoff weapons we use have a longer range when launched from high altitude—Longhorn's range is thirty percent greater, and Lancelot's range is almost fifty percent greater. Second, we're stealthier and faster now—we don't need to go low, even against pretty substantial fighter coverage or advanced SAM systems. Third, we make great use of smaller attack-and-reconnaissance drones that map out the enemy defenses pretty well, long before we go in. What threats we can't destroy, we circumnavigate. And, of course, flying away from the cumulogranite is safer—"

"Whoa. Pardon me, boys. I was with you on the first reason, but not the last three reasons," Daren said. "You're already relying on a lot of technology to do the job for you. There's no reason to hang it out even further by staying up high in a heavily defended area. We should practice going low at every opportunity. We can build a certification program. Certain equipment status and training proficiency earns a crew the distinction of going low, into the heavier-defended areas; other not-so-qualified guys can stay up high and lob in cruise missiles. And 'safety' seems a funny thing to be considering when we're talking about going to war or employing weapons like this. We should—"

"Let's concentrate on the basic flight-training program you're going to undergo, Colonel," Long said. "Flight characteristics for the first couple flights, then emergency procedures, then air refueling."

"We're not doing air refueling today *either?*"

"Is English not your primary language, Colonel?" Long asked perturbedly. "You've got to master the basics before you do the more advanced procedures. I built this training program to get new crew members with no recent B-1 experience up to maximum proficiency in minimum time. After air refueling, we'll move on to instrument-pattern work, visual-pattern work, and then we go into the strike stuff." He got to his feet. "You haven't been operational in many years, Colonel, and even when you were, you were . . . less than reliable." He hesitated, looked at Grey, then made a wordless show about not revealing what he was thinking. "Do it my way, Colonel. Is that clear?"

"Sure, John," Daren replied. Long looked as if he really, *really* wanted to chew on Mace for calling him by his first name in front of the younger officer, but decided to save it for later.

After the protracted, uncomfortable pause ended, Grey glanced over at the crumpled-up paper by the wastebasket. "I see you passed your bold-print test," he said. "Outstanding." It made Daren wonder what Long did with the tests that weren't perfect—probably kept a file to use against the crewdogs. "We have about an hour until we step, so let's talk about local procedures before we get into discussing stalls, falls, crashes, and dashes for a few moments." Grey handed out flight plans, kneeboard cards, target-prediction cards, and weather sheets, all organized and stapled together. "I went ahead and filed our flight plan, got the weather—"

"Hold it a second. We do all that as a *crew*, Lieutenant."

"Yes, sir, but I thought since the weather's clear in a million, we're not going terrain-following, and we've got the MOA and ranges to ourselves, we'd spend a bit more time talking about the plane, you know, getting acquainted. . . ."

"You don't freelance training missions, Lieutenant," Long interjected hotly. "You're going to fly a two-hundred-million-dollar supersonic bomber, not go on a fucking date with a Russian tennis babe." He flipped through the briefing cards—they were complete, perfectly legible, and perfectly organized. Grey was right: The weather for everything west of the Rockies, and every alternate military field within a thousand miles, was clear as a bell with no restrictions. "But now that you've completely screwed up the sequence, you might as well proceed. Let's go. You don't have all day."

"Yes, sir." Grey handed Daren more checklist pages. "Here is a list of local frequencies, step procedures, taxi and departure procedures, phone numbers in case the duty officer is on the fritz—"

"Got 'em," Daren said. "I got all that stuff from General Furness, too. I studied them last night, but be sure to watch my back in case I screw something up."

Grey nodded, impressed. Daren noticed that even Long was nodding approvingly. That made Daren feel good—until Long added, "I hear you and Rebecca used to be a hot and heavy item, Colonel."

The motherfucker, Daren thought, bringing something like that up in front of a junior officer. "Let me tell you about Rebecca, John," he said with a conspiratorial smile. He motioned Long to lean toward him. When he did, Daren stuck his face in Long's and said loud enough for Grey to hear, "None of your *fucking* business, Colonel."

Long's head snapped back as if Mace had head-butted him. He narrowed his eyes and opened his mouth as if he were going to yell at Mace, then shut it, embarrassed, opened it again as if he'd reconsidered, then blinked in confusion. Daren didn't wait for him to sort it out any further. "Let's get on with the briefing, Zane," he prompted, still glaring at Long.

"Yes, *sir,*" Grey said, hiding a very amused and pleased smile. About time someone told off the DO, he thought.

"Open your 'plastic brains' to the air-work checklist, and let's get started."

As Grey began his briefing, Long made a big show of checking his watch, then slipped out of his seat and exited the lounge.

"Sorry about that, Zane," Daren said after Long had left. "He had it coming."

"I didn't see a thing, sir," Grey said with a smile.

"Who peed in his cornflakes this morning?"

"I hate to say it, sir," Grey said, "but I didn't see anything out of the ordinary."

"Oh, shit."

"Exactly."

"So tell me, what was it like to play in the NCAA championships, Zane?" Daren asked excitedly. "Man, it was very cool to watch. You running halfway up the bleachers to save that last volley and then spiking the ball *from the bleachers* was awesome. First volleyball game I ever saw on TV."

"It was like living a dream, sir," Grey said. "I look at the trophies and pictures on the wall, and I still can't believe we did it."

"So the question the whole male world wants to know: Anna or Gabrielle? Or both together?"

"That has the *highest* classification level, sir," Grey said. But his mischievous smile told Daren everything he wanted to know.

"And tell me, what's it like working here?"

Grey's smile grew even wider. "It's another dream come true," he said sincerely. "In a lot of ways it's pretty austere—nothing as cushy as how we had it in pilot training. But the stuff we're doing is two or three generations beyond anything else I've ever seen. You really feel like you're riding the wave into the future."

"Sounds good to me. And how about the brass?"

"They're okay. Even Colonel Long is a good guy—and I'm not just saying that to cover my butt either," Grey said with a sly smile. "You can't help but work in the Lair or in the command center and not be aware of the awesome things we're doing. I think that feeling extends to everyone, from General McLanahan on down. This place is special, and everyone knows it, but it's so . . . you know, *out there, unworldly*—that no one cops an attitude around here. I think we all realize that this is so high-tech and futuristic that we can all be shelved in a heartbeat, so we're all trying hard not to screw up."

"I think I understand," Daren said. "Makes me wonder why I'm here—but I guess I'm thankful to be anywhere."

They bullshitted for a few more minutes. Grey asked the questions this time; Daren knew he was collecting "intel" to share with his squadron mates on the new boss.

Finally Grey said, "It's just about step time, sir. We'd better get going."

"Hold on, Zane," Daren said. "You mean to tell me I'm really going to go through this flight-orientation program?"

"That's my understanding, sir."

"Call me 'Daren' when the bosses aren't around, or 'skipper,' or 'lead'—anything but 'sir,' okay, Zane?" Daren asked. "You're making me feel pretty damned old."

"Colonel Long mapped out your orientation program, skipper. What do you have in mind?"

"Well, I'll tell you," Daren said. "My dad was a cutter skipper in the Coast Guard, one of the big Bear-class boats, and what he said was the most important thing for the boss to do: use all your toys."

"Sir?"

"If you got guns, shoot 'em; if you have a helicopter, fly in it; if the captain has a barge, take it out and cruise around in it. I've got a bunch of B-1 bombers here—I want to fly 'em. I've got weapons, I assume—I want to pop a few off. I don't just want to bore holes in the sky—I want to drop some iron and make things blow up in a loud, messy fashion. Let's go *flying*."

"What about the colonel's orientation program, sir?"

"Screw it. General McLanahan told me that my job is to stand up this unit, and that's what I'll do—but in my own way. You game?"

"Absolutely, sir."

"Outstanding." He touched the earpiece in his right ear and said, "Duty Officer, schedule a low-level route, an air-refueling anchor, and live air- and ground-attack-weapon range time. Stand by for training ordnance load."

"Yes, Colonel Mace," the computer responded. "Standing by."

"Uh . . . sir, don't you remember? We don't go low-level anymore?"

"Well, shit, I think I'm dating myself every time I open my damn mouth around here," Daren said. "But we'll see how it goes. Who knows, maybe I have a couple tricks you youngsters might need to learn."

"Roger that, sir," Grey said eagerly.

"Colonel Mace, this is the duty officer," Mace heard in his earpiece.

"Duty Officer, go ahead," Mace responded. He was really getting the hang of this computerized duty-officer system—the creepiness of talking to a machine as if it were a human being was quickly wearing off the more he discovered how well the thing worked and how useful it could be.

"Colonel Mace, I have been advised that live-weapon air-to-ground range times are available this afternoon in the Tonopah complex. A Bobcat tanker crew is available this afternoon as well. Please advise."

"Duty Officer, put the Bobcat tanker on my schedule," Daren said. To Grey he said, "We got the Tonopah range for this afternoon."

"Ask the duty officer if they can get us a surface-to-surface rocket launch, too," Grey chimed in.

"Duty Officer, ask the Tonopah range director if they can get us a surface-to-surface target rocket launch for our range time," Daren asked.

"Please stand by, Colonel Mace. . . . Colonel Mace, I have been advised that no surface-to-surface launch targets are available at the Tonopah complex. They can give you ground targets only."

"No rockets—ground targets only," Daren said to Grey.

"No problem. We can bring our own air targets—if Colonel Long doesn't have a fit that we changed his training schedule," Grey said excitedly. He was starting to adopt a Southern California "surfer dude" accent. He would lose his shirt, Daren knew, in any poker game. "We can upload a couple Wolverine missiles to use as fast-moving long-range targets, and maybe a FlightHawk to use as a slow-moving air-to-air target."

"Good," Daren said. "So we'll have two Wolverines in the forward bay."

"Make it four," Grey said.

"Okay, four," Daren said. "One FlightHawk in the aft bay and a rotary launcher with two Scorpions, two Anacondas, and . . . what's the third target for?"

"Lancelot," Grey said. "Two Lancelots. You *are* cleared to use Lancelots, aren't you, sir?"

"Let's find out," Daren said. He touched his earpiece again. "Duty Officer, am I cleared to launch Lancelot missiles?"

"Stand by, Colonel Mace. . . . That is affirmative, sir. You are cleared to employ all expendables authorized for the squadron."

"Cool," Daren remarked. "Can't wait to pop one of those babies off. What do you have for precision-guided standoff missiles nowadays, Zane?"

"We fly the AGM-165B Longhorn for short-range, operator-aimed, precision-guided missions," Grey replied.

"Outstanding. Duty Officer, I want one FlightHawk unarmed target UCAV with telemetry, four unarmed Wolverine target cruise missiles with telemetry, two Scorpion missiles with telemetry payloads, two Anaconda missiles with telemetry, two Longhorn missiles with target-marking warheads, and two Lancelot missiles with telemetry payloads loaded in my sortie right away," he said into his earpiece. "Request two ground targets on the Tonopah range—"

"One fixed, one moving," Grey said. He was getting into it now.

"One fixed target, one moving target."

"Yes, Colonel Mace. Please stand by, I will request authorization." The reply did not take long. "Colonel Mace, Colonel Long has denied your request for training weapons for your sortie."

"Duty Officer, pass the request to General Furness," Daren responded.

"Yes, Colonel Mace. Please stand by."

"Oh, crap," Grey muttered. "The shit's going to hit the fan now, sir."

He was right. It did not take long for John Long to burst back into the lounge, his eyes burning with anger. "You son of a bitch!" Long shouted. "What is all this shit about uploading weapons and getting range time? Your task for today is basic flight orientation—"

"I can't be wasting time on that stuff, John."

"You will do it because *I said so!*" Long shouted. "I built your training syllabus, and you will follow it *to the letter!* Is that clear?"

"John, I'm a bombardier," Daren said. "I need some range time, I need to fly the jet, and I need to blow some shit up."

"You can practice all that stuff in the simulators," Long said. "Now, forget this request for flight time and—"

"I passed my request on to General Furness."

"You . . . *what?*" Long gasped, dumbstruck. "You went over my head? *How dare you,* you son of a bitch? You're out of line, Colonel!"

"John, I told you, I'll get your Vampires up and running, and a hell of a lot faster than you've got programmed into your timetables," Mace said, getting to his feet to make a stand in front of the operations-group commander. "But I'm not going to be stuck doing stalls and approaches. I'm a navigator, a bombardier, a systems officer—"

"You will do it my way, Colonel, or you won't do it at all!" Long barked.

"I need to get up to speed as quickly as I can on employing this squadron for combat," Daren said. "I'll venture a guess and say that all the other squadron commanders here have extensive experience in their weapon systems."

"The rest of my squadron commanders seemed to have been more successful in progressing in their careers, that's why."

Daren let that jab roll off his chin. "I'll also venture a guess and say that, next to Generals McLanahan and Furness, you are the most experienced person on this base in the EB-1A."

Not exactly true, Long thought, but he did not deny that guess either.

"So I need to do everything I can to learn about the Vampire, and that doesn't mean waste time with pilot shit. Let me do my thing, John. I promise, this unit will be fully qualified in all aspects. But I need to do it my way."

"Colonel Mace, this is the duty officer," the computerized female voice said. "General Furness has approved your request for aerial refueling, low-level training, and live weapons on your sortie. I will coordinate your request with your squadron munitions officer. . . . Colonel Mace, I am advised by your squadron munitions officer that your request will be handled immediately."

"Duty Officer, get an estimated time to completion from Captain Weathers on uploading the weapons and relay my sortie timing to me and Lieutenant Grey." Captain Weathers was the chief of the squadron munitions department.

"Yes, Colonel Mace." Seconds later: "Colonel Mace, I have a preliminary estimated time of completion from munitions and have planned your sortie timing. Your new step time is eighteen hundred hours Zulu."

Pretty good, Mace thought, uploading a stack of air-to-air and air-to-ground missiles and unmanned combat aircraft in a B-1 bomber in less than six hours without any notice was shit-hot in any unit, and especially good for a brand-new squadron. "Duty Officer, have Captain Weathers meet us at the aircraft during preflight to brief me on the weapons."

"Yes, Colonel Mace. Your updated flight-planning materials are available on any terminal using your password. Be advised, your new sortie timing may exceed authorized peacetime-crew duty-day regulations."

"Duty Officer, request a waiver of crew duty-day regulations."

"Yes, Colonel Mace." Moments later John Long got the request in his earpiece.

"You going to approve it, John?" Daren asked. "Or should I go to the general again?"

"You think you can just do whatever you feel like here?" Long growled, his voice shaking with anger. "I guess we know why you've been stuck in purgatory all these years since you screwed the pooch in the Sandbox, huh?" He turned and stormed out of the lounge.

Moments later the duty officer reported, "Colonel Mace, Colonel Long has authorized extension of crew duty day to sixteen hours."

Daren responded with a polite "Thank you," even though it was only a machine on the other end of the line.

Dean Grey looked at Mace for several moments, hoping he would fill in some details; when he didn't, the curiosity got the better of him. "You were in Desert Storm, sir?" he asked.

"Yep." Mace realized with a faint shock that Grey was barely in his teens when that war started.

"Flying what?"

"The Aardvark. SAC version."

"The FB-111? I didn't think we used any Strategic Air Command 111s in Desert Storm."

"We did—and I strongly advise you to not ask any more questions about it," Daren said seriously. He noticed Grey's concerned expression. "It's still classified, and it'll give you nightmares. We'd better get going with planning this sortie."

"Yes, *sir!*" Grey said happily. "I'll show you how to use the duty officer and planning computers. You won't believe how fast we can spin a sortie like this." He paused, looking at Daren carefully, then asked, "Do you have a call sign we can use, sir?"

"I'm old school, Zane—I was around when we had a Strategic Air Command, and we in SAC didn't get call signs back then. I guess the squadron's going to have to name me."

"We can do that, skipper," Grey said with an evil smile. "And we'll try not to stick with 'Pappy' or 'Granddad.'"

"I'd appreciate that. Let's go."

Six hours was barely enough time to do all the planning they needed for this flight, even with the computerized duty officer's help, but as the morning wore on and more and more crew members filtered into the squadron, Daren got more and more help. His squadron was small, only seventy-two members altogether, and it was indeed young, mostly first lieutenants, with only one or two captains. The enlisted corps was young, too. But they were all eager to impress their new boss and to show what they could accomplish. In less than three hours Daren was sitting down with Long, Grey, and another Vampire crew they'd be flying with for the first few hours, briefing a marathon six-hour sortie. They then took an elevator in the squadron hangar down to the Lair to begin the aircraft preflight.

They completed a briefing with the crew chief, another impossibly young Air National Guard sergeant, then proceeded to do a walkaround inspection and preflight the weapons. They were met by Captain Willy "Wonka" Weathers, the squadron munitions officer. "Glad to meet you, Wonka," Daren said, shaking his hand. "Thanks to you and your guys for hustling for me."

"It's our pleasure, sir," Weathers replied, smiling broadly. "Frankly, it's the first hurry-up job we've had here in the Lair. We've been involved with so much engineering support and mate testing that we forget we're supposed to be a combat unit, getting ready to go to war. I'm grateful for the chance to put my BB-stackers into action. Any no-notice taskings you want to give us is okay with us."

"That's what I like to hear," Daren said. "I enjoy lots of no-notice exercises."

"Outstanding, sir," Weathers said. He motioned to the forward bomb bay. "Allow me to give you a little brief on our babies here, sir. First time you've seen any of these weapons?"

"I've read about them and did some planning with all except Lancelot," Daren replied. "I heard about Lancelot from the Korea conflict, but nothing in detail."

"Well, this will be quick and dirty. We've got lots of briefings lined up for you, but the best way to get acquainted with these babies is to touch them and use them," Weathers said. "Fortunately, General McLanahan and General Furness believe in making holes in targets rather than just boring holes in the sky."

Weathers started with the forward bomb bay. "AGM-177 Wolverine attack cruise missiles, configured today with recovery and telemetry stuff," he said. "About three thousand pounds apiece, turbojet engine, cruise speed of about four hundred knots, loiter time thirty minutes after a one-hundred-mile, low-level cruise. Mission-adaptive-skin flight controls, highly maneuverable. Imaging infrared and millimeter-wave radar sensors, satellite datalink. Payload of about two hundred and fifty pounds in three weapons bays, plus defensive expendables, plus an enclosed payload bay for a terminal warhead or any mix of weapons, sensors, cameras, radio relay, and so forth. You can program it to act like a low-level attacker, like a maneuvering fighter up high, or like a ballistic missile. Please, make sure your attack computer is programmed for a training miss—these babies are one point six million bucks each, without payloads."

"Roger that."

"We loaded your Wolverines in the forward bomb bay on this sortie. We usually put them on rotary launchers, but we're normally not allowed to use RLs in training."

"Rotary launchers are designed to carry twenty thousand pounds of munitions and rotate them at ten rpms at temperatures down to minus fifty degrees while maneuvering at up to nine Gs," Daren said. Weathers began to smile and nod appreciatively at his new boss's obviously extensive knowledge of the weapons equipment. "You can't let them sit around. You use them or lose them. From now on they fly on every sortie, with training shapes loaded, but empty if absolutely necessary. If we can't get range time, we'll rig up a range right here on the base."

"Excellent. They need to be hooked up to hydraulic power and air-conditioning systems regularly to keep the bearings and seals tight. Anyway, we can put four in clip-in racks or six on an RL."

They moved to the center bomb bay. "Rotary launcher with Longhorns, Anaconda, Scorpion, and Lancelot—the ultimate aerial-combat payload," Weathers said proudly. "AIM-120 Scorpion medium-range air-to-air missile, triple-mode active radar, passive radar, and infrared guidance, fifty-pound directed-frag warhead, max range thirty-five miles. AGM-165 Longhorn air-to-ground guided-attack missile, enhanced longer-range version of the Maverick, two-hundred-pound thermium-nitrate warhead, sixty-mile range, millimeter-wave radar autoguidance or imaging infrared guidance—our Longhorns are enhanced with a target-handoff capability from the laser-radar attack system where we can input target coordinates and launch the missile, then refine aiming as it closes in.

"AIM-152 Anaconda long-range hypersonic air-to-air missile. Ramjet engine, max speed Mach five, max range one hundred and fifty miles. Only a fifty-pound warhead, too, despite its size, but if this thing hits you going Mach five, the impact will knock the biggest plane into next year.

"Finally, the ABM-3 Lancelot anti-ballistic-missile missile," Weathers said, pride gushing in his voice. "Basically an air-launched Patriot missile, triple-mode guidance, max range about three hundred miles at optimum launch parameters. The big bad boy in Lancelot is the plasma-yield warhead. In earth's atmosphere the warhead has the punch of a twenty-thousand-pound high explosive, but above sixty miles altitude the plasma field will vaporize anything within five to ten miles—no radiation, no heat, not even any noise, just complete obliteration. You should schedule to see a plasma-yield detonation as soon as you can—you won't forget it. Today, of course, we just have telemetry payloads."

They moved to the aft bomb bay of the EB-1C Vampire. "Last but not least, the U/MF-3 FlightHawk," Weathers said. "Long-range, long-endurance stealthy unmanned combat aircraft, used for an entire laundry list of jobs: attack, recon, decoy, deception, jamming, SEAD, you name it. We have a longer-range, stealthier version called StealthHawk that's just now being deployed. We can put four on a rotary launcher." Weathers turned to Mace. "That's it, sir. You've got quite a mission coming up. I'll be with you in the virtual cockpit monitoring your progress if you need any help, but if you follow the prompts from the attack computer and take your time, you won't have any trouble. Anything else for me, sir?"

"Just one thing," Daren said. "If any of your troops would like to strap on the jet with us, we'd love to take them along."

"You're *kidding?*" Weathers gasped. "Two of my guys get to ride with you on this mission?" Daren thought Weathers might volunteer himself, but, like a good officer and leader, he turned and whistled at a couple of his techs, who trotted over. "Colonel Mace, I'm happy to introduce you to Staff Sergeant Marty Banyan and Senior Airman Todd Meadows, by far the best weapon-jammers in the entire Air National Guard. They were the first ones on the line this morning before oh-six-hundred; they were responsible for getting this package uploaded in record time. Sergeant Banyan, Airman Meadows, Colonel Mace, our new squadron CO."

Daren shook hands with the eager, awestruck airmen. "Captain Weathers picked you to take a ride with us this afternoon, guys, if you're up for it."

Both Banyan's and Meadows's eyes became as big as soccer balls.

"You bet I am, sir!" Meadows shouted enthusiastically.

"I've worked on B-1s for almost five years," Banyan enthused, "but I've never been up in one. I've been waiting for this chance for years!"

"Outstanding. We start engines in about an hour. Captain, if you'd give Life Support a heads-up, we'll get these boys some flight gear ASAP. Report back as fast as you can."

"Yes, *sir!*" both techs shouted, and they hurried off to stow their tools.

"That was a great thing you did, sir," Weathers said after he had the duty officer alert the Life Support shop to get ready to brief and equip the two weapons loaders for their flight. "We're always looking for all the ways we can find to motivate our troops. As I said, I'll be in the virtual cockpit monitoring your weapon releases and performance. Good luck and happy shooting." He shook his squadron commander's hand, gave him a salute—a rather strange thing to do, Mace thought, being eighty feet underground; were they indoors or outdoors or what?—and then drove off to look in on the other bombers getting ready for launch.

"Good going, sir," Grey said proudly. "I'd say you scored some points today."

"And I haven't done a damn thing," Daren said with a wry smile. "Shit, if I ever thought being a squadron commander was as easy as just treating the troops like professionals, I'd have done it a long time ago."

Grey led Daren on the power-off preflight in the cockpit, then back down the tall entry ladder to do a walk-around inspection. This was the most bizarre experience—getting ready to fly an aircraft while underground. Afterward, when the two weapons loaders had met up with them, Grey briefed the flight and ground crews on their departure procedures, and then they climbed up inside the bomber.

While Grey made sure Banyan and Meadows were properly strapped in and were given a safety and procedures briefing on the ejection and escape equipment—most of which the two B-1 veterans seemed very aware of already—Daren moved forward and began to "build his nest"—put all his checklists, charts, and gear in exactly the places he wanted them. Grey ran through a quick console orientation—quick because there was very little to review. The system was so automated that there were very few human-activated switches left. "We monitor and check everything," Zane said, "and let the computers do their thing. Two minutes to power-up. The computer does power-on checks itself on the mission schedule. Make sure you're ready—things happen fast from here on. Sing out if you see any anomalies. Otherwise, sit back and enjoy the ride."

As power-up time approached, Daren silently prayed the old airman's prayer: God, please don't let me screw up. "O-kay," Daren said nervously.

"Crew, this is Bobcat Two-three," the computer spoke a few moments later. *"Check in when ready for power-up."*

"Bobcat Two-three, AC is ready for power-up."

"A 'please' would be nice," Daren quipped. He keyed his mike button and spoke, "Bobcat Two-three, MC is ready for power-up."

"Power-up commencing," the computer responded, and immediately the monitors on the back wall came to life and lines and lines of computer reports started to scroll

across the screens as the computer ran through its built-in checks. Daren watched, absolutely fascinated, as the aircraft proceeded with its power-on system checks. The before-engine-start checklist ran the same way as the power-on checklist. Less than five minutes later, the computer reported ready for engine start.

"So far so good, guys," Grey said after the computer completed its checks. "Ready for a tow to the surface." Engines were not started, and aircraft did not taxi on their own power, inside the Lair unless absolutely necessary. After Grey called the flight leader and reported ready, ground crews hooked a tow bar up to the bomber's nose gear and pulled the bomber out of its parking spot with a large aircraft tug.

Moving inside the Lair, Daren thought, was like driving a big SUV inside an underground parking garage with very low ceilings—it seemed as if every girder and piece of concrete above them was sure to hit the vertical stabilizer, and even with the wings fully swept, the wingtips seemed to pass just a few inches away from the other parked jets. He instinctively ducked his head when approaching a structural crosspiece in the ceiling.

Daren saw B-52 bombers as they were towed past, including a couple with huge rounded-nose turrets. "Those must be the Dragons," he said. "Airborne lasers on B-52 bombers. Incredible."

"Yep," Grey said. "Fucking amazing jets. They're still Strato-Pigs, but—my God—when that laser lets go, it still sends a chill down my spine."

"Who's the squadron commander?"

"Colonel Nancy Cheshire," Zane replied. "She's one of General McLanahan's test pilots from Dreamland. The Fifty-second Squadron is technically not activated yet, but they're organized and run just like the other flying units. Just two aircraft, and neither will be mission-ready for at least another year, but they've already flown a bunch of sorties, and we know they work. I'd like to have one on every sortie I fly over Indian country," Zane added.

The Vampire was pulled alongside the lead EB-1C bomber, and the tow bars were disconnected. "Okay, we'll motor up to level two and start engines there," Zane said. Level two had special exhaust chambers that channeled the exhaust away more efficiently than did the passive system used in the main complex. "After that, the computer will do the before-takeoff checks, then motor up to the surface, get a last-chance inspection, and then we go." It was weird to be staring straight ahead at solid rock directly in front of the EB-1C's windscreen, and Daren was thankful when the engines were started, the last of the pre-takeoff checklists were done, and they were raised all the way to the surface.

It was mostly sunny but windy on the surface, with an occasional cloud of dust blowing past the windscreen. "Lovely day in Battle Mountain, guys," Grey said. They noticed that Rebecca Furness and John Long themselves were doing the last-chance inspection—Daren could still see Long scowling at him from inside the car.

"Bobcat flight."

"Two's ready," Grey replied. On intercom: "Ready, guys?"

"MC is ready," Daren announced.

"Banyan ready."

"Meadows ready. Let's light this candle!"

"MC, you have the aircraft," Zane announced.

"Me? Are you kidding?"

"Best way to learn, sir," Grey said. "No matter how much you want to freelance the training program, sir, you're going to have to do a check ride, and part of the check for the MC is a takeoff, landing, stabilized precontact position behind the tanker, instrument approach, and visual approach. Might as well get as much stick time as you can."

"Too bad takeoffs aren't automated, too, like everything else," Daren commented.

"They are," Grey said. "The system actually does a very good formation takeoff. But we don't do autotakeoffs or much formation stuff anymore. Besides, I like hand-flying the jet every mission, and takeoff seems like a good time to do it. Doing takeoffs is a good way to get a feel for the jet. Besides, if the system decides to burp on takeoff, there's less chance of an accident."

"In that case how about I just watch the first one?"

"I'll watch your gauges," Grey urged him. "Take thirty-second spacing behind the leader, fan right twenty degrees, turn when he makes his turn, and go into trail on him. I'll be right here if you need me, sir. We'll fly with the mission-adaptive stuff on—you won't believe how smooth and easy it is."

"I haven't done a takeoff in many, many moons," Mace muttered.

"It's as simple as becoming aware of when she's ready to fly," Grey said encouragingly. "We know what the book says the takeoff run should be, and it's pretty accurate, but the Vampire is like a thoroughbred racehorse—you've got to be sensitive to when it's hesitant, when it's ready to run, and when to give it full rein. Rotate around one-fifty, climb to one or two hundred feet in ground effect, raise the gear, and then lower the nose until we reach three hundred knots. Once you hit three hundred, raise the nose and maintain three-fifty. As long as you maintain at least two thousand feet per minute, which should be no problem at our gross weight, we'll clear the mountains easily. I'll back you up on heading and keep an eye out for the leader. Ready?"

"Ready—I guess," Daren said.

"You got the aircraft," Zane said, giving the control stick a shake.

Oh, shit, Daren thought. Here we go. "I have the aircraft," he acknowledged, shaking his control stick in reply.

The pilot of the lead EB-1C Vampire bomber got clearance for takeoff, taxied off the elevator to the end of the runway, lined up on centerline, locked brakes, lit afterburners, released brakes, and shot down the runway.

A few seconds after the leader lifted off, Daren locked the brakes and smoothly moved the throttles forward. He paused at the first detent, then smoothly moved the throttles into the afterburner zone. "Good nozzle swing . . . zone five, now . . . brakes off."

The Vampire bomber leaped forward as if it were shot from a catapult. Daren was pressed hard in his seat. The pressure on his chest was surprising, much more than it had been in the supersonic FB-111. It was hard to believe that a plane this big could accelerate so fast. It seemed only seconds later that Zane announced, "Coming up on rotate speed . . . rotating, now." Suddenly the Vampire broke ground and soared into the air like an arrow fired into the sky. "Positive rate . . . positive altimeter . . . gear moving." Daren checked that all the gear lights were out—and by the time he did, the bomber had reached almost three hundred knots.

"Watch your airspeed—there's your barber-pole max V," Grey said. "Don't be afraid to pull it up. The faster we get to altitude, the better."

"Guess I'm a little rusty," Daren commented. He pulled back more on the stick and retrimmed but found he had to pull and retrim every ten seconds or so to keep the bomber at three-fifty. They were now climbing at well over eight thousand feet per minute. "Christ, she's like a bat out of hell," Daren muttered.

"You got that right, sir," Grey agreed. "Mission-adaptive technology. The whole airframe becomes a lift-producing device until we hit three hundred knots, and then the computer takes it away little by little, till just a small part of the wing and fuselage produces lift. That way there's no induced drag caused by a lot of lift-producing surfaces. Sounds weird, but it's true. The faster we go, the faster we *can* go. Above four hundred knots almost none of the wing and a tiny fraction of the fuselage is producing lift—the rest is just knifing through the air at zero angle of attack."

A few moments later Zane put his right hand on the control stick. "Good job, sir," he said. He shook the stick. "I have the aircraft. I'll do the rejoin, check over the leader, then let you try some formation. It'll get you warmed up for the air refueling."

"You got the aircraft," Daren said. His palms felt clammy inside his gloves. Damn, things happened *fast* in this machine!

It did not take long to catch up to the leader, and soon Zane maneuvered his bomber into route formation, five hundred meters to the right, a hundred meters behind, and a hundred meters above the leader. He got on the interplane radio frequency to the other aircraft. "Lead, this is Two, clear me in to fingertip," he radioed.

"You're cleared in to fingertip," the leader radioed.

Grey performed an initial join-up, closing in to about a half mile away from the leader's right wingtip. "That's a pretty good combat spread position," he said. He then made an imperceptible stick movement, and slowly they slid toward the leader until the two planes were less than a hundred feet apart. They looked the leader's aircraft over; then Grey ducked underneath and repositioned himself on the other side. "Want to give it a try, sir?"

"Think I'm ready, Zane?"

"We'll shortly find out, sir."

"What's the trick to fingertip in the Vampire, Zane?"

"The mission-adaptive computers dampen out most of the bow wave but accentuate the wingtip vortices, so we set up a little farther out than normal. We can't really tuck it in as tight as a T-38 Talon or T-1 Jayhawk. Nice and easy is the key. I know you have formation experience in the F-111s and various trainer aircraft. With mission-adaptive technology, controlling the Vampire in close is easier than on any other aircraft. All it takes is a light touch on the controls."

Daren flexed his neck muscles, shifted slightly in his seat, and looked as if he was taking a deep, nervous breath—but they hadn't moved an inch yet. "Anytime you're ready, sir," Grey prompted him. He was just about to give Mace a few more basic pointers on how to close in to fingertip position when, before Grey or anyone else realized what happened, they were flying within just a few feet of each other, wingtips overlapping. *"I've got the aircraft! I've got the aircraft!"* Grey shouted.

"No," Daren said calmly. "Hands off."

"Two, you guys are a little close," the lead mission commander radioed.

"We're fine," Daren responded. Grey quickly realized that Mace hadn't overcorrected or made a mistake—he was purposely tucked in close, the leader's left wing casting a shadow on the second Vampire. But Mace was in there so close and so tight that it felt as if they were one aircraft.

"I see what you mean about the wingtip vortices. The trick would be to keep the vortices away from the flight-control surfaces. Look—I'll move out a few feet. Put your hand on the stick." When Grey put his hand lightly on the control stick, Daren moved the bomber an imperceptible amount away from the leader. "See that?"

"No."

"Turn off the mission-adaptive computer for a sec."

"What?"

"I said, turn off the MA computer, Zane."

"You want to move away first?"

"No." To Grey's horror, Daren keyed his voice-control button: "MAT to standby." There was a slight burble that caused a thrill of panic to shoot up and down Grey's spine, but their position did not change one bit. "See it now? The mission-adaptive system masks it out quite a bit. Look— it'll go away." He slid in four feet closer, so close that Grey could see the whites in the lead AC's eyes. "See? It's gone. You really got to get it in there tight, but the vortices just spill out over the top of our fuselage and overboard along our slipstream." Daren keyed the interplane channel mike button: "Lead, give me a standard rate turn," he radioed. "Either direction."

There was a *long* pause, but finally: "Roger. Coming left."

The lead Vampire made an ultracautious, much less than standard-rate turn, and the second Vampire turned with him. "See this, Zane?" Daren said. "Once you're in tight enough to let the vortices spill over the fuselage instead of the wings, the vortices actually help keep you in place." He moved his hand until he had just one finger and one thumb on the controls. "She's practically flying herself. I wouldn't unzip and take a pee, but this gives you enough of a breather to refocus your eyes, check a caution message, or get a kink out." They turned right to get back on course, and Mace's Vampire stuck with the leader as if it were welded to him. "Let's see what it's like on the other side." On interplane he radioed, "Lead, Two's crossing under to the other wing."

"Is that you flying, Zane?"

"Negative. It's the new guy."

"Say again?"

"It's the new MC flying," Zane said proudly. "He's got liquid nitrogen for blood."

Still in the turn, Daren crossed under the lead EB-1, close enough so that they could see seams in the composite fibersteel skin. "Wow. Feel this, Zane—I'm dead in between both wingtip vortices, and it's as smooth as a baby's bottom here." All Zane could think about was smacking into the underside of the lead plane—they were closer than precontact position from an aerial-refueling tanker. But he took the controls and found it incredibly steady. No sign of turbulence or cross-controlling at all. Daren tried it with the mission-adaptive system on, and it was even smoother.

He backed away to a more reasonable position. "Nice job in the groove, Nitro," the pilot of the lead bomber remarked.

"I think you've just been named, sir," Grey said.

" 'Nitro,' huh? It's a helluva lot better than 'Pappy,' " Daren said. He moved away to route-formation position and gave control back to the flight-control computer.

"Shit-hot job, sir," Grey said. "I got the impression you didn't like flying."

"Nah," Daren said. "Just because I don't think mission commanders need to be experts in flying the jet, or because I think I shouldn't be wasting time learning flight characteristics, doesn't mean I *can't* fly. But I prefer dropping bombs, my friend. I'll get our range clearance, and then we'll go in and have some *real* fun!"

BATTLE MOUNTAIN AIR RESERVE BASE
Later that afternoon

Daren had to struggle to keep up with the squadron as they headed down the aircraft-parking ramp for the finish line. His newest squadron joint activity: letting everyone off at 4:00 P.M. on Friday afternoon and doing a five-kilometer run around the runway, followed by a tailgate beer and soda party hosted by one of the squadron's duty flights, rotated each week. He was heartened to see everyone who was not on critical duty, and even a few others who had a quick-response responsibility, out for the run. He was also pleasantly surprised when Patrick McLanahan, David Luger, and a bunch of other Air Battle Force types joined in the run with Rebecca Furness, John Long, and a few other wing personnel he hadn't even met yet.

The afternoon air was cold and dry, much different from the humid air in the District of Columbia and Alabama, but his body was finally getting accustomed to the dryness and altitude, and Daren felt he acquitted himself well despite obviously being the old man in the group. He felt that more than just a few folks had to slow up so they wouldn't completely wax their squadron commander, and there was a big clump of squadron personnel who finished beside Daren and Rebecca. John Long, a three-per-day cigar smoker, dropped out after three kilometers, the minimum distance for the twice-annual Air Force aerobics test; almost no one else dropped out, although a few had to stop and take some deep breaths and rest aching legs.

Daren first chose a large bottle of icy-cold water after the run, but then he took one look at the disappointed faces of his squadron, put it back, and pulled out a bottle of beer instead, then handed one to Rebecca. This gave the go-ahead for everyone else, and the partying started in earnest. "Good move, Colonel," Rebecca said as they walked along the dirt beside the Security Forces building. "You saw that everyone wanted a beer, but no one was going to partake unless you did first. Very heads-up of you to switch."

"Thanks."

"I've seen a lot of that lately. You seem very in tune with your troops. I see you playing basketball and having chow with the enlisted people, playing cards with the NCOs, turning wrenches with the maintenance guys, and shooting rifles and pistols on the range with the Security Forces. I know it means a lot to them to see you around." She paused, then said, "But *I* don't see much of you these days. The general's big project?"

"He's got me plugged in night and day." There were lots of generals on base, Daren thought, but everyone knew that "the" general was Patrick McLanahan. "Lots of meetings and trips to TTR." The Tonopah Test Range was the flight test and research base in southwestern Nevada that served as the medium-security conduit between the unclassified flight testing done at Edwards Air Force Base in Southern California and the supersecret research work done at the High Technology Aerospace Weapons Center, or HAWC, near Las Vegas.

"Everything going all right?"

"I think we'll have it dialed in soon," Daren said. "The general is a hard-charger."

"Good candidate for a nervous breakdown."

"His head is screwed on right, I think," Daren said. "He's spending more time with his kid. He even showed up for the squadron run."

"I couldn't believe it myself."

"I wasn't surprised. He works hard, but he's starting to gain a bit more perspective, I think."

"That'll be a switch."

They fell silent again, nursing their beers. Finally Daren said, "How about dinner tonight? I think the Owl Club is doing cowboy poetry in the dining room. Should be a rip-roarin' time in the old town!" That was pure sarcasm. There was not much to do in Battle Mountain after hours; cowboy poetry was a special treat.

"I . . . I don't think so, Daren," Rebecca said uneasily.

"You're allowed to spend time with your squadron commanders while off duty."

"I know that. It's just—"

"This is the first time I've even spoken to you outside meetings and briefings, Becky, and we've still got several hundred airmen around us," Daren said. "Something a little more relaxed and private would be nice."

"I'm not ready to start seeing you, Daren."

"Not even for dinner and some wine?"

"When did we *ever* get together for 'just' dinner?"

He smiled in spite of himself. "Well, I certainly didn't mind when things turned in that direction."

"And that's why I'm saying no, Daren. I'm afraid our whole relationship outside of work revolves around sex. I'm not ready for that yet."

"It doesn't have to end up with us in the sack, Becky."

"I just don't want to take the chance," she said. She motioned to the rest of the large crowd of runners a few dozen yards away. "I think I'm comfortable enough around you right now."

"You're not giving me very much credit here."

"I'll apologize—if you tell me you didn't think about it when you asked me out." Daren smiled again. "I thought so."

"Hey, it doesn't mean I was planning to carry you up to a hotel room and throw you on the bed after dinner,"

Daren said. "If it happened, then . . . I'd be very happy. If it didn't—"

"You'd try again," Rebecca finished for him. "Problem is, I'm not sure if I'm ready for the pursuit right now . . . and I'm not sure what I'd be feeling if I said yes." He looked away. "And if you cared about me at all, you'd respect that."

"I do," Daren said earnestly. "But it won't stop me from thinking about it—or trying again." She had no response to that. Daren couldn't tell if it meant "Don't bother" or "I'd like that." He looked over the aircraft-parking ramp, wishing he could throw the beer bottle across with all his strength. "Are you ever going to tell me about you and Rinc Seaver?" he asked sharply.

"No. And I advise you not to bring up *that* topic again," she said, and she walked quickly away.

As he watched her move off, his mind flashed briefly on Amber back at Donatella's—and then he shook his head, finished his beer, and went to get another.

While over at the tailgate, Patrick McLanahan met up with him. "Good idea doing a run," he said. Daren noticed with amusement that McLanahan's sweatshirt was heavily sweat-stained. "The tailgate party makes it even better."

"Thanks for turning out, sir," Daren said. "Been a while since you've done any running?"

"I've been allowed to skate."

"I see."

"I saw the rundown on your familiarization ride today with Lieutenant Grey. Very good shooting," Patrick said.

"Thank you, sir. With precision-guided weapons and the systems you have on board your B-1s here, a person's got to have a pretty good excuse to miss."

"Youth. New systems. Not intuitive enough. I've heard lots of excuses," Patrick said. "It takes a skilled operator to simply walk into a Vampire, manage the aircraft, manage the systems, and release good weapons. You're a good stick, too. You watered your wingman's eyes with your formation flying."

"Thanks."

McLanahan pulled Mace away from the others circling the beer. "You're doing an outstanding job getting the virtual-cockpit stuff ready on the Vampires, too," Patrick went on when they were by themselves. "It's coming together great."

"I think we'll be done well before your deadline, sir."

"Unfortunately, we're going to be taking a break for a few days. We have a special mission—and I want you to fly it."

"You got it, sir. Where are we going?"

McLanahan looked around to see if anyone was in earshot, then: "Turkmenistan."

Daren didn't look surprised. "I had a feeling things were heating up out there," he said. "When do we brief?"

"We'll brief the mission itself in the plane after we're airborne," Patrick said. "Crew rest for you starts as soon as you finish that beer. Show time in the Lair is oh-two-hundred, wheels-up at oh-three-hundred."

Daren drained his beer. "Cool," he said simply. "I'll be there. Who's my aircraft commander?"

"You worked well with Lieutenant Grey this morning," Patrick said, "but we need someone with a little more experience."

"Don't tell me—I know."

Patrick glanced at Rebecca heading for her Yukon in the parking lot, then back at Daren. "You two going to be okay?"

"Yes, sir. If not, we'll have lots of time en route to discuss things."

"That's for sure. See you in the Lair."

"May I make a suggestion, sir?"

"Of course."

"Let's turn this mission into an operational test flight," Daren said. "Let's use everything we've put together. It can work, I know it."

Patrick thought about it for a moment—but only for a moment. "Good idea," he said. "We'll still have a live crew on board, but we'll run it as if they're not on board. We'll have to let everyone in the One-eleventh in on it. . . ."

"It'll work, sir," Daren said. "It'll be great."

Patrick fell silent again, then said, "Fine. But I'll fly as mission commander."

"Sir . . ."

"No argument. This mission and this system are completely off the books. No one flies experimental aircraft until I fly it first. I might even bar Rebecca from flying it, but she'd argue so loud and long that I know there'd be no point."

"Sir, the original idea behind this whole plan was to make it so you wouldn't *have* to fly missions like this."

"That's not why I set up this program!"

"I didn't mean it like a selfish act, sir—I know you wouldn't start something like this just for yourself," Daren said. "But the original motivating factor behind all of this was creating a weapon system that didn't rely on human factors to complete the mission. You have too much invested in this program—emotionally as well as careerwise—to be completely effective."

"That's enough, Colonel," Patrick snapped. "I'm the MC on this mission, and that's it. You will be the virtual mission commander; we'll put Colonel Long and Lieutenant Grey in as the virtual aircraft commanders. I'm sure Dr. Jon Masters will want to be present as well; Captain Weathers will be on call as the weapons officer."

"Not going to let me be the hero, eh, sir?"

"You so sure we'll end up with a hero once this is over, Colonel?" Patrick asked.

"Damn straight, sir."

Patrick clasped Daren on the shoulder. "Your confidence is infectious, Mace. All right, let's do it."

THREE

KERKI ARMY AIR BASE, TURKMENISTAN
Early the next morning

I t's true, sir—they're gone," the platoon lieutenant reported. "The trucks and armored vehicles are all abandoned. We saw some stragglers camped out a few kilometers away, carrying wounded, but they ran off as we approached. They did not appear to be carrying weapons, so we let them go."

The commander of Kerki Army Air Base glanced at his lead helicopter pilot. "What did you see?" he asked.

"The same, sir," the pilot reported. "About a dozen light armored vehicles, four small tanks, two large main battle tanks, two dozen supply trucks, the two towed antiaircraft weapons—all scattered across the road and abandoned. Some appeared to be torched."

"We did see evidence of scouts or infiltrators on the base, sir," the captain in charge of base security added. "Perhaps they got a look at our preparations for a counterattack and fled."

"Did you see any of their pickups?"

"We found a few nearby, broken down and abandoned,

but all the rest of them are gone," the scout platoon leader reported. "They are faster and more maintainable than armored vehicles—better getaway vehicles."

"I'm well aware of that, Lieutenant," the commander said irritably. "But I don't believe for one moment that they've fled just because their scouts saw us getting some helicopters ready to fly. That Afghan terrorist who calls himself General Zarazi is a berserker, but he is crafty and unconventional. He had several hundred men less than twenty kilometers from here—they have to be nearby. I want search teams sent out after them immediately."

"Then we shall postpone the assault, sir?"

"Of course. If their vehicles are abandoned, why bother attacking them?" What he did not say was that it was too expensive and too hard on the machines to fly them; he had to save the equipment, fuel, and ammunition for more direct threats. "Redeploy your men and search the area surrounding the base—they have to be moving in on us. If you find any, squeeze them until they talk. Make an example of a few of them." The officers nodded enthusiastically and hurried off.

The call came just a few minutes later: "Colonel, we've captured several terrorists—including the leader, Zarazi!" The base commander hurried out to meet with his men. Sure enough, they had several scraggly-looking men kneeling on the dirt floor, hands cuffed behind their backs. All of them appeared to have been beaten. "Good work, Captain," the commander said. "Did you get anything out of them?"

"We haven't started questioning them yet, sir," the security chief replied. "They came in like that, dragging themselves to the front gate. Looks like they were beaten pretty badly by their own men."

"So much for honor among thieves," the commander

sneered. "Which one is Zarazi?" The captain pointed him out. "How do you know this?"

"We overheard one of the others addressing him as 'General.' He is clothed a bit better than the others, and he is the only one with a holster for a sidearm. We took fingerprints—we expect an answer back from Interior Ministry headquarters on his identity soon."

"Let me know the minute it comes in." The commander stepped over to Zarazi. "You are General Zarazi?" he asked in Russian. No response. The base commander reared back and smashed his fist into the back of his captive's head, and Zarazi pitched forward, his face crunching into the dirt. "Now is not the time to act brave, scum. Either you talk, or you die." Zarazi struggled back to his knees but said nothing.

The colonel dragged another man by his hair over in front of Zarazi. "You. What is this man's name?" He did not reply. The colonel drew his pistol, placed the muzzle on the back of the second man's head, and pulled the trigger. A mass of bone, hair, blood, and brains spattered across Zarazi's body. Thankfully, the bullet lodged in the ground and did not ricochet around the small building. "I will continue to execute your men one by one in front of you until you talk."

"Aslayop!" Zarazi shouted in Russian, blinking to try to get the gory mess out of his eyes. "You murderous donkeyfucker!"

"Do I have your attention now? Are you Zarazi?"

"Yes, God damn you!"

The base commander ordered the others taken out to the detention facility, and soon he and the captain of security were alone with Zarazi.

"You are one bold man, Zarazi—stupid, but bold," the colonel said. "You've killed scores of loyal Turkmen soldiers, shanghaied dozens more, destroyed several pieces of military equipment, and stolen hundreds of millions of manats' worth of equipment. What is the point of this rampage you're on? What is your objective?"

"After putting a bullet into your head, just as you did to poor Ahmed there? Destruction of your pissant cowardly country."

"Destruction? Why? What did we ever do to you?"

"You and your corrupt government sat back and did nothing while the United States, the infidels, and the Zionists raped my country," Zarazi said. "The infidels drove all my people out of our homeland, and you did nothing. My people tried to seek shelter and help in your country, and you did worse than nothing—you caged them up like rabid animals. You deserve to die, slowly and painfully, and God has chosen me to carry out this task."

"Unfortunately, my insane friend, you have failed," the base commander said. "You shall be brought to military headquarters at Ashkhabad, interrogated, then executed. Take him away."

"Don't you want to hear what will happen if I am taken away, Colonel?"

"Your men will attack my base? Let them try."

"No—I mean, what will happen to your *family* if I am taken away."

The base commander's face turned to stone, and he gulped involuntarily. It took just an instant, but the steel returned to his face, and he raised his pistol and pointed it at Zarazi's right temple. "If you thought that would buy you more time, you were wrong, asshole," he growled. "You just bought yourself a visit to a firing squad, right here at Kerki."

"I have already surrendered my life to Allah. I am confident he will receive me into heaven," Zarazi said. "I will meet your four sons, your wife, your two sisters, and your *min'etka*—Kaliali, I believe her name is—there. Soon afterward you will join them."

"You fucking bastard!" the base commander shouted, grabbing Zarazi by the hair and pulling him to his feet. "What in hell have you done?"

"While your men were searching the desert for me, my men were moving into Kerki, Khatab, and Kizyl-arvat, capturing your family members," Zarazi said. "Your men are not very happy with you, Colonel, especially the enlisted men. They were more than happy to tell me all about your families in great detail, after they swore loyalty to me and joined my brigade."

The base commander threw Zarazi back down on the ground, then went over to a wall phone and dialed. After a few moments his men could see their commander's eyes bulging in terror. He replaced the receiver on its cradle with a shaking hand. A nod from him, and Zarazi was lifted up to his feet.

"You'll never get away with this, criminal," the commander spoke. "The police and the military will hunt your men down and slaughter them."

"Then they will find your family members dead beside them," Zarazi said. "I told you, Colonel, we are all prepared to die to complete our mission and fulfill our destiny. You cannot threaten us with pain or death, because we know at the end of it comes everlasting peace and happiness with God. But your children—surely they are too young to die? The oldest has just turned twenty-two, and the youngest is still in his teens—why, his whole life is still ahead of him. And your girlfriend could very well be your daughter—"

The commander punched Zarazi in the face as hard as his shaking, spasmodic muscles could manage. Zarazi only smiled. He knew by the force of the blow that the Turkmen officer was done fighting.

"You fucking bastard . . ." the commander murmured.

"The same fate awaits your officers' families as well," Zarazi said. "We targeted at least two dozen of your officers' and senior enlisted men's households. We will butcher them all if you do not do as I say."

"What in hell do you want?"

"Simple: for you and your men to walk off this base, unarmed," Zarazi said. "When I am satisfied that you and your men are far enough away and no threat to me, I will order my men to release your families."

"How do I know that you'll do as you say?"

"You do not know," Zarazi said. "That is my insurance. I promise you, I will slaughter them if you do not obey me—of that you can be certain."

"Do you seriously expect me and my men simply to walk off this base and leave it to you and your scavengers? Are you delusional?"

"I expect you to act like men," Zarazi said. "Either execute me for daring to touch your families, and then prepare to mourn the loss of your loved ones, or obey me, evacuate this base, and save your families. Asking stupid questions is a waste of my time. You decide. You have until dawn. If my men do not hear from me by then, they will assume I have been killed and will proceed with my last instructions: kill the captives and escape."

"You . . . sick . . . bastard. I hope you rot in hell for this." But the commander nodded to the guard, who hauled Zarazi to his feet and removed the handcuffs.

"Do not worry about my place in the afterlife, Colonel. I believe it has been reserved for me by God," Zarazi said. "But now I have one more request."

"We are leaving this place so we can save our families. What more do you want?"

Zarazi looked at the guards surrounding him. As if with

a silent command, one of the guards handed over his AK-74 assault rifle to Zarazi.

"What do you think you're doing, Corporal?" the security chief asked.

"He is doing what I think most of your men assigned here will choose to do—join my regiment, rather than slink away with you," Zarazi said. "Now, as for my one last request, Colonel, I ask that you sacrifice yourself in forgiveness for the murder of my comrade."

"What?" The commander's eyes were round with fear, and he looked at the others, hoping for some sign of support. He got none—not even from his security chief and certainly not from the conscripts. They seemed to be very, very pleased to watch their commanding officer die. "You fucking bastard. Kill me if you want. But if you even so much as approach any member of my family, I swear, I will arise from the grave and haunt you through eternity." And at that, the base commander grabbed the muzzle of the rifle and steered it under his chin. "Let's get it over with, bastard," he growled, looking at Zarazi with quivering lips but also with pure hatred in his eyes.

"This is the first brave thing you have done, Colonel— unfortunately, it is the last, too," Zarazi said as he pulled the trigger. Then he slung the weapon over his shoulder while the ringing of the shot, the acrid smell of gunpowder, and the sickening sound of the body hitting the floor, minus most of its head, settled. He turned to the security chief and said, "It appears you are in charge now, Major. I suggest you call the company commanders, have them assemble their troops outside the front gate, and prepare to move out."

By the time dawn began to break over Mount Ayrybaba, the ten-thousand-foot mountain that sat on the border between Turkmenistan and Uzbekistan, the Turkmen troops had assembled outside the gates of Kerki Air Base. To General Zarazi's joy, more than four-fifths of the Turkmen soldiers, including a good number of pilots and officers, remained behind. The Turkmen conscripts were very unhappy with their treatment by the elitist professional soldiers; the younger professional soldiers who were not part of the new quasi-Russian regime in Turkmenistan also chose to remain.

Jalaluddin Turabi, who had met up with Zarazi shortly after the deadline passed, administered the oath via loudspeaker to almost two thousand Turkmen troops assembled in front of base headquarters. They had already organized themselves into companies, chosen new unit commanders, and torn the Turkmen patches and flags off their uniforms. Zarazi, still bloodied by his treatment at the dead commander's hand, led the assembled force in prayer. He then ordered the men to return to their barracks and for the company commanders and senior noncommissioned officers to meet him in headquarters.

"Allah has blessed us and answered our prayers, gentlemen," he began. "Our crusade to build a haven for warriors of Islam begins right here, right now. It is our duty to organize and secure this area, prepare to fight off any challengers to our authority, and work to spread the word of God throughout this country."

Turabi watched the newcomers carefully and, to his great surprise, noticed that a good many of the new officers sat in rapt attention, gazing at Zarazi like he was some sort of demigod. What was wrong with these men? he wondered. Could their lives be so screwed up out here in the wilderness that they would be willing to betray their country this easily and quickly and join up with a foreigner?

Zarazi stood before a large wall map of eastern Turkmenistan. "Our first objective will be to secure the Kizyl-arvat hydroelectric dam. This dam supplies power to all of eastern Turkmenistan as well as southern Uzbekistan. Once we take this facility, we also control the Turkmen oil and natural-gas pipeline that connects to Afghanistan and Pakistan, and we also control several irrigation and fresh-water pumping stations for the region. The oil facilities shall be destroyed immediately."

"Destroyed?" Turabi asked. He said it louder than he meant. He didn't want the men assembled before them to see any sign of confusion or disagreement in the leadership, but they hadn't discussed this move beforehand. "Wakil, we can hold those pipelines and wells for ransom. The Turkmen or whoever built them will pay us handsomely to keep them in operation."

Zarazi glared at Turabi as if the man had pissed on his boots. "And if they don't, Colonel?"

"*Then* we destroy them," Turabi said. "But I think they'll pay to keep their precious oil flowing. That means more money we can send back to our clans. Let's give it a try, at least."

Zarazi looked as if he were going to order Turabi to be silent—he appeared angry enough even to strike him—but instead he held his anger in check and nodded. "Very well, Colonel. I shall leave that task in your hands. Make contact with the Turkmen oil minister or their Western puppet masters and tell them that if they want their oil to keep flowing, they will pay."

"Yes, General," Turabi said loudly, thinking that he'd better do whatever he could to show everyone that Zarazi was back in command. "I'll make the pricks pay out their asses."

"Our greatest threat is the infantry base at Gaurdak," Zarazi continued after giving Turabi a final warning glare. "They have a full brigade there, do they not?"

One of the Turkmen officers shot to his feet. "Master,

they are authorized to brigade strength, but they have been unable to get enough equipment and supplies to fully equip a brigade," the man said, standing at ramrod attention. "Most have not been paid in many weeks; most of the officers, like ourselves, have not been paid in many months. They have had many desertions and crimes against the local population. Many of the soldiers have resorted to stealing from the locals to feed themselves or selling fuel and equipment to smugglers. Their overall readiness is very poor."

"Stealing from the people we are dedicating ourselves to liberate and protect will not be tolerated in my army, is that clear?" Zarazi said sternly. "But I also hereby command that anyone who does not declare himself a true servant of God shall not be entitled to own land, property, or resources under our jurisdiction or protection. That includes the water, the oil and gas through the pipelines, the power that flows from the hydroelectric power plant—everything. If it is under our protection, then either outsiders must swear allegiance to us and our cause, or they must pay for these resources."

Now he had *all* their attention, Turabi noticed. Zarazi had a good number of men here who believed that he was some sort of holy warrior, but most of them were just tired of the old commander and wanted to be paid. Zarazi was promising them a paycheck. He was definitely in business now.

Zarazi outlined his wishes for patrols, security, and reporting to him, then dismissed the company commanders and their senior noncommissioned officers. The officer who spoke up in front of the others, a transportation and supply officer named Lieutenant Aman Orazov, remained behind, along with Turabi. Orazov was a tall, heavyset man with long, unkempt hair, no mustache or beard, and filthy boots and uniform—Turabi worried the guy might be infested with lice. "It is a great honor to serve you, master," Orazov said in halting Pashtun. "I am proud to be part of your command."

"You are a loyal and brave servant . . . *Captain* Orazov," Zarazi said. The scruffy-looking clerk looked as if he were going to kiss Zarazi's hand—and then, disgustingly, he did. "I hope you are correct about the base at Gaurdak."

"I am, master," Orazov said. "I do not think they will be a threat to us. They are even more isolated than Kerki; they do a great deal of black-market trading with smugglers and villagers from Uzbekistan and Afghanistan. I think you will find many who support our cause."

"We shall see," Zarazi said.

"My concern would be for the major and the other company commanders that you are allowing to walk free, master," Orazov said. "I would be afraid they will spread lies and wild stories about you. They should not be allowed to reach Chärjew." Chärjew was the location of the largest military base in eastern Turkmenistan, about 180 kilometers upriver. The Turkmen zealot's eyes brightened, and he fairly rocked from foot to foot in anticipation. "I shall kill them for you, master. Let me organize an attack. We outnumber them. It would be my very great pleasure to lead your loyal Turkmen soldiers on an attack against the oppressors from whom you have liberated us."

Jalaluddin Turabi could scarcely believe it, but Wakil Zarazi was actually nodding in thought at this peasant's psychopathic ramblings. Thankfully, Zarazi responded, "No, Captain. I am grateful for your enthusiasm and drive, but those men are not yet our enemy, only our adversaries. If they organize and return to do battle, you shall lead our forces against them."

Zarazi glanced at Turabi. Was he looking for approval or afraid his second in command would object to his giving a command to a Turkman? Turabi remained indifferent.

"I have given my word they shall not be harmed if they surrender—so it shall be. Now, go. Organize your men and report to me when they are ready for my inspection."

The guy could not stop bowing as he made his way out of the room.

After everyone else had departed, Turabi regarded his leader and longtime superior officer with a mixture of caution and admiration. Zarazi was standing on the platform, staring out through a window at the sunshine streaming in. "I like the plan to take Gaurdak," Turabi said. "Taking the hydro complex at Kizyl-arvat is also a good plan. We can threaten to blow the plant if we get attacked. I hope that Orazov character is right about the readiness at the base. We'll need every advantage if we're going to split our force to take the hydro plant and do an assault on Gaurdak."

Zarazi was silent. It was as if he hadn't even heard him, which infuriated Turabi.

"Excuse me, *General*," he snapped, the edge in the invented title obvious in his voice, "but what is the objective here? What do you hope to achieve?"

"What is it *you* wish to achieve here, Colonel?" Zarazi asked without turning to face him.

"Wakil, our orders from our leaders were to procure money, weapons, and equipment that can be sold to support the Al Qaeda forces in northern Afghanistan," Turabi said. "Our tribal leaders pledged to do this, and you were given specific instructions to go out and obtain these things. That was the whole purpose of attacking that convoy. That is the only reason these men agreed to leave their homes and wives and children and fight for you—our clan leaders ordered us to raise money for Al Qaeda.

"You have succeeded far more than anyone could have imagined: You have taken over an entire Turkmen army aviation base," Turabi went on. "You have men and equipment of enormous power and value. Don't you realize, Wakil? If you return to our tribal home of Jarghan with even a fraction of these tanks and guns, you will be promoted to the tribal council. If you succeed in bringing back even one of these helicopters, you will most assuredly be made a chieftain. You will be allowed to lead your own clan and be equal to all the other sheikhs and *shuras*.

"But now you're talking about attacking more Turkmen military bases and hydroelectric plants. I agree with subduing Gaurdak—they could cause us trouble when we start heading for home—but why are we wasting time and energy attacking dams, power plants, and pipelines? We might be able to squeeze a few manats out of the people here, but we stand an even greater risk of being trapped inside Turkmenistan, with their whole fucking army, such as it is, coming down on top of us. No one will come to rescue us if we are surrounded."

"Our mission has changed, Colonel," Zarazi intoned.

"Oh?"

"We shall not leave Turkmenistan," Zarazi said. "We are here to liberate this country and these people, not loot them."

"We have received orders from the tribal council to—"

"I have received orders from God," Zarazi interjected heatedly. "God has ordered me to take this country. He demonstrated that He is watching over me by saving me from the American attack aircraft, and He guides my hand and my tongue as I lead His faithful across the wastelands to victory. Our success is proof of His love for our cause and us."

"Wakil . . . General, we are successful mostly because the Turkmen forces are weak in this area," Turabi said. "There's nothing but empty desert out here. Their aviation battalion has been sitting on their asses doing nothing for ten years. They rout a few smugglers every now and then, take bribes from Northern Alliance forces or Taliban—whichever side wants to cross the frontier to escape the other—guard one river and a few oil pipelines, and go back for another nap. We haven't faced the real Turkmen army yet."

"Colonel, are you *afraid?*" Zarazi asked. "Are you scared of battle?"

"First of all, Wakil, I'm not a colonel, and you're not a general," Turabi snapped, allowing his anger at being called a coward to erupt despite the warnings in his brain *not* to allow it. "We gave ourselves military titles as a joke, remember? Whatever the rank of whomever we encountered, we gave ourselves a rank one or two over him. Now, for some damned reason, we're senior officers! We might as well be wearing a chestful of medals, white gloves, and riding breeches.

"Get this straight, Wakil: We're not military men," Turabi went on ferociously. "We're jihadi. We fight for our tribes and for our mullahs, not for a nation. And we sure as hell don't invade other countries, occupy military bases, and capture dams and power plants. And to answer your question—yes, I *am* scared! I'm scared of any operation that has no real objective! I'm scared of any operation that runs counter to what we have pledged our lives and our future to support and defend! I'm—"

"You will be *silent,* Colonel," Zarazi snapped. "My intentions are plain: We will occupy this territory in the name of God and build a refuge for the faithful warriors of Allah, just as Afghanistan once was, before the Americans and Zionists arrived. You either do as I command or you leave. I will not have you questioning my vision or usurping my command."

"Then I will go back to Jarghan, Wakil," Turabi said. "I didn't leave my wife and children and travel three hundred kilometers across this shithole of a country so I can play nursemaid to a bunch of chest-thumping desert rats from all over the Muslim world, like your new friend Orazov." He scanned Zarazi's face, searching for danger signs—and definitely finding them.

Turabi averted his eyes momentarily, apologetically—it was not a good thing at all to abandon your leader deep inside enemy territory, he knew, even if you thought he was crazy—and added, "I am going to inspect the site where our scouts saw smoke this morning. It might be a Turkmen helicopter patrol from Chärjew or Mary that crash-landed out there, or it might be whomever those antiaircraft missile batteries were firing at last night. I shall be back by dawn, and then I will form a company-size rear guard and move to Jarghan." Without waiting for a response, Turabi turned and walked away.

Zarazi stood for several long moments on the dais, pondering what Turabi had just said. Then he stopped daydreaming and half turned to his right. "What is it, Captain?" he asked the man approaching silently behind him.

Aman Orazov halted, his breath catching in his throat. "I . . . I beg your pardon, master," he stammered. "I . . . I could not help but overhear. . . ."

"Speak," Zarazi prompted him. When the man remained silent, Zarazi turned and faced the Turkmen officer, noting that now Orazov was wearing a sidearm and that the flap covering the holster was unfastened. He had also pinned on captain's rank, obviously stolen from someone else on post. "You wish to tell me that Colonel Turabi is unfaithful and does not deserve to be part of our mission," Zarazi said.

"He is a coward and a disgrace before God," Orazov said. "How dare he question you? How dare he snap at you like a child?"

"His faith has been shaken because of the danger and because of our rapid success in battle."

"He is a *coward,* master," Orazov spit. "He deserves to be punished."

"Punished?" Zarazi looked carefully at Orazov, then at the sidearm, then back at the Turkman. "Perhaps . . ."

"Let me, master," Orazov said. "I will deal with the colonel for what he has said to you."

Zarazi smiled and nodded. "And so you shall, Captain—but not now. I need the colonel and his men to help take Gaurdak and to start our push westward. Afterward he and any other unbelievers will be dealt with."

"Yes, master," Orazov said. "I shall keep close watch on the colonel. When you give the command, I shall strike."

"He will be keeping close watch on you as well, Captain," Zarazi warned him. "He and his men are skillful killers. They distrust you and all Turkmen."

Orazov smiled confidently. "Do not worry, sir. He has great reason to fear us. I shall be alert and ready at all times." He bowed again, then departed.

Wakil Mohammad Zarazi watched Orazov leave, then walked back to the large map of Turkmenistan and the surrounding region. Kerki: an easy conquest. Gaurdak: easy as well. Chärjew: not easy at all, their first encounter with Russian officers, and their first encounter with Turkmen regulars. But once Chärjew was taken, they could sweep across the Kara Kum Desert right up to the suburbs of Mary, the largest city in eastern Turkmenistan, with a force almost as large as Turkmenistan's itself. Even if the Turkmen government made a stand at Mary—Zarazi had no fantasies about being powerful enough to take that combined Turkmen and Russian stronghold—he would control nearly one-half of Turkmenistan's oil and gas reserves.

More important, he would control some of the richest land in Central Asia: most of the Amu Darya River plains located inside Turkmenistan, the Kara Kum Canal that ran across the Kara Kum Desert between Mary and Kerki, and the Gaurdak plains, which were extensively irrigated and which grew a wide variety of food and plant products, especially cotton. Even if he was forced to retreat east of the sixty-third meridian, he could still easily control the eastern third of the nation from Chärjew.

The excitement ran through Zarazi's body like an electric current. He could do this, he told himself. If he stayed faithful to God and ran this brigade with passion and relentlessness, he could become the undisputed warlord of eastern Turkmenistan, as powerful as the president. He could create a Pashtun stronghold, a haven for Taliban and their sympathizers from all over the Muslim world.

All he had to do was keep his men in line—or dead— starting with his former friend and fellow tribesman, Jalaluddin Turabi.

TRANSCAL PETROLEUM CORPORATION HEADQUARTERS, WEST SACRAMENTO, CALIFORNIA
That same time

"Ladies and gentlemen, here he is, back from his very successful round-the-world travels! Please welcome to West Sacramento, the next president of the United States, Kevin Martindale!" The men and women at the table rose to their feet and clapped as the former president of the United States, Kevin Martindale, entered the boardroom, followed by two Secret Service agents. The large, ornate room echoed from the applause and cheers as Martindale strode to the head of the massive oak conference table, shaking hands with a few of the board members—retired politicians and military men—that he recognized. Behind them, through the floor-to-ceiling windows, the city of Sacramento sparkled in the clear, sunny winter afternoon, with the Tower Bridge, Discovery Park, the confluence of the American and Sacramento Rivers all presenting the perfect backdrop to this special meeting.

William O. Hitchcock, the president and CEO of Trans-Cal Petroleum, added his applause to his fellow board members' after shaking the former president's hand warmly. He allowed the applause to continue for almost thirty seconds, then invited the board members to sit. "Members of the board of directors of TransCal, I need not remind you that the name of the enemy in our business is OPEC. But for every dragon that terrorizes the kingdom, there is a dragon slayer—and I am proud to say that America's dragon slayer is this man, the once and future president of the United States, Kevin Martindale." Again Hitchcock let the applause run another several seconds, until Martindale finally held up his hands in surrender.

"While the OPEC ministers were publicly threatening to cut production to absolute bare minimums, President Martindale was meeting with each of them, securing special delivery and storage arrangements that will ensure TransCal's supply and distribution contracts for years to come," Hitchcock went on. "With his help we have received very good assurances that prices will remain stable; that no member, no matter how large or powerful, will exceed the production limits; and that there will be enough markets and enough profits available to all, whether a member of OPEC or not. We are happy and proud that he is on our side, and we are honored to be able to support his drive to be only the second man in history to be voted back in as president of the United States after being voted out. My friends, please join me once again in welcoming home and thanking our good friend, Kevin Martindale."

After the third round of applause died away and Martindale greeted each of the board members personally, Hitchcock escorted the former president to his office, which was only a bit smaller than the boardroom. Any walls not composed of glass to take advantage of the spectacular city views were covered with rare and beautiful artwork, the immense faux fireplace was New Hampshire granite and Italian marble, the furniture was rich Spanish leather and polished California redwood. Martindale settled onto one of the expansive sofas with a tumbler of orange juice and sparkling water; Hitchcock offered the former president a cigar and helped himself to ice water and a Davidoff. "Good to have you back in the U.S. of A., Kevin," Hitchcock said as they lit up. "Your trip was more successful than we could possibly have hoped."

"Thanks, Bill," Martindale said. "I was happy to do it. I love the road, and I love confronting some of these Third World big shots. They think the world is scared of the name 'OPEC,' and I love seeing them squirm in front of the other delegates."

"Ten countries in less than a week. You must be whipped."

"I've forgotten how much traveling charges my batteries," Martindale said. It was true. He didn't look at all like a guy who had probably rung up a year's worth of frequent-flier miles in less than a week. "I'm ready to head on out again—as long as I'm not neglecting my national and state party obligations."

"Don't you worry about the state delegations. We're coordinating all your appearances and fund-raisers," Hitchcock said. "They know they have to be well organized and busting their butts before you'll even consider setting foot in their districts, and it's pumping up the candidates and the party committees to work extra hard to show us some impressive canvassing and donor numbers. They're gearing up well, but they won't be truly organized until the summer party convention. So we have a few months to go on the foreign-affairs track, and the press is lapping it up. Thorn is still nowhere to be seen on the radar screen, so the foreign-affairs field is all yours."

"I just can't figure that guy out," Martindale said, sipping his drink. "He's smart, tough, energetic—"

"He's all that, all right—but only on whatever planet he's really from," Hitchcock said. "On this planet he's a zero. Don't worry about him right now. We have some other fish to fry." He sat on the edge of his desk and looked seriously at the former president. William Hitchcock was young, very good-looking, and enormously wealthy, mostly from inheritances and an oil business that thrived on adversity. He was a newcomer in politics, but he attacked it with the same drive and take-no-prisoners attitude he applied to dealing with all problems in business—use every weapon in his arsenal to win.

The former president was his newest and by far his most potent weapon. Kevin Martindale wanted badly to reenter politics. But his fiasco with his not-so-secret mercenary group known as the Night Stalkers made political contributions dry up quickly. Whispers around Washington said that the former president was financing and leading a group of ex-commandos called "the Night Stalkers" on vigilante and mercenary missions all around the world. But rather than being considered a Robin Hood with his band of merry thieves, Martindale and the Night Stalkers were considered homegrown American terrorists. Enter William Hitchcock. As a partner in an African oil cartel, Hitchcock had hired the Night Stalkers to investigate and stop a Libyan incursion into Egypt, and he saw firsthand the power, charisma, and energy Kevin Martindale possessed. Their goals meshed perfectly: William Hitchcock wanted political influence, and Kevin Martindale needed financial backing for another run at the White House.

"What's up?" Martindale asked.

"A potential shit storm in Turkmenistan," Hitchcock said.

"Let me guess: The Russians are squawking that you're moving too quickly, and they want you to give up some of your fields. No problem. After what my Night Stalkers did to Sen'kov's plans in the Balkans, the Russians won't give us any hassles."

"I *wish* it was the Russians! I've already got their payola money in the budget," Hitchcock said. "We've got Taliban problems."

"Oh, shit, that's not good," Martindale exclaimed. "Threatening your pipelines?"

"A small band of insurgents from Afghanistan kicking ass and taking names. They're knocking down Turkmen army bases, capturing weapons, and recruiting followers faster and easier than the Pied Piper," Hitchcock said. "Problem is, the Turkmen government isn't doing anything to stop them. In fact, I think the government might secretly be supporting them."

"And the Russians would love to see the Taliban blow up some of your facilities."

"Exactly. We need to convince the Turkmen government to fight these Taliban bastards, but without involving the Russian army. I know that your administration negotiated the original deal with Niyazov for those oil leases. Can you go back to Ashkhabad and try to convince the government to turn these Taliban assholes away?"

"That should be no problem," Martindale said. "You realize that it might be in our best interests to make contact with the Taliban leaders themselves—grease their palms a little bit to keep them from just torching your pipelines?"

"I was hoping to avoid that . . . but, yes, I'll agree to it," Hitchcock said. "The Turkmen think those Taliban insurgents won't dare take on the regular-army bases at Chärjew—that they'll just take over a few pumping stations in the east, collect some ransom money, and split. But these guys keep moving westward, and they're growing in strength. If they take Chärjew, they could gain control of almost half our facilities in Turkmenistan."

"No problem," Martindale said confidently. "I'll speak with Gurizev and find out what he has in mind. Knowing him the way I do, I'll bet he'll be crying to the Russians to stop the Taliban, but I know he'll take help—and money—anywhere he can find it. But unless I miss my guess, we won't have to rely on the Turkmen. Most Taliban raiding parties stay in the field just long enough to collect money for their tribes. We pay them enough, and they'll be gone like a puff of smoke back to whatever caves they came from."

"So you'll go to Turkmenistan, then?"

Martindale looked a little apprehensive. "I'm not so sure that'll do any good," he said. "The Turkmen don't like outsiders, especially Westerners, and they like their under-the-table deals done well beyond arm's length. Besides, frankly, that place gives me the creeps. I'd rather go in with a pretty strong security advance team."

"No chance of Thorn providing anything like that," Hitchcock pointed out. "What about your Night Stalkers?"

Martindale took a pensive sip of his drink. "Disbanded. They got beat up pretty bad in Libya before they finally slapped down Zuwayy. Thorn offered to return their military rank and privileges to them, and they took it. But that's exactly who I'd like to bring with me." He nodded confidently at Hitchcock, trying to hide his feelings of dread. "Don't worry. I'll start the ball rolling from here— the threat of my coming to Turkmenistan should force Gurizev to cooperate. If necessary, I'll go to Ashkhabad and explain the facts of life to him. As for the Taliban, just be prepared to offer them some 'protection money,' and they'll leave your pipelines alone. Of course, the fact that we're 'forced' to pay protection money will be another strike against Thorn. After all, what kind of president will Thomas Thorn be if he won't send in troops to protect American economic interests overseas?"

"You don't think he would intervene, do you?"

"I don't see any evidence at all that he's inclined to do so," Martindale said. "But he's got some tough advisers and military leaders working for him who could convince him otherwise. You never know with him. But I wouldn't count on Thorn doing a damned thing. If we can convince Gurizev to send some troops in, and at the same time pay the Taliban fighters some protection money, I think your pipelines will be safe."

"Excellent," Hitchcock said, the relief evident in his voice. "Thank you. I knew I could count on you, Kevin."

"Just be sure my campaign war chest stays topped off," Martindale reminded him.

"My pleasure . . . Mr. President," Hitchcock said. "You won't have to worry about money as long as you're out there on TransCal's behalf."

"Good," Martindale said, finishing his drink and getting to his feet. The Secret Service agents immediately announced that their charge was on the move. "I'll get started right away. Put an extra three million in the operations account—that should be more than enough."

"You got it. I'll be sure your campaign account has a few extra million in there for your 'consulting help' on this as well," Hitchcock said. He shook hands warmly with the former president. "It's a pleasure working with you, Mr. President." As they shook hands, Hitchcock added, "I'm still open to heading your reelection campaign, Kevin, and eventually running your White House staff."

"I know, Bill," Martindale said. "But you don't know the White House battleground well enough yet."

"TransCal has a hundred times more employees than the White House, and I run every aspect of the company," Hitchcock said. "I can do the job. You've gotta give me the chance."

"I know you want this, Bill, but trust me, you're not ready for the political spotlight yet," Martindale said earnestly. "You can't run the White House like a Fortune 500 company—the bureaucrats, the political hacks, and the press inside the Beltway will drive you to homicide in no time. You're helping me now more than you know. Once we make it back to Sixteen Hundred Pennsylvania Avenue, I'll bring you in on everything. But for now you're more effective behind the scenes."

"Okay—for now, Kevin," Hitchcock said, obviously disappointed. "But I want to assure you, I'm more than just deep pockets. Let me prove it to you. You won't be sorry."

"Thanks, William. You're definitely on my short list. But unfortunately, no matter how much money you have, we can't do it without the party's support, and that means taking actions and formulating policies with which the party can build a strong nationwide platform—and we can't start picking staff and appointees without the party's input. Let's keep our eyes on our plan and timetable. We maintain the momentum going in foreign affairs, energy policy, and the military; we stay in the media spotlight, and the party will be kissing our boots and agreeing to anything we want before you know it. They'll be begging us to make you chief of the White House staff."

"Sounds good to me, Kevin. Sounds good to me."

They shook hands again. "Don't worry about Turkmenistan, Bill. It'll all be over in a couple days, and we'll come out of it smelling just fine. It's in the bag. Thorn will be sitting around cross-legged, confused, and clueless while we solve yet another brewing foreign crisis right under his nose."

"What if he or his administration is already doing something about Turkmenistan?" Hitchcock asked. "How do you know we're in the lead on this problem?"

Martindale shrugged and replied with a smile, "I'll ask him. I'm the former president of the United States—I should be able to make some inquiries and get some briefings from his staff. Besides, Thorn believes in open government. He or his staff will tell me everything. And if that doesn't work, I'll just send my spies into the White House and find out everything my own way."

BATTLE MOUNTAIN AIR RESERVE BASE, NEVADA
Early that morning

"With all due respect, Rebecca, this is the most harebrained stunt I've ever heard of," Colonel John Long, operations-group commander of the 111th Bombardment Wing, snapped. He was standing out on the underground flight line of Battle Mountain Air Reserve Base with Rebecca Furness, Patrick McLanahan, Dean Grey, and the ground team, getting ready to brief the ground crew prior to their flight mission. Long and Major Samuel "Flamer" Pogue were to fly in the second EB-1C, parked beside Rebecca's, as the alternate mission aircraft.

"You've made your opinion plain to everyone, Long Dong," Rebecca said quietly. "Keep it to yourself."

"It's my job to point out potential policy mistakes by our senior officers," Long retorted, raising his voice so everyone could hear and plainly refusing to take the hint, "and this is one perfect example. Completely untested, unverified, a disaster waiting to happen."

"We copy all, Colonel," Patrick McLanahan interjected. He wanted to chew the guy out for voicing his opinion like that in front of the entire ground crew, but he didn't want to quash debate, no matter how unprofessionally it was initiated. Instead he only glanced at Long, nodded, and said, "John, we've discussed this decision for two days now. We've staffed it up and down as best we could."

"General, we had no choice but to meet your arbitrary deadline," Long insisted. "I'm concerned that *you're* more concerned with dazzling your friends in the Pentagon and meeting a deadline than with crew safety, and I'm afraid this will end in a real disaster."

"You've made your view very clear," Patrick said. "I'm taking full responsibility for this test. Your career won't suffer if it fails."

"I'm concerned about this wing, not about my career."

"Then that will be a *first,*" Patrick said acidly. "Now, I *strongly* encourage you to keep your opinions to yourself unless asked directly for them. Is that understood, Colonel?"

"Yes, *sir,*" Long shot back. "Loud and clear, *sir.*"

Rebecca and Patrick finished their Form 781 logbook review and crew briefing, then began a walk-around inspection of the aircraft. The forward bomb bay held a rotary launcher carrying four AIM-150 Anaconda long-range, radar-guided, air-to-air missiles and four AIM-120 medium-range, radar-guided missiles. The aft bomb bay held a rotary launcher with eight AGM-165 Longhorn TV- and imaging-infrared-guided attack missiles. The center bomb bay held two AGM-177 Wolverine attack missiles loaded into air-retrieval baskets. Patrick knew that the Wolverines' bomb bays each held four AGM-211 mini-Maverick guided missiles.

"I hate to say it, General, but Long is right—this is crazy," Rebecca said to Patrick once they were out of earshot of the ground crew.

"It'll work fine," Patrick said.

"There is an army of engineers and test pilots at Edwards whose job it is to test stuff like this, Patrick," she said. "Why don't we let them do their damned jobs?"

"Rebecca, if you feel so strongly about this, why are you going along?"

"The same reason you're going—because it's *our* plan and *our* program, and we don't put others in harm's way unless we're willing to take the lead and do it ourselves," Rebecca replied. "Besides, they're *my* planes, and if you crash one, it's *my* ass. We have some skilled fliers in our unit, but they're newborns compared to us. They've never been in a B-1 bomber that's trying to kill them. But there are a dozen crewdogs at Edwards or Dreamland who would give a month's pay to fly some test missions for us. Why don't we just take the bird down there and let them do it?"

"You know why—because no one at Edwards or anywhere else will waste one gallon of jet fuel or spare one man-hour to work this project without a fully authorized budget."

"Except me. Me and my budget are the expendable ones, right?"

"I've given you lots of opportunities to back out of this project, Rebecca," Patrick said. He stopped and looked at her seriously. "You and John Long seem to delight in busting my ass and branding me as the bad guy, the one that breaks the rules but gets away with it every time. Fair enough—I'll accept that criticism. But both of you can put the brakes on this at any time with one phone call to General Magness at Eighth Air Force or General Craig at Air Reserve Forces Command. You haven't done it. You've chewed me out in front of every officer on this base. Long steps right up to the brink of insubordination without even blinking. He's done everything but put an ad in the *Reno Gazette-Journal*.

"But you never made the call, and I think I know the reason: You're hoping this works. Every new wing commander wants two things: for no one to screw up too badly, and to make a name for him- or herself in order to stand out above all the other commanders. In relative peacetime it's even more important to shine. Long wants his first star so badly it hurts, and you can trade on your reputation as the first female combat pilot only so long."

"That's not true, General," Rebecca said—but her voice had no force, no authority behind it. She knew he was right.

"We can debate this all day, but it won't make any difference," Patrick went on. "We have the skill and knowledge to make this work. But you're the aircraft commander, the final authority. If you disagree, call a stop to it." He waited, hands on hips. When she turned her flashlight up at the emergency landing gear blowdown bottle gauges, continuing the preflight, he nodded and said, "All right then, let's *do* it."

They finished their walk-around inspection, then climbed the steep entry ladder behind the tall nose-gear strut and made their way to the cockpit. After preflighting his ejection seat and strapping himself in, Patrick quickly "built his nest," then waited for the action to start.

Rebecca joined him a few moments later. After strapping herself in, she pulled out her checklist, strapped it onto her right leg, flipped to the BEFORE APU START page, and began—then stopped herself. She ignored the checklist and sat back, crossing her arms on her chest in exasperation— and maybe a little bit of fear.

"Pretty bizarre way to go to war," she muttered.

"Pretty bizarre way to go to war," Dean "Zane" Grey muttered. He was seated at a metal desk inside the VC— virtual-cockpit—trailer, staring at two blank flat-panel LCD computer monitors. It was a tight squeeze inside the trailer. In the center of the interior were two seats in front of the metal desk; flanking them were two more seats with full computer keyboards, a trackball, and large flat-panel LCD monitors. On Daren Mace's side, he had a "super-cockpit" display—a twelve-by-twenty-four-inch full-color plasma screen on which he could call up thousands of pieces of data—everything from engine readouts to laser-radar images to satellite images—and display them on Windows- or Macintosh-like panes on the display. All other room inside the trailer was taken up by electronics racks, air-conditioning units, power supplies, and wiring. It was stuffy and confining, far worse than the real air-plane ever was. It made Grey a little anxious—no, a *lot* anxious.

"Well, this is very cool," Zane said, "but I'm ready to get going. So where is everything? Flight controls? Gauges?"

"Right here," Daren Mace said. He handed Zane a thin, lightweight helmet resembling a bicyclist's safety helmet, with an integrated headset and wraparound semitransparent visor encircling the front. Daren then handed him a pair of thin gloves. They all took seats. Putting on the helmets helped to kill the noise of electronics-cooling fans and air-conditioning compressors.

"How cool is this!" Zane repeated. A few moments after turning on the system, he saw a three-dimensional electronic image of an ultramodern B-1 bomber cockpit. No conventional instruments—everything was voice-controlled and monitored via large, full-color, multifunctional electronics displays. He was able to reach out and "touch" the MFDs and move the control stick. "Man, this is unbelievable!"

"We can shift the view to anything you'd like to see—charts, satellite imagery, tech orders, sensor information—anything," Daren said. "Calling up info and 'talking' to the plane is easy—just preface every command with 'Vampire.' Voice commands are easy and intuitive. We have a catalog of abbreviated commands, but for most commands just a simple order will do. Try to use the same tone of voice, with no inflections. You'll get the hang of it soon enough."

"Very nice," Zane exclaimed as he got settled in. "It's like a fancy video game, only a lot noisier. Almost as noisy as the plane, I think."

"General McLanahan wants to build a nicer command-and-control facility here at Battle Mountain," Daren said, "but we have to prove this thing can work first." He spent several minutes explaining how to enter commands into the system—voice commands, touching floating buttons or menus, touching the screen with virtual fingers, or using eye-pointing techniques to activate virtual buttons and switches on the instrument panel.

"You almost don't need arms and legs to fly this thing," Zane commented.

"It was designed at Dreamland by a guy who lost the use of his legs in a plane crash," Daren responded. "Zen Stockard. He's a buddy of mine. There was a phase where everything designed there was based on virtual-reality or advanced neural-transfer technology, simply because that was the best way for paraplegics to be able to use the gear. You don't need to be an aviator to fly them either—the computers do most of the flying, even the air refueling. We use crew chiefs and techs to fly Global Hawk all the time. Let's report in and get the show on the road."

"I'm ready, boss," Zane said excitedly. "VAC is up," he said on intercom, addressing himself as the "virtual aircraft commander."

"VMC is up," Daren reported as the "virtual mission commander."

"The guinea pigs are in place," Rebecca responded. "I mean, AC is up."

"MC is up," Patrick said. "The guinea pigs here resent that."

"VE ready," replied Jon Masters from the seat beside Patrick, reporting in as the "virtual engineer." Dr. Jon Masters, a boyish-looking man in his mid-thirties who had several hundred patents to his name long before most kids his age had graduated from high school, was the chief engineer and CEO of Sky Masters Inc., a small high-tech engineering firm that developed state-of-the-art communications, weapons, and satellite technology, including the virtual cockpit. Patrick McLanahan had known Jon Masters for many years and had been a vice president of Sky Masters Inc. after he had been involuntarily separated from the Air Force.

"Okay, folks, here we go," Daren said. "VAC, you have the aircraft."

"Oh, shit, here we go," Zane muttered. In a shaky but loud voice, he commanded, "Vampire, battery power on." Instantly the lights inside the EB-1C Vampire's cockpit came on. He tuned in several radios and got permission to start the plane's APU, or auxiliary power unit; then: "Vampire, before-APU-start checklist."

In the cockpit, Rebecca barely noticed the response. All

the checklist items—eleven steps, which normally took about a minute to perform—were done with a rapid flicker of warning and caution lights. Within three seconds the computer responded, *"Vampire ready for APU start."*

"Wow" was all Rebecca could say.

"Shit-hot," Zane exclaimed. "Vampire, get me a double cheeseburger, no pickles."

"Would you like fries with that?" the computer responded.

"What?"

"You youngsters are so predictable. That was one of the first responses I programmed into the voice-recognition software," Jon Masters said gleefully. Jon was only a few years older than the "youngsters," so he knew them very well.

"Can we get on with it?" Rebecca asked. "This thing is giving me the creeps."

"Roger," Zane said happily. "Vampire, APU start."

The checklists ran quickly and smoothly, and in a fraction of the time it normally took to get ready for engine start, the Vampire bomber was ready. They had to wait for Long and Pogue to finish their checklists, done in a more conventional manner. The bombers were then towed to an elevator and hoisted to the second level, where they started the engines and performed a before-takeoff check; shortly thereafter the two bombers were raised to the surface.

"So how do I taxi this thing, boss?" Zane asked.

"You don't. The computer does," Daren replied.

"O-kay. Vampire, taxi for takeoff," Zane spoke.

"Laser radar is on and radiating, very low power, short range," Patrick reported. Just then the Vampire bomber's throttles slowly advanced, and the plane crept forward.

It was slow going, but eventually the Vampire taxied itself out of the hammerhead and onto the end of the runway. *"Vampire in takeoff position, eleven thousand four hundred feet remaining,"* the computer reported. *"Partial power takeoff performance okay."*

"The LADAR maps out the edges of the runway and automatically puts you on the centerline, then measures the distance to the first set of obstacles—in this case, the edge of the overrun," Jon Masters explained. "The laser radar also measures nearby terrain and samples the atmosphere and plugs the information into the air-data computer for takeoff-performance computations."

"So what the heck do *I* do?" Zane asked.

"You get to choose the type of takeoff," Patrick McLanahan said.

"Can't I make my own takeoff?"

"The computer can make about a dozen different takeoffs: max performance, minimum interval, unimproved field, max altitude, partial power, noise abatement—you name it," Masters said. "You just tell it which one and it'll do it."

"So can I, Doc, so can I," Zane said. "How do I work this thing?"

"Rest your arm on the armrest," Daren said. Grey did. "Vampire, cockpit adjust," Daren spoke. In an instant the cockpit flight controls rearranged themselves to fit Grey's hands. "In the virtual cockpit, the controls come to *you*—not the other way around."

"I love it!" Zane exclaimed happily. The rudder pedals did the same, and when it came time to flip a switch or punch a button, all he had to do was extend a finger. The control panel came to his finger, then moved again so he could clearly see the display, then moved out of the way so he could "look" out the window or "see" other instruments. Zane experimentally "stirred the pot"—moved the control stick in a wide circle to check the flight-control surfaces—and watched the control-surface indicators move.

"Not so hard," Rebecca said. "You're banging the control surfaces around too much."

"Keep in mind that you don't have any control-stick feel," Daren pointed out. "You have to use the indicators and the flight instruments to tell you how you're doing—no 'seat of the pants' flying. Use your cameras on the takeoff roll, but if you go into the clouds, transition quickly to your instruments." Daren got takeoff clearance from the air base's robot "control tower": "You're cleared for takeoff, VAC."

"Here we go, boys and girls," Zane said. He put his hands on the "throttles" and slowly pushed them forward—too fast. He moved them more slowly, stopping just as he advanced into zone-one afterburner, then released brakes as he slowly advanced them further into zone five.

He felt as if nothing were happening—and then, before he realized it, the computer said, *"Vampire, rotate speed, ready, ready, now."* Zane wasn't ready for it. He pulled back on the stick—nothing happened. He pulled back more . . . still nothing—and then suddenly the nose shot skyward.

"Get the nose down, Lieutenant," Rebecca warned. "You overrotated."

"Sorry, sorry," Zane said. He released some of the back pressure.

"Too much!" Rebecca shouted. "Nose up!" They were less than fifty feet aboveground. Zane pulled back on the stick—and started another PIO, or "pilot-induced oscillation." Rebecca cried out, "I've got it!"

"Let Zane fix it, Rebecca," Daren said calmly. "Nice and easy with the controls, Zane," he said softly. "There's a slight delay in the datalink—be ready for it. Put in a control movement, then keep an eye on it. Everything you see is delayed slightly from what the plane's doing. Use your instruments, but be aware of the delay."

"Vampire, configuration warning," the computer announced.

"You wanted to do the takeoff, Zane. You're the one who has to remember to clean up the plane," Daren said.

"Shit, yeah," Zane muttered. "Vampire, after-takeoff checklist." Immediately the landing gear started retracting, lights turned themselves off, the air-traffic-control transponder activated, and the mission-adaptive flight controls changed from takeoff to en route climb configuration.

"After-takeoff check complete," the computer reported seconds later.

"This is totally cool," Zane said. He experimentally turned the plane side to side. "Once you get used to the delay, it's not bad at all."

"Speak for yourself," Rebecca said nervously as she watched her bomber do its random gyrations. "It figures you young kids would enjoy it—it's like playing a big video game, right, Zane?"

"Yes, ma'am. How about we see if it'll do a roll?"

"You do and I'll court-martial you—and then I'll kill you."

"Enough fun. Let's fly this thing like it was meant to be flown," Daren said. "Vampire, activate flight plan one, standard en route climb."

"Vampire, flight plan one activated," the computer responded.

Zane released his grip on the stick, and the autopilot took over, immediately reducing the throttles out of afterburner, reducing the climb rate, and turning to the first waypoint.

"Two's airborne, tied on radar," John Long reported.

Daren watched in utter amazement. "I simply can't believe this," Daren said incredulously. "I'm sitting here flying a three-hundred-thousand-pound supersonic attack bomber from a trailer on the ground in the middle of nowhere in northern Nevada. It's unbelievable."

"It's totally cool from here," Jon Masters said. "It's better than a video game. It's hard to believe that's a real machine out there. We should—" Just then he noticed a flashing message on a computer screen. "We got a fault in the primary datalink computer," Masters said.

"What happened?" Patrick asked.

"Master computer fault. It automatically shifted control to the secondary computer," Jon replied. "We got an automatic reboot of the primary computer. It'll take a couple minutes to come up."

"How about we put this thing on the ground now, boys?" Rebecca asked. "We'll let the wingman take over."

"We've got four redundant, independent operating computers driving the datalink and aircraft controls, plus an emergency system that will force the aircraft to execute a direct return to base, no matter what systems are damaged," Masters said. "The system did exactly what it was supposed to do—hand off control to another good computer, restart itself, and then, if it checks out, wait in line for a handoff."

"*Another* handoff? You mean we could lose *more* computers?"

"We plan on the worst and hope for the best, General," Masters said. "Aha . . . the first computer came back up, so we've got four good computers again. We're back in business."

"Doctor, you're not exactly filling me with confidence," Rebecca said. "Everyone remember: This is my wing's bird. I signed for it, and I decide when this test mission ends."

"Roger, ma'am," Zane said. "Now, just sit back and relax and enjoy the ride."

KARA KUM DESERT, EASTERN TURKMENISTAN
That evening

Only his tracked vehicles had the capability to go across the open desert, so Jalaluddin Turabi had no choice but to split up his force. He divided his group into three: Two would encamp along the Kizyl-Tabadkan highway, divided by fifteen kilometers, ready to move toward each other if trouble appeared; the third force, led by Turabi himself, would trek across the desert to the crash site. Because of weather and their upcoming battle at Gaurdak, helicopter support would not be available until dawn—Turabi was effectively on his own. He had some working night-vision goggles, and the weather was improving, so he decided to start out in the relative coolness and cover of night and head toward the crash site, using only a compass and prayers to guide him.

It took an hour to travel the first twenty kilometers, driving an old Soviet-era MT-LB multipurpose tracked vehicle they'd captured in Kerki. He deployed an even older GSh-575 tracked vehicle—actually a ZSU-23/4 self-propelled antiaircraft-gun system, with the antiaircraft guns unusable and deactivated long ago—out three hundred meters ahead of the MT-LB as a scout; this vehicle managed to throw a track every five to ten kilometers, which made for even slower going. Several times Turabi ordered his men to abandon the vehicle and hide when his scout heard jet aircraft nearby, but they were never able to pinpoint its location after the echo of the roar of their own engines faded away. Nerves were on edge.

About three hours before dawn, they reached the place where Turabi thought the smoke had come from, but there was no sign of a crash. There was nothing else to do but start a search pattern. Using both tracked vehicles, they set up a search grid and moved out, crisscrossing the desert with soldiers on foot continually moving the grid in different directions, overlapping slightly at the ends.

After an hour they still hadn't come across the wreckage. "This is insane," Turabi muttered after he received the last report. "I swear to God I saw a crash out here. I have traveled the deserts for most of my life—I do not imagine such things." He turned to his senior sergeant, Abdul Dendara. "What am I missing here, Abdul?"

"If you saw smoke, sir, there has to be surface wreckage. Aircraft or weapons that bury themselves in the sand don't release enough smoke to spot from a distance," Dendara said. "I checked to be sure the men were probing underneath the sand. There was a short but pretty strong storm that came through here yesterday—the wreckage could be lying just under the surface." He looked around. Of course, in the darkness, there was little to see. "No landmarks, no exact position—maybe we're not at the right spot, sir."

Turabi swore under his breath, pulled out his map, and examined it in the subdued red beam of his flashlight. "All right. Let's shift five kilometers to the south and do another grid search. We search for one more hour, then we pack up and head back to join up with the rest of the battalion."

Turabi radioed for the MT-LB, which picked him up a few minutes later. Following his compass, he steered the driver south, then started to set up another grid-pattern search. It would take several minutes for the other members of his detail to move to the new position, so he decided he would need to get out there and start searching himself if he ever wanted to finish this grid and get back to Kerki by dawn. He fixed a bayonet onto his AK-47 assault rifle and started probing the sand with his red-lensed flashlight, looking for evidence of debris.

He soon realized how difficult this search really was. He knew he could step within centimeters of a critical piece of evidence and never see it, or he could step on a land mine and be legless in an instant. He knew he had to use every sense he possessed, and maybe even some kind of extrasensory perception, to accomplish this task. He waved the MT-LB away from him so he wouldn't be distracted by its engine noise, diesel exhaust, and the occasional shouts of the men on board.

Finally it was relatively quiet. Turabi's night vision improved, and soon he could start seeing objects on the ground that were not directly in the flashlight's beam. He could still smell the armored personnel carrier's exhaust smoke, and he picked up his radio to order the MT-LB farther away.

But he stopped, the radio a few centimeters from his lips, his finger on the push-to-talk switch. Yes, he could still smell engine exhaust—but he was upwind of the MT-LB now. He shouldn't be able to smell it. It had to be something else. He used his nose like an automatic direction finder triangulating on a radio beacon, steering himself to the source of the smell.

Minutes later he saw it: a mass of metal, blackened and lumpish but definitely an aircraft engine. It was a cruise missile turbojet engine, not more than forty or fifty kilos, about the size of a bedroll. He'd found it! He swept the flashlight beam around excitedly. There were other pieces of debris nearby, too—including a large fuselage piece. It was here! He slung his AK-47 onto his shoulder, put the walkie-talkie up to his lips, and keyed the mike button. "Dahab Two, this is One. I found some wreckage of a small aircraft or cruise missile. I'm a half klick south of the new grid locus. Join on me and—"

At that instant he heard a faint *fwoooosh!* sound. He dropped to one knee, the flashlight replacing the radio in his left hand, held far out to his side, and his Tokarev TT-33 in his right hand. The muzzle of the Tokarev followed the flashlight beam turned in the direction of the sound. Nothing. No sounds of footsteps running on desert sand, no vehicle sounds. He quickly extinguished the flashlight and picked up the radio: "Dahab, Dahab, alert! Someone else is out here!"

Suddenly a brilliant curtain of stars obscured his vision, and he was unable to tell up from down. The harder he struggled to stay on his feet, the faster he found himself sprawled in the sand. He still felt as if he were upright, crouching low, but he felt the hard-baked sand in his face and knew he was on the ground. He was wide awake and still breathing, but he couldn't make any of his limbs respond—and he heard voices. Voices, machinelike but definitely human. Voices *in English!*

"One down, all clear," Colonel Hal Briggs reported. "He found the StealthHawk. He may have gotten off a report." He quickly changed the scene in his electronic visor to the imaging infrared sensor aboard the number-one Stealth-Hawk unmanned combat aerial vehicle that was orbiting overhead. "We've got company. That armored personnel carrier is headed this way. Give me control of Hawk One."

"Roger that," responded Daren Mace, back in the virtual command trailer at Battle Mountain Air Reserve Base. He pressed a button on his console and spoke, "Hawk One, transfer control to Tin Man One."

"StealthHawk flight-control transfer to Tin Man One, stop transfer," the computer responded. Seconds later: *"StealthHawk flight-control transfer to Tin Man One complete, awaiting commands."*

"Hawk One, sitrep," Briggs ordered.

The response took only moments: *"Warning, unidenti-fied moving armored vehicle, bearing zero-six-two de-grees, range one point three miles, heading two-seven-three degrees, speed twenty-one knots, designate Tango One. Warning, unidentified stationary armored vehicle, bear-ing zero-one-four degrees, three point one miles, designate Tango Two. Tango Two now turning south, accelerating, speed now one-five knots. Warning, numerous infantry tar-gets approaching at slow speed, range three miles, bear-ing zero-one-six."*

Briggs used his eye-pointing system to place a target cursor over the image of the nearest vehicle in the Stealth-Hawk's scan—the MT-LB—then pointed to the menu se-lection for voice commands and spoke, "Hawk One, attack this target."

"Attack Tango One, stop attack," the StealthHawk re-sponded. Moments later it peeled away from its patrol or-bit and swooped in on the target. The StealthHawk's attack was flawless. It locked on to the target shape and fired a mini-Maverick missile at it, sending it down through the thin upper skin of the armored vehicle atop the hottest portion of the vehicle—the engine compart-ment. The engine exploded in a brilliant burst of fire. Three men were able to run clear before the entire vehicle was engulfed in flames.

"We got a kill!" Hal Briggs said. "Way to go! Man, I'm starting to like these gadgets you guys make, Doc."

"We aim to please," Jon Masters said from Battle Mountain.

"Hawk One, sitrep."

"Tango One immobilized," the drone reported. *"Tango Two turning west bearing three-five-zero, two point eight miles. Unidentified numerous infantry targets still pro-ceeding southbound bearing zero-one-six."*

"Looks like the second APC is going to stay away and check us out before he attacks," Briggs surmised. "Hawk One, proceed to ten-mile cover patrol at one-five thousand feet."

"Hawk One proceeding to ten-mile cover patrol, stop command." The StealthHawk began a "wobbly circle" flight pattern around Briggs's position, changing the center of the circular orbit by several hundred feet each time so it would not pinpoint Briggs's location as it circled overhead.

Daren nodded happily. "The StealthHawk found all the targets and prosecuted a successful attack by voice command from the ground!" he crowed. "Excellent!"

"Okay, Sarge, you got the last target," Briggs said.

"Yes, sir." Sergeant Major Chris Wohl leveled his electromagnetic rail gun, centered the electronic gunsight on the second armored personnel carrier, and fired. A sausage-size tungsten-steel projectile shot from the muzzle at an incredible ten thousand feet per second. The projectile had no explosive warhead—it didn't need one. At that velocity the projectile easily pierced the GSh-575 vehicle's armor, went through one Taliban fighter inside as if he were as thin as a soap bubble, pierced the engine block, passed outside through a drive wheel, and buried itself two hundred feet into the sand before it finally stopped. The armored vehicle's engine cracked, then blew apart like an overinflated balloon.

"Target neutralized," Wohl reported matter-of-factly.

"Tango Two neutralized," the StealthHawk reported moments later.

"No shit," Wohl commented. He stepped over and motioned to the Taliban fighter lying on the ground. "I think he's awake. He probably saw everything. Should we take him with us?"

"Stand by. Three, this is One. How much stuff have you recovered so far?"

"I've got about two hundred pounds of components, One," responded Air Force Lieutenant Mark Bastian, one of Hal Briggs's first officers assigned to the First Air Battle Force Ground Operations team. At six feet four inches tall, Bastian was one of the tallest men ever to wear the Tin Man electronic battle armor. "I need to separate out about another three hundred pounds."

"Roger that. Two, we won't have room on the Dasher for a prisoner. Question him, get any info you can on him, then make sure he stays near what's left of his APC and let's get ready for extraction."

From his spot on the desert floor, Jalaluddin Turabi watched the death of his first armored vehicle, then heard the death of his second. He could finally move his arms and legs, but it was as if his own body now weighed thousands of kilograms—he had absolutely no strength in any of his muscles.

The two strange figures in the dark outfits and full bug-eyed helmets marched in front of him. While the one with the large, futuristic-looking rifle stood guard, the other stopped to examine pieces of the crashed aircraft. Turabi was surprised when the figure picked up the cruise-missile engine as effortlessly as if he had picked up a pebble. Who were these men? They had to be Americans—only they had this kind of technology. Either Americans or Martians.

The figure with the large rifle approached him. *"Ismak eh?"* it asked him in Arabic.

"I won't tell you anything," Turabi said. "Who are you? Why are you attacking us?" At that he felt a surge of electricity flowing through his temples, seemingly trying to push his very eyeballs out of their sockets. Turabi screamed.

"What is your name?" the figure repeated.

"Turabi. Jalaluddin Turabi."

The electric shock ceased. "Are you Taliban?"

Turabi said nothing—but when the electric shock recommenced, he couldn't help but blurt out his response. "Yes, damn you! I am Taliban!"

"What is the name of your commanding officer?"

"General."

"General what?"

"Just 'General.' "

The electric shock started again, not as bad as before, but Turabi remembered how bad it could be. "His name?"

Turabi kept silent until he thought he might scream again from the pain. "Wakil Mohammad Zarazi." The pain instantly ceased. Turabi prayed he would black out, but the figure apparently knew how to control the electric shocks well enough to keep his victims conscious.

"What is your rank?"

"I do not have any rank. I am jihadi."

"But your commanding officer is a general?"

"He calls himself a general, yes. But we are jihadi. We are Taliban. We are servants of God and loyal members of our clan."

"This whole operation is a jihad?" Even with his voice electronically altered, Turabi could hear the surprise in the stranger's voice. "You invaded Turkmenistan because you're on a jihad?"

"We left our homes and villages in Afghanistan and came into Turkmenistan to escape you Americans and your robot killing machines!" Turabi shouted angrily. "We stayed in Turkmenistan because we found loyal soldiers and sympathizers. It was easier to keep moving west than it was to head back to our own homeland."

The figure paused, and it sounded to Turabi as if he might be speaking inside his helmet to his comrades. Then the man asked, "How many in this jihadi army of yours?"

"We are no threat to you."

"I said, how many?"

"Several thousand. I don't know. We get more defectors every day. The Turkmen will fight for whoever pays them more money."

"What is your objective after taking Kerki?"

"Whatever the general wants. He says God gives him instructions and guides him to victory."

"Wa'if hena min fadlak," the figure said to him in a monotone, machinelike electronic voice.

"Where do you expect me to go, Mr. Robot?" Turabi responded. "You have destroyed two vehicles and killed my soldiers. The rest of my army is a hundred kilometers from this place."

But the menacing figure had already strode away. Turabi snatched up a chunk of metal, a piece of his destroyed armored personnel carrier, and threw it at the figure. He didn't even turn—but a blue-white bolt of electricity shot out from an electrode atop his shoulders and hit the chunk of metal, causing it to burst in midair like an overripe melon. Who in God's holy name were these men?

The MV-32 Pave Dasher tilt-jet aircraft moved in from its hiding place a few miles away from the crash site, picked up the Tin Men and the critical components of the downed StealthHawk unmanned combat air vehicle, and headed off. But just as they did, Patrick did a long-range scan of the area with the laser radar aboard the EB-1C Vampire. *"Two unidentified airborne contacts, seven o'clock, thirty-one miles, level at one thousand feet above ground, air-*

speed one hundred thirty knots," the attack computer reported. "*Designate bogeys one and two.*"

"You got these newcomers, Daren?" Patrick asked.

"Yes, sir, I see them," Daren responded. "Vampire, IFF check on bogeys."

"*Negative IFF,*" the computer responded. The Vampire could send out coded interrogation signals and scan for a response from a friendly aircraft using the IFF, or "Identification Friend or Foe" system—if it did not receive a response, the aircraft was considered hostile. "*Designate as bandits one and two.*"

"Attack bandit one," Daren ordered. He waited, then said more insistently, "I said, attack bandit one, Vampire. I say again, attack bandit one, Vampire."

Zane looked at Daren with surprise. "Uh . . . sir?"

Daren held up a finger, but Zane pressed.

"You forgot to say the magic word, boss."

"I know—just wanted to see if the computer would go off on its own," Daren explained.

"Let's not screw around here, guys," Rebecca warned. "We can test the gear once our guys are out of Indian country."

"It was just a test, Rebecca," Daren said. "Vampire, attack bandit one. Hang on, crew."

"*Engaging bandit one,*" the computer responded. The bomber immediately threw itself into a hard right turn and accelerated to zone-five afterburner.

"Weapons arming," Patrick reported as he scanned the readouts on his multifunction display. He had barely moved from the position he assumed on takeoff—hands firmly holding on to his ejection seat's armrests, feet locked together, as if ready for the ejection sequence. "Scorpion missile powered up. Continuity check in progress . . . continuity and connectivity checks on all weapons."

"Thirty seconds to attack," the computer responded. Then: *"Attack aborted."* The Vampire rolled wings-level and maintained its present altitude.

"Weapons just safed themselves," Patrick reported. "Jon . . . ?"

"Second computer crumped," Masters said immediately. "Third computer couldn't accept control with weapons armed. The next computer should assume control any second."

"Vampire, pursue bandit one, close to ten miles in trail at flight level one-five-zero," Daren ordered. There was no response. "Vampire, close to ten miles in trail on bandit one at flight level one-five-zero. It's not accepting commands, guys."

"Wait until the third computer assumes control," Jon said.

" 'Wait'? What do you mean, 'wait'?" Rebecca asked.

"Computer transfer complete," Masters said. "Everything should be okay now."

"Vampire, close to ten miles in trail on bandit one at flight level zero-five-zero," Daren ordered. The bomber immediately started a steep dive, and seconds later it passed the speed of sound. "Coming up on missile launch . . . ready . . . doors should be coming open. . . ."

"Won't happen," Patrick said. "You didn't reissue the attack command."

"Another glitch?" Rebecca moaned.

"It's not a glitch," Masters said. "The computer is programmed not to remember attack commands in case of a computer malfunction. They have to be reissued to be sure the computer doesn't execute a bogus attack command."

"Hold on a second," Rebecca said. "We'd better let this one go until we—"

But at the same time, Daren was already talking to the computer: "Vampire, attack bandit one," he ordered.

"I said *hold on a second!*" Rebecca shouted. She reached forward, grasped the control stick, and squeezed the paddle switch. Instantly she felt the pressure of the flight controls in her hands. "I've got the aircraft!"

"Rebecca, let the VC take the aircraft back," Daren said.

"Hey, it's *'General'* to you, mister!" she shot back. "And no one tells me what to do on my aircraft, especially not barely qualified navigators sitting on the ground!

"Now, in case you boys haven't noticed, in case you were too busy gawking over your computers, we were on a five-degree, nose-low descent, going Mach one point two, about ten seconds before going below the emergency-descent altitude for this area and fifteen seconds from dying in a smoking hole in the earth. *The plane is trying to kill us,* and you're arguing over computer logic."

"Rebecca, this is our first test," Patrick said. "Let's let the system work so we can flush out the bugs. Let it—"

" 'Flush out the bugs'? How many lives are you willing to risk to 'flush out the bugs'?" Rebecca retorted. "*This is not my job,* General! You may have spent the past several years stuck on the lake 'flushing out bugs' in new, untested, and potentially dangerous aircraft, but I haven't!" Even angry as she was, Rebecca knew better than to talk about McLanahan's previous assignment—deputy commander of the High Technology Aerospace Weapons Center at Groom Lake, now known as Elliott Air Force Base. "I train hard so I can employ operational aircraft in the most effective and efficient ways possible."

"So you're terminating the test flight, General?" Daren Mace asked.

In response Rebecca pulled the throttles back to 80 percent power and flicked two switches on her left instrument panel to the off position—the WEAPONS CONSENT switch and the DATALINK ACTIVE switch. "I've got the aircraft. The test is terminated. Get those incoming bandits, General."

"Roger, AC," Patrick responded. He wasted no time at all locking up the lead helicopter—but he found a few moments later that they were not pursuing the Pave Dasher, but rather flying toward their comrades at the UCAV crash site. "The bandits are no threat," he announced. "Weapons safe." He immediately called up their egress flight plan and gave Rebecca autopilot steering commands. She did not relinquish control of the aircraft until they were well out over the Arabian Sea.

The StealthHawk drone launched by Furness and McLanahan stayed in the vicinity until the Pave Dasher was safely out over the Arabian Sea and there was no sign of pursuit. By this time Pogue and Long in the second EB-1C had refueled on Diego Garcia and were back up on air patrol, guarding the salvage ship that the Pave Dasher used as a forward base. The Pave Dasher safely landed on the ship, refueled, and flew on to Diego Garcia.

In the meantime Furness and McLanahan continued slowly on toward Diego Garcia, flying more slowly than normal because they wanted their StealthHawk to stay in close formation. They had already been in the air for almost two days, and they were looking forward to downtime on the isolated tropical island in the Indian Ocean. But they had a few other tasks to perform first.

"Rebecca, let's see if the virtual cockpit can steer the StealthHawk into docking position," Patrick asked on intercom.

"I don't know, Patrick. With live weapons on board, I'd rather set her down."

"But we're not scheduled to offload weapons on Diego. We're just going in for crew rest, debriefing, refueling, and then we're off again," Patrick reminded her. "This is a good time to test it out."

"I don't think so, sir."

It sounded to Patrick that Rebecca was just tired, not really objecting to a test. It also sounded as if maybe she wanted to see what else this system could do. "It'll just be to predocking position, not all the way in the sling," Patrick pressed. "Let's give it a try."

"You just can't take no for an answer, can you, sir?" Rebecca asked derisively. Again, to Patrick, it didn't sound like an objection. "All right, all right, do it. Just don't knock us out of the sky, okay?"

"Okay, time for the rest of the test," Patrick announced on the command frequency. "Reel it in, Daren."

"Roger," Daren Mace responded from the virtual cockpit. "Hawk One, rejoin on Vampire One, left fingertip formation."

"Hawk One beginning rejoin with Vampire One, stop rejoin." After a moment the StealthHawk started a rapid climb and headed toward the EB-1C Vampire.

"This is the part I can't handle," Rebecca said.

"It'll work," Patrick reassured her. He had to force down a bit of doubt in his own voice, but he was able to repeat, "It'll work."

It worked better than they could have imagined. The StealthHawk climbed and accelerated until it was almost at the EB-1C Vampire's altitude, then quickly slid in until it was flying precisely two hundred feet beside Rebecca Furness's window and fifty feet below the Vampire's altitude. "I have the StealthHawk in sight," she reported. The StealthHawk looked perfectly normal in the dawn sky, hanging in tightly in a modified fingertip-formation position. "It looks in the green."

"Aft bay doors coming open, docking web coming out," Daren said. He opened the aft bay doors by remote control, then ordered, "Hawk One, translate to predock position on Vampire One."

"Hawk One translating to predock position Vampire One, stop translate," the UCAV responded. Then, as everyone watched on remote cameras, the StealthHawk slid back and across underneath the EB-1C.

"Oh, shit, I can practically feel that sucker under me," Rebecca breathed.

"Steady, Becky," Patrick said, but he found he could not talk in a normal tone of voice either.

The StealthHawk continued moving underneath the bomber until it was centered precisely in the opening of the aft bomb bay, then slowly, excruciatingly, began climbing. They could see the StealthHawk buck and burble as it corrected its flight path through the bomber's slipstream. But both the Vampire and the StealthHawk used mission-adaptive "smart skin," and their flight-control computers were able to both smooth out and dampen out the other's slipstream and wake turbulence. The Stealth-Hawk nosed toward a large composite material half-shell framework called the "docking web" that had been extended into the slipstream. It seemed like a millennium later, but finally the StealthHawk announced, *"Hawk One stabilized in predock position."*

"Yeah, baby!" Jon Masters shouted. "That's my boy!"

"Looks good," Rebecca said. "Now move it back so I can see it."

"Roger. Hawk One, translate to left fingertip position," Daren ordered.

"Hawk One translating to left fingertip position, stop translate." The StealthHawk obeyed and appeared a few moments later back on Rebecca's side of the plane.

"That's good, Dr. Masters," Rebecca said. She finally took what felt like her first full breath of air in a very long time. "Let's let it land on Diego Garcia."

"Rebecca, I think we should try a docking," Daren said.

"That wasn't in the flight-test plan."

"The ship and the UCAV are doing better than we ever expected," Daren responded. "Let's give it a try."

"Let's stick with the plan, guys," Rebecca argued. "We'll have lots of opportunities to dock it when we don't have live ordnance on board. If we take any damage from the UCAV and we can't jettison the remaining weapons, they'll never let us land on Diego Garcia—we'll have to ditch the Vampire."

"Rebecca, let's try it," Patrick said. "The apparatus is in place, and the predock join-up looked nice and steady. It'll work."

Rebecca thought about it for a moment. Her hesitation was all the prompting Patrick McLanahan needed.

"You're clear to do a docking, Daren," he said.

"Roger *that!*" Daren responded happily. "Hawk One, dock with Vampire One, center bomb bay."

"Hawk One docking with Vampire One center bay, stop docking," the StealthHawk responded. Rebecca stared at the UCAV as it flew out of sight, and soon the strange feeling of being able to feel the little robot plane as if it were flying around her own body returned.

The StealthHawk maneuvered itself back underneath the Vampire bomber's aft bomb bay, stabilized in predock position for a few seconds, then slowly continued its climb. Now Patrick and Rebecca could both feel a tiny shudder in the Vampire's airframe, a slight vibration that couldn't be dampened out by the mission-adaptive system. "Here it comes," Patrick breathed. "Here it comes. . . ."

Slowly, slowly, the StealthHawk climbed until it nestled inside the half-shell framework of the docking web. A powerful electromagnet activated, pulling the nose up into a latching mechanism that held tightly to the UCAV; then soft composite tubular frames extended out from under the docking web, completely encircling the UCAV. The turbulence from the web started to make the StealthHawk buck and fishtail inside the web, but by the time the turbulence got bad enough that the mission-adaptive system couldn't counteract it, the web had captured the UCAV, the turbojet engine had shut down, and the StealthHawk was pulled inside the aft bomb bay and the bomb doors closed.

"We nabbed it!" Jon Masters shouted. "It worked! We got it!"

"I don't friggin' believe it," Rebecca murmured as she saw the StealthHawk safely back inside the bomb bay in her TV monitor. "We retrieved it." She reached across and clasped hands with Patrick McLanahan. "General, I know there will come a time when that will be routine," she said cross-cockpit, "but, I swear to God, that was the most nerve-racking thing I've ever done."

"Excellent job. Thanks for agreeing to do it," Patrick said. "Ready to finish the test flight?"

"I don't suppose there's any way you'll agree to terminate this and let us take it back to the barn?" Rebecca asked.

"We're on a roll, Rebecca," Patrick said. "You're the aircraft commander, so whatever you say goes, but I say let's finish this test."

Rebecca nodded, took another deep breath, and said, "Okay, guys, let's go to the next evolution—before I run out of adrenaline."

"Roger, boss," Zane said happily. "VAC has the aircraft, proceeding to the air-refueling anchor."

Zane then flew the EB-1C Vampire bomber south toward a designated military operating area east of the island of Diego Garcia. A Sky Masters Inc. launch-and-control aircraft, a modified DC-10 airliner, was waiting for them with its refueling boom extended.

"Here's the big test, guys," Daren said. To the computer he ordered, "Vampire, translate to precontact position on the tanker."

"Vampire translating to precontact position, stop translate." The bomber immediately climbed until it was five hundred feet below the tanker, accelerated until it was one thousand feet in trail, then slowly climbed and decelerated until it was ten feet below and ten feet behind the boom's nozzle. *"Stabilized precontact,"* the computer reported.

"How is it doing that?" Grey asked.

"The laser radar paints an exact picture of the entire tanker, including its boom," Patrick explained, "and measures the tanker's exact distance, speed, and altitude."

"Isn't hitting the refueling boom with laser beams dangerous?"

"About as dangerous as shining a TV remote in your eyes," Daren chimed in. "The laser's power reduces as the range decreases, so there's no danger. Let's do the checklists, Zane."

"Roger. Vampire, precontact checklist."

The air-refueling slipway door opened, and several lights were illuminated on the overhead instrument panel. *"Precontact checklist complete,"* the computer responded moments later.

"Vampire, translate to contact position," Zane ordered.

"Vampire translating to contact position, stop translate." The Vampire bomber began a slow climb and a very slow acceleration. Patrick and Rebecca watched as the DC-10's air-refueling director lights—two lines of lights under the tanker's belly that told a pilot where he was in the refueling envelope—activated, ordering the receiver to move up and forward with a green light toward the lower edge of the light display. As the bomber moved closer, the green light moved forward toward the center of the light display, and another green flashing light inched its way from the lower UP bar toward the center. Rebecca had her right hand poised on the control stick, her little finger automatically lining up with the "paddle switch"—

a lever on the front of the control stick that would disconnect the VC from aircraft control completely and immediately.

"Coming up on contact position," Daren said.

The boom's nozzle looked like a huge cannon pointing directly at their foreheads. "This is nutso," Rebecca whispered. "This is crazy. . . ."

"Steady, Rebecca," Patrick said on intercom. "Easy . . ."

The boom hove dangerously close to the bomber's radome, coming mere inches away from hitting. The boom operator grabbed it away just in time. "That was close," Rebecca said.

"We're still moving in," Daren said. "Almost there . . ."

Patrick wasn't sure if it was the tanker or the Vampire that did it, but the tanker abruptly seemed to pull away. The Vampire made a sudden acceleration, and as it sped up it also climbed sharply. The boom operator, not expecting the sudden movement, had to yank the boom out of the way. The nozzle seemed close enough for Furness and McLanahan to clearly see the scratches around the business end.

Just as Patrick breathed a sigh of relief that the nozzle was well clear, he heard Rebecca shout, *"Boom strike!"*

"Vampire, *breakaway!"* Daren said immediately. The bomber instantly decelerated, dropping a thousand feet behind and five hundred feet below the tanker in just a few seconds. At the same instant Rebecca squeezed the paddle switch, taking complete manual control of the bomber, and flicked off the datalink switches.

Patrick turned to Rebecca and said cross-cockpit, "Are you sure the boom hit us, Rebecca?"

"Pretty damned sure," she replied excitedly.

"No damage observed on the boom," radioed the boom operator in the pod in the tail of the DC-10. "No observed damage to the receiver. Let me reset my system, stand by. . . . System reset. Vampire, you're cleared to precontact position."

Patrick loosened his straps so he could lean forward and carefully look out the windscreen. "I don't see any damage," he said. "Let's give it another try."

"I've got a better idea—let's *not*," Rebecca said angrily cross-cockpit. "We had a boom strike. No more refueling until we get on the ground and check it out."

"Rebecca . . ." Daren began.

"That's *'General'* to you, Colonel Mace!" Rebecca snapped on intercom. After a few moments' stunned silence, she continued, "For those of you who don't speak English or have conveniently forgotten the regs, a boom strike means no more refueling unless it's an emergency or there are no suitable landing alternates available. We're done for the day. Postrefueling checklist, *now*." Patrick had no choice but to comply, and a few minutes later, after again reporting no visible damage, the boom operator cleared the Vampire to depart.

DEARBORN, MICHIGAN
The next morning

The president of the United States, Thomas Thorn, reached under the floorboards in the rear of the big sports utility vehicle and extracted a large gray case, resembling a footlocker. With photographers snapping away like crazy, the president set the case on the ground, took another case proffered him from Secretary of Defense Robert Goff, set it inside the SUV in place of the first, closed the floorboards, then closed the rear hatch, giving it a slap. Moments later the SUV rumbled to life. The president knelt beside the SUV's exhaust pipe, touched it, and even put his face uncomfortably close to it, smiling the entire time. The cameramen hungrily snapped away.

Thorn removed a pair of work gloves as he approached the podium. "That, my friends, is how easy it is to replace a Sky Masters fuel cell," he said. "This vehicle can now travel at legal highway speeds for another seven hundred miles—about twice the range of gasoline-powered vehicles. And its exhaust is completely clean, with nothing but water vapor as its only combustion by-product. It is my intention that every government vehicle purchased from now on will be powered only by non-petroleum-based fuels such as fuel cells, if Congress approves my alternative fuels vehicle purchase program bill." He turned to the SUV heading down the automobile test track. "There goes the car of the future, ladies and gentlemen."

And then, as if on cue, the SUV sputtered, coughed a few times, then coasted another few dozen yards before coming to a stop. A small army of technicians and engineers rushed to it, some carrying spare fuel-cell cases. A few moments later, after a change of the fuel-cell locker, the SUV began to move, then began sputtering and jerking ahead. Finally the techs and engineers began ignominiously pushing it off to the side of the track.

"Well, I think that illustrates the status of my bill so far: starting strong, showing a lot of promise, then running out of steam and needing an extra boost," the president said gamely. "But I am bound and determined not to let a few setbacks stop this bill. Finding alternative sources of energy for America is a priority of mine as well as of the American people, and I've resolved to see it through." The president pointed to one of the reporters arrayed around the podium, indicating he was ready to take questions.

"Mr. President, does your bill supporting and encouraging development of all nonpetroleum forms of energy include nuclear and coal, both of which have the danger of seriously polluting the environment?"

"It does," the president responded. "I'm confident we have the technology to control hazardous waste and by-products from both forms of energy production, and I want the federal government to encourage such development through increased tax deductions and lowered tax rates on income for energy production using alternative sources."

"Mr. President, even if this bill passes, it'll take several years, maybe even decades, for the economic benefits to be felt from some of these technologies," another reporter said. "What do you intend to do to ensure America's need for petroleum-based energy until then?"

"As I have always done, I will encourage domestic oil production, conservation, and further development of renewable sources of energy such as solar, wind, geothermal, hydroelectric, and tidal," the president said. "My administration has already sponsored two dozen bills to encourage these initiatives." He knew where this line of questioning was leading.

"It seems that you are pushing for domestic oil production and all these other alternative and renewable energy sources, Mr. President," the reporter followed up, "because your foreign policy is in disarray and you cannot ensure adequate supplies of fossil fuel for the future from foreign sources. Your comments?"

"I would very much disagree with your characterization," Thorn replied. "My foreign policy position in regard to adequate supply of petroleum products is simple: We will deal fairly with any nation that deals fairly with us. We will not be held hostage by any nation that seeks to exploit how much oil we import from it."

"Sir, former president Kevin Martindale has met with

the oil ministers of most of the OPEC countries convening this week in Caracas, Venezuela, including Saudi Arabia, Russia, Iran, and most of the Central Asian states," another reporter said. "It appears that President Martindale is lining up support for increased oil production and more secure supply chains. In sharp contrast, sir, your trade representative is still in Washington, and Secretary of State Kercheval hasn't been seen or heard from in days. Can you explain this?"

"I don't think there's anything to explain. No one from my administration was invited to the OPEC meeting, and Secretary Kercheval is busy with other projects," Thorn replied. "I don't see the need to send trade representatives to hang around the hotels and conference halls in Caracas like some rock groupies. If any of the oil ministers wish to speak with me, they know how to contact me."

"Are you characterizing President Martindale's presence in Caracas as his being like a *rock groupie?*" another reporter shouted incredulously.

"As for the former president: He's a private citizen and free to travel and meet with whomever he chooses," Thorn went on, ignoring the question. "Everyone, I'm sure, understands that he does not speak for the U.S. government."

"Mr. President, with the removal of U.S. troops from overseas bases and the American withdrawal from most mutual-defense agreements, the popularity of and confidence in the U.S. are at an all-time low," another reporter said. "Recently TransCal Petroleum said in a press release that a group of Taliban fighters from Afghanistan have invaded a neighboring country, Turkmenistan, and are threatening to take over the oil-drilling and -distribution facilities built by TransCal for the Turkmen government." The president nodded. "TransCal execs claim that the Turkmen government is powerless to stop the insurgents, and that, because your administration refuses to get involved, they might be forced to pay 'protection money' to the Taliban to keep the oil flowing. What's your response?"

"I've been thoroughly briefed on the situation in Turkmenistan," the president said. "The situation there is extremely unclear. These Taliban fighters are marching quite easily and virtually unopposed through most of the eastern part of the country, gaining tremendous popular support. My question is, why is this happening? Until we know the answer, I see no use in sending in U.S. troops to protect their pipelines."

"But TransCal Petroleum, an American company, is losing millions of dollars a day—"

"I will not commit fighting forces to any sovereign nation unless it is in the defense of the people and the nation of the United States of America," Thorn said resolutely. "The Founding Fathers created a military force with one and only one objective in mind: the defense of the United States. With the information I have currently, I am not yet convinced that these Taliban insurgents pose a risk to Americans here at home or overseas."

Several more questions were shouted at him, so many that he could not sort them out. He saw Robert Goff nervously fidgeting. Things were starting to get out of control, the photo opportunity lost, and it was time to move on. "In closing, ladies and gentlemen, I'd like to say that it is innovations such as Sky Masters's fuel-cell project that will ensure America's energy independence and keep us from getting entangled in risky and murky conflicts overseas. America can be strong and energy-independent with the right combination of creative thinking, science, and support from the people and the government. I urge support for my alternative fuels vehicle purchase program bill and my other initiatives that are designed to promote and encourage development of dependable, sustainable sources of energy. Thanks very much, and God bless." He ignored a loud volley of shouted questions, most of which began to sound more like threats or challenges than mere questions.

The president took several minutes to shake hands—designed to let the live-news outlets terminate their coverage of his press conference while he was pressing the flesh, instead of showing him retreating—and was then escorted to a waiting car to be taken to the airport. There was silence for several minutes after everyone was on board. Finally Robert Goff said, "I apologize for that snafu with the fuel cell, Mr. President. We tested that exchange a half dozen times today alone, and it worked perfectly every time."

"Those things happen, Robert," Thorn said, smiling. "Don't worry about it."

He turned to watch the televised coverage of the event. The satellite-TV station was showing video of the president with his face next to the exhaust pipe of the SUV, and one of the commentators made a crude remark about the "president's energy policy being full of hot air" and "high in the ozone."

"Wish I could've thought of another way to show how safe the emissions from those fuel-cell engines are without sticking my face near that tailpipe," Thorn said wryly.

"We'll be sure we explain to all the media outlets the point you were trying to make," Goff said. "That commentator has got his head up his ass anyway."

"So Martindale is scoring some points in his trip to Venezuela, eh?"

"Sir, Martindale is on TransCal Petroleum's bankroll to the tune of millions. He probably should be registered as a TransCal lobbyist," Goff said disgustedly. "He's spending that money down in Caracas, in the Middle East, in the Balkans, and in Central Asia, trying to gain support for

TransCal production deals. Most of those countries still think he's running the Night Stalkers and will attack if he doesn't get to meet with the oil ministers."

"It wouldn't surprise me if he was still involved," Thorn said. Kevin Martindale's leadership of a group of high-tech mercenaries was one of the biggest nonscandals in years. It made him a roguish legend in America and definitely did not hurt his reelection chances.

"Well, the intimidation factor is definitely working. Most of those countries in turn are financing his reelection campaign." Thorn was about to say something, but Goff anticipated the remark. "I can't prove it, but I know it's happening. He's hoping that more and more countries warm up to him so it looks like he has support overseas. More support overseas means more American companies feel better backing Martindale for president because it means a stronger dollar and more American clout overseas, which he's hoping translates to more donations and support here at home."

"Sounds logical to me."

Goff looked at Thorn quizzically. "Sir, it's easy for candidates to throw lots of money around to court companies and governments for support. They're not on the front lines every day," Goff reminded the president. "This plan of Martindale's will backfire because everyone knows who Martindale really is. He talks about peace and harmony and friendship, and then *boom!*—he sends in the Marines or the stealth bombers and blows the crap out of anyone and everyone who gets in his way. He's a backstabber, sir, and everyone knows it."

Thomas Thorn stared blankly at the TV. "Would it work in Turkmenistan, I wonder?" he asked at last.

"What? Sending in the Marines against those Taliban?"

"I was thinking of the bombers," Thorn said. He pressed a button on a computer keyboard, and the TV image changed to the military briefing page. "Status report on McLanahan's recovery mission in Turkmenistan: complete success, complete withdrawal of the cruise missile, all personnel extracted, no casualties."

"The guy's good—there's no doubt about that," Goff said. He waited to see if the president was going to say anything more; when he did not, Goff asked, "What are you thinking, Thomas?"

Thorn was silent for a long time. Finally he said, "Nothing."

"Having some second thoughts about getting involved in Central Asia?"

"No," he replied quickly—too quickly, Goff suspected. When he noticed his friend, adviser, and secretary of defense looking questioningly at him, Thorn added, "Martindale is wrong, Robert. The solution to what's happening in Turkmenistan does not lie in military force."

"I happen to agree—for now," Goff said. "The problem remains: Martindale is on the offensive politically. He's in Venezuela talking to world petroleum ministers, grabbing headlines, and making himself look like a leader. The word is he'll be heading to Kuwait City to address a meeting of the Gulf States Security Council—the first American ever to do so since the Gulf War. He probably *won't* be talking about Central Asia at that particular time. That might be a good opportunity."

Thorn looked at Goff, then said, "To make a diplomatic move in Turkmenistan?" Goff nodded. "The only way to do that would be to send a high-level delegation."

"It should be Kercheval. But he doesn't deserve it now, does he?" Thorn closed his eyes—they both knew the answer to that one. "Maureen Hershel is a good choice. Turkmenistan is Muslim, but it's run mostly by Soviet-era bureaucrats who know they have to deal with high-ranking women in today's world. She's smart, tough, and, best of all, she knows when to keep her mouth shut."

"Time's running out. If that Taliban insurgent army gets their grips on the capital, Turkmenistan could fall fast."

"Let's give her the go-ahead right away, then," Goff said. "Let her staff start laying the groundwork for a diplomatic visit and high-level talks." Thorn nodded his approval. Goff added, "You might even consider bringing a military liaison along. Turkmenistan's military is very small and run by Russian officers."

Thorn looked at Goff, then smiled. "You mean McLanahan?"

"Why not? McLanahan has pretty good name recognition and respect here in the U.S., but at the same time he's not very well known overseas. He'll have the luxury of relative anonymity. He can look around and talk to folks without calling too much attention to himself. I know you don't care about political stuff, but the fact remains, McLanahan has pretty good poll numbers—about where Colin Powell was when he was Reagan's national security adviser."

"Let's not get into a discussion again about asking McLanahan to be my national security adviser," Thorn groaned. "I've already got *you* to tell me where I'm screwing up." The president thought about it for a moment, then shook his head. "There's an old saying in the military: 'Screw up and move up.' McLanahan has done his share of bad decision making lately. I'm not so sure he deserves a plum posting like that."

Goff shrugged. He certainly couldn't argue. "I'll draw up a list of candidates and send it over to State, then present it to you for your approval," he said.

"I'll let Miss Hershel pick her own attachés from your list."

Goff nodded. That was the way Thorn did business—

pick good people, then delegate authority to them. It was faster, less stressful on him, and made his staff feel like they were part of the action every step of the way. "In the meantime why don't we talk to McLanahan and get his thoughts about what's going on over there."

"Why him in particular?"

"Because he's smart, and he's in command of a unit that could very well be the tip of the spear if we decide to move out there," Goff said. "Besides, he's on the way. We're heading to Lake Tahoe for that environmental-summit thing. There's plenty of time to reposition the support crews to Battle Mountain. I'll have General Venti transmit a request for an operational assessment from McLanahan's unit. We can have Miss Hershel accompany us out there. You can look over McLanahan's unit and get a briefing directly from him."

"You're high on this guy, aren't you, Robert?" Thorn asked. "Why?"

Goff shrugged. "The same reason I'm high on you, my friend," he replied with an uneasy smile. "You both have the strength of your convictions. You both know what you believe is right, and you're not afraid to fight for it." His eyes danced a bit, and he added, "Besides, I have a feeling it'll be like the unstoppable force meeting the immovable object when you two get together. Patrick McLanahan on his own home turf, versus the commander in chief. I already know who'll win—but it'll still be fun to watch you two get in each other's faces."

FOUR

The massive shape of Air Force One appeared through the snowstorm like a giant fantasy bird and touched down on Battle Mountain's long runway in a puff of snow. One-eleventh Bomb Wing Security Forces units, including armored personnel carriers, were stationed along the infields and taxiways to escort the plane to its parking spot. The winds were right down the runway but gusting well over twenty knots, blowing snow nearly horizontally and creating large drifts on the runway and taxiway edges. Despite the poor visibility, Air Force One taxied quickly over to a designated spot several hundred meters in front of the base-operations building and shut down engines.

A set of covered airstairs was wheeled over to the entry door, and a few moments later President of the United States Thomas Thorn, Secretary of Defense Robert Goff, and Deputy Secretary of State Maureen Hershel emerged. Patrick met them at the bottom of the stairs, saluted, then shook hands with each of them. "Welcome to Battle

Mountain, Mr. President, Mr. Secretary, Miss Deputy Secretary," he said.

"Lovely weather you're having here, General," Robert Goff groused.

"We don't build military bases on the waterfront in San Francisco anymore, sir," Patrick said. "This weather suits us just fine."

Goff looked unimpressed as he turned up the collar of his overcoat and motioned toward a nearby armored Suburban belonging to the Secret Service. "Thanks for parking us so far away from your base-ops building, General," he complained. "Is that our vehicle? Let's get the hell out of this snowstorm."

"Not necessary, sir," Patrick said. He raised his head slightly, as if making a request of God, and said, "Ready on elevator three, surface to main ramp level."

"What did you say, Gen—" Goff stopped in midsentence—because he felt the earth move beneath his feet. *"What in hell was that?* An earthquake . . . ?" And then he noticed that the entire parking spot, VC-25 and all, started to descend into the earth.

The Secret Service agents seemed right on the brink of panic, but the president held up his hands as he saw the look on McLanahan's face. "Very interesting, General," he said.

"This is why working here in the middle of the high deserts of northern Nevada in a snowstorm is no big deal for us, sir," Patrick said. Goff and Hershel gasped in astonishment as a six-inch slab of steel and concrete slid over the opening overhead, blocking out the wind and snow.

"I'll bet you had one hell of a time convincing Congress to fund *this*," Hershel said.

"Thankfully, it was funded back in the Eisenhower administration. I don't think I would've stood a chance."

"No shit," Goff muttered.

Thorn, Goff, Hershel, and their entourage were taken

aboard electric cars and shown around the vast underground aircraft-parking ramp. They received tours of all the aircraft. They were especially impressed with the two AL-52 Dragon airborne-laser aircraft. "Unbelievable," Thorn said. "There they are—laser weapons aboard combat aircraft. *Star Wars* for real."

"They're not officially operational," Patrick explained, "but the first one was used successfully over Libya. It and the second one are being modified with the plasma-pumped solid-state lasers. They have fifty percent more power than the original chemical-oxygen-iodine laser design, nearly two megawatts of power—enough to destroy airborne or space targets as small as a Sidewinder missile three hundred miles away or ground targets up to one hundred miles away."

"What do they cost, General?" Maureen Hershel asked.

"Almost a billion dollars, ma'am," Patrick replied, "plus ten thousand dollars per flight hour to fly them and about fifty thousand dollars to fire the laser each time."

"So on a typical patrol mission . . ."

"Twelve-hour patrol sortie, two hundred engagements . . . over ten million dollars per sortie, not including the air-refueling tanker support."

"Ouch."

"It's cheap compared to what it would cost to field enough aircraft to do all those attack jobs at once," Patrick said.

He turned and got the opportunity to study the young woman for the first time. He'd seen her often on TV, of course, and was intrigued from the first moment he heard of her and her background. Shoulder-length brown hair, blue eyes behind rimless reading glasses, mid- to late forties, a bit above average height, trim and shapely, wearing good-looking but casual slacks, jacket, and all-terrain boots—unlike the president and secretary of defense, she looked like she'd come to take a tour of a military base.

"For maximum coverage in a hot combat zone," Patrick said to her, "we would field three to four aircraft: two in an orbit about a hundred miles from the forward edge of the battle area and one or two aircraft that cycle with the others—one in transit, one on the ground undergoing maintenance and crew rest."

"You need to think of a way to do it with less," Thorn said. "Those two birds may be all you ever get. Maybe not even that."

"We could do it with two aircraft, sir, but we wouldn't have total coverage," Patrick said. "An interim solution is to place a few EB-1C Vampire airborne battleships up, armed with Lancelot anti-ballistic-missile weapons and Anaconda long-range air-to-air missiles."

"So now we're talking about maybe two squadrons of planes just for the anti-ballistic-missile job," Goff summarized.

"The EB-52 Megafortresses will be capable of doing the long-range precision standoff bombing missions, and the EB-1C Vampires can also serve as long-range bombers. We can launch fast with a lot of firepower and swing easily from mission to mission."

"It just doesn't seem likely we'd ever be able to justify that kind of expense, Patrick."

"Here's how, sir: One engagement could destroy a single multiple-warhead ballistic missile, saving as many as twelve cities or military bases from annihilation," Patrick explained. "A single laser shot could destroy a fifty-million-dollar bomber or a hundred-million-dollar spy satellite. I don't like focusing on the numbers, sir, because they usually tell only part of the story, but in this case, the numbers show that the Dragon is a superb force-multiplying combat system."

"Most of Congress can't get past the purchase price, let alone the cost per sortie," Secretary of Defense Goff said. "And when they realize they're paying a billion dollars for a plane that was probably built before most of them were born—let me just say it's a very tough sell."

"I'd be happy to help try to make the sale, sir," Patrick said. "We can dazzle them."

"Well, dazzle *us* first before you go volunteering to take on Congress," Goff said.

"Yes, *sir*," Patrick said enthusiastically.

There was an odd assortment of other aircraft in the underground parking ramp: C-130 Hercules transports with weird, winglike spy antennae attached to various parts of the fuselage, wings, and stabilizers; huge helicopters with an assortment of radomes and sensor turrets on the nose; and two transport planes that had engines attached to their short, stubby wingtips. "Okay, stop," Robert Goff said. "I recognize the Commando Solo C-130 psyops plane and the MH-53 Pave Low special-ops helicopter, but what in the heck are *those?*"

"We call it the MV-32 Pave Dasher—our modification of the CV-22 Osprey tilt-rotor aircraft," Patrick explained. "The standard V-22 has turboprops. This one uses fanjet engines that swivel on the wingtips to provide vertical flight as well as high-speed forward flight. The fanjets give it much more lifting power as well as twice the forward speed of the Osprey. The MV-32 Pave Dasher can insert six Battle Force teams—twenty-four heavily armed combat troops—about two thousand miles, or farther with aerial refueling."

"I don't recall those planes being authorized or funded," Goff pointed out. He noticed Patrick's expres-

sion. "I see—another of your freelance, no-cost acquisi-
tions. From Sky Masters Inc., I suppose?"

"One of their development partners, yes, sir."

"McLanahan's private little air force again, eh, General?" President Thorn asked.

They continued through a series of wide corridors cut
out of the rock and stopped at a set of large steel doors on
immense hinges, reminiscent of the huge, vaultlike doors
at the entrance to the North American Aerospace Defense
Command's underground command center at Cheyenne
Mountain. The doors looked tired and gray, definitely
old—but inside, the large room looked modern and well
lit, like a brand-new auditorium or theater.

Brigadier General David Luger, Colonel John Long,
Lieutenant Colonel Nancy Cheshire, Lieutenant Colonel
Hal Briggs, and Sergeant Major Chris Wohl were lined up
in front of the stage inside the auditorium, surrounded by
Secret Service agents. "Mr. President, Miss Secretary, Mr.
Secretary, I'd like to introduce you to the rest of the com-
mand here." Thorn, Hershel, and Goff stepped over to
where the others were waiting. "I'd like to introduce you
to my second in command, Brigadier General David
Luger."

The VIPs shook hands with Luger. "It's an honor to
meet you, General," Robert Goff said. He looked at Luger
solemnly, glanced at Patrick, then added, "The last two
surviving members of the Old Dog crew. Two living leg-
ends. I'm glad to have you both around."

David Luger, tall and lanky and towering over Goff,
looked bowed as he realized that it was true: There were
only two of the original six crew members of the first "Old
Dog" mission left. "It's good to be here, sir," he said.

"This is Brigadier General Rebecca Furness, commander of the One-eleventh Attack Wing; Colonel John

Long, the operations-group commander; Colonel Daren Mace, commander of the Fifty-first Attack Squadron with the EB-1C Vampires; and Lieutenant Colonel Nancy Cheshire, commander of the Fifty-second Attack Squadron with the EB-52 Megafortresses and the AL-52 Dragons."

"The first female combat pilot—another living legend. Nice to meet you, Rebecca," Goff said, shaking Rebecca's hand enthusiastically. He shook Long's hand but did not address him—obviously an astute judge of character, Patrick thought. "Nice to see you again, Daren," Goff said, shaking Daren's hand warmly. "I was pleased with the work you did out at Beale."

"Thank you, sir," Daren replied.

"I hope you'll find a home out here—" Goff said. He paused, glanced at McLanahan, then added, "If they haven't scared you too much already."

"That may be possible to do, sir, but not yet."

"Colonel, I'm looking forward to seeing what your airborne-laser aircraft are capable of," Goff said, shaking Nancy's hand. Nancy Cheshire was tall, athletic bordering on muscular, with strawberry-blond hair, shining green eyes, and an ever-present smile. She was the senior test pilot in the experimental B-52 bombers at Dreamland, accepting her first operational command to get the chance to keep on flying her beloved super-B-52s and work with Patrick McLanahan.

"Finally," Patrick went on, "Colonel Hal Briggs and Sergeant Major Chris Wohl, Air Battle Force ground operations."

Maureen Hershel stared at Chris Wohl in wonderment. Hal was wearing his Air Force Class-A blue uniform, but Chris Wohl was wearing a strange black outfit that resembled high-tech scuba diver's gear, with a thin backpack, thick boots and belt, and tubes running along the arms and legs. "What in the world is this?" she asked, touching the strange material.

"It's called BERP—Ballistic Electro-Reactive Process, ma'am," Hal Briggs replied. "Electronic armor. It responds to being sharply struck by instantly hardening into an almost impenetrable protective shield that can withstand attack by up to thirty-seven-millimeter cannon shells. The tubes you see outside the armor are part of the powered exoskeleton, which uses microhydraulic actuators to activate the armor and enhance the wearer's strength. These electrodes on the shoulders emit directional bursts of electrical energy out as far as fifty feet, which can paralyze an attacker. The boots contain a gas thruster system that can help the wearer jump several hundred feet. The backpack contains a power-generating and rechargeable-battery system, plus worldwide communications and sensor equipment. This is what the well-dressed commando will be wearing this century."

"They call themselves the Tin Men, Maureen," Goff said, shaking hands with Briggs and Wohl. His voice was filled with tension and seriousness, but his handshake and eyes were friendly. "They've proven themselves extraordinarily effective in many different scenarios, but they've also given us a lot of headaches since we've taken office. Isn't that right, gentlemen?"

"That's one of our specialties, sir," Hal Briggs said. "We aim to please."

"I for one don't think it's funny, Colonel," President Thorn said. "You successfully dragged the United States into a shooting war with Russia and nearly got us into a shooting war with Libya—all for a few lousy dollars. If it weren't for General McLanahan's interceding on your behalf, you'd all be in prison right now." Briggs and Wohl said nothing but remained at parade rest, eyes caged forward. "Well? What do you have to say for yourselves?"

"I'm happy to have the opportunity to create some havoc for *you* now, sir," Briggs said.

"Same here, sir," Wohl chimed in.

Thorn looked Wohl up and down. "I was a commando, too, Sergeant Major," he said. "I spent a month crawling on my belly in Iraq before and during Desert Storm with nothing but a laser designator and a bad attitude. But not once in all the battles and all the shit we took did I ever consider turning my back on my country or the Army."

He stared both Wohl and Briggs in the eyes, his chin jutting out, his jaw clenched. "You left the Corps and fought for an outlaw organization," he went on angrily. "Both of you renounced your oaths and went to work for what I believe was a criminal organization—a group that stole money, committed murder and mayhem, and absconded with government property. You nearly caused a world war with your antics. You didn't deserve to come back into the *country,* let alone come back into the U.S. armed forces and get a promotion."

"You gave my men and me full exoneration and full restoration of our rank and privileges, sir. . . ." Patrick interjected.

"That's right—I gave your ranks back to you," Thorn said heatedly. "I gave them back because you acquitted yourselves with honor in Libya. But you haven't won the right to think you're some kind of bad-ass fighting men now." Thorn turned and saw Wohl glaring at him. He turned and faced the big Marine nose-to-nose. "You have something to say to me, Sergeant Major?"

"Yes, sir," Wohl said. His eyes remained caged, not looking directly at the president's. "But I choose not to say it."

"Go ahead, Sergeant Major," Thorn pressed. "You have permission to speak freely. Tell us why you chose to leave your post without being properly relieved, and why you think you deserve to come back into my country's armed forces—instead of spending the rest of your life in prison."

Wohl's eyes angrily snapped over to Thorn's. That was the reaction Thorn was waiting for.

"Go ahead, Sergeant Major, say it," Thorn goaded him. "Give me a reason to toss your ass in Leavenworth, where it belongs."

Wohl wisely, thankfully remained silent.

"You assassinated Pavel Kazakov in Iceland, didn't you, you murderous son of a bitch?" Thorn asked in a low, ominous voice.

"Excuse me, sir—" Hal Briggs interjected.

"Shut up, Colonel," Thorn ordered. "I haven't even started with *you* yet." He turned again to Wohl. "You're a wild dog, Wohl." He jabbed at Wohl's chest and was surprised when the material he thought was fabric felt as hard as titanium—he could have *all* his Secret Service agents nearby, he realized ruefully, and they wouldn't be able to stop this guy. That made him a little nervous—no, it made him a *lot scared*—but he knew he couldn't dare let that show, so he pressed on. "There's an Interpol warrant for your arrest for Kazakov's murder, did you know that? He was under United Nations protection. You cut his head off, didn't you? Whose idea was it to kill Kazakov? Yours or Briggs's?" Still no response. *"Answer me!"*

"My men prefer to do their talking on the battlefield, Mr. President," Patrick McLanahan said forcefully, quickly interjecting his voice between them—he could practically feel the heat from Wohl's temples as his anger mounted. No one, not even the president of the United States, would be allowed to get into Chris Wohl's face unscathed for very long. "Sergeant Major Wohl isn't a debater. He follows orders, leads men into battle, and kills with extraordinary efficiency."

Thorn looked into Wohl's eyes and instantly believed what Patrick was telling him.

"If you'd like a briefing on our prior activities and the reasons behind them, sir, I'd be happy to accommodate you at any time."

"I'm not interested in dog and pony shows, and I'm sure as hell not interested in excuses," Thorn said. "I'm letting you know that I'm still not convinced that you're fighting for the United States of America. You have a long way to go before that happens."

"Sir, we're ready to demonstrate our capabilities—and our loyalty—anytime, anywhere."

"That's why we're here, General," Goff said. He waited to see if the president had anything more to say; when Thorn remained silent, Goff said to Patrick, "Okay, Patrick, show us around."

"Yes, sir. We call this the BATMAN, or Battle Management Center," Patrick said. They were in a huge room, like an auditorium, complete with tiered seating, a stage, and even three glassed-in balcony sections. Sixteen four-by-three-foot color plasma displays seamlessly hung together on the forward wall above the stage; a few of them were out of order, but the view was still spectacular. "Here in the center are consoles for the commanders and leadership. Behind the commanders are the support staffs, linked together by fiber-optic networks—intelligence, operations, communications, logistics, weather, and manpower. The rear of the tiered section is the virtual-cockpit command center, where teams will be able to control up to six long-range bombers plus a dozen unmanned combat air vehicles or monitor the automated progress of dozens of unmanned aircraft. Up above is the battle staff area; on either side of that are areas for joint forces or civil commanders; and on either side of BATMAN are observer areas, which can be closed off if necessary."

"When is all this going to be finished, General?" Hershel asked.

"We're mission-capable now, ma'am," Patrick replied. "We already have worldwide communications capability here via high-frequency radio, the Internet, secure fiber-optic landline, and secure satellite. All the datalinks aren't set up yet, but most of the hardware is in place, and it's just a matter of programming in the links. At this point we're about at the level where command posts were in the 1980s. In two months we'll be up to date. In three to six months—with the right funding—we'll be state-of-the-art, able to control entire squadrons of unmanned aircraft and collect and analyze real-time reconnaissance and intelligence data from all over the world."

"I've seen better, General—I'm not impressed," Thorn said impatiently. "If I recall correctly, you were tasked only with investigating how your experimental aircraft and weapons could interface with today's tactical air squadrons. We gave you back all your toys with the idea that they would be merged into other existing combat units on an as-needed basis. It looks to me like you're building your own military unit here, using General Furness's planes."

"That's inaccurate, sir," Patrick said. "I don't control any of these aircraft. The B-1s and KC-135s belong to General Furness; the B-52s belong to the High Technology Aerospace Weapons Center.

"As I understand them, sir, my orders were to discover ways to integrate the EB-52 Megafortress, EB-1C Vampire, AL-52 Dragon, and other weapons, aircraft, satellites, and sensors developed at HAWC with existing forces," Patrick went on. He knew he was quoting his orders word for word. "I was also given the task of standing up this facility for use as an alternate national military and civil emergency command center and secure evacuation location for the national command authority. I'm ready to brief the National Command Authority at any time on how these weapon systems and this facility can be integrated into the total force structure. I assembled a team of experts on unmanned aircraft development, on my own authority and budget, and I—"

"What you consider 'your authority' is highly questionable to me, General," Thorn interjected. "You must be taking money from other projects and programs to help fund your project—maybe even taking money from General Furness here. Is that what you're doing, General McLanahan? You *are* doing flight tests with General Furness's unmanned B-1 bombers? You want to create an entire wing of robot planes, all controlled from this place?"

Patrick looked over at John Long, who was looking directly at him with a grin on his face. He should've expected the rat bastard to drop a dime on him, Patrick thought. "Yes, sir," Patrick said. "That's what I'm doing here."

Rebecca cut in quickly, "Sir, I fully authorized General McLanahan's use of wing resources for his—"

"I seriously doubt it, General Furness," Thorn said. "I'll look into that issue myself." Thorn and McLanahan stared at each other for a few moments. Then Thorn asked, "So tell me, General—did it work?"

"No, sir," Patrick replied, "it did not."

David, Rebecca, Daren, and even John Long looked at McLanahan in surprise. "It *didn't work?*" Thorn retorted. "Not at all? Any of it?"

"The tests proved what we already knew about the StealthHawk unmanned combat air vehicle system—it's a mostly reliable and effective weapon system," Patrick elaborated. "Unfortunately, the tests we performed regarding unmanned full-size bomber aircraft being used both as a mothership and as an attack platform were unsuccessful. Although we were able to launch and retrieve a StealthHawk UCAV remotely, we were unable to complete an aerial refueling, which was our main objective."

Thorn looked at the surprised expressions of the officers before him—something wasn't quite jibing. He gave them a few heartbeats to speak, perhaps come to McLanahan's defense . . . but they did not.

"Too bad, General," he said finally. He wasn't about to prompt anyone for more information. If they didn't want to be forthcoming for some reason—meaning, if they didn't believe in the project enough to back the boss—he certainly wasn't going to do it for them. "I hope all you've wasted is a little jet fuel."

"I would like to see the full results of your flight tests," Goff interjected.

"Secretary Goff gave you an assignment recently, General," the president asked. "Got something for us?"

"Yes, sir," Patrick replied. "My deputy, General Luger, has the information you requested."

"Then let's get started." They all took seats, and Patrick motioned to David Luger.

"Good morning, Mr. President, Mr. Secretary, Miss Deputy Secretary," Luger began. "Last week, on orders transmitted to the First Air Battle Force from the Joint Chiefs of Staff deputy commander for operations, I was directed by General McLanahan to perform an operational air-battle assessment of the eastern Turkmenistan region, concentrating specifically on recent military maneuvers by a group of insurgents identified by the CIA as the same Taliban fighters we interdicted in Operation Hilltop a couple weeks ago," Luger said. "An air-battle assessment is a tasking whereby we identify and classify threats in a specific area using our own surveillance assets, combined with national and international sources, and then develop a plan of action to counter the threats. I looked at all threats posed by these insurgents but primarily focused on the threat to U.S. interests—national and civil as well as military—in Central Asia.

"In general, sir, we identify no credible threat to U.S. military interests in Central Asia and only minor military threats to U.S. interests in neighboring areas such as the Persian Gulf, Indian Ocean, or Black Sea regions. However, we have identified an imminent and serious threat to U.S. commercial interests in Turkmenistan that could have grave repercussions in the entire region and neighboring regions."

"You mean those insurgents and the threat to Trans-Cal's pipelines," Maureen Hershel interjected.

"Yes, ma'am," Luger acknowledged. "In short, the TransCal pipelines—all of them—are effectively right now in the hands of the insurgents, and at this point they fully control them. They can shut them down, blow them up, hold them hostage, keep them running—whatever they want to do. The Turkmen army is virtually incapable of resisting them any longer."

"It's worse than we thought, then," Goff said.

"The insurgents control fifty percent of all the pipelines in the entire country—nearly ninety-five percent of the lines not owned by Russian oil companies," Luger said. "Duty Officer, slide number one." Several of the screens in front of them came to life, showing a map of Turkmenistan, the border region with Uzbekistan highlighted. "Here is a map of all of TransCal's pipelines—five billion dollars' worth, a joint venture by TransCal and the Turkmen government, transporting crude oil and natural gas from Turkmenistan's substantial known oil and gas fields to a few refineries, but mostly to users in twelve neighboring countries and to shipment points in Pakistan. Turkmenistan itself uses only about three percent of what it produces. Overall, the pipelines are modern, aboveground, well hardened against earthquake and storms, and mostly remotely monitored, with quarterly visual inspections.

"The biggest pipelines—both oil and gas lines—run right along the entire Turkmen-Uzbek border. As you can see, most of these lines are controlled by the insurgents, from the Tajikistan border to Chärjew. TransCal also has a pipeline system running from their wells in Uzbekistan south to the city of Mary, then south through Afghanistan to Pakistani ports on the Gulf of Oman; all the lines from Chärjew to Mary are under insurgent control, which means they control the lines south of there as well.

"The insurgents also control the TransCal pipelines running along the Kara Kum Canal, which runs east-west from the Iranian to the Uzbek borders. That canal is important in irrigation, flood control, and transportation in most of southern Turkmenistan. The insurgents can now cut off all petroleum deliveries running to the east and south, including oil and natural gas to Central Asia and the Indian subcontinent—we estimate nearly two hundred thousand barrels of crude oil and fifty million cubic feet of natural gas per day.

"TransCal has responded to the insurgents by paying them what amounts to 'protection' money," Luger went on. "We have located sizable numbers of Taliban forces, including Turkmen soldiers hired by the Taliban or by Turkmen defectors, at every pumping and control station east of the sixty-second-degree east longitude—over a hundred switches, pumping stations, check-valve stations, power stations, and control stations spread out across forty thousand square miles. We estimate that the numbers of Taliban troops are at least fifteen to eighteen thousand—over a third the size of the regular Turkmen army."

"So you're saying it'll be real tough to kill these Taliban, is that what you're telling me, General?" Thorn asked irritably.

"The problem isn't with killing them—the problem is what they'll do once they find out they're under attack," Dave Luger said. "Their forces are spread out over three hundred miles of pipeline. If Battalion A comes under attack, Battalion C a hundred miles away might have orders to blow up a pumping station or the pipeline itself."

"I don't need you to present me with problems, son. I need you to give me answers," Thorn said.

"The answer, sir: concentrate our forces on the most vital points in each section of the pipelines," Luger went on. "We've identified six of the most vital upstream points. We can verify our analysis with TransCal, but this is our best guess. Duty Officer, next slide." Six red triangles appeared on the map of Turkmenistan. "The most critical one is in Chärjew. It controls pipelines running east-west along the Amu Darya River and north-south from Uzbekistan. If we can take control of these six points, but especially the main control center in Chärjew, the insurgents can blow up almost every foot of the rest of the pipelines, and there won't be a major spill. The second most important control center is in Bayramaly, east of the city of Mary. This one controls oil flowing north-south to Pakistan through Afghanistan and also east-west."

"Let me guess—you have six teams standing by ready to go," Thorn said.

"Yes, sir," Luger said. He motioned to Hal Briggs. "Colonel?"

"Thank you, sir," Hal Briggs began, stepping forward. "Mr. President, Mr. Secretary, Miss Deputy Secretary, I'm Colonel Hal Briggs, commander of the Air Battle Force ground forces. The Air Battle Force concept puts together massive airpower with small, well-equipped, and highly mobile ground forces for its operations. We believe, and we can demonstrate, that this concept will be the primary way in which many conflicts are fought in the foreseeable future. The Air Battle Force concept emphasizes speed, precision striking power, and adaptability to a wide range of conflicts, from small-scale protective and defensive missions such as an embassy emergency, to antiterrorist operations, to military operations in urban terrain, to an all-out air, ground, naval, and space battle.

"In Turkmenistan we intend to field ten strike teams," Briggs said. "Six teams will take the petro-control stations that General Luger mentioned; two teams will be in charge of securing the airfield at Chärjew, which will become our base of operations; two teams will man the supply aircraft and roam across the battle area, augmenting other teams as necessary."

"Ten teams? Do you mean ten *battalions*? Ten brigades?" Defense Secretary Goff asked in surprise. "What do you intend to do? Insert the entire One Hundred and First Airborne Division into Turkmenistan?"

"No, sir. I intend to insert ten Battle Force teams—one hundred men and women," Hal Briggs replied.

"*One hundred?* Are you kidding me?" Thorn asked incredulously. "You intend to capture those positions with just one—" And then he saw Chris Wohl, in the Tin Man battle armor with the microhydraulic exoskeleton, step over to Hal Briggs, and he understood. Wohl had put on his helmet during the briefing, so the visitors were getting the absolute full effect of the Tin Man battle armor system. "You've got *one hundred* soldiers with that getup?"

"Not quite, sir," Briggs explained. "Each Battle Force team consists of five men with complete Tin Man battle-armor systems, plus three men with advanced combat-armor systems, or ACAS, and two conventionally equipped commandos. ACAS provides improved ballistic protection and the same communications and sensor capability—several steps up from standard-issue infantry units, but not as capable as the Tin Man system. Eventually all team members will have Tin Man systems, but we aren't ramped up to that level yet.

"The principal technologies behind the Air Battle Force teams is high-speed mobility, high-tech precision weapons, and advanced sensor capabilities," Briggs said. "The Tin Man systems are designed for mobility and hitting power, and we're relying on them to hold the positions with support from ACAS troops."

"It still seems pretty unlikely you can cover that entire pipe with one hundred guys, Colonel," Hershel observed.

"Ma'am, combined with the air-operations force, we can," Briggs said. "The Battle Force ground teams' assignment will be to break the grip of the Taliban on the six most vital control stations of the pipeline system, plus Chärjew Airport. The air-operations teams will be above us to take out any Taliban troop concentrations, but we need to be careful not to bomb too closely to the pipelines for fear of causing the very catastrophe we're trying to prevent."

"The air-operations force will initially consist of StealthHawk unmanned stealth combat air vehicles flying round-the-clock patrols over eastern Turkmenistan," David Luger said. "The StealthHawks are launched by EB-52 bombers, EB-1C bombers, and other support aircraft. The unmanned aircraft serve as both reconnaissance and defensive attack platforms to protect the ground forces. If necessary, the patrols will be augmented by manned EB-52 Megafortress and EB-1C Vampire bomber attacks on Turkmen air-defense locations, protected by AL-52 Dragon airborne-laser aircraft. Once we have control of the skies over eastern Turkmenistan, we can withdraw the manned aircraft."

"Sounds like you've got it all worked out," President Thorn said sourly. "But I know for damned sure that if it sounds too easy, there's always a catch." He turned to Patrick McLanahan and asked pointedly, "What's the catch here, General?"

"The catch, sir, is that the Air Battle Force's mission is to go in fast and hit hard—we're not set up to protect or hold territory," Patrick responded. "We can defend those positions only for so long. Eventually you need to send in Marines or regular-army units to take over until Turkmen forces get reorganized."

"If there's even a Turkmen government to command them," Acting Secretary of State Hershel added.

"Frankly, Miss Hershel, if the Turkmen government doesn't want to play, we shouldn't be in there risking American lives to defend them—or TransCal's oil," Thorn said. "TransCal can continue to pay protection money, or they can bug out, too. We go in with friendly forces solidly behind us or we don't go in at all."

"Roger that, sir," Patrick McLanahan agreed enthusiastically. "The Gurizev regime is staunchly pro-Russian."

"Yes, but who speaks for the Turkmen people?" Maureen Hershel asked. "You've mentioned a lot about TransCal and the Russians, but what about the people?"

"The people seem to be siding with the Taliban insurgents more and more," David Luger responded. "In general, the Taliban insurgents have treated the people of Turkmenistan and army conscripts with kindness and generosity, and at the same time they've shown how brutal they could be with the professional Turkmen soldiers and the Russians."

"Sounds like two different people calling the shots to me," Maureen Hershel said. "Maybe the Taliban leader is the brutal one and the military guy knows better than to alienate the people while occupying their land."

"I think you're right, Miss Hershel," Patrick said. "Sergeant Major Wohl interrogated one of the Taliban commanders on our last mission inside Turkmenistan, and his observations are in line with that."

"Oh? Mind filling us in, Sergeant Major?" Goff asked.

Chris Wohl removed his Tin Man helmet before he responded. "I spoke with a man who called himself Jalaluddin Turabi, sir. He said his commander's name is Wakil Mohammad Zarazi. We ran their names through intelligence files. Both men have been trained by foreign countries for military and terrorist operations, but Wakil Zarazi was identified and specially trained as a religious zealot. We don't know much more about them, except for this: When I interrogated Turabi, he described himself as a jihadi—a holy warrior. He mentioned Zarazi's rank—a general—but said he himself did not have any rank, although he was clearly the leader of the detachment we encountered. He seemed to indicate that Zarazi was on some kind of quest, some sort of mission—not a jihad, or at least not the same holy war that Turabi thought he was on."

"We consider this a fairly significant ideological break," Patrick said. "Taliban soldiers on a jihad are usually tasked with disrupting enemy lines of communication and obtaining money and supplies for their clans. This appears to be what Turabi's mission is. But Zarazi is obviously doing far more. If politicians like Gurizev and fighters like Turabi can be convinced to side with the West in exchange for a greater share in the oil profits and a greater voice in their government, maybe they can be convinced to accept U.S. military and financial assistance in setting up a representative government."

Now I understand why this guy is being considered as President Thomas Thorn's national security adviser, Maureen Hershel thought. That is exactly the kind of half-military, half-political strategic advice Thorn needs—but he rarely gets it because he's beleaguered with the minutiae of the kind of administration he designed. Thomas Thorn didn't believe in getting the United States involved with other countries' problems, so he had no one in his inner circle thinking or studying those problems and how it might benefit the United States to help.

"General McLanahan, you haven't told me anything that leads me to think we need to change our position on Central Asia," Thorn said. "I don't see that a military option is called for."

"We would suggest other options: either support Gurizev's government, the one that signed the deals with TransCal Petroleum, or replace it," Patrick McLanahan suggested.

"Replace it with what?" Hershel asked. "Gurizev is little more than a dictator."

"Why not start with Jalaluddin Turabi?" Patrick replied.

"Turabi—you mean *support a Taliban insurgent as the new president of Turkmenistan?*" Robert Goff exclaimed. "We've spent several years and billions of dollars trying to eliminate the Taliban. Surely you can't expect us to support a Taliban terrorist to be president?"

"Based on the sergeant major's observations, I believe that Turabi is a senior officer in this Taliban army—maybe even the deputy commander," Patrick said. "It's possible he could be the real military brains behind this operation as well. If so, he embarked on this mission simply because he's obligated to follow his leader, Zarazi, in supporting their clan. Zarazi pushes them forward, but it's Turabi who actually accomplishes the missions. Zarazi kills with vengeance; Turabi is praised for his kindness, compassion, and generosity. Zarazi is a zealot, a wild ideological dog—he probably can't be bargained with. Turabi is the clearheaded one. If he's approachable and interested, we should try to make a deal with him."

Robert Goff shook his head and muttered something that sounded like "That's crazy," but Hershel nodded thoughtfully at McLanahan. "I think it's an interesting idea," she said. "I think it's worth a trip out to Turkmenistan to try to make contact with him."

"If I know President Martindale, he'll be on his way out there to do the same thing," Patrick observed. "He'll try to get Gurizev to crack down harder on the insurgents, but he'll also try to contact the insurgent leaders—first to bribe them into not blowing up the pipelines and then to feel them out as a possible replacement regime to Gurizev."

"Interesting idea," Thorn said acidly. "Did your buddy Kevin Martindale tell you that himself?" Patrick McLanahan's face turned grim. The activities of the former president of the United States were a very unpleasant topic between them all.

Three years earlier, following the successful development of the Tin Man battle-armor system by Sky Masters Inc., then-president Kevin Martindale sought to build the first Air Battle Force: small teams of high-tech commandos that could devastate the enemy with high-speed maneuverability and advanced weaponry, supported by stealth aircraft. It would be unnecessary to spend months mobilizing thousands of troops for overseas deployment when a force of a few dozen Tin Men could do the job just as well.

Kevin Martindale did not get reelected to the White House—but the Air Battle Force concept didn't die. Instead, as an ex-president, Martindale assembled the team code-named "the Night Stalkers"—former special-operations operators, led by Patrick's brother, Paul McLanahan, in the Tin Man battle-armor system. They acted as high-tech mercenary soldiers, pursuing the world's worst criminals and terrorists.

Their audacity and disregard for the rules of law made

them many enemies, including President Thomas Thorn and his advisers, but the organization was highly successful. Eventually Patrick's and his friends' public support for the organization embarrassed the White House to the extent that they were all involuntarily retired from active duty. Patrick, David, Hal, and Chris soon joined the Night Stalkers, and Sky Masters Inc., the private defense contractor run by Jon Masters, supported them as well. The group soon became the "firemen" in the world-crisis scene—they carried out the nasty, unpleasant search-and-destroy missions that most other nations, including Thomas Thorn and the United States, refused or were unable to tackle. This proved to be doubly embarrassing for men like Lester Busick, Edward Kercheval, and Robert Goff, who were members of Thorn's administration but who openly advocated more U.S. involvement in world hot spots.

But it was soon obvious that the Night Stalkers weren't going to survive. In order to finance their global operation, the Night Stalkers often had to steal from their victims. Patrick McLanahan himself tortured, then threatened to kill one international terrorist, Pavel Kazakov, unless he was paid half a billion dollars. As pleased as the world community was to see killers like Kazakov in prison, the extortion tactics left a dark stain on the Night Stalkers' reputation.

The group later turned to mercenary work, being paid by wealthy corporations to spy on foreign governments and raid foreign military installations that threatened the company's interests. That turned out to be the last straw. Now every government was afraid of being hit by the Night Stalkers. The group wasn't fighting for justice or retribution anymore—they were fighting for money. The U.S. government cracked down on them, arresting several associates and closing down Sky Masters Inc. for a short time. Martindale disbanded the team shortly thereafter. McLanahan, Luger, Briggs, and Wohl were allowed to return to active military duty.

"He did not, sir—but I'm sure he would have," Patrick said now in answer to the president's question.

"How the hell can you give that bastard any credit at all, General?" Thorn asked. "You lost your wife and your brother in Libya, thanks to that son of a bitch Martindale." Maureen Hershel stared at Thorn, then McLanahan, in total shock. Obviously she hadn't heard the stories yet.

"Sir, I give President Martindale credit for the courage to act," Patrick said. "We did what we thought was right. We had the power to do something, and we did it. We didn't wait around for some government to do it for us."

"Fine. You made the deserts of Libya and Egypt safe for multinational oil companies to make tremendous profits off blood oil," Thorn said. "Was it worth the lives of your family, General?"

"You said you're here for your own edification, Mr. President," Patrick said. "If you won't get involved in Turkmenistan, why bother coming here and getting this briefing? Is it disrespectful, wrong, or even treasonous to plan and prepare for action even if your boss, the so-called leader of the free world, doesn't want to get involved?"

"You're talking about your commander in chief, General," Robert Goff said pointedly. He couldn't get too angry with McLanahan—he mostly agreed with him, after all—but he couldn't let him get away with talking so freely either. "Let's get off this subject, shall we?"

Thorn gave Patrick a stern glare but let the matter drop.

"CIA just briefed the White House that they think Russia might be a player again in Turkmenistan," Goff informed them. "Kurban Gurizev is staunchly pro-Russian, anti-West, and anti-Muslim. CIA feels that if the insurgents threaten the oil coming out of Turkmenistan, the

Russian army could intervene—in fact, their intervention would be *welcomed* by Gurizev as a way to cement his hold on the government."

"And if the Taliban insurgents continue to beat down the Turkmen army—what little remains of it—it would almost certainly draw Russia into the conflict," Patrick said. He thought for a moment. "Russia has a couple fighter wings, weapon ranges, and a large air-combat-training facility at Mary in Turkmenistan. It's equivalent to the Navy's Strike and Air Warfare Center at Naval Air Station Fallon or the Air Force's Air Warfare Center at Nellis Air Force Base. Elements of Russia's Caspian Sea Flotilla are still based in Turkmenistan, including a marine infantry brigade and special-operations battalion, and Russian officers still serve in many Turkmen military units as contract workers."

"But we're told the Russian military has completely departed Turkmenistan, and there is virtually no integration between the Turkmen and Russian armies," Goff said. "What's the threat, Patrick?"

"It's a perceived threat, sir, not a real one," Patrick replied. "Turkmenistan was an important Soviet republic, and it still is a major source of cheap oil that Russia relies on for its own use and for export. If Turkmenistan were lost to a bunch of Muslim extremist insurgents, with Russian officers in charge of the military and with Russian military forces still on the ground there, it would be a major embarrassment for Russia."

Both Thorn and Goff fell silent, deep in thought.

"Interesting analysis, gentlemen," President Thorn said at last. "Your observations seem to dovetail very well with CIA's." He turned to Hershel and added, "A diplomatic mission to Turkmenistan might be in order right away." He nodded to Luger, Briggs, and Wohl. "Thank you, gentlemen. I'd like to speak with General McLanahan for a few moments." He shook hands with each one of them, even Chris Wohl's armored hand, as they departed.

Thorn, Hershel, and Goff conferred with one another apart from the military personnel; Patrick walked the others to the door so he could stay respectfully out of earshot. "What do you think's going on, Muck?" Dave Luger asked.

"I think we watered their eyes," Patrick replied, "and we're going to be very busy in the next several weeks. I want a staff meeting set up for thirteen hundred hours. Let's talk about what we have and what we don't have."

"You got it."

"General McLanahan," Secretary Goff called out. Patrick, Rebecca, and then John Long joined Thorn, Hershel, and Goff. "We thank you very much for the tour, General," he said. "We're on our way."

"Yes, sir. I'll see to it that your aircraft is brought up to the surface and made ready right away."

"General Furness," President Thorn asked, "what is your opinion of General McLanahan's program here?"

"My opinion, sir?"

"What do you *think,* General?" Thorn asked pointedly. "Do you think he has something there, or do you think he was too far out in left field to come up with anything practical?"

Rebecca looked uncomfortable for a moment, then replied, "Sir, General McLanahan has always been an unconventional thinker. Ever since he first set foot on my base in Reno, he baffles, irritates, and frustrates me with the ideas he comes up with and the gadgets he devises to get the job done. I call it unconventional; some might call it innovative. I don't know how he does it, but he gets the job done."

"Damning with faint praise?" Goff remarked. "I'm not following you, General. Is this whole idea something that needs to be explored further, or do you just want to get your base and wing and planes back and put together your unit the way you see fit?"

"Sir, I don't quite know what to make of this unmanned-attack-plane idea," she replied. "I've been training and leading aircrews into battle for twelve years. In my estimation a human being behind the controls will always be better than a machine. Had we not been at the controls of that EB-1, I feel fairly certain—not positive, but fairly certain—that we could have lost a two-hundred-million-dollar plane."

She paused for a moment, then added, "And yes, I'll admit, I was very aware of the fact that it was *my* plane, one of only a few that belonged to *my* wing. This is my first wing-level command, something I've always wanted, and, frankly, I don't relish sharing the spotlight with Patrick McLanahan. General McLanahan has an annoying habit of smelling like he came out of a French whorehouse even after emerging out of absolute train wrecks. Pardon me, sir, but what I meant to say is—"

"We know what you mean, General. We've been there," Thorn said with a faint smile.

"At one point in our nation's history, sir, they said a woman didn't have what was needed to take a warplane into combat," Rebecca went on. "They said women were too nurturing, not strong enough, not aggressive enough, too overcome by emotions and feelings and too ingrained as the ones who give birth and build nests to make effective destroyers. I'm happy to say we proved them wrong."

"So what *are* you saying, General?"

"I'm saying that General McLanahan's project needs more study and more experimentation," she replied. "One test flight is not enough to prove his theories either way. And . . . and it only makes sense to use my wing's aircraft, facilities, and budget to continue the experiments. General McLanahan and General Luger have been working with my wing's aircraft for years. We're still in the process of developing an EB-1C Vampire training program for instructors. We're at least six months from finalizing a curriculum and training students. Our aircraft and facilities are underutilized."

"So what are you recommending?" Goff asked.

"I'm recommending that my unit's budget be recast and our mission redefined to make General McLanahan's Air Battle Force concept operational as soon as possible," Rebecca said. "If it works, we may never need to send an American into harm's way again. The fliers I know consider it their *duty* to fly into harm's way, and as long as they know and understand the mission and the objective, they'll do it time after time. But that's my old-school opinion. If the future of air combat means remotely piloted planes and satellite-guided, unmanned, bomb-carrying drones, then I'd be proud to have my wing lead the way."

Robert Goff nodded in agreement—but Thomas Thorn looked at first confused, then angry.

"Listen, I'm sure I'm not getting the whole story here," he said, "but I've seen what I came here to see. I'm still going to do an investigation on whether or not you misappropriated any funds, General McLanahan, or whether your use of private experimental aircraft puts the government at risk." He looked at all three of them, then added, "I do like the analysis you did regarding Central Asia, and I think you might have some weapon systems here that can be of use if this incident starts to get serious. Secretary Goff, you handle this affair as you see fit."

"Very good, sir."

Thorn nodded, then looked the three military officers in the eye. "Maybe you kids aren't as dishonest, backstabbing, treacherous, and confused as I was led to believe." And then he paused, looked right at John Long, and stared at him long enough for everyone to fully understand exactly who it was that had led him to believe those things. Long squirmed, but there was nowhere to hide.

"I don't know what to make of all this, but I can tell you one thing: I don't like sidewinders. I like my fights out in the open. That'll be all, Colonel." Long saluted; Thorn did not return the salute. "Right now I pretty much feel like a damned gopher. Someone show me the fastest way to some sunshine." David Luger and the head of the Presidential Protection Detail motioned toward the waiting electric cars. "Robert, Maureen, a word with you, please."

Rebecca Furness went over to Patrick when Goff, Hershel, and the president stepped away to confer among themselves. "You know, I can't figure you out sometimes, McLanahan," she said.

"What do you mean?"

"Why didn't you tell them what you think, Patrick?" she asked. "I know you don't think the plane was in danger. I know for *damned* sure you don't think there was a boom strike. In fact, none of the maintenance guys, at Diego Garcia or here, found any evidence of a boom strike."

"It doesn't matter what I'd tell them."

"Doesn't matter? You know as well as I do that if you told them, they might give you another chance to test your virtual-cockpit stuff. . . ."

"Rebecca, they would expect me to say exactly that. They would expect me to support my program no matter what happened or what my staff report read," Patrick said. "But I can't ignore my senior officers. I may not agree with your observations, Rebecca, but I'm not going to tell the National Command Authority that you're wrong and I'm right, just because I'm wearing two stars. I have more respect for you and your years of experience than that. If you say the test was not successful and the only argument I have is 'I disagree,' I'm not going to push a bad position. We live to fight another day."

The president stepped on board the electric car after a few moments, while Robert Goff and Maureen Hershel went back over to Patrick. "The president is leaving it up to me," Goff said. "I want this unit made mission-ready as soon as possible. How soon can you have your mission statement, timetable, and budget built, General?"

"We can have it sent to the chairman's office in two days," Patrick said.

"Make it one day, Patrick, and I'll sit down with General Venti and get it moving," Goff said. "And I want to see your detailed plan for Turkmenistan, should the president decide to intervene. I'm not promising you any more money or very much support, but any plan that doesn't involve sending in a lot of troops or equipment while still getting the job done will definitely merit the president's attention."

"I'll transmit General Luger's report to your office immediately, sir."

"Your damned report frankly scared the shit out of us, General," Goff added. "The CIA pussyfooted on their report, of course. They either won't commit to any conclusions or put every possible conclusion, no matter how unlikely, in their summaries. You folks came up with clear observations, logical conclusions, a direct plan of action, realistic problem scenarios, and even some political directions to pursue as we head down the military track. I like that.

"And I believe that the president admired your candor and honesty with each other," Goff went on. "You two definitely have a history together, and most of it has not been pleasant. You're both chasing different and most times opposing objectives, but you eventually realize the need to work together so you can achieve them. You haven't killed each other, so that must mean you have some respect for one another. It's like mixing hydrogen and oxygen: If you do it wrong, it blows up in your face, and if you do it right, you get life-sustaining water. Just when we think putting you two together is going to blow up in everyone's faces, you come together and make something happen." He shook his head and said, "Shit, this mole hole of yours is starting to affect my brain, McLanahan. I'm starting to sound like Mark Twain's stupid brother. Let's get the hell out of this bat cave, Maureen, and let these kids get back to work."

The last to depart was Maureen Hershel. She shook hands with Patrick McLanahan. "I don't understand everything about your aircraft and the weapons you have here, General," she said, "but I'm fascinated with the electronic-armor technology. The power at your disposal with such a system appears immense. One man equals a dozen soldiers—and then some."

"That's the idea. Use technology as force multipliers," Patrick said. "There's no need to bring a huge security force when one properly equipped man can do the job."

"Very interesting," she said. "I might be calling on you for help someday."

"We're ready to help any way we can."

"And"—she looked into his eyes as if uncertain, then went on—"and I don't want to pry. . . ."

"It's all right," Patrick said. "Ask me anything, Miss Deputy Secretary."

"Please don't call me that. I'm Maureen to you," she said.

"Thank you . . . Maureen." And for the first time since she met him, McLanahan smiled. It was still a tired, war-weary smile, but it seemed to change the mood of the underground facility as dramatically and as surely as if a giant hand had ripped the place open and let sunshine come streaming in.

"I don't know what happened with you and your family

and President Martindale," Hershel went on. "I've heard the rumors about some of the former president's activities since leaving office, but I assumed they were just rumors. I would like to extend my sympathy to you, even if I don't quite know all the circumstances. If you could someday explain it to me, I'd like to hear what happened. *Your* version of it."

"It's not something I'd care to relate, ma'am—"

"Maureen. Please."

"Maureen, it's not a story I'd care to tell. But if it would help explain what we do and how we intend to use the Air Battle Force in future conflicts . . . then, yes, I could tell you what happened."

"Thank you, General," she said, touching his arm. "Believe me, it's not idle curiosity. If you don't feel comfortable talking about it, you shouldn't say anything at all."

"Thank you, Maureen," Patrick said. "I'll make myself available to tell you everything—soon."

"Thank you again." She paused, then added, "And I suppose I can expect the confirmation hearings to start soon on your nomination as President Thorn's first national security adviser?"

"I haven't been asked, and I doubt if I ever will," Patrick said.

"Your name is still being bandied about on Capitol Hill. I think you'd find a surprising number in Congress ready to support you. President Thorn will never be seen as anyone with a strong military-affairs mind-set, despite his military background. On the other hand, you have a very impressive—and enticingly mysterious—one. Don't count yourself out too soon."

"I'm not counting myself in or out at all, Miss Hershel. I've got too big a job here."

"Yes, you do," she agreed. "I'll be watching for you in Washington, though. Good luck, General."

THE FAIRMONT HOTEL, SAN FRANCISCO, CALIFORNIA
Days later

So it's true, Kevin Martindale remarked silently to himself as he entered the luxurious hotel suite. There's been a shake-up. Kercheval's gone.

Maureen Hershel got to her feet, put on her best smile, and extended her hand long before she reached her visitor. "President Martindale, welcome," she said. "I'm Maureen Hershel. I apologize that Secretary Kercheval couldn't be here, but he asked his staff to brief you and for me to answer any questions you had personally."

"Thank you."

Kevin Martindale had a chance to look the woman over as she crossed the opulent Sherwood Suite to greet him. Wearing a conservative but expensively cut suit tailored just above the knee, a silky beige low-cut blouse underneath, and Italian shoes, she looked like a junior partner in a wealthy law firm instead of a State Department official. Her handshake was firm but brief.

"I'm sure I'm in good hands, Miss Hershel. How are you today?"

"Fine, thank you," she said in a friendly and only slightly officious tone. "Please have a seat. I'm told you wanted to forgo the usual meet-and-greet photos."

"I hope you don't mind," Martindale said, in a tone that obviously indicated he didn't much care if she minded or not.

"Not at all." She paused for a heartbeat, then asked, "But would you mind telling me why, Mr. President?"

The question took him aback for a moment, but he looked her straight in the eye and replied, "Frankly, I don't expect you to give me any of the answers I'm looking for. And since this is otherwise not a social visit, I thought it best to skip the usual smiling faces and glad-handing pretexts."

"I see." Now it was her turn to look Kevin Martindale over. The young former president of the United States had been a force on the American political scene for many years. He was portrayed as everything President Thomas Thorn was not: brash, headstrong, opinionated, hard-charging, and forceful. It was almost as if the American people, anxious and maybe even fearful of the future emerging because of Thorn's laissez-faire attitude toward foreign affairs, were wistfully thinking back to the respect and power as portrayed by the government during the Martindale administration.

But only recently had he become a celebrity personality as well. It helped that Kevin Martindale was young, hand-some, wealthy, single, and had at one time been one of the most powerful men on earth. His well-publicized divorce while vice president, and his steady stream of starlet girl-friends during his single term as chief executive, only served to keep him in the public eye. But now that he was back in the political hunt, his name and face appeared in all sorts of media outlets these days, not just the super-market tabloids.

Maureen gave Martindale his choice of seats in the sit-ting area of the suite—even the armchair opposite hers, as her equal—but instead he chose the far side of the long sofa. She dismissed the official State Department photog-rapher with a polite nod, then, playing the hostess, ges-tured at a nearby serving cart. "Coffee? Tea?"

"No, thank you."

"Coffee for me," she said, then sat down in the plush armchair at the head of the sitting area in front of the fire-place. She crossed her legs, held the cup in both hands, and took a sip as her guest made himself comfortable.

Martindale reached into a jacket pocket and withdrew a

Davidoff Double R Churchill. "Do you mind, Miss Deputy Secretary? I know there's no smoking in the Fairmont these days, but I also know that Mr. Kercheval enjoys a good cigar, so I brought mine and a few for him."

"Not at all," she said, quickly and neutrally.

He clipped his cigar, then, as an afterthought, reached into his pocket and withdrew another. "Do you indulge, Miss Deputy Secretary?"

"No," she said coolly.

He chuckled with a distinct air of superiority. "Thought I'd better ask. Equality for women should extend to things like fine cigars, should it not?"

"It has nothing to do with equality—just taste," she responded.

He shrugged, uncertain of what she meant by that, and put the second cigar back in his pocket. He withdrew a silver lighter and was about to touch the flame to his cigar when he stopped in surprise—as Hershel pulled her own cigar from her inside breast pocket.

"But it's not because I don't like cigars. I just don't like *those* cigars. I prefer Lars Tetens to Davidoffs." She pulled her own clippers and lighter from her pocket. "The Tesshu Deluxe Robusto is my favorite. Made in New York. I was introduced to them by a German vice air marshal. You'd have thought he'd discovered the New World by how much he raved about them. They take some getting used to, but they *are* worth the effort." The pungent aroma of the Lars Teten quickly, easily overpowered the Davidoff. Martindale couldn't help but look on in amazement as the woman puffed away happily on the rich, strong cigar.

"I hope you're having a pleasant trip out here to the West Coast, Miss Hershel."

"Fine, thank you, Mr. President."

"Kevin. Please. Thorn is 'Mr. President' now."

"Thank you, Kevin. And I'm Maureen."

Martindale nodded. "I thank you for meeting with me."

"Not at all." She eased back in her chair, then surprised him again by casually throwing the elbow of her left arm onto the chair back and propping her head on her left thumb, with the cigar between the forefinger and middle finger of the same hand.

"I wanted to discuss a very important matter confronting the United States, Maureen."

"The situation in Turkmenistan."

"Exactly," he said. "You know, of course, about the invasion by those Taliban fighters."

"Yes." She turned away from him to take another deep draw from the cigar, and she did not look back at him as she released the smoke from her lips. "The fighters seem to be growing in strength and taking new territory almost at will. I'd say the situation is extremely fluid."

"'Fluid'? Miss Hershel, the situation is critical out there!" Martindale retorted. "The Taliban insurgents now control three-quarters of the American-built oil and gas pipelines in Turkmenistan!"

"They control three-quarters of the pipelines in the eastern half of the country, approximately eight thousand linear miles, plus eight distribution facilities, sixteen pumping facilities, and two power-production facilities," Hershel said, still looking away from Martindale, reeling off the information as if she were reading it in the clouds of cigar smoke swirling around her head. "They control all of product distribution to Uzbekistan and Pakistan and about half of the distribution to Iran, Afghanistan, and Kazakhstan."

"It's a serious development, Maureen." Martindale slapped his Davidoff into an ashtray on the table next to him with an angry jab; he couldn't taste it anyway over the overpowering scent of the Lars Teten. "Many folks around the world consider this conflict to be President Thorn's first major foreign emergency test, one that directly affects American business interests. I'm impressed that you have such a command of the data, Maureen, but what I'd like to know is, what exactly does the president intend to do about it?"

Hershel finally turned toward her guest, undocking her head from her thumb but staying back in her chair. "The president has made his views clear, Mr. Martindale," she said. "The Turkmen government hasn't asked the United States for help." Martindale was about to speak, but Hershel quickly said, "We know about the Taliban and their moves on the oil and hydroelectric facilities. Even so, the president does not feel that this insurgency is a threat to any vital national interests—"

"Not a threat!" Martindale retorted. "If this doesn't qualify as a threat, I'm not sure what would."

"The insurgents haven't taken anything," Hershel said calmly. "TransCal is paying the leader of that Taliban group to leave the pipelines alone and functioning—protection money—and that's exactly what they're doing. Product is flowing; TransCal is still making money. In fact, with the current spike in oil prices with no corresponding decrease in production, I would say TransCal is enjoying some substantial windfall profits. Their stock has gone up by seventeen percent in the past month, if I'm not mistaken—although why their dividend predictions have gone down so drastically is still a mystery. Less than a dollar a share in dividends from a company making record profits and hasn't paid below a dollar a share in almost ten years?"

"I would guess that they're preserving capital to keep their business afloat if those pipelines are destroyed."

Maureen said nothing, just studied Martindale over her cigar and nodded noncommittally, wondering if he'd gotten that information directly from the horse's mouth.

TransCal may have already spoken to Martindale about supporting his run for the presidency in exchange for his promising more protection for their overseas ventures.

"The point, Maureen, is that our government should be doing more to protect the interests of Americans overseas, including business interests," Martindale said. "We shouldn't have to pay 'protection money'—we should be doing whatever is necessary to ensure that foreign governments and businesses live up to their contracts and promises."

"Mr. Martindale," Hershel said, letting the pungent smoke stream out of her mouth slowly and seductively, "the president feels, and I agree, that if we tried to enter this conflict with military might, the insurgents would destroy the pipelines, just as the Iraqis did as they were forced to withdraw from Kuwait." She put down the cigar after taking another long draw. "But in any case, even if the United States *was* able to wipe out all the insurgents without causing any damage to the pipelines, what then? The Turkmen government is obviously not strong enough to protect the pipelines. If another group of Taliban came in, we'd be faced with the same dilemma. Do you suggest the United States set up a permanent presence in Turkmenistan to protect the pipelines?"

"If that's what it takes, *yes!*"

"Mr. President . . . Kevin, you should realize that's not possible," Hershel said calmly. The more wound up Martindale got, the calmer and more introspective Maureen made herself. "The United States is not in the business of providing mercenary services for the benefit of private companies."

"No one is asking the United States to supply mercenaries," Martindale argued. "The United States should use its military power and influence to restrain other outside powers from disrupting the business of the legitimate government. We had a *deal* with President Niyazov. TransCal spent almost eight billion dollars to build those pipelines and infrastructure—"

"Kurban Gurizev is in power now."

"Gurizev is a Russian stooge," Martindale said acidly. "He was against the TransCal deal right from the start. He wants to increase his own wealth and prestige by getting the Russians back into Turkmenistan so they'll back him as president. Then TransCal will be forced to renegotiate the contract with the Turkmen government."

"That sounds very likely," Hershel said matter-of-factly.

Martindale stared wide-eyed at the deputy secretary of state. "I'm glad you find favor in my analysis," he said sarcastically. "Does that sound fair to you, Maureen?"

"From TransCal's point of view, I shouldn't think so," she replied. "From Gurizev's perspective it sounds like a perfectly reasonable and rational idea." She could see Martindale getting angrier by the second. "Kevin, I'm sure TransCal knew what they were getting into when they made this deal. I'm sure they knew that Turkmenistan was and still is a virtual dictatorship. TransCal knew about Gurizev and all his close ties to the Russian government, they knew that the Russians still extracted huge amounts of oil and gas from the country, and they knew that the Russian army still had a large presence there. They knew the risk—as did your government, sir. Yet you met with President Niyazov and brokered this deal for TransCal."

Hershel's staff had definitely done their homework before this meeting. He wondered if Maureen Hershel had even touched cigars until this meeting was set up.

"Why isn't the CIA keeping you better informed on what's happening out there?" he asked, hoping to change the subject quickly.

"We have assets everywhere, as you know," Hershel said, "but we can't see everything. However, I'm sure

TransCal was briefed and fully understood the risks when they signed the deal with President Niyazov."

"Frankly, Maureen, we were able to sign a deal back then because my government made it very clear that it would enforce the law, no matter where in the world it was violated," Martindale said acidly. "If Thorn showed even a fraction of the backbone my government had, we probably wouldn't be in this mess."

"I can't comment on that."

"Well, I can, and that's how I see it." Martindale paused for a moment, then sat back, picked up his cigar and puffed it to life again. "Tell me, Miss Hershel," he asked, "what happened to Secretary Kercheval?"

"Nothing has happened to Secretary Kercheval," she replied.

"There's a rumor around that he's taking medication for Parkinson's disease."

"He was given a completely clean bill of health in his last physical. He hasn't told us a thing about Parkinson's."

"There's also a rumor that he's extremely displeased with President Thorn's overall handling of foreign affairs and that he may retire rather than continue to serve in this administration."

"I've heard nothing of the kind."

"There seem to be an awful lot of ugly rumors circulating around all of a sudden, Miss Hershel—and they correspond closely to your frequent appearances at the White House recently. How do all these rumors get started, Maureen?"

"You should know, Kevin." She shifted slightly, an amused glimmer in her eyes. "You talked about it on *Crossfire* last week, remember?"

"Will Secretary of State Kercheval resign over the Turkmenistan issue?"

She retrieved her cigar and sat back in her seat, her eyes

riveted on his. She knew he was trying to interrogate her, and she sent up a cloud of cigar smoke as a screen in front of her. "No," she replied.

"Are you being considered to replace Kercheval, like it says in the press?"

"I've been asked to spearhead a State Department position paper on Central Asian affairs for Secretary of State Kercheval," Hershel replied. "I retain my position as deputy secretary of state. Mr. Kercheval is still in charge of the State Department, a valuable member of the administration, and a trusted adviser and friend of the president. That's all."

"Sounds like a carefully scripted talking point—as if you were preparing for the Sunday talk shows," Martindale said.

Hershel said nothing, only stared at him through the cloud of pungent smoke.

"You have been with the State Department for seven years, but the FBI Counterintelligence Operations Office for twelve. Why did you leave that office?"

"Counterintelligence—like the military, I believe— serves diplomacy," Maureen replied. "I preferred to be on the policy side of diplomacy rather than on the operations side."

"But you were a good spy-catcher, Maureen—one of the best, according to my sources," Martindale said.

She did not respond—except with her eyes. Those very blue eyes suddenly adopted what soldiers called the "thousand-yard stare," as if she were reliving some event triggered by his question, watching the replay as if it were being projected onto the back of Martindale's skull and she was looking right through him at it. The cloud of Lars Teten smoke only served to heighten the sense of mystery and danger.

"You miss it, don't you, Maureen?" Martindale asked in a low, almost seductive voice.

Again she did not reply—but he could see his response in her eyes.

"Maureen," he went on, "what sorts of efforts has the president directed the State Department to pursue on the diplomatic front in regard to Turkmenistan?"

"My study is one response," Maureen said. "But the president usually doesn't direct anyone to do anything. He tells the cabinet what he will support and what he expects, and they go forth and do the job."

"The chief of staff doesn't coordinate efforts between the cabinet members . . . ?"

"The vice president acts as chief of staff, and, yes, he does have meetings and coordinates activity via e-mail, but the cabinet officers call the shots and then report directly to the president."

"I'm curious, Maureen: How does the cabinet know if what they're doing is what the president wants done?"

"It's not that kind of organization, Kevin. The president just lets the cabinet members do their jobs. They listen to the president, he tells them what he's thinking, and . . . they leave and go back to their offices and do what they think needs to be done."

"How does that system work for you?"

"I'm new at this, but it seems to work just fine, every day."

"It doesn't seem to be working fine now, does it?" Martindale commented. "And it didn't work in Egypt, or Libya, or Kosovo, or Russia. It seems like Thorn's foreign policy is a hopeless mess."

"That's not an accurate characterization at all."

"So I'll rephrase my question, Maureen: What are *you* doing about the Turkmen situation?"

"I'm in daily contact with the foreign minister from Turkmenistan and delegates from the United Nations," she replied. "We are also in contact with representatives of all the other parties involved, including the Taliban, who are represented by the Saudi Arabian embassy."

"And?"

"And we're trying to get an official sense of exactly what the different factions have in mind before we issue a policy statement to the American people," Hershel replied. "The president believes in carefully studying a situation; getting official, nonofficial, and intelligence information; and reaching a consensus with his advisers before making a decision."

"Sounds like a fancy way of saying Thorn's not sure what he wants to do and he's stalling for time."

"Again I disagree with your characterization." She paused, then asked, "If I may ask, sir, what's *your* opinion regarding this matter?"

"I believe the United States is the greatest nation on earth and the protector of liberty, freedom, justice, and democracy for the rest of the world," Martindale said. "I also believe in concepts as simple as 'a deal's a deal.' If Gurizev thinks he can hand over control of eight billion dollars of *American* pipe and petroleum infrastructure to the Russians, or if these Taliban insurgents think they can disguise their invasion of Turkmenistan as a fight for freedom and take *American* pipelines, they're *seriously* mistaken."

"First of all, Kevin, the Americans don't own those pipelines—the people of Turkmenistan own them," Hershel said. She held up a folder that had been sitting on the table beside her. "TransCal takes forty percent of all the income they earn from crude, refined products, flowage, duties, transshipment, storage, and even futures, for the next fifty years, in exchange for the cost of building and maintaining that system. A pretty sweet deal. According to the IRS, they've already recouped half their investment in Turkmenistan's oil industry in just three years, and by the looks of it they'll move into the black in less than two years."

"And I'd like to make sure they have a chance to make it there," Martindale said.

"With the help of the U.S. military," Hershel said.

"Like you said, Maureen, the military is an important extension of foreign policy."

"May I ask you, Kevin, if the CEO of TransCal Petroleum, William Hitchcock, has decided to spearhead your reelection campaign?"

"Bill Hitchcock and I are old friends. He's a successful businessman and strategist, and he's supported me and the party for years," Martindale said. "If he offered, I would consider myself lucky to have him in my corner, in a variety of capacities. But I'm not here discussing Turkmenistan because TransCal's pipelines are in great jeopardy—although they *are*. I'm here because intervening on their behalf is the *right* thing to do. The military is supposed to protect the American people."

"The people, yes—not their bank accounts."

Martindale just stared at Maureen without commenting.

"Speaking for myself, Kevin, I don't see that many differences between my opinion of President Thorn and your position. President Thorn wants justice and freedom, too, but he doesn't believe in using the military in every conflict, especially overseas. What do you think you'd be doing right now?"

"I certainly can't speculate on that, because I don't have access to the information you have." He saw Hershel smile. It was well known that Martindale kept himself actively involved in foreign affairs, even to the point of supporting a quasi-mercenary group known as the Night Stalkers to perform clandestine paramilitary operations all over the world. "But I think I'd be taking a much more active leadership role—conferring closely with allies, sending high-ranking officials to Turkmenistan to talk face-to-face with those involved, and speaking more openly and forcefully on the subject to the American people at every opportunity. I think President Thorn has his work cut out for himself just *winning back* some allies. He's done practically everything possible to destroy our alliance structure."

"So you think I should be on the plane right now to Turkmenistan?"

"I think if President Thorn cared at all about American business and American prestige overseas, not to mention the faith and trust the American people have in him and his government, he should have put you on a plane to Turkmenistan last month."

Hershel nodded, then turned and called, "Isadora?"

A moment later a tall, dark-haired woman appeared, dressed in a business outfit every bit as nice as Maureen's. Martindale leaped to his feet as if propelled by a hydraulic lift—he couldn't take his eyes off the woman.

"Mr. Martindale, may I present Assistant Deputy Secretary of State Isadora Meiling. Izzy, this is Kevin H. Martindale." He aimed his *People* magazine smile at her, drinking in her deep, dark eyes. "Let's get authorization and clearance for that SAM flight to Ashkhabad, Turkmenistan, right away."

"Yes, ma'am." She favored Martindale with a mind-blowing smile and hurried off.

As mesmerized as Martindale was, his attention was drawn away by the shock of Hershel's order. "You . . . you're going to Turkmenistan? *Now?*"

"Right now."

"What about your preparation? Don't you have security arrangements to make, briefings to organize, meetings to set up with foreign office officials, communiqués to the embassies, coordination of agreements and position papers . . . ?"

"The planning for this trip was already in the works," Hershel said. "I'm sure we'll overnight in Washington, maybe meet with the director of Central Intelligence and get the latest situation reports. That'll give the staff a day or two to organize. But it's a long flight to Turkmenistan. I imagine we'll be busy the entire way."

"What about your appearances scheduled for the West Coast?"

"I think this is much more important, don't you?" Hershel asked sincerely, watching Martindale carefully.

Martindale did not—*could* not—answer. He would never pass up any large political rallies or appearances, especially with major West Coast media involved, in favor of going to a shithole like Turkmenistan with virtually no press and the possibility of considerable personal danger involved. But if he said it wasn't important, he would be contradicting himself.

He didn't need to answer. Maureen Hershel could see the dilemma in his face. Instead of replying, he asked, "How do you know the Turkmen government will even allow you into the country?"

"You're right. They might not like a State Department official poking her nose into their backroom dealing." She looked over at Martindale. "But there's one way to entice them to agree to see us."

"What's that? Offer them financial assistance?"

"Even better than that—I should bring *you* along. Would you like to accompany us, Kevin?"

"*Me?* Go to Turkmenistan with you? Now?"

"I'm going to make the last scheduled appearance here in San Francisco, but right after that we'll be off," Hershel said. "I figure in about three hours. What do you say?" Martindale hesitated. "I'm sure Miss Meiling will be busy, but I think she'd enjoy your company."

He could think of a dozen things he had on his schedule that couldn't be missed, and with no prep and no real agenda, the trip would likely be a total flop. There wasn't even a guarantee that Hershel would be allowed to meet with any of the principals involved. But the opportunity to get a glimpse of the inner workings of Thorn's foreign-policy team in action couldn't be missed either. And, naturally, the happy thought of spending some time with Isadora Meiling sealed the deal. "Of course, Miss Deputy Secretary. I'd be happy to accompany you."

"Good. I'll tell her you'll be accompanying us. I'm sure she'll be thrilled."

"I do have one question," Martindale said.

"Fire away."

"What are your rules about disclosing conversations discussed during the trip?"

"You mean are we going to allow you to talk to the press about what you see and hear on this trip?"

Martindale said nothing, but Hershel knew his silence meant yes.

"President Thorn believes in completely open and honest disclosure with all American citizens, even potential political adversaries. We may exclude you from some discussions, but if you see or hear anything, you're free to discuss it or mention it to anyone you choose."

"Thank you. I appreciate the president's position." *I would never allow the same,* he thought, *but if Thorn wanted to deal his cards faceup like this, all the better.* "At the same time I assume that the president will make as much political hay as he can about my participation in this trip."

"I suppose it's possible—to the extent that the president makes any political hay at all," Hershel said. "But who knows? Maybe you'll see something in this administration that appeals to you, and we can convince you to support the president's reelection campaign?"

"If the president wanted my help, he could have asked me."

"The president doesn't often ask for help, especially from those he considers political rivals," Hershel said. "Perhaps he was wrong in this case?"

"It sounds as if *you're* heading up Thorn's reelection campaign, Maureen."

"If the president asked me to do so, I'd be honored." Hershel smiled and nodded. "Very good. I'll leave you to head back and get ready for the trip. A car will pick you up." She shook hands with him. "I think this will be an educational journey for both of us."

He shook her hand and then, as they were heading for the door of her hotel suite, asked, "Miss Hershel, Turkmenistan is a . . . rather dangerous place right now. Do you think it's wise to be going there at this time?"

"I suppose if we go and we come back safe, folks will say it was a successful and worthwhile trip—and if we get hurt or killed, they'll say it was a stupid move," she replied. She shrugged. "I can't really answer that question, Kevin. I know we have work to do out there, and I think at this stage in the game, a personal visit is warranted. I guess we can't always go on diplomatic missions like this only when it's safe, can we?" She shook his hand again. "It'll be fine, Kevin. I'll see you on the plane." She hurried off, leaving him alone in stunned silence.

What in hell did I just get myself into? he thought grimly.

"Pompous ass," Maureen Hershel said to Isadora Meiling as she returned to her makeshift office in an adjacent room. "Still, I have to give the bastard credit. He agreed to go on the trip, even though he knows how dangerous it is."

"I'm wondering if *you* fully understand how dangerous it is, ma'am," Meiling said. She held up a red-covered folder marked CLASSIFIED. "Latest intelligence reports state that Russian transports are arriving in the capital, offloading a lot of Russian officers and communications equipment. CIA speculates the Russians are putting together a wartime command infrastructure. And there's something about Iranian troops moving toward the borders, maybe preparing for some kind of military action."

"Izzy, I let myself get sucked into this. It's too late to back down now," Hershel said.

"You most certainly do have options—starting with canceling this trip. Deep down inside, Martindale will be breathing a sigh of relief if you cancel. Then *he* won't be putting his tight ass on the line."

"But then he'll be publicly slamming me for backing down in the face of the war threat and not doing enough to stabilize the situation," Hershel said. "I have to go."

"Please bring along some security," Meiling said. "At least a couple platoons of Marines, in addition to the security staff at the embassy. We'll request the reinforcements right away."

Hershel thought for a moment, then smiled. "No. I've got a better idea. Get General McLanahan at Battle Mountain Air Reserve Base on the line for me. Tell him I need some security support right away."

"Battle Mountain is an Air Reserve base. They don't have troops stationed there. You mean Quantico or Cherry Point—"

"No. McLanahan has the forces I want," Hershel said. "And he won't need another logistics flight to move them, either. He'll have them ready and waiting for us in Washington by the time we get back, you'll see. We'll need diplomatic credentials for them. Make sure they have those ready for us."

"That'll take time. Turkmenistan doesn't process those kinds of requests quickly—no one in Central Asia does."

"But I predict Mr. Martindale won't have any difficulty getting a visa," Hershel mused. "Credential McLanahan's people as embassy security personnel."

"That'll use up our only allotted short-notice personnel-changeover slot for this year." To help prevent introducing spies into their countries and to help the nation's internal security apparatus to track foreigners, Turkmenistan, like many other countries, allowed embassy security personnel to change only once per year if there was less than thirty days' notice.

"That can't be helped," Hershel said. "I don't think Turkmenistan will be a very friendly place in the near future anyway. We might end up pulling everyone out soon. And if we can ultimately help that country, they'll agree to give us all the personnel we want."

"You're going to take a supplemental security force to Turkmenistan on board your own plane? That's impossible. An embassy-reinforcement team usually deploys in a separate C-141 or C-17. . . ."

"They'll come in our plane," Hershel said with a smile, "and they'll look like the rest of us—until they get inside the embassy. Get Patrick—I mean General McLanahan— on the line for me right now."

" 'Patrick,' huh?" Izzy Meiling asked with a mischievous smile as she used a secure telephone to dial the communications center at the federal building in San Francisco. "Someone out there in Nevada made an impression on you, I see."

"He's definitely off-limits until I can find out what's happened to him over the past few months—something very tragic and horrible," Maureen said. "The guy might have scar tissue in place of his heart, and that's the *last* thing I need in my life."

"But you care enough to find out?"

"I want *him* to tell me what's happened, not some Pentagon intelligence wonk," Maureen said. "But . . . yes, I think he's worth pursuing. Anyone who can stand up to the president of the United States when he's on the warpath has got some nerves of steel."

"Not to mention a big pair of you-know-whats," Izzy said.

"Get him on the phone and wipe that smirk off your face, sister, or I'll sic Kevin Martindale on you again."

"Hey, I can put up with a lot of nonsense for the kind of money that guy has," Meiling said. "A *whole* lot."

FIVE

For the thousandth time in just the past few days, Jalaluddin Turabi asked himself why he was there, why he chose to march with Zarazi's army into the heart of this godforsaken country. Why in hell was he standing on this armored personnel carrier, protected only by several thousand acres of cotton—while what appeared to be the entire Turkmen army was marching toward them? Wakil Mohammad Zarazi's campaign to capture the western half of Turkmenistan and turn it into a training ground for Muslim holy warriors did indeed seem to be blessed. Except now the blessings of Allah were going to be severely put to the test.

Up to that morning their campaign seemed to be not only blessed but plainly miraculous. They captured Gaurdak with barely a shot fired. After their victory at Kerki, the Turkmen soldiers at Gaurdak fairly rushed into their arms. Their army nearly doubled in size overnight. They had over six thousand fighters plus dozens of attack and scout helicopters, weapons of all kinds, from pistols to self-propelled artillery pieces, and vehicles ranging from motorcycles to main battle tanks.

Turabi was simply caught up in the emotion of their victories. When the army started marching westward along the Amu Darya River, he couldn't help but come along. His original idea was to remain behind at Gaurdak, in charge of the "rear guard," and then prepare to bug out at the first sign of a Turkmen army counterattack. However, they had captured the hearts and souls of not just the Turkmen army, but the people there as well—there was clearly no need for a rear guard. Zarazi's army started moving westward, and Turabi could do nothing but march as well.

When Zarazi's brigade was one day's march away from Chärjew, the largest city on the Amu Darya River and a major nexus for oil and gas transshipments across Central Asia, an armored personnel carrier, its fifty-seven-millimeter cannon removed and a white flag flying in its place on the turret, came out onto the main highway to meet them. A young man wearing a leather jacket, a bump helmet over a pair of headphones, and knee-high tanker boots was standing in the APC's cupola. Zarazi, Turabi, and Orazov—the Russian-speaking Turkmen traitor was now seemingly inseparable from Zarazi—rode out in their own APC, with the cannon installed, to meet him.

"I am Captain Rizov," the young Russian officer said. Orazov translated the Russian for Zarazi. "I am aide-de-camp for the commander of the Turkmen Seventeenth Mechanized Infantry Brigade, Colonel Yuri Borokov."

"Why couldn't the colonel come out here himself?"

"Colonel Borokov does not negotiate with terrorists," Rizov said. He was remarkably calm, Turabi noticed—the confidence and fearlessness of youth, no doubt. Rizov had probably never been in battle and thought he was invincible sitting in that little APC. "He is busy planning his operation to grind your little band of raiders into the sand. I offered to negotiate on behalf of the colonel and the people of Chärjew."

"Then your colonel is a coward for sending a junior officer to do his dirty work for him," Zarazi said. "You have shown great courage by coming out here alone and unarmed. I admire that. You do not deserve to die. You may withdraw; I guarantee your safety."

"Thank you for the compliment, sir, but I don't need your guarantees. What I need is your cooperation to avoid any violence," Rizov said. "If you move your forces any farther west, Colonel Borokov will attack without warning. That is *my* guarantee."

"I could use a young, courageous fighter like you in my force, Captain," Zarazi said. "You could command one of my tank companies."

"Then I'd be commanding a company of corpses," Rizov said. "You cannot hope to win an assault against Turkmen regulars. The Seventeenth has a total fighting force of eight thousand soldiers in seven combat battalions—"

"My intelligence says the Seventeenth has a total of *thirteen* thousand soldiers in *eleven* combat and three support battalions, Captain," Zarazi interrupted. "Elements of the Twenty-second Infantry Brigade from Mary joined up with you yesterday, along with three reserve battalions—old men and youngsters, hardly real fighting men, but still a fairly successful call-up of reserve forces for a country with virtually no army at all. In addition, the Fourth Attack Wing from Ashkhabad, with one squadron each of MiG-23 and Sukhoi-25 bombers, has reportedly been deployed to Mary and should be ready to begin close air-support operations by tomorrow. I am told you moved an artillery company to Khodzhayli, but even my most conservative intelligence estimates cannot tell me if the unit is ready to fight or even if the batteries are real or just fakes. I congratulate you for trying to disguise your numbers, but I am very well informed of Turkmen troop movements. Is there anything I've left out, Captain?"

Rizov fell silent for a moment. Zarazi had indeed left a few things out, but Rizov was amazed at what the Taliban fighter *did* know. "What is it you wish in Chärjew, sir?"

"If you join my army, Captain, you will learn everything," Zarazi said. "Because of your courage, you may still withdraw with safety if you refuse to join me. But I warn you: If you do not join my army, you will be killed the next time we meet."

"Sir, I did not come here to listen to threats," Rizov said. "I agreed to come out here like this to learn what you want. We know that TransCal company officials are prepared to offer you large sums of money to keep their pipelines safe. I understand their concern. They make more money if the lines are undamaged and their product is flowing. Frankly, I believe that the Turkmen government thinks similarly. If you agree not to harm the lines and withdraw, the Turkmen government will see to it that you are paid, promptly and generously."

"So your commander will *pay me* not to fight? What kind of soldier is he, Captain?"

"A practical one, sir," Rizov said. "If it is money you are after in Turkmenistan, then we offer it to you. I am carrying a sizable amount with me right now. Withdraw your forces immediately, and by the time you reach the Afghan border, I will deliver it to you."

"How much are you carrying?" Jalaluddin Turabi shouted.

"Quiet, you idiot, or I will have you shot," Zarazi growled, speaking out of a corner of his mouth and not turning toward Turabi so as to not indicate that there was any discord in their ranks.

"We are here to gather funds for our tribe and for the Al Qaeda cells that we support," Turabi said in a low voice. "If he is offering money, we should take it."

"I said *shut up,* Colonel. *Now,*" Zarazi ordered.

"I am authorized to pay you one hundred thousand dollars in gold bullion if you agree not to move any farther west," Rizov said. He still had his tanker's helmet on, but Turabi could tell by his expression and by his tone of voice that he had indeed heard Zarazi's angry comment and was pleased that they were arguing. "A helicopter from Ashkhabad will deliver another two hundred thousand dollars in gold to the town of Mukry, on the Afghan border south of Gaurdak. You may even have the helicopter to transport the gold out."

"One hundred thousand dollars just to *hold our position?*" Turabi exclaimed to Zarazi. "Offer to do it for five hundred thousand, Wakil, and it's a deal."

"I said be quiet," Zarazi snapped.

"We'll take two hundred thousand now, and three hundred thousand when we reach Mukry!" Turabi shouted to the Russian. "All in gold bullion. If we see anyone but you, the deal is off and we will lay siege to Chärjew."

"I warned you, Turabi . . . !"

"Done!" Rizov shouted back. "I have fifteen kilos of gold bullion on board right here. Stand by, and I will unload it." Rizov motioned to someone inside the armored personnel carrier, and soon a young soldier carried what looked like a steel footlocker out of the APC and started walking toward Zarazi's vehicle.

Orazov was visibly shaking in excitement. "General, let me go get the money," he said. "When I bring it back, let's kill that bastard and take his APC." He leaped off the APC and headed for the steel case.

"Stay where you are, Orazov," Turabi said. "Can't you smell a trap?"

"A trap?"

"Do you really think the Turkmen carry fifteen kilos of gold around in military vehicles, you fucking idiot?" Turabi asked. "It's a trap."

The Turkmen soldier carried the steel case several meters in front of his APC, then laid it on the highway, undid the latch, opened it, and stood up. Turabi could see something sparkly inside. "There's your down payment," Rizov shouted, "and that is also the line over which you may not cross. The deal is off if you move past that box." He gave an order, and the soldier started heading back to his APC.

"Thank you, Captain," Turabi said. "Now, if your man there would be so kind as to dump the contents of the box on the pavement?"

"Excuse me, sir?" Rizov asked. He barked another order, and the soldier started running back to the APC.

Turabi reached over to the twenty-three-millimeter cannon beside him, cocked the action, aimed, and pulled the trigger. The steel box jumped and danced on the pavement—and then a gush of thick white gas began to stream out of the shattered steel box.

"*Gas!*" Orazov screamed. "They booby-trapped that case!"

"Get us out of here!" Zarazi shouted. As Turabi laid down machine-gun fire on the Turkmen APC, the driver threw the transmission into reverse, and they roared backward. The gas was spreading quickly, probably with some sort of aerosol propellant to disperse it faster.

The Turkmen soldier was hit in the leg by Turabi's machine-gun fire, and he pitched forward, screaming in pain. Rizov's APC was in full reverse by now, too. Soon the white gas reached the soldier—and within seconds he was flopping and writhing on the ground like a fish caught in a gill net. Just when Turabi thought he was going to break his neck with the force of his convulsions, he lay still. "Allah have mercy . . . !"

"I don't think we'll be facing any untrained Turkmen border guards or conscripts from here on out," Wakil Zarazi said as they roared away from the area. "The Russians play to win."

They soon found out that the artillery batteries set up at Khodzhayli Airport southeast of Chärjew were not fakes when the barrage started, just after midnight. The attack was initiated with strings of starburst illuminators over their positions, followed by rounds that appeared to miss them by very wide margins. "Good thing the Turkmen can't shoot," someone remarked.

"Have you never seen an artillery attack before?" Zarazi said. "The illuminators were dead-on. If they fired standard rounds, we'd have been chewed up pretty bad. The rounds that are falling short are not high explosives— they are seeding the area with mines."

"Mines?"

"Antivehicle and antipersonnel mines," Zarazi said. "They are surrounding our positions very well, even to our rear. If we panic and move without sweeping our escape paths, we'll blow ourselves up. The shelling will start within a few minutes, and they'll be very accurate, I assure you."

"I hope Turabi is in position," Aman Orazov muttered. He had volunteered for the mission that Turabi had been sent on. He was still in shock from being duped so easily by the Turkmen, and now he was smarting from not being chosen to lead this raid. "If he fails, we're going to have a very, very long night."

* * *

Turabi and his light-infantry platoons had departed imme-diately after the attempted Russian nerve-gas attack, driv-ing light vehicles across the rocky sands toward Chärjew, spread out on either side of the highway.

They first investigated the small airfield at Chauder, but it had been recently abandoned—no doubt the Russians thought it would be the first to fall—and moved back to a more defensible position. Turabi ordered a second secu-rity company to move forward, search for mines and booby traps, and take the airfield.

Their first firefight was with a Turkmen security pla-toon at a power substation northeast of Sayat, and it was here that the Taliban fighters first learned what the Turk-men army was really made of. Although outnumbered three to one, the Turkmen held on to that tiny five-acre substation as if it were the birthplace of the prophet Muhammad. The fighting lasted almost a half hour. Turabi lost five men and had three wounded, including himself—a ricocheting bullet, mostly spent, hit him on the cheek, causing him to momentarily lose vision in his left eye.

He could not afford to take any more losses like that to-night, Turabi thought ruefully. He left the remnants of one decimated platoon behind to tend to the wounded, called for replacements, slapped a fresh bandage on his cheek, and moved on.

They quickly approached the airfield at Khodzhayli, skirting the village of Sakar and then fanning out for their assault. Turabi stationed mortar squads east and west of the airport, then split up his platoons, forming a semicir-cle southwest of the airfield. The plan was to have his mor-tar platoons start walking in mortar rounds and then have his rifle and machine-gun platoons pick off any security teams and any other targets of opportunity. Turabi knew he was outnumbered, so his objective wasn't to attack the artillery-battery security forces; all he had to do was prevent the security teams from closing in to the mortar teams until they could knock out or disrupt the fire batteries and then cover their escape.

Like most plans, Turabi's didn't survive first contact.

The eastern mortar platoon managed to set up just a few dozen meters from a Turkmen machine-gun squad that was either sleeping or just not paying attention, so as soon as the first mortar was launched, the platoon was under fire. Instantly, Turabi was laying in only half the number of rounds he thought necessary to take out the artillery site, and his team was under attack. His men started engaging the Turkmen security forces right away, and soon the mortar platoon was able to resume firing, but just thirty seconds into their operation the entire Turkmen army was converging on them. The Turkmen defenders were using troops in "spider holes" to spread their forces out more and keep them out of the line of fire—as soon as a soldier reported contact, a nearby machine-gun nest behind him opened fire over his head. As long as the soldier did not stick more than his head, shoulders, and rifle out of the hole, he was safe.

"Use your smoke! Use your smoke!" Turabi shouted on the radio. Their smoke grenades were very effective—the smoke hung close to the ground, obscuring the Turkmen's sight. Finding the spider holes turned out to be relatively easy: The Turkmen had dug them in an almost perfect circle, so once one of Turabi's men made contact, all they had to do was search left and right for another hole. But the machine-gun fire, although not accurate—the gunner could not see his target, although he knew they were out there—was devastating. One by one his men were going down, usually clipped in the upper thigh or near the waist by big twenty-three-millimeter shells. The screams of his own men, dying and maimed, started to engulf him. Surrounded by smoke, sand, stones, and dead comrades,

Turabi felt disorganized, disoriented, and helpless—but he kept on moving forward.

He practically fell into a spider hole, plopping right down onto the headless body of a Turkmen soldier. He scrambled out of the blood and gore, keeping down below the rim of the hole while machine-gun fire zinged all around him. He reloaded and checked his ammo—just four magazines left, plus his sidearm with two extra mags. He had used up over half his ammo already, and they hadn't hit one thing at the airport. Turabi had to assume, since he was frugal with his ammo, that his men were probably much lower. Once he used up another mag, he decided, they would pull back. This attack was going nowhere.

Then he saw it: a field telephone, a simple, old-style crank-and-talk box. The Turkmen soldiers didn't even have radios out here! Turabi found the dead soldier's headphones, rubbed the blood and brains out of the ear cups, and put them on.

He was desperate—he could think of only one thing to try. He cranked the phone and, summoning all his Russian-language skills, pressed the talk button and shouted, *"Astanavleevat'sya! Eta vazmooteeteel'no!"* he shouted, doing his best impersonation of a pissed-off Russian officer. "Who in hell are you shooting at?"

Someone responded, in even worse Russian than his.

"I cannot understand you!"

"Sir, there are intruders in the perimeter!" the Turkmen soldier said in terrible Russian.

"I hope to hell you haven't attacked my security detail returning from patrol!" Turabi shouted, trying to run his words together to make it sound more authentic. "Now I want every one of you to get up out of those damned holes, without your weapon, and search for the wounded! I am sending trucks out to assist. If you come out of your holes

with your weapons, you're likely to be shot by my men—
or your own! Now, get moving!"

"Da, tovarisch," the soldier responded. He heard frantic calls in Turkmen broadcast on the phone. Turabi
peeked out of his hole—and sure enough the Turkmen
soldiers were standing up and searching the ground
around them with big, boxlike flashlights. Hold your fire,
damn it, Turabi silently ordered his men as he pulled his
pistol out of his holster, hold your fire. . . .

They did. And then as if by another silent command,
shots rang out all around him all at once, and the Turkmen
soldiers fell.

"Viper team, Alpha, report," Turabi radioed.

"East One point secure, three down."

"Center One point secure, four down."

"West One point secure, three down."

One by one, each of the platoons reported in. The east
mortar platoon, the only one attacked as soon as it started
launching rounds, suffered the worst casualties. Only two
of the twelve members survived, and they had lost all their
tubes and mortar rounds. Out of almost a hundred men
who attacked the airport, they had lost thirty-one—but
they had killed over a hundred Turkmen soldiers.

"What are we going to do now, Colonel?" Turabi's second in command said. "More Turkmen security forces
will be on their way any moment."

"We're not going to wait for them," Turabi said. A few
soldiers hung their heads—in exhaustion or shame, it was
hard to tell. "We're going to take those artillery batteries.
Have everyone find a Turkmen uniform and weapon, and
get ready to move."

About thirty minutes before sunrise, General Zarazi himself strode into the communications center. Captain Aman

Orazov put down a pair of headphones and met the general. "Well?" Zarazi asked.

"Still no contact with Colonel Turabi," Orazov said. "Khamsa Company has not had contact with Turabi either since they took up positions at the power substation north of Chauder."

"The last report was Turabi's company making contact at Khodzhayli?"

"Yes, sir," Orazov replied. "Several platoons encountered a dug-in company-size security force surrounding the airport. Looks like the colonel marched right into an ambush. Their forces were of equal size, but Turabi lost several men at the substation, so he was undermanned." He paused, then said, "*I* should have led that force, sir. I know my country's tactics. I could have gotten around a simple spider-hole security perimeter. And getting ambushed by a couple scout platoons at that substation—how could he let that happen? He couldn't see a force that size in a small, enclosed area?"

"This was not Turabi's shining moment," Zarazi had to admit.

"The colonel is very good at smash-and-grab, small-unit guerrilla tactics against paramilitary forces, sir, but conducting a raid with a company-size force against army regulars is another matter," Orazov said. "Turabi's company may have been wiped out completely. We should consider the very great possibility that some of our men, perhaps even the colonel himself, will have been captured. If that is so, they will use unspeakable methods to extract information from them. We must assume that the Russians and Turkmen know our current position, manpower, and order of battle."

Zarazi turned away and stared into a corner of the communications tent. "We . . . we must make preparations to shift forces . . . move forward, perhaps to Chauder. . . ."

"We do need to shift positions, sir, but we should not go forward—we need to *retreat*," Orazov said. "Those men at Chauder and at the substation are dead when the Turkmen begin their counterattack. We should pull back to Esenmengli—"

"*Esenmengli?* That's . . . that's *seventy kilometers!*"

"We have no choice, sir!" Orazov said. "Turabi has failed, and his failure has stalled our entire offensive. We can't afford to waste time crossing the river to Imeni Kalinina. If we're caught while we're crossing, we'll be slaughtered. The only stronghold on this side of the river we can retreat to is Esenmengli."

Zarazi turned and straightened his shoulders. "Very well—*Major*," he said. "Deploy security forces along the river to assist in the withdrawal of our remaining forces at Chauder. Then give the order to move quickly to Esenmengli."

"Yes, sir," Orazov said proudly. "Once we are secure, sir, I will be honored to lead the men in a new offensive. Just give the order, sir."

"I am disappointed in Turabi," Zarazi muttered. "He has proven himself a good fighter in the past, but it should have been obvious to me that his heart was not in this campaign. My friendship for him blinded me to the reality of the situation."

"The deficiency was in Turabi, sir, not you," Orazov said. "But the battle is not yet lost. We can still—"

At that moment they heard a loud *boom!* off in the distance, followed by several more in rapid succession.

"*Artillery!*" Orazov screamed. "The Turkmen artillery positions at Khodzhayli—they started up again! This can only be a prelude to a full-scale attack on our position! We need to get out of here!"

"Launch the attack helicopters! Commence attacking the artillery positions and any advancing armor immediately with everything we've got!" Zarazi shouted. "Notify all battalions to prepare to repel attack!" Just then he stopped and listened. He could hear the artillery pieces booming in the distance—but no rounds had fallen yet. "What is going on? Whose artillery *is* that?"

Orazov picked up the headphones again to listen to the reports coming in from their security patrols and scouts. His eyes widened in surprise a few moments later.

"What is it, Major?"

"The scout helicopters report the artillery units at Khodzhayli are . . . *they are firing toward Chärjew!*" Orazov exclaimed. "The scouts report heavy aircraft losses and heavy bombardment of armor-marshaling areas at Chärjew Airport. They report—" He paused, listening intently. "Sir, Turkmen infantry units are in full retreat! Entire companies . . . no, entire *battalions!*—are evacuating north into Farab and Imeni Stalina . . . some reportedly even crossing the border into Uzbekistan!"

He listened further, his eyes flickering in dejection. He removed the headphones and handed them to Zarazi. "It's Colonel Turabi, sir. He is requesting that all available fighting forces be moved up immediately—to *Khodzhayli*. He is at the airport now and has it under his control. He expects to have the airport at Chärjew under his control by the time our forces reach Khodzhayli. City officials, TransCal executives, and Colonel Borokov, the Russian in charge of the garrison, have already been in contact with him, asking for terms."

Zarazi rushed out of the communications tent to issue orders to his troops, leaving Orazov behind. The other men in the tent looked at the Turkmen turncoat, and he could see the accusations in their eyes: You are the coward here, Orazov, not Turabi. Jalaluddin Turabi had just proved he was worthy of respect and admiration. All they were showing Orazov now was contempt.

There was only one way to win General Wakil Zarazi's trust back, Orazov decided—get rid of Jalaluddin Turabi.

THE KREMLIN, MOSCOW, RUSSIAN FEDERATION
That morning

"It is confirmed, sir," Army General Nikolai Stepashin, commander of the Ministry of State Security of the Russian Federation and the Commonwealth of Independent States, reported as he strode into the president's office. The president of the Russian Federation was on the speakerphone and scowled as the intelligence chief spoke. "The city of Chärjew is in the hands of the Taliban insurgents as we speak."

"Finally you confirm what I have been telling you for days now, Mr. President!" cried the voice on the other end of the phone, belonging to the president of the Republic of Turkmenistan, Kurban Gurizev. "And I'm telling you now, they are marching on the city of Mary. They'll be there in less than three days. I need help to crush these Taliban bastards, Mr. President, and I need it *now!*"

Russian Federation president Valentin Gennadievich Sen'kov made a disgusted snorting sound, aimed directly at his minister of foreign affairs, Ivan Ivanovich Filippov. " 'No threat'—is that what you told us, Ivan?" Sen'kov sneered. "Those Taliban are just a bunch of rabble-rousers? Scroungers? Desert rats? Isn't that what you told us only two days ago?"

"Mr. President, the Ministry of Defense and the Ministry of State Security agreed with my assessment—that this Taliban incursion was nothing more than a small, isolated band chased out of Afghanistan by American and

United Nations forces," Filippov said. "They should have been crushed days ago by the Turkmen army—"

"The Turkmen army is joining them!" Sen'kov exploded. "Shit, I wish the Red Army had such good recruiting numbers! They've taken three Turkmen military bases— one of which was commanded by *Russian officers*—as easily as if they were getting a fifty-ruble blow job on Ostankino Prospekt. Their army almost exceeds the size of the *entire Turkmen army!* What in hell is going on out there?"

"The field commander, a man named Turabi, is apparently the key," Stepashin said. "He's young, fearless, and very popular with the locals. The leader of the Taliban group, a weirdo named Zarazi, is the idealistic firebrand— Turabi is the real brains behind their operation."

"I don't give a shit!" Gurizev said over the speaker-phone. "Mr. President, these Taliban are threatening to turn this country into another Chechnya, another Afghanistan! Do you want the rest of the world to see a handful of half-starved Taliban greasers occupy another former Russian republic? We'll be the laughingstock of the entire world!"

"Sir, it's nothing to be concerned about," Minister of Foreign Affairs Filippov said calmly, ignoring Gurizev. "These Taliban don't want to take the country. All they want is money or stuff they can sell for money. As soon as they get a bankroll, something big enough that'll buy them a clan leadership position back home, they'll be gone."

"Is that what you thought of Afghanistan, too, Minister Filippov?" Gurizev asked.

"Sir, there's absolutely no comparison here," Filippov said. "These insurgents are raiders, not invaders. It'll be over in forty-eight hours, sir, I guarantee it. If they don't burn themselves out by marching across the Kara Kum

Desert, they'll take some more protection money from the Americans and leave."

"What do the Americans have to do with this?"

"In order to keep the oil flowing, the Americans have been willing to pay the Taliban to keep the pipelines open—and pay them handsomely," Filippov said. "The Taliban don't want territory—they want money, funds they can take back to their tribes to fund whatever criminal operation they're involved in."

"I tell you, Mr. President, the Taliban want to take the *country,* just like they took Afghanistan," Gurizev said on the speakerphone. "If they were only doing it for the money, they'd have stopped in Kizyl-arvat. I tell you, they want to take the city of Mary, then march on Ashkhabad itself."

"Stop whining, Gurizev," Sen'kov said. "That *will not* be allowed to happen." He looked warily at his military chief of staff. "What do you think, General?" he asked.

"I agree with President Gurizev, sir. We should move immediately to reinforce our military units in Mary," General Anatoliy Gryzlov said. He did not have the same close personal relationship with Sen'kov that Zhurbenko had. Gryzlov was a career military officer and showed an open dislike for politics, especially Valentin Sen'kov's cutthroat style of politics. "President Gurizev is right—we cannot afford to underestimate these Taliban. Any more forward movement by them toward the capital will be seen as weakness on our part. And if they even threaten Mary, let alone *take* the city, we might as well evacuate the entire country—it'll be a worse disaster than Afghanistan."

"You're exaggerating, General."

"Sir, let's not take the chance," Gryzlov said. "We can quietly move tactical air assets to our training base at Mary and not attract any attention from the Americans or anyone else."

"Air assets? The same 'air assets' you used on Vedeno?"

"My operation was approved by the Defense Ministry and this office—"

"Your plan said nothing about firebombing an entire village with supersonic bombers!" Minister of Defense Bukayev said. "Shit, next time you'll ask to use a rifle and drop a nuclear weapon instead!"

"If that's what it takes!" General Gryzlov retorted. "Sir, this new threat in Turkmenistan is a direct threat to the Turkmen and an indirect but very real threat to Russia. We have a mutual security agreement with Turkmenistan, the first ever signed with a former republic. We need to honor that. We need to move forcefully and decisively, *right now*."

"We are not going to firebomb some ragheads scratching across the desert."

"What better time and place to do it, sir?" Gryzlov asked. "High visibility, low chance of collateral damage, a purely defensive move in support of a neighbor and ally—we're even helping the Americans!"

"Don't try your hand at politics here, General—you're no good at it," Sen'kov interrupted. "I suggest you send out probes to keep watch and maybe harass the Taliban as they move. Eventually they'll get tired of being plinked off one by one and decide to leave."

"I don't want to get our forces bogged down in guerrilla warfare with a bunch of fucking desert reptiles, sir," Gryzlov said. "We lost the advantage in Afghanistan not because we used airpower but because we didn't use *enough* airpower. If we go in, we must go in not just with adequate force but with *overwhelming* force."

"We don't need an invasion force to take out a handful of ragheads in the open desert."

"We can't take the chance, sir," Gryzlov emphasized. "Let's move into Turkmenistan in force. Let's not make the mistakes we did in Chechnya or Afghanistan. I can send three wings of heavy bombers over those rebels in twelve hours and wipe out their armor, artillery, and air defenses *in one night*. I can have thirty thousand troops on the ground in Turkmenistan in two weeks, which should be more than enough to destroy what's left of the Taliban. In two months I can have another fifty thousand troops in place. We can protect every drop of oil we pump out of that place."

"And have the entire world watching on CNN while we bomb the hell out of a bunch of desert ragheads?" Sen'kov retorted. "Out of the question. You can send in commando teams to keep an eye on those pigfuckers, but I don't want to slaughter them unless I absolutely have to."

"Sir, they've already killed Turkmeni and even Russian troops," Gryzlov said. "We're fully justified in sending in troops to destroy them. We should—"

"Denied!" Sen'kov said. "I want our troop movements kept quiet. I don't want to be accused of starting another Chechen-style holocaust. Is that clear?"

"Yes, sir." Sen'kov motioned at the door, and Gryzlov got the hell out of there quickly.

"Mr. President, you have a right to help defend Turkmenistan," Kurban Gurizev said. "Russia helped build this country, and we still have a sizable Russian population here. You don't need to tiptoe around the damned Americans and their pipelines. They are raping our country—the entire world knows it."

"No one seemed to mind when Niyazov signed that oil project with the Americans and cut Russia out completely."

"Most people don't know the details of the TransCal deal," Gurizev said. "At least Russia pays for Turkmen oil, instead of leaching off every barrel pumped by someone else. I may have been born in this country, Minister, but my loyalties are with Mother Russia—as long as you are there to back me up. Otherwise, I have no difficulty at all in accepting the American oil companies' money."

"Don't try to play both sides here, Gurizev," Sen'kov said. "We'll back you against these Taliban, but we don't want to hear about you making any special backroom deals with the Americans. Your future is in Russia. That's what you wanted, and that's what we agreed to, once the Russian oil companies can take over those new oil and gas fields discovered by the Americans. You just play this game exactly how we planned it and you'll get your reward—a first-class ticket back to Russia, with the money you've embezzled from the Turkmen treasury safe in your pocket."

Gurizev quickly decided to change the subject. He was dismayed to learn that the Russians knew about the frequent "enhanced-benefit receipts" he'd been drawing from the treasury. "The Americans have asked to meet with myself, the Russian ambassador, and even the Taliban leader," Gurizev said. "I think it would be unwise not to allow them to visit—it might help defuse the situation here. What do you want me to tell them?"

"Tell them the situation is extremely dangerous and the government cannot guarantee their safety," Sen'kov said. "If they still want to come, let them—but do everything you can to discourage it."

"I should let the Americans meet with those Taliban?"

"Damn it, I hope to hell you've killed those Taliban insects long before the Americans arrive," Sen'kov said angrily.

"I don't know what to say to an American delegation—"

"Gurizev, you simply tell them you are serving your country," Sen'kov said. "Just get your picture taken with whomever they send, then let your underlings handle it. Your job for now is to mobilize that army of yours and squash those Taliban insurgents—*immediately*." He terminated the call with an angry stab on a button. "He had better get off his ass and do something, or we'll have to replace him—sooner rather than later."

"Sir, General Gryzlov seemed pretty adamant about sending in a powerful force to knock back those Taliban outside Mary," Minister of Defense Bukayev said. "Maybe we should let him mobilize a good-size force. No one in the world would argue if we sent several air regiments to Mary. We still have a sizable training force in Turkmenistan."

"The general needs to have his insubordinate ass kicked!" Sen'kov shouted. "I have become the hellmaster of Chechnya in the world press because of him! Now he thinks I'm going to approve of another similar operation in Turkmenistan? He's crazy! If he can't handle this operation with a few commando units, he shouldn't be in charge of the Russian military."

OUTSIDE MARY, REPUBLIC OF TURKMENISTAN
Days later

Jalaluddin Turabi had to admit that the swelling tide of victory was compelling, even addictive. Wakil Mohammad Zarazi's little band of Taliban raiders had turned into a real army now, with over twelve thousand fighters and another two thousand support personnel spread out over much of eastern Turkmenistan. They left a garrison of a thousand troops and support personnel in Chärjew to guard that vital city against the Russian and Turkmen forces that had fled the country across the border into Uzbekistan, but it was doubtful if that was even necessary—their victory in Chärjew had been complete.

The people of Chärjew were solidly behind Zarazi for one simple reason: Zarazi had money, and lots of it. He had made a deal with the American officials of TransCal

Petroleum to keep the pipelines and pumping stations safe and had been paid well. Zarazi wisely disbursed the money to the Turkmen officials of Chärjew in exchange for loyalty, and it had worked. Zarazi could safely leave the security of the pipelines to local police and militia, with only a token force of his loyal soldiers to oversee things and watch for any incursions from the north. Zarazi also gave quite a bit of money to the local population as well as to his soldiers. His flanks were secure.

It had been the perfect opportunity for Turabi to leave Zarazi and take command of the garrison at Chärjew. Except for his raid on Khodzhayli Airport, where almost a hundred Turkmen and Russians had been killed or wounded, Turabi had gone easy on the Turkmen army as he moved into Chärjew, and the Turkmen people seemed thankful for that. He could have easily, quietly watched Zarazi's back as he moved his ever-growing army down the main highway toward their ultimate clash at Mary. Why did he not ask Zarazi if he could stay behind in Chärjew?

Two reasons: fear and curiosity. Yes, he was afraid of Wakil Zarazi. When his old friend and leader told him to do something, he did it. Zarazi did have some sort of powerful effect on Turabi. It was more than clan loyalty: Turabi was genuinely afraid of Zarazi's going drunk, or even crazy, with the power he was accumulating. He hated to think what Zarazi would do if he sensed any weakness or betrayal in any of his senior officers.

Turabi was also very much afraid of Aman Orazov, their Russian-Turkmen turncoat who had maneuvered himself in as Zarazi's confidant and adviser, almost on a par with Jalaluddin Turabi himself. Since the successful occupation of Chärjew, when everyone else seemed to treat Turabi like some kind of battlefield genius, Orazov had been standoffish, perfunctory, and even hostile toward Turabi. Was it because Turabi took on Turkmen regular-army soldiers and defeated them—or was it because he was far more popular with the Turkmen, even ones he'd defeated in battle, than Orazov ever was?

Whatever he thought or whatever the hell was going on, one thing was certain: Wakil Zarazi was marching on Mary, the largest and most important city in eastern Turk-menistan—and their destiny.

Zarazi's army of about ten thousand soldiers had reached the outskirts of the Turkmen city of Bayramaly, about thirty kilometers east of Mary. This area was part of the expansive Merv oasis, one of the largest oases in Cen-tral Asia and an important stopover on the ancient Silk Road that ran between Istanbul, Turkey, and Shanghai, China. The city itself was in the center of the oasis, fed by a number of natural and man-made irrigation ditches that connected the Kara Kum Canal, a large irrigation project completed by the Soviets, and the Murgab River that flowed south.

Turabi had never seen anything like it: cotton every-where, as far as the eye could see. Thousands upon thou-sands of acres of white plants dotted the landscape on either side of the highway ahead of them, which made it look as if an immense, fluffy white blanket had been laid across the harsh desert. "My God—they can hide an en-tire corps in those fields," Turabi said, studying the terrain with field glasses. "It looks like tough maneuvering in that stuff besides. We're too accustomed to maneuvering in the desert."

"God will show us the way to victory," Zarazi said woodenly.

Turabi looked at his former friend and tribal leader with an exasperated expression. Then, sensing he was being watched, he turned—and saw Aman Orazov staring at him. That rat bastard was constantly hovering around when he was with Zarazi, watching—and surely reporting—Turabi's every word, action, or expression to Zarazi.

"Do you not believe that it is God's will we should be victorious, Colonel?" Orazov asked suspiciously.

Turabi ignored him. "Even so . . . I've deployed the Fifth and Ninth Motorized Rifles and the Second Air Mobile to reconnoiter those cotton fields north and south. I asked for a report on soil conditions and any problems they encounter driving through that stuff. The last thing we want is for a ton of unpicked cotton jamming up our tracks."

"Very well, Jala," Zarazi said. "All good precautions."

Turabi looked at Zarazi with faint surprise. "Thank you, sir," he said. He hesitated before speaking his mind, then said, "You know, Wakil, that's the first time in weeks you've called me by my first name. It felt good. Just like in our youth."

"Our youth," Zarazi said with a chuckle. "It seems like centuries since we played in the corrals and fields of our youth."

"It seems like centuries since we crossed the border into this godforsaken country," Turabi said.

Zarazi looked at Turabi with a serious expression. Turabi thought he was going to get chewed out again for using God's name disrespectfully—but instead Zarazi said, "I know what you mean, Jalaluddin."

Well, this was certainly a change in attitude, Turabi thought. "It's a shitty business, Wakil. We're far from home, far from our wives and children."

"I feel my life is changing here, Jalaluddin," Zarazi said. "I . . . I don't know what it means. I have felt the hand of God on my shoulder before—but I don't feel it now. I don't think He has abandoned me, but . . . but I don't hear His voice right now. We stand here, on the threshold of the enemy, and I can't hear Him. I don't know if this is a test of my faith or if He thinks we can do this task using our own poor mortal brains."

"It's called precombat jitters, Wakil," Turabi said. This was amazing, a relief, *wonderful*—for the first time in many days, Zarazi wasn't talking like some kind of religious zealot. He sounded like a regular guy, like any other military commander ready to step onto the field of battle and face the enemy. It was a welcome and heartening change. "We've done everything we need to do. We've deployed our scouts, deployed troops to our rear to guard against flanking maneuvers and protect our best escape route, and set up reserve forces. We've got pretty decent intelligence, and we're still getting good recruits coming forward to join our army, even though we're closing in on Mary. We've done everything we need to do."

"Will it be enough?"

"That's something I can't answer, Wakil," Turabi said. He paused for a moment, then said, "Wakil . . . my friend . . . listen to me. Why don't we pull back to Chärjew? If you feel there's something we missed in our planning, let's fall back, regroup, get some fresh intelligence reports, build our forces a bit more, and plan it again."

"You mean . . . you mean *retreat?*"

"Wakil, running away in a disorganized fashion is a retreat. Pulling back in an orderly fashion with three full companies as our rear guard is not," Turabi said. "Chärjew is ours, Wakil—that's undisputed. We have our hands on the taps of fifty thousand barrels of oil and five million cubic meters of natural gas *per day* there. We have the twelfth-largest company in America paying us thousands of dollars a day to 'guard' their pipelines. We're in control in Chärjew, Wakil. Out here we're not in control of anything, not even what's sticking to our tank treads. The apprehension you feel is a soldier's sixth sense. It tells you when danger is nearby. Listen to it."

Wakil looked at Turabi—then, to Turabi's joy, looked behind him, back to the northeast, toward Chärjew. It was such a slight movement, such a casual thing, but to Turabi it spoke volumes.

They had marched almost two hundred kilometers from Chärjew in less than a week across the barren, burning Kara Kum Desert to get here, fighting off attacks to their flanks by Turkmen guerrillas, chasing away scouts, burying their dead, taking captives and executing spies, and planning their final assault—and not once in all those days had Wakil Mohammad Zarazi ever looked backward. He hadn't looked backward once since getting jumped by American bombers in northern Afghanistan, since he'd first heard the word of God and set out on this quest.

"We can set up the rear guard in Ravnina. We found good water supplies there, the terrain is a bit higher, and we're far enough away from the canal so we don't have to set up security posts there," Turabi said quickly, excitedly. He had been working out the details in his head for days— but for an escape, not for a withdrawal. This was better than he could ever have hoped. "We leave Second Battalion and Second Air Mobile there, and we pull back—a little at a time, so the Turkmen don't realize what's happening. The two units deploy along the Halach oil fields east and west—we know we can hide a battalion-size force among all those wells. In three days we can be back in Chärjew, and we fortify the ten-kilometer perimeter I set up after leaving Chauder. As we pull back, we pull the rear guards in. They'll pull back to a safe, secure perimeter and be relieved. Once they're rested and rearmed, we push the perimeter out to twenty kilometers. Now we control everything east of the sixty-third meridian. Solid as a rock."

Zarazi was silent for a long moment. Turabi looked at Orazov and saw nothing but hatred and loathing in his eyes. Keep quiet, you asshole, Turabi said silently. Keep quiet or I'll kill you. . . .

"We do not need to pull back, General," Orazov said. "Mary Airport is less than thirty kilometers right in front of us. We haven't seen more than a few helicopter probes come our way since we moved into position. We can take Mary, sir, just as easily as we took Chärjew."

"*We* didn't take Chärjew, Orazov—*I* took it," Turabi snapped. "And there was nothing easy about it. I lost a lot of good men, one out of every five of my force. But Chärjew will be nothing compared to the battle that awaits us in Mary. The Russians will be waiting with their close-air-support fighters and—"

"What fighters? We haven't seen one fighter since leaving Chärjew."

"They are there, Orazov, we know it."

"They were there at Chärjew, too—many of them. But not one lifted off to oppose us."

"They were flown into Chärjew to scare us away, but the pilots left as soon as they got out of their planes," Turabi said. "Those planes were worthless anyway—a bunch of old Sukhoi-17 bombers, over thirty years old and not very well maintained. They were never a threat to us."

"They were a very great threat when we first planned the assault on Chärjew."

"Our intelligence said the Turkmen had asked the Russians to bring up their Sukhoi-24s and MiG-27s—*the ones based at Mary,*" Turabi argued. "They brought up the relics instead. That means the first-line fighters and bombers are probably still in Mary. And we *still* don't know exactly what the Americans are doing in Turkmenistan."

"Ah, yes, your ghostly Americans," Orazov said derisively. "You say you saw only two men, but they destroyed two armored vehicles, killed a half dozen men—but did nothing to you but question you."

"Shut up, damn you," Turabi snapped. "The Americans were there to retrieve their crashed aircraft or cruise missile or spy plane—whatever it was that got shot down."

"So you say," Orazov said dryly. "Or did you really lead your men into a minefield, as the helicopter-patrol officers surmised . . . ?"

"Go to hell, Orazov."

"In any case we haven't seen any evidence of American soldiers in Turkmenistan—if they ever existed in the first place," Orazov said to Zarazi. "They probably came in just to retrieve their cruise missile. There's nothing to be concerned about."

"*Nothing to be concerned about?* We are facing five to ten thousand Turkmen and Russian soldiers to the west, and we might have these American supersoldiers to the east—or at the very least over our heads with their spy planes and satellites." Turabi turned to Zarazi. "I'll take my scout company into Mary and find out exactly what's happening, Wakil. But if you are considering a pullback to a more defensible position, sir, I recommend we proceed immediately. We need to shift the vanguard to defensive positions and move the main force forty kilometers north along the highway to get across the Kara Kum Canal. That's a hard day's march."

"What is it with you, Colonel?" Orazov asked. "Why are you so bent on retreating all of a sudden?"

"Because any fool can see we are overextended in this position, with a large entrenched force up ahead of us," Turabi retorted. "We barely have enough supplies to last us three days while we're on the march. If we go into battle, we'll use up all our supplies in less than a day."

"Are you calling the general a fool, Turabi?"

"I am no expert in maneuver warfare," Turabi went on, ignoring Orazov's remark, "but I do know that hundreds of successful campaigns have been lost when an army marches beyond its secure supply lines. We are well beyond that point *now,* Wakil. It now takes more than a day to bring in enough fuel for our helicopters, armor, and vehicles. One interruption in our supply lines and we'll have no choice but to retreat—and *that's* when the chaos and confusion start."

For the first time since the battle of Chauder, Zarazi looked confused and . . . yes, a little frightened. The change was amazing, Turabi thought. He didn't know for sure, but perhaps this was the beginning of the long march home.

"General, we must attack, and do it *now,*" Orazov insisted. "Let's not wait any longer. We should move with all possible speed to within artillery range of Mary Airport and begin the assault."

"That would be suicide!" Turabi retorted. "Wakil, we have incomplete intelligence, our air defenses are not in place, and, as I've told you repeatedly, our supply lines are stretched to the limit—"

"Address him as 'General' or 'sir,' Colonel," Orazov said angrily.

"Shut up, you bastard!" Turabi exploded. "You don't know what you're—"

At that moment a siren began to wail throughout the headquarters company—the air-raid siren. Turabi's blood turned cold. It was too late. He thought for certain they had one more day. They were at the extreme edge of effective combat range of the Mi-24 attack helicopters based at Mary. Turabi believed that the Russians would wait until they attempted their assault on their objective, the oil-control facility at Bayramaly. That would give the big Hind-D attack helicopters several more weapons to carry into the attack, several more minutes over the target area. But surprise was everything in battle—and the Russians had just achieved it.

"*Gunships!* Helicopter gunships to the south!" one of the command-post lieutenants shouted. "Sir, spotters have detected two formations of three, about fifteen kilometers out."

"Not even a full squadron. It might be a feint," Turabi said. He motioned for the radio handset and shouted, "This is Colonel Turabi. Clear this net! I said *clear this net immediately!*" He waited a few moments for the excited chatter to die down. Then: "Echo Company, Echo Company, alert your scouts and make sure they're ready to deal with the main body. If it's coming, they'll be rushing in from the north.

"Break. All antiaircraft crews, all antiaircraft crews, listen up. Do not panic when you see the damned Hinds. If you keep your cool, you'll have a good chance. Dismount your man-portable missile crews, disperse and hide in every crack and crevice you can find, and go to remotes on your gun units. The Hinds like big targets out in the open—don't give them one. Relax and get hits. Vanguard units, don't break out of formation until you see the enemy break first, and don't start radioing artillery-grid coordinates until you see their attack formation take shape. I want our artillery to drop ordnance on where they *are,* not where they *were.*" He threw the headset into Orazov's face. "You wanted a fight, Orazov, you got one now." Turabi ran off to the command truck, not waiting to see if Zarazi or Orazov followed.

They did not.

Turabi sat in the commander's seat, in front of a large Plexiglas board with a grid showing the location of all their units. Behind the transparent board were communications technicians receiving reports from scouts and brigade commanders; another technician quickly drew and erased the symbols on the board, writing backward so Turabi on the other side could see them properly, as the battle progressed. On either side of the commander's seats were the deputy's seat and seats for communications officers and other advisers and specialists. Turabi could speak with anyone in his team, from a rifle-platoon leader to a battalion commander, by flicking a switch.

It was happening exactly as he'd envisioned it: a classic Soviet-style envelopment attack. Two flights of helicopter gunships were sweeping in from the south; a small formation of light tanks, just a dozen spotted so far, were heading up the highway toward them. But these were just the diversions—the main-objective force had still not been spotted. "Echo Three, this is Green One," Turabi radioed to one of the scout platoons that was the farthest north and west, "what do you see? They should be right in front of you."

"Negative contact, Green One," the leader of the three-tank scout platoon reported.

Either the platoon was not where it was plotted on the board, Turabi thought, or the Turkmen forces were coming in from even farther north than he'd anticipated. "Echo, this is Green One, move one of your platoons straight north, straight north, right to that H-1 access road. They have to be coming in from farther north—your scouts are too close in and too far west."

"Echo acknowledges," the scout-company commander radioed back.

Turabi studied the board for a few moments, counting scout units, then flipped the channel selector: "Airborne Two, this is Green One, I don't see any of your units up. What's the problem?"

"Green One, we lost the diesel-powered pump for the refueling bladders," the helicopter-company commander radioed back. The helicopters were refueled from giant twenty-thousand-deciliter collapsible rubber bladders, resembling tire inner tubes, using high-volume, diesel-powered pumps. They could have all the fuel they needed available—but if the pumps went out, getting the fuel into the aircraft's fuel tanks was long, hard work. "Our first chopper should be airborne in five to ten minutes."

"Two, if you ever again fail to report a malfunction like that in a timely manner, I'll have your eyeballs for breakfast!" Turabi shouted. "Break. Airborne Three, how fast can you get a cover aircraft over to grid three-zero-Charlie?"

"Green One, stand by," the commander of another helicopter company reported. After a short but utterly nerve-racking wait: "Green One, I'll send a unit in right now, ETE three minutes. He can be on station for about five minutes before he bingos."

"Very well, Airborne Three. Break. Airborne Two, get your aircraft in the air as soon as you can, or—"

A tremendous explosion outside shook the command-post vehicle so hard that Turabi almost flew out of his seat. *"What was that?"* he shouted, struggling back to his seat.

"A bomb!" someone else shouted. "At least a two-hundred-kilo gravity bomb! It hit the radar truck!"

An antiradar missile or TV-guided missile, Turabi thought. Too big for a small, helicopter-fired missile, Turabi knew—it had to be from a fixed-wing aircraft. And if it was TV-guided, it could just as easily have hit the command-post truck—that would have been a juicier target. No one had reported any low-level bombers inbound, so it had to be a cruise missile, launched from high altitude, or a long-range guided missile. "Switch to the number-two radar van and recalibrate," Turabi directed, "then order them to go to intermittent operation." It took several moments, but finally he could see the radars up front in the command vehicle come back to life. They were still in the fight, but down to their last radar array.

"Should we retreat, sir?" the operations officer asked nervously, shouting his question out at the top of his lungs even though Turabi was only a couple meters away. "I think we should get out of here *now!*"

"No one is retreating, Captain—not yet," Turabi said quickly. No, he thought, they should have retreated *days* ago—it was way too late now. "Calm yourself. Go get a report on that impact area. Have someone check for chemical or biological weapons. Pressurize the command cab." Turabi had to swallow hard as the pressure quickly built up in the command-post truck. If those last weapons dropped nearby had chemical or biological weapons aboard, the positive pressure inside the cab would help keep toxic chemicals from seeping inside. On the commandwide net, Turabi radioed, "All units, I think that was an antiradar-missile attack. Check for biochem weapons and report. Bravo Three, Bravo Three, wheel north to H-1 and engage targets."

"No targets spotted yet, Green One."

"They'll be there!" Turabi insisted. "Bravo Four, back up Bravo Three to the north. Bravo Six, move forward and take Five's position on the tail, and do it *right now,*" Turabi ordered. "Prepare to move to the west to engage the enemy's left flank if they come in from the north. Acknowledge."

Another long pause, more confusion on the network. Turabi thought the reserve unit had bugged out already. But finally: "Acknowledged, Green One, Bravo Six is on the move."

"Very well. Move up as fast as you can. Break. Bravo Five, take Bravo Two's position on the left flank and move forward *fast*. Airborne One, take the point. Airborne Two, get your birds fueled and move north to cover Bravo Three and Four, and you'd better have them all up in ten minutes or I'm going to rip your head off and shit down your throat! Airborne Three, don't engage those Hinds—go around them and see if you can get them to follow you. They have to be low on fuel. Get Chärjew to start moving fuel down here on the double!"

He thought for another moment. There was no supply line behind them anymore, Turabi knew. They would either make it to Bayramaly and their objective, the petroleum-control station outside the city, or they would get smashed out here. If they ran out of fuel, they weren't going to get any more from Chärjew in time. The reserve force, Battalion Six, had to move up to join the fighting. If they didn't advance, they were going to turn and run back to Chärjew on first contact.

"Bravo One and Bravo Two, move out and engage the point vehicles. Blast them the hell off the highway, and don't dance with them—those Hinds will be after you before too long. I want both One and Two at the objective point in one hour, or we're going to get chewed to pieces. Let's get moving, or we'll die out here in the desert."

He held on as the command vehicle lurched forward, wheeled sharply left up and down over the edge of the highway, and drove several dozen meters away into the cotton fields. Moments later another explosion shook the area—and, yes, it had landed two hundred meters northeast on the highway, exactly where they'd be if they'd pulled back and stayed on the highway. Crap, this was getting hairy now. Turabi could practically feel a TV- or laser-guided bomb on its way for the command-post vehicle right now.

"Fast-movers!" the senior watch officer shouted. "Sukhoi-24s, at least two inbound!"

"Inbound PGM attack!" Turabi radioed. "Radars to standby! All units pop smoke." Not only could the tanks and heavier armored personnel carriers obscure themselves with smoke from their exhaust stacks, but they could also fire volleys of smoke grenades several dozen meters away to make it appear as if there were more vehicles than there really were. He didn't know if it would fool sophisticated sensors, but it was the only countermeasure his forces had.

"SAM-12 Bravo One," the ops officer reported. One of the air-defense units in the lead battalion was launching surface-to-air missiles, their mobile 2K12 "Cub" missiles. "Another SAM-12 Bravo One . . . SAM-12, three missiles away, Bravo One." That was a typical Cub engagement, Turabi knew, but he had ordered the operators to launch only one missile at a time to try to save missiles. Each battalion had only six systems—nine missiles total—to counter all the high-powered fighter-bombers at Mary. "Got one!" the ops officer crowed. "SAM-33 Bravo One engaging." The SAM-33, or 9K33 Osa, or "Wasp," was a short-range, low-altitude capable antiaircraft-missile system—that meant that the aircraft had blown past the longer-range Cub missile system and had to be engaged by the shorter-range, close-in Wasp. "Triple-A-Six-Mike Bravo One engaging radar." Now the self-propelled antiaircraft guns were responding. The enemy aircraft were coming in fast.

"How many aircraft, damn it?" Turabi shouted. "Where are they?"

"Got another one!" the comm officer crowed. "Sukhoi-24s, coming in low! They—"

They heard it almost simultaneously: the hiss of a high-speed jet passing very close by, like a fast-approaching swarm of angry bees racing across the desert, followed by two sonic booms that rattled everything not welded in place, followed by a string of large explosions. One or two bombs landed close enough to make the command-post vehicle jump a meter or two off the ground, and Turabi wasn't sure which direction was up—they could have been blasted on their side or blasted to hell, for all he knew. The lights went out inside the cab, and there was nothing but a loud squeal in his headphones. An electrical fire started someplace—the cab started filling with acidy fumes.

"Power!" Turabi shouted. "Get the power on!" Someone tried to push past him in the darkness—one of the techs who sat behind the Plexiglas board, panicking and rushing toward the exit. Turabi shoved him back through the hinged board. "Get back to your station!" he shouted. "Get some battery lights on and get the generator restarted! Do it *now!*"

"They're dead!" the tech shouted. When the inside battery lights finally snapped on, Turabi could see the whites of the man's eyes, huge with fear. Turabi saw that the tech had opened up the slit between the command-post cab and the driver's cab, and a thick curl of smoke was drifting in. That's where the acrid electrical smell was coming from. "The front of the truck . . . God help us, they're all *dead!*"

The armor plating between the cabs had probably saved them from the same fate met by the drivers. "Close that shutter and *get the power back on!*" Turabi shouted. The fact that he stayed in the command-post vehicle seemed to boost the spirits of his men, and after a few moments they started working together once again. Soon the generator power was back on and the radios came back to life, and even the frightened techs behind the Plexiglas were updating the tactical-grid display with their grease pencils, writing backward with extraordinary speed and clarity.

"Green One, Green One, this is Bravo Three, how do you read me?"

"Loud and clear now, Bravo Three," Turabi responded. "We were knocked off the air for a minute. Did you make contact?"

"Affirmative! Looks like eight heavy-tank platoons in a staggered W formation, coming in hard from the north-northwest. We are engaging."

"Bravo Three, acknowledged. Engage from your position. If you need to break contact, pull straight back to the south. Bravo Four and Airborne Three should be moving in any minute to back you up from the east, and Bravo Six should be moving in from the north. Don't let them break out past you—keep them in front of you. Acknowledge." No reply. "Bravo Three, acknowledge."

A skull-piercing shriek of pain and the roar of an explosion and fire suddenly broke the chatter over the command net. Oh, shit—the leader of Bravo Three or one of the other company commanders on the net had been hit, and his last dying action was to keep his fingers pressed onto the mike button so everyone on the net could hear his death scream. That was not good. "Airborne Three, this is Green One, what do you see?"

"We are engaging enemy tanks on the northwest grid," the helicopter flight commander reported. "Bravo Three looks like they took several direct hits. The Turkmen are coming with T-72s and maybe even T-80s—they're shooting on the run." The biggest tank Zarazi's force had was a T-64, which had a 125-millimeter smoothbore cannon and autoloader like the T-72, but it did not have a sophisticated laser-aiming computer, so it had to stop to fire its gun; most of Zarazi's tank force were much older T-55s and T-54s, whose 100-millimeter main guns probably wouldn't even put a dent in a T-72's 120-millimeter reactive armor.

"Roger, Air Three. I can see one platoon of Bravo Four moving in fast from the north, but I can't see the rest of Four, and there's no sign of Six. I will . . . shit . . . oh, shit—" And then his radio cut off as well.

"Airborne Three, come in."

"This is Airborne Three-Two," a different voice said.

One of the wingmen had taken over on the net. "Lead took a hit. Looks like the armor coming in from the north brought some SAMs with them. We are engaging. I see only four tanks from Bravo Four coming in to help Bravo Three. They're going to get chewed to pieces here in about twenty minutes if they don't get more help."

"Roger, Airborne Three. Did you hear that, Bravo Four? Get in there and help, *right now!*"

"Green One, this is Bravo One, we have pushed off the enemy force on the highway—they are scattering. The highway is clear. Do you want us to head north to help Bravo Three? Over."

"Is Bravo Two still with you?"

"They are engaging the Hinds off to the south, but I think the Hinds might be withdrawing to the southwest. We appear clear to the south. I haven't heard from Bravo Two, but I think they lost only one or two units from the Hind attack."

"Roger that. Stand by. Break. Bravo Two, this is Green One, are you up on the net?"

"Affirmative, Green One. It looks like the Hinds only had cannons and marking rockets and just a few missiles. They swept in, fired a few rounds, then headed away."

"Roger. Bravo Two, you take the highway and make best speed to the objective. Don't stop to fight, just get to the control station and take it as soon as you can. Take as much air defense as you can. Keep an eye to the south— they might try another attack once the Hinds depart. Acknowledge."

"Roger, Green One. We're on the move. Our air defense will have to catch up with us. They'll cover our six."

"Roger that. Break. Bravo One, wheel north and attack the enemy's right flank. Get a good positive ID before you shoot—elements of Bravo Four are moving in behind the enemy formation. You'll be face-to-face." He hoped.

"Acknowledged. We're on the move."

Turabi took a moment to plant the image of the battle-field in his mind. It was not looking good. "Airborne Three, what's the status of Bravo Three?"

There was a slight pause, then, "Sorry, Colonel."

Turabi swore loudly—an entire company of tanks, destroyed in less than fifteen minutes. Their entire northern flank was exposed now.

"Airborne Three is breaking contact to reload," came the report. "We've got elements of Airborne Two moving in. I think I saw one more platoon of Bravo Four moving in, but no sign of the rest of them and no sign of Bravo Six."

"Bravo Six, what is your position? Can you see the enemy forces? They should be about ten kilometers in front of you." No response. Damn it, Turabi swore, silently this time. They bugged out, probably back up the highway toward their reinforced ammo dump and supply depot at Ravnina. They were going to pay for that! "Bravo Four, have you made—"

"SAM-12 Bravo Two . . . SAM-12 Bravo Two, south-west!"

"Green One, Green One, many fast-movers, many fast-movers coming in from the southwest, going supersonic, very low altitude!" The Russians had waited until their Mi-24 Hinds moved out of the way and the left flank moved up, and then they swooped in with a force of fighter-bombers.

"Pop smoke! Pop smoke!" He was about to order the driver to move positions, but he remembered that the drivers were dead, the engine and front of their command-post vehicle blasted apart. There was no longer any choice—they were sitting ducks here. He pounded on the Plexiglas board with a fist. "Evacuate the command cab! Get moving!" The techs behind the glass needed no encouragement. They had the board opened and were racing out of the cab as soon as the metal stairs were lowered into place. Turabi remembered to grab the backpack radio and map case just before he leaped out of the vehicle.

The screening smoke was gagging and oily-tasting, so thick that at first Turabi didn't know which way to run— but soon the explosions started again, and he ran straight ahead until an explosion tossed him off his feet as if the hard-baked desert floor were a carpet that had just been pulled out from under him. He felt white-hot pieces of flying metal rip into his uniform and bounce off his helmet, and the soles of his boots seemed hot enough to melt. The last explosion felt like being hit with a hundred-kilo bag of sand, and he could do nothing else but close his eyes and scream.

Once the ringing in his ears stopped, he willed his legs to start working again and managed to crawl over to his command-post vehicle. It had taken an indirect hit that had turned the ten-ton vehicle over on its side and blown out all its tires. The drivers' cab was indeed burned out by what appeared to be a rocket or small missile. The bomb crater was fairly deep and was no longer smoldering, so Turabi crawled down inside it. The height was perfect— all but the very top of his head was underground. He thought it a little strange to be headquartered in his enemy's bomb crater, but there was no time to worry about that now. He set up the portable radio, extending the antenna as far over the crater rim as he could, and spread out his chart, holding it open with bomb fragments.

The network was eerily quiet. This did not feel good at all. "Bravo One, Green One."

"Green One, this is Bravo One." Again it was a different voice on the radio, much younger and panicky-sounding—the company commander and perhaps a platoon commander or two had probably been killed by now. "Are you all right, sir?"

Suddenly the net was coming alive again—it was as if all the units were waiting for someone to take charge. He couldn't blame his men too much. A month ago his most senior and battle-hardened commanders were little more than half-starved bandits driving Toyota pickups across the desert. They had to learn how to be tank commanders by watching, listening, following orders, and having the courage to take the fight right to the enemy. "The CP took a hit, and the crew scattered," Turabi said, after he cleared the chatter off the command net again. "What's your situation?"

"We are engaging the Turkmen right flank," the company commander reported. "The *nafahm* Bravo Four finally showed up in force and is engaging the enemy left. Air Two and Three are trying to keep the center from breaking through. No word at all from Bravo Three or Bravo Six."

So they were still in the fight—good. It showed that competent warriors could still be effective even without a command post bugging them every five minutes. Turabi tried Bravo Six, the rear company, again—still no response. *Haramzadeh!* Bastards!

"Incoming!" someone shouted. Turabi turned toward a hissing sound—just in time to see what looked like an immense dart or a small fighter jet drop out of the sky only a few hundred meters away. He knew he should be diving to the bottom of the crater, but the sight of such a large object moving so fast, hitting the earth so close to him was eerily fascinating. He didn't know if it was a downed Russian jet or a cruise missile—but soon it didn't matter. There was another powerful explosion, except this time it didn't feel like anything. Darkness closed in around him as if an "off" switch had been thrown in his brain.

Turabi awoke lying on the hard desert floor. At first he

couldn't open his eyes, and when he finally could, they stung from the billows of smoke wafting into his face. Someone was pouring water on top of his bare head. Every part of his body ached, and his face felt burned and raw. The smoke was gone, but his throat and lungs still felt coarse, and he could neither cough the congestion away nor take a deep enough breath to try harder.

His hands touched something brittle, yet it gave easily to pressure. Turabi knew that the tank was to his right, so he felt to his left to go around it. There was more brittle material that way. He felt farther left—and found a human arm. His fingers moved on their own now. He soon felt a torso, and then a chest. The corpse was not wearing a uniform—it was wearing robes. It was one of his men, a Taliban. He soon realized that the first thing he'd felt was the head, blasted open and burned.

Turabi quickly rolled to his other side, but moments later he encountered another body, this one even more heavily mangled and burned than the first. He realized with shock that he had been deliberately placed in the midst of a line of Taliban corpses.

"Try to stay still, sir," he heard a familiar voice say. He turned and saw his first sergeant and aide, Abdul Dendara, sitting nearby. His face was almost completely black from smoke and burns, and his clothing was in tatters.

"What happened?" Turabi asked. "Have we been overrun?"

"Overrun?" Dendara looked puzzled for a long moment, and then his eyes brightened. "You don't know, sir?" he asked incredulously. "Of course not—you've been unconscious, maybe even in a coma, for most of the day. Your forces were victorious, sir!"

"What?"

"You had the Turkmen on the run. It's a good thing your

helicopters came in when they did, because you were no more than even most of the battle, but you deployed your forces brilliantly and had the upper hand. The Turkmen ran like scared mice, with the Russians leading the retreat. The city of Mary is yours, sir. Congratulations."

SIX

BATTLE MOUNTAIN AIR RESERVE BASE
BATTLE MANAGEMENT CENTER
That same time

Four of the sixteen large, full-color screens at the back of the Battle Management Center at Battle Mountain Air Reserve Base filled with the image of the chairman of the Joint Chiefs of Staff, Air Force General Richard Venti, speaking through the secure videoteleconference system in his office. Venti's uniform blouse and tie were gone, and a large glass of something with ice sat on the desk; Patrick couldn't see if it was just water or some after-hours beverage. Venti was absently juggling a fat Montblanc pen in his fingers, a habit he picked up from the endless mission briefings and debriefings he'd sat through during his Cold War fighter-pilot days pulling alert in Europe. "Go ahead, folks," he said. "I see you fine now. Secretary Goff asked me to handle your request. He's standing by on a secure line if we need him."

Patrick McLanahan sat forward at the command console. With him were David Luger, Rebecca Furness, Daren Mace, and John Long. "Sir, I've received a request from

Deputy Secretary of State Hershel to provide security support for her upcoming trip to Bahrain and Turkmenistan."

"We've received the request as well," Venti said. "I got
approval from SECDEF. Any problems on your end?"

"Just one, sir: I don't think it's enough," Patrick
McLanahan replied.

"Explain."

"Sir, as part of the operational review of the situation in
Turkmenistan, we launched a constellation of reconnaissance and eavesdropping satellites to monitor the situation
there," Patrick said. "We recently monitored a major battle
between the Taliban insurgents and Turkmen regulars
against the city of Mary, and we believe that the insurgents
will have the city in their control within a matter of
hours—and that means Russia will be directly threatened."

"I received your report from Air Force, Patrick," Venti
said, "but, as I said in my reply, I don't see the hazard here
other than what Deputy Secretary Hershel has already accepted. The Turkmen capital doesn't appear to be in danger currently. This would be a good time to initiate a
diplomatic mission. If the fighting starts to spread west,
I'm sure State will order an evacuation."

"But I believe that the situation *has* become much
worse, sir, even in the past two days," Patrick said. "Flying
a diplomatic mission into Turkmenistan right now might
be an important thing to do to try to get control of this Taliban uprising and the possible repercussions should Russia counterattack, but it still places Deputy Secretary
Hershel and President Martindale in grave danger."

"It's part of the job," Venti said. "If she or the president
thought they'd be in real danger, I suppose they would send
some other representative. The State Department deals
with these kinds of dangers every day." It was obvious in
his voice that he wanted to wrap up this discussion—or
maybe he didn't really believe what he was saying himself.

"Thanks for your concern, Patrick. I'll forward your report to State. Anything else?"

"No, sir."

Venti stopped and looked at Patrick for a rather long moment. "Just for my edification, General: In case the situation did get worse between now and when Deputy Secretary Hershel's plane flies over Turkmenistan, what else would you have in mind?" He turned and typed something on his computer terminal, then read a page or two. "I have your entire unit mission plan right here in front of me, which I received from General Luger. Is this what you're talking about?"

"Sir, the Air Battle Force ground team has been mobilized. I would simply implement the rest of the total force," Patrick explained. "The Air Battle Force travels and fights as a team, not as individuals. I agreed to provide security support for Deputy Secretary Hershel because I'm anxious to prove what our ground team can do, but the idea is to deploy as a team, even if the other elements are never utilized."

"So you're suggesting . . . ?"

"I should be authorized to deploy the rest of the Air Battle Force," Patrick said. "One Air Battle team, deployed and ready for action in-theater, with the rest of the Air Battle Force deployed to Diego Garcia or on fast alert here to back up the first team if necessary."

Patrick could see General Venti wearily rubbing his temples, then leaning back in his seat. "I'll need to read over your unit mission plan again, Patrick, before I up-channel this."

"Sir, Hershel is already on her way to Bahrain for updates and consultations. She goes on to Turkmenistan in under forty-eight hours," Patrick said. "That gives us less than one day before we need to deploy—"

"I know, Patrick, I know," Venti said irritably. "But

there just hasn't been time to study all this. We were concerned about *funding* further development of your unit, not about actually *deploying* it in so short a time."

"Sir . . ."

"Patrick, relax," Venti interrupted. "I'll call the staff together and we'll get this on the secretary's desk right away, along with your report and your recommendations. But we can't accomplish everything instantly. If need be, we can recommend that Hershel's mission be postponed. But in all likelihood everything will proceed normally. She and Martindale will meet with the Turkmen government and the ambassadors from the different nations involved, then get the hell out of there. The Turkmen and Russians aren't crazy—they wouldn't dare threaten a U.S. diplomatic mission."

"Yes, sir" was all Patrick could say.

Venti shook his head. "You did good work here, Patrick. Very heads-up—the kind of information I need from my field commanders. But the civilian side, especially the diplomatic side, is a whole other world. Sometimes everything we do is simply not enough. Our job is to give them the data and our recommended course of action. *They* make the decisions."

"Yes, sir," Patrick responded neutrally.

Patrick's tone of voice rang an alarm in Richard Venti's head, and his attention immediately snapped back to the video screen. "General, I advise you to think carefully before you plan your next moves," he said. Furness and Long could feel the weight of his stare even through the secure videoconference link. "I know you want to help, and you're doing so right now. But remember your recent history. I like the planning you and your staff do, and I encourage you to continue. But every time you decide to embark on some unauthorized activity, someone ends up getting hurt—usually yourself."

"I understand, sir."

"Make sure that you do, General. Anything else for me?"

"No, sir. Thank you for your time."

"Thanks for your reports. I'll be in touch."

The connection terminated. Patrick immediately called up the aircraft status board and a chart detailing the current locations of all the Air Battle Force's and 111th Wing's airborne aircraft. He ignored the alarmed shuffling Colonel Long was doing behind him. "General Luger."

"Sir?"

"Generate and deploy the First Air Battle team immediately, and assume combat air-patrol operations over Turkmenistan. Assemble and deploy a combat-support group to Diego Garcia, and prepare ramp space and support facilities at Diego Garcia for combat operations. Then generate the Second Air Battle Team, and deploy them to Diego Garcia, configuration Gold."

"What?" John Long exclaimed.

"Yes, *sir,*" Luger responded, glaring at Long. He immediately sat down at the deputy commander's console and began typing in instructions. Seconds later Rebecca Furness turned away from the others as the duty officer called on her earpiece to notify her that her wing's aircraft were being recalled and tasked with a mission and deployment by the Air Battle Force.

"Excuse me, General, but didn't you hear what the chairman said?" Long asked incredulously. "He said *no unauthorized activity.* I was standing right here, and I didn't hear him authorize you to send any aircraft anywhere!"

"John . . ." Rebecca started.

"What is it with you, McLanahan?" Long dug in. "Do you think this Air Force exists for your own personal pleasure?"

"Colonel . . ."

"Or have you completely gone *insane?*"

"Colonel Long!" Rebecca snapped.

Long turned to her in surprise.

"An L-hour has been declared by the Air Battle Force. Issue an immediate recall of all wing personnel and aircraft—"

"Rebecca, *what are you doing?*"

"Then generate the Alpha and Bravo Force aircraft in configuration Gold," she went on, setting a timer on her watch—she knew that the duty officer would keep track of aircraft generation timing, but old habits died hard with veteran commanders like herself. "The Alpha Force crews should be ready for the prelaunch mission brief in L plus ten hours; the Bravo Force should be ready to go on ground alert in L plus eighteen. The wing battle staff will meet in the BATMAN in thirty minutes. An L-hour directs a Reserve Forces call-up, so you better notify the Nevada adjutant general and the governor of Nevada that the wing is commencing a full combat generation, and make sure they understand this is not an exercise."

"Rebecca, we have absolutely no authority to be doing this," Long sputtered. "It's patently illegal. McLanahan is going to make a fool out of us *again!*"

"Colonel Long, I haven't heard you order the duty officer to issue a wing recall."

"And you won't, until we have a chance to talk," Long shot back.

"Duty Officer," Rebecca called, "notify Colonel Mace that he is now the wing operations-group commander. Colonel Long will assume the duties of the Fifty-first Squadron commander."

"Yes, General Furness," the electronic duty officer responded.

"Rebecca, damn it, listen to me!" Long shouted. He took her by the arm and physically moved her away from McLanahan and Luger.

Rebecca's eyes blazed, but she let him have his say.

"Rebecca, you can't do any of this. You can't follow an order knowing it's illegal. You've been through this before with McLanahan, and you've gotten busted. Don't trash your career again for the likes of *them*."

"Colonel Long, you are to report back to the BATMAN in utility uniform and organize the Fifty-first Squadron recall until the battle-staff meeting—"

"I've got something to say first."

Rebecca closed her eyes, then turned away from him and spoke: "Duty Officer, have Security Forces report to the BATMAN immediately and escort Colonel Long to his office, situation code yellow."

"'Yellow'? What do you think I am, damn it, a *terrorist?*"

"You've disobeyed orders and shown absolute disregard for rank or authority," Rebecca said. "In my opinion you are not in full control of your emotions or senses, and I determine you are a risk to wing assets. Duty Officer, Colonel Long is to remain confined to his office incommunicado until further notice. Rescind my order making Colonel Long the Fifty-first's commander—show his specialty code as Eight-X. Notify Lieutenant Colonel Ricardo that he is now the Fifty-first Squadron's commander."

"Yes, General Furness."

"God damn you, Rebecca—you're fucking out of your mind!" Long shouted.

"Duty Officer, correction, show Colonel Long's specialty code now as Nine-X," Rebecca ordered. The Eight-series codes were reserved for special-duty officers—usually officers stuck in an office somewhere insignificant until they could be reassigned or ousted, or for medical patients in hospitals. It was bad enough going from a Zero-series code—a commander—to an Eight-series. But the Nine-series specialty codes were reserved for officers doing time in prison, under investigation for criminal activities, or undergoing psychiatric treatment—untrainable, unpromotable, and unassignable. Long had just been sent to the Air Force's version of purgatory.

Moments later two Security Forces officers stepped quickly into the room. Both were pulling on leather gloves. After putting on his gloves, one of the officers pulled a stun gun out of its sheath, keeping it in view just long enough for Long to know he had it in his hand. The other officer took Long by the upper arm to lead him away; when Long tried to shrug off the officer's hand, the first officer immediately pinned Long's other arm behind him, and together, the two officers handcuffed Long's arms behind his back and led him away.

At first McLanahan and Luger made absolutely no mention of the entire event once Rebecca had sat back down at her console and logged in. But after a few minutes Patrick half turned to her and asked, "Isn't that going to leave the Fifty-first short of aircraft commanders, Rebecca?"

"Who cares?" she replied. "We don't need aircrew members to fly my planes anymore, remember?" She looked at McLanahan and said, "I'm taking the first Air Battle team to Turkmenistan."

"I need you here."

"I'm going with the general, sir," Daren Mace said.

"I need you *both* here."

"Sir, I know what you're going to say, but you know it's not the right thing to do," Rebecca said. "The virtual-cockpit control stuff is just too unpredictable and new to rely on with this mission. I'll fly with your unmanned toys, sir, but I'll insist on personally commanding the rest of the force. If you don't like it, too bad—sir."

Patrick looked at both Furness and Mace, then nodded. "I wish I were going with you, that's all."

"Say that more than once, sir, and I'll put you on a

crew," Rebecca said. She smiled, then added, "You've had your fun, Major General McLanahan. I've got a bunch of youngsters on this base who want a piece of the action now. You built this place as your command center—you should use it."

TWO HUNDRED KILOMETERS NORTHEAST OF MARY, REPUBLIC OF TURKMENISTAN
Later that day

A string of six Russian Mi-6 transport helicopters swept in at high speed toward Mary. They flew less than a rotor's diameter above the desert floor, high enough to minimize the dust cloud kicked up by their huge blades but low enough to avoid detection by ground-based radars.

The Mi-6 transport helicopter, first rolled out almost fifty years earlier, was one of the world's largest, a perfect example of the old Soviet drive to build bigger and bigger war machines. Fitted with external wings to help provide lift and plenty of hardpoints for extended-range fuel tanks, the immense Mi-6 transports were the Russian army's most important heavy-lift helicopter. Each one carried forty fully armed combat troops and two BMD airborne-combat vehicles. The assault group had deployed from its base in Volgograd, refueled in Astrakhan on the Caspian Sea, and had launched again with other helicopters carrying enormous fuel bladders. They landed in the wastelands of central Uzbekistan completely undetected by anyone, refueled from the bladders, and then began its assault into southwestern Turkmenistan.

For the Russian helicopter pilots manning the big transport and attack choppers on this mission, flying in this region of the world was a whole new experience. They truly believed that life for most of the people living in these wastelands couldn't have changed much in the past thousand years. Case in point: the camel caravans they encountered in Uzbekistan and Turkmenistan.

As they raced across the desert, they saw dozens of groups of nomads scattered across the landscape. The gunners in the Mi-24 Hind attack helicopters locked up every one of them in their infrared targeting systems, ready to blast them to pieces—and at first, in Uzbekistan, a few groups did get blasted. But when they zoomed in on them with their telescopic sights, it turned out they really *were* just camel caravans traveling across the burning desert sands. Here it was, the twenty-first century, and there were still nomads riding their camels, the animals piled high with crates, blankets, and other odds and ends to trade or sell. No use in wasting precious ammunition on them.

Fifty kilometers outside Mary, the formation moved into trail position and descended lower to the desert floor in an attempt to hide themselves from patrols. All radio frequencies were silent. Once in a while the gunship crews would spot an explosion far on the horizon or receive a brief squeak on the threat-warning receiver, but there was no sign whatsoever of the presence of Taliban forces. The pilots had to be careful now—there were more oil wells in this area, and they were definitely flying low enough now to run into them—and the clouds of dust kicked up by their rotors were starting to limit visibility for the trailing helicopters.

"Approaching infiltration point," the company commander announced. "Prepare for dismount."

"Target, target, two o'clock!" one of the Mi-6 pilots shouted.

The lead gunship pilot swung his telescopic sensor in

that direction—but it turned out to be a camel. The sight was so funny that the pilot couldn't help laughing. The big animal was truly comical, madly dashing away from the approaching helicopters, a few rugs and blankets that had broken loose from its back streaming behind it. As the pilot watched, the poor animal ran headlong into a fence surrounding a cluster of oil wells and collapsed in a tangle of legs and neck on the barbed wire. "No target," the pilot said. "Another damned camel."

"What should we do about those camel caravans we find out here?" the gunship pilot asked. "If the noise spooks those animals so bad, they could attract attention or set off an alarm in those oil well compounds."

"Next time you see them, take them out," the commander ordered.

Sure enough a few moments later the gunship pilot spotted several more groups of camel nomads huddled around some abandoned oil wells. "How in the hell can those people live out here like that?" he asked his gunner as he zoomed in the infrared image and centered his thirty-millimeter cannon's crosshairs on the first group. "They're fifty kilometers from the nearest shelter. No water, no food, no—"

The nomads started to move. A camel clambered to its feet and trundled off—and right behind where the camel had lain, the gunship commander clearly saw a man raise something to his shoulder. Seconds later a flash of light obscured the scene—but he knew what it was. "Missile attack!" he shouted. "We're under—"

The SA-14 antiaircraft missile hit the engine compartment of the hovering lead gunship, tearing the engines to pieces in a millisecond and sending the big helicopter spinning out of control sideways across the desert. In rapid succession a dozen more shoulder-fired antiaircraft missiles shot out across the night sky, and almost all of them found their targets. In seconds all the Russian heli-copters were on the ground. Only two of the half dozen Mi-6 transports and one Mi-24 gunship landed upright, and three of the fully loaded Mi-6s were on fire. A few troops ran out of the other downed helicopters, some carrying wounded.

"Open fire, fire at will," Jalaluddin Turabi ordered on his command radio. The six antiaircraft squads deployed around the area threw aside their SA-14 launchers and un-covered their thirty-seven-millimeter machine guns from their hiding places in the sand, mounted them, and began firing at the survivors. A few Russian commandos re-turned fire, but in a matter of minutes the battle was over.

Turabi and his security forces carefully approached the hulks of the downed helicopters. The echoes of gunshots and the crackle and groaning of burning metal and burn-ing Russian soldiers disturbed the desert stillness. Their grim job took nearly an hour—examining and, if neces-sary, dispatching almost three hundred Russian comman-dos strewn across the desert floor. "Three officers and twenty-one enlisted recovered alive, four armored person-nel carriers still operational," reported one of Turabi's se-nior platoon chiefs. "One helicopter gunship may be flyable. Want to try to fly it out of here, sir?"

"Burn it," Turabi said. "Get the prisoners to Mary, and get replacement missiles and ammo sent out here on the double. This might be only the first wave of Russian troops moving into this area—we need to be ready in case the second assault is inbound." Turabi had fought the Rus-sians before, as a youngster recruited into the Afghan re-sistance in the 1980s, and he knew that they rarely moved in small numbers. When they moved into an area, they usually did it with large, overwhelming force, giving themselves at least a ten-to-one numerical advantage.

"Yes, sir," the platoon chief said. "Outstanding job, sir.

It was a perfectly executed ambush. Brilliant idea using the camels to disguise our positions. The Russians must've actually thought we were a bunch of desert rats. They flew right up to us as if they didn't even know we were here."

Turabi surveyed the area. The massive burned hulks of the Mi-6 helicopters looked like the carcasses of some sort of prehistoric dinosaurs littering the desert. The smell of burning flesh and jet fuel was almost overpowering, but Turabi had seen too much death on this campaign to be sickened by it now. He scowled at his senior chief. "Two months ago, Anwar, we *were* nothing but a bunch of desert rats," Turabi said. "But at least we had a purpose and a mission. What are we now? Nothing but a bunch of invaders and murderers."

"We are soldiers."

"Soldiers fight to defend their homes and repel aggressors," Turabi said. "We do neither. We attack and pillage and kill, for no apparent reason. That makes us marauders, not heroes."

"Tomorrow we might be as dead and crispy as those Russians," the chief said. "Tonight we are victorious. That is good enough for me right now." He bowed his head briefly in respect and left to carry out Turabi's orders, obviously uncomfortable with the direction this discussion was taking.

Jalaluddin Turabi had to remind himself—*again*—to be careful about verbalizing his doubts and inner conflicts with his men. It was a very successful operation, well planned and executed. Their losses had been minimal; the Russians' overconfidence cost them dearly. It was necessary for the men to know he was proud of their courage and discipline. Instead he had moaned to the senior chief about how all of this was a waste. How were the men supposed to react after hearing something like that?

This war was far from over, Turabi reminded himself, and he was farther than ever from home. He had to rely on these men, and they had to rely on him, if they had any chance whatsoever of making it home again.

MINISTRY OF DEFENSE, FRUNZE EMBANKMENT, MOSCOW, RUSSIAN FEDERATION
A short time later

"Oh . . . my . . . God," faltered General Anatoliy Gryzlov, chief of staff of the Russian military forces. He immediately slammed the phone down, jumped from his seat, and dashed to his private elevator, which took him down to the underground Central Military Command Center at Frunze Embankment. "What in hell happened out there in Turkmenistan?" he thundered as soon as he entered the chamber.

"An ambush. They were waiting for us, sir," the senior controller replied. "We're repositioning satellites to get a better look at the northeast quadrant of Mary, but we feel it was a freak occurrence—our forces were just in the wrong place at the wrong time. The opposing force could not have been more than company size, well hidden, and armed with shoulder-fired antiaircraft missiles."

"Ni pizdf!" Gryzlov swore, banging a fist on the desk. He thought for a moment, but he had already made up his mind long before he reached the command center. "Get the entire staff in here immediately. I was briefed on an air-invasion plan as a contingency operation—I want that plan set in motion immediately. I want all the airspace around Turkmenistan closed off and ten tactical-attack air

regiments on the ground in Mary and Ashkhabad within forty-eight hours." He picked up the direct line to the president's office in the Kremlin. "I want to speak with him *immediately*—I don't care who he's meeting with."

"What in hell is so important, General?" Sen'kov said a few minutes later when he came on the line. "I'm in a very important meeting with—"

"Mr. President, I lost three hundred soldiers last night in Turkmenistan."

"*Sraka,*" Sen'kov muttered. The line was silent for a moment, and then Gryzlov could hear Sen'kov ordering the room cleared. "All right, damn it, get over here as fast as you can."

"I will tell you what happened and what I will do about it *now,* Mr. President. I'm not going to waste more time taking crap from you!"

"Watch your tongue, General!"

"*Yimu adin huy kto ty yest!*" Gryzlov said. "I don't care who the hell you are now, sir. All I care about is teaching those Taliban bastards the dangers of raising a weapon at a Russian soldier!"

"Relax, General. Get over here and—"

"Sir, I'm sending in an air strike against the known Taliban positions in Mary," Gryzlov interrupted. "First I'm going to order a complete air blockade of Turkmenistan. No one enters or leaves the country without my express permission."

"The American secretary of state's delegation is due to arrive in twenty-four hours."

"The Turkmen foreign ministry should warn that delegation not to attempt to enter the country, especially around Mary," Gryzlov said. "I will not allow even one beat-up old crop duster to interfere with my operation. It will be in the Americans' best interest to stay well away from Turkmenistan. President Thorn is *famous* for staying away from trouble—make him understand that it would be wise to stay out of this conflict."

"What are you planning on doing next?"

"I'm going to commence round-the-clock heavy aerial bombardment until satellite imagery detects no movement of Taliban armored or mechanized forces," Gryzlov replied. "Then I'm going to drop an entire battalion of paratroopers with artillery on that city, retake the airfield, and set up a secure forward command center in Mary. I'm going to insert a brigade of mechanized infantry into Mary and retake the city. I'm going to repeat the entire process with Chärjew, then Kizyl-arvat, and finally Gaurdak."

"What in God's name is your objective here, Gryzlov? Do you want to destroy all those cities? Do you intend to take the entire *country?*"

"My objective will be to eliminate all Taliban and any other subversive elements in Turkmenistan and retake the oil fields and pipelines," Gryzlov said. "Russia will be criticized for attacking Turkmenistan with such overwhelming force—but I don't care. I will retake control of the country quickly and effectively." Gryzlov paused, waiting to see if Sen'kov was going to object. When he did not, Gryzlov continued, "Sir, the warning order will be transmitted to the district headquarters immediately, and the execution order will be on your desk in fifteen minutes. I expect you to sign the order. I plan on launching the first air strike in less than eight hours from now."

There was a very long pause, almost a full minute. Gryzlov was growing angrier by the second, until: "Very well, General. Issue the warning order, then get the execution order on my desk immediately. I am prepared to sign it. But, General?"

"Sir?"

"You will be very careful in the future to consult with the Defense Ministry and myself before making any more such plans," Sen'kov warned. "I don't like your tone, and I don't like being told what to do."

"Sir, at this moment I don't much care what you like," Gryzlov said. "You told me you were so afraid of Turkmenistan's turning into another Kosovo or Chechnya, and then you tied my hands behind my back—"

"Watch your tone of voice, General!"

"I will *not,* sir!" Gryzlov shot back. "I am putting you on notice from now on, sir, that the Russian military *will not tolerate* any more political equivocating or half commitments where vital Russian interests or Russian military forces are involved! If my men are attacked again, I will act—and if I do not receive one hundred percent backing from the Kremlin, I will see to it that there are leaders in place who *will* back the military!"

"You are out of line, Gryzlov!" Sen'kov cried. "One more word out of you and you'll find yourself in a Siberian prison beside Zhurbenko!"

"Don't threaten me, Mr. President," Gryzlov said. "As long as my men and women guard your offices, support influential members of the Duma, and monitor your phones and computers, you will not threaten me! My soldiers know I will die before I fail to support them, and I know they will die to support me. That is all *you* need to remember. I'll have that execution order on your desk in ten minutes. It had better be back on my desk in twenty minutes, or the next target for my bombers will be the Kremlin!"

Valentin Sen'kov replaced the phone on its cradle. His foreign minister, Ivan Filippov, stared at him in complete amazement. "Was that General Gryzlov shouting on the phone?" he asked. "I could hear it all the way from here!"

"The commandos he sent to Turkmenistan—"

"The ones he sent in to sneak into Mary and reconnoiter the Taliban positions—I remember," Filippov said. "What about them? Were they successful?" He looked at Sen'kov's horrified, incredulous expression. "Some of them get hurt?"

"All of them . . . got dead," Sen'kov breathed.

"What?" Filippov cried, rising to his feet. "All of them? How many . . . ?"

"Three hundred."

Filippov was too stunned to speak.

"Gryzlov is shutting down the airspace over Turkmenistan, and he's going to send in a large bomber force," Sen'kov went on. "You need to contact the American foreign ministry and the White House right away, notify them what happened, and tell them that for our protection we are imposing a blockade of Turkmen airspace."

"Sir, we didn't discuss doing that—not even as a contingency," Filippov said. "Besides, we can't legally just close off another country's airspace. My advice would be to let a bunch of journalists in to see what those Taliban raiders did. Then the world might be more on our side when we're ready to strike."

"General Gryzlov is sending over an execution order for me to sign right now," Sen'kov said. "He's already issued a warning order to his bomber forces."

"Well, fuck him until you decide what you want to do first," Filippov said. "He's not the—" Filippov stopped and looked at Sen'kov with a perplexed expression that quickly turned to shock. "Wait a minute . . . Gryzlov was *yelling* at you on the phone just now? He was telling you what he was going to do, and he ordered you to comply?"

"He threatened me," Sen'kov said.

Filippov had never seen the president so scared before—in fact, he thought he'd never seen *anyone* so scared before, even Zhurbenko just before they hauled him away to prison.

"He threatened to kill me, blow up the Kremlin—and he's serious, Ivan. He's not crazy—he's dead serious."

"He needs to be arrested—no, he needs to be disposed of!" Filippov cried. "Threatening the president of the federation, threatening the lives of government officials—who in hell does he think he is?"

"Who's going to dispose of him, Ivan? You? Me? He's threatened to turn every uniformed man and woman against me. And after what happened in the Balkans, I don't think the Duma or the bureaucrats will stand in his way."

"Don't let him bullshit you, sir," Filippov said. "The MVD Interior Troops and the OMON special-assignments command forces assigned to protect you are not under his command—they're part of the Interior Ministry."

"That's . . . what? A few thousand troops? Maybe ten thousand? He controls over a *million* battle-ready troops."

"He doesn't command them—he runs the general staff," Filippov said. "He can't get on the radio or TV tomorrow and *order* all those troops to do what he . . ."

But Filippov's voice trailed off, and Sen'kov immediately knew why. They both knew that General Anatoliy Gryzlov might just be popular enough to do exactly that: get on TV and the nationwide radio system, address the Russian people, order a coup, and roll his tanks into Red Square to take over the government.

Tomorrow. Maybe even *tonight.*

"What are you going to do?" Filippov breathed.

"We're going to do exactly what he told us to do," Sen'kov said nervously. "We are going to get Gurizev to immediately rescind his invitation for the Americans to visit Ashkhabad, and we're going to announce an air cordon of Turkmenistan. And then we're going to let Gryzlov pound the hell out of those Taliban." Sen'kov thought for a moment, then added, "And we are going to use every opportunity, quietly and publicly, to distance ourselves from this military action."

"But you've got to sign the execution order."

"I said I *would* sign it, but Gryzlov said he was going to deploy his troops immediately and attack as soon as they were in place," Sen'kov said. "I think we could arrange for Gryzlov's office to *think* I signed the order. . . ."

"So if the attacks work, you can show you signed on to the plan," Filippov said. "And if it doesn't work . . ."

"I'll show I didn't sign the order, which makes Gryzlov look even more like a berserker than he already is."

"But if Gryzlov finds out that you double-crossed him?"

"We'll just have to be sure that he's taken care of before that happens," Valentin Sen'kov said. "We'll start building a 'watch file' on Gryzlov with the Interior Ministry and the Federal Security Bureau." The Federal Security Bureau was the new name of the old Komitet Gosudarstvennoy Bezopasnoti, or KGB, the main foreign- and internal-security and intelligence agency in Russia, whose commander reported directly to the president. "I'll need a copy and transcript of his tirade on the phone to me. That'll show the world that the man's insane. Then I won't be accused of murder—I'll be praised for ridding the world of yet another mad dog."

OVER THE MEDITERRANEAN SEA
A short time later

Assistant Deputy Secretary of State Isadora Meiling stepped quietly past the sleeping berths occupied by former president Kevin Martindale. Oh, God, she thought. All she could think about was sneaking in there and giving him a kiss—or maybe something more. What was it about that guy anyway? His supernatural silver locks? The tight ass? Or the sheer power that seemed to ooze from every pore of his body?

She knocked twice on a locked door, swiped her passkey on the lock, and went inside to the private cabin in the rear of the Air Force C-32A transport, a modified VIP version of the commercial Boeing 757 airliner. The private VIP cabin had a walkway on the port side of the aircraft, making room for two soundproof sleeping quarters on the starboard side. The cabin then opened up into the main working area. There was a large semicircular desk, a small eight-person conference area in front of the desk with a table and laptop computer hookups, another desk on the starboard side, and electronic and office equipment in glass-enclosed soundproof racks. Two aides were working away at their computers; behind them Deputy Secretary of State Maureen Hershel was also busy typing on her laptop.

She looked up and noticed the worried look on Meiling's face. "What do you have, Izzy?" she asked.

Meiling glanced around to see who else might be in the room.

"Martindale is finally taking a nap. I've never seen people use the phone as much as he and his staff do—he probably had every transponder channel on every satellite in earth orbit tied up. So what do you have?"

"The latest from Turkmenistan," Meiling replied. She placed a folder on Hershel's desk. "Late yesterday some Turkmen and Russian military forces attacked those Taliban insurgents."

"What was the outcome?" Hershel asked, opening the folder and studying the maps. "Anything left of the Taliban?"

"The *Turkmen* units and their Russian officer corps got slaughtered," Meiling said.

Hershel's jaw dropped in surprise.

"Sixty percent casualties in less than half a day. The Taliban insurgents are firmly in control of the city of Mary and the TransCal Petroleum lines."

"Oh, shit," Maureen said. "Well, that's what General McLanahan predicted all along. We can expect the rest of his predictions to come true, too—including the Russians' counterattack. Anything else?"

"The Russians' counterattack, ma'am." She dropped another folder on Hershel's desk. "Shortly after the battle outside Mary, the Russians tried to insert about three hundred commandos northeast of the city."

" 'Tried'?"

"The Taliban troops were waiting for them," Izzy said. She tapped the folder with a long, red-painted fingernail. "Looks like every Russian helicopter was shot down, and every Russian soldier is either dead or captured. The satellite photos, sent from Battle Mountain, are pretty explicit."

"My God." Maureen thought for a moment. "Ask Colonel Briggs to come in here."

The tall, good-looking black officer was brought into the VIP cabin within moments, followed by Sergeant Major Chris Wohl. Maureen handed Briggs the message form.

"Your thoughts, Colonel?" she asked.

Briggs studied the reports for a few moments, then handed them to Chris Wohl. "Any word from the Turkmen foreign ministry?" Briggs asked.

"Just the warning that insurgents have taken Mary."

"Has Turkmenistan revoked our overflight authorization?"

"No," Isadora Meiling said. She turned to Hershel and said, "The closest divert base is Athens. Ankara, Turkey, is ahead, or we can reverse course and go to Rome."

Hershel looked puzzled. "Land in Europe? We've already got clearance to land in Bahrain, and we've got permission to land in Ashkhabad. Why do we need to reverse course?"

"*Why?* A major shooting war just started in Turkmenistan!"

"I agree with the deputy secretary," Briggs said. "If everyone is going to respect our diplomatic credentials, we should keep on pressing forward."

"Land in Turkmenistan? *In the middle of a war?* Excuse me, Colonel, but that sounds crazy," Meiling said incredulously. "Is there any guarantee that the Taliban or the Russians are going to respect our credentials? Is someone's air-to-air or surface-to-air missile going to respect our credentials before it blows us out of the sky?"

"Good points," Chris Wohl said.

Izzy Meiling nodded and smiled at the big Marine—and Hal Briggs nearly fell over in a dead faint when he saw Wohl nod and even appear to favor her with a half smile in return. When Chris Wohl was on the job, he usually remained as serious as a nuclear war. That microscopic smile was the closest Hal had ever seen the big Marine come to emotionally connecting with a woman—Hal hesitated to call it a "flirt"—in eleven years of working with the guy.

"It might be safer to land in some neighboring country—the United Nations base at Samarkand in Uzbekistan would be my first choice—and proceed by land or helicopter, or conclude your business by phone, or have the principals come to you," Wohl added.

"All good suggestions—except I don't feel we have the time," Hershel said. "I know there's a risk involved, but I want to proceed."

There was a knock at the door. Meiling checked the peephole. "It's President Martindale." The phone rang at that moment, and Hershel picked it up immediately as she waved for Meiling to let Martindale in. "Hershel . . . okay, operator, going secure." She pushed a button on her phone and waited for the beeping and hissing to stop. "Yes, I'm secure, thank you, operator. . . . I'll stand by."

A few moments later: "Maureen?"

"Yes, Mr. President."

"I don't suppose I can assume that because your plane hasn't diverted, you didn't get the word."

"I got the information on the attacks on the city of Mary and the Taliban ambushing those Russian commandos, Mr. President," Hershel replied. "But unless they revoke our landing permission, I intend to complete this mission."

"Miss Hershel, you know I try not to involve myself in my staff's decision making, but this is one instance when I think the smart thing would be to postpone your trip to Turkmenistan until things have calmed down."

"I'll talk it over with my staff, sir."

"But your inclination is to go ahead with the trip."

"It is, Mr. President."

Maureen heard the president sigh, but he did not contradict her. Instead he said, "I heard you brought along some . . . help."

Not one word of advice, second-guessing, or questioning—Maureen liked that. This was a president who trusted his staff, all right. "I hope that's okay, sir."

"It was a good call. What's your plan?"

"If we're allowed to land, I'm going to meet with Gurizev," Hershel replied. "If they refuse, I'll make a courtesy call to Niyazov—maybe he'll have some information. Then I'll meet with the Russian ambassador, if he's still in the capital. And then I'll try to meet with the Taliban general."

"And what about your new 'security personnel'? What are their plans, once they get to Turkmenistan?"

"*Their* plans, sir?"

"In light of what's happened in Turkmenistan these past few days, Miss Hershel, I think they'll be more effective on their own, not tied to your embassy staff or your travel contingent," the president said.

Hershel looked at Briggs and Wohl—and only then realized that they were probably not going to want to stick around just to baby-sit her. "I think I see what you mean, sir. I'll find out and let you know."

"Sounds fine, Maureen," the president said. "Keep me advised. Good luck."

"Thank you, Mr. President." And like that the call was over. Maureen looked at the receiver as if wondering if that was really all he had to say, then put the receiver back on its cradle. "The president wished us luck."

"What's happened, Maureen?" Kevin Martindale asked. He saw Briggs and Wohl and extended a hand. "How are you boys doing?"

"Very well, sir," Hal Briggs replied.

"Mr. President," Chris Wohl chimed in, as warm as he ever was—which was never very warm at all.

"I heard that Thorn reinstated you and gave you promotions. I'm glad to hear it."

"Thanks to you, I hear, sir," Briggs said.

"Just trying to undo the mess I caused by signing us on to that deal in Africa," Martindale said. "I know I'll never undo the pain I've caused Patrick. How is he?"

"Just fine, sir."

Maureen Hershel's face brightened when she heard Patrick's name. "I didn't realize you knew each other," she said.

"We go back a long way," Martindale said. "I didn't know they were part of this trip, but, by God, I'm glad they're here." He clasped Wohl on the shoulder. "I hope you brought all the gear with you."

"We did, sir."

"And Patrick . . . ?"

"Standing by, sir."

"Excellent." He turned to Hershel. "What's happened, Maureen?"

"Things are getting pretty tense over in Turkmenistan, Mr. President," Hershel said. "There's been a skirmish—" She stopped, then said, "No, I won't try to soft-pedal this. Sir, there's been a serious development. The Taliban insurgents decimated a Turkmen army force outside the city of Mary."

"My God," Martindale breathed. "Thorn should expect the Russians to counterattack, maybe try to land some commandos behind the Taliban forces in the city, maybe send some long-range bombers to pound the crap out of them like they did in Chechnya—"

"The Russians apparently tried to airlift about three hundred commandos into the outskirts of Mary," Maureen said. "Some Taliban forces ambushed them with shoulder-fired antiaircraft missiles. All of the Russians were either killed or captured."

"So it's war," Martindale muttered. "Have we been ordered to turn around? Have our landing or overflight rights been canceled?"

"No, sir."

"Did Thorn *order* you to turn around?"

"The president advised me to postpone the trip," Hershel replied, "but he said it was my call."

"And?"

"The conflict happened almost two hundred miles from the capital—I think we'll be all right," Hershel said. "But I'm more concerned about your safety, Mr. President. I'm concerned about not making it to Turkmenistan."

"I only need to know one thing: Is Patrick McLanahan on the case?" Martindale asked.

Maureen Hershel blinked in surprise. "He happened to be the first person I called when I planned this trip."

"You did exactly the right thing, Maureen," Martindale said, barely disguising a sigh of relief. "I can guarantee that the general has been doing little else but watching over things in Turkmenistan since you first called."

That made Maureen Hershel feel very good, and she wasn't ashamed to let everyone see it. "Then I recommend we continue the mission," she said. "If overflight or landing privileges are revoked, we'll need to reassess." She turned to Briggs and Wohl. "What do you gents need from me? Satellite phones? Computers?"

"Access to our equipment," Briggs said. "We may have you take a few folks off the manifest in Bahrain and make the necessary calls to Ashkhabad."

"Some of you aren't going to Turkmenistan with us?"

"Oh, we'll be there, ma'am—just not as part of your contingent," Briggs said with a smile. "We might have the need to move rapidly, and it would be easier if we weren't forced to stay with the group."

Maureen held up a hand. "I didn't hear that," she said. "You're sick, you need a wisdom tooth pulled, you're going to have a baby—just tell me what I'm supposed to tell the Turkmen government and I'll do it."

"Don't worry, ma'am, we'll be nearby," Briggs said. "You just make all your visits and keep to your schedule— we'll do the rest."

"We especially want you to insist that the Turkmen government allow you to travel outside the capital to meet with the Taliban fighters," Wohl added.

"I wouldn't count on that."

"Then we'll take a meeting anyway—*our* way," Wohl said.

His voice made Maureen Hershel's skin turn cold and

break into goose bumps. She was amused to see it had the same effect on Isadora Meiling—except hers didn't appear to be goose bumps of fear, but goose bumps of pleasure. Izzy Meiling, who had her pick of any man in Washington, D.C.—falling for a broken-faced, gravel-voiced, jarhead Marine? Well, why the hell not?

NORTHWEST OF MARY, TURKMENISTAN
That same time

The twelve Russian Tupolev-160 "Blackjack" bombers had flown all the way from Engels Air Base for this mission. The Blackjacks carried a maximum load of twenty-four Kh-15P long-range attack missiles on rotary launchers. Each of the missiles had three-hundred-kilogram fuel-air explosive warheads, designed to knock down and kill any Taliban forces not in the safety of shelters. The Russians wanted to preserve as much as possible of the infrastructure at the two major airports at Mary for the eventual invasion forces that would soon follow.

The Blackjacks attacked from long range and low altitude. The Taliban and Turkmen defenders, manning early-warning radars and air-defense missile and artillery units, had virtually no warning. Coming in at supersonic speeds in an almost vertical dive onto their preprogrammed targets, the Kh-15 missiles were almost undetectable. All the missiles were programmed to explode about three hundred meters aboveground so the blast and fire effects of the fuel-air warheads would not create large craters in the runways or aircraft parking areas but would be sure to kill anyone unlucky enough to be out in the open.

The Blackjacks, however, were only the first wave.

Twelve Tupolev-22M bombers, also from Engels Air Base, swept in behind the Blackjack bombers. The "Backfires" carried twelve Kh-25MP medium-range antiradar missiles on external pylons under the engine intakes and on the fixed-wing pivot points, plus an APK-8 radar-emitter pod on the centerline hardpoint that would feed precise range and bearing information to the missiles. Cruising in a low-altitude orbit north of Mary, the Backfires acted as "red rovers" for each other: When one bomber was targeted by an air-defense missile or antiaircraft artillery radar, another Backfire would swoop in from a different direction and fire a missile. Operating in four three-ship hunter-killer packs, the Backfire bombers made short work of dozens of air-defense units operated by the relatively inexperienced Taliban fighters.

With the radar-guided air defenses down around Mary, the third wave of bombers cruised in—twelve more Backfire bombers, each carrying twelve RBK-500 dispensers bearing area-denial mines and antitank and antipersonnel cluster bombs. They flew virtually unopposed over Mary Airport. Each cluster bomb was designed to explode either on contact, if it was disturbed, or automatically within seven days. If any Taliban should escape the first two attacks and were rushed enough not to sweep carefully for mines, the cluster bombs and mines would get them—but each one would destroy itself before the Russian invasion forces moved in.

"I have heard the blessed news!" Wakil Mohammad Zarazi exclaimed as he strode into his alternate headquarters, which was far from the airfield and had survived the assault.

Major Aman Orazov did not try to rise from his seat as

his commanding officer entered the room. His head and neck were wrapped tightly in bandages, and he winced from the pain of shrapnel wounds to his neck and shoulders as he took deep drags on a thick hand-rolled cigarette, which had a little opium sprinkled in with the tobacco to help dull the pain.

"An entire company of Russian commandos, sent to hell by Turabi and his soldiers." Zarazi looked at Orazov as if it was the first time he had seen him. "What happened to you, Major?"

"I was caught in the initial firebomb attack," Orazov replied. "I watched an entire truckload of our soldiers incinerated before my eyes." He did not bother looking up at Zarazi. "Where were you, General?" he asked.

"In the shelters, of course," Zarazi replied. "You saw to the deployment of the mobile antiaircraft units, as I directed?"

"Most of them made it out," Orazov said. "I ordered the operators not to turn on their radars until someone spotted aircraft near the airfields."

"You told them not to engage the Russians? *Why?*"

"Because if it was just a standoff antiradar-missile attack, General, the Russian missiles can kill each radar-equipped unit from over thirty kilometers away," Orazov said angrily. "The launch aircraft would be well out of range of our air-defense weapons, but our radars would be easy targets for their antiradar weapons."

"Then you countermanded *my* order, Major," Zarazi said, "because *I* ordered the men to attack and keep on attacking until every one of those godless Russian scum were dead."

"Then you sealed their fates, Zarazi," Orazov said, "because I would guess that every unit that turned on its radar was hit by a missile and destroyed."

If Zarazi noticed that Orazov had not addressed him as "sir," "General," or "master," as he usually did, he did not indicate it. "Deploy the rest of the air-defense units around the airfields," he ordered, "and this time make sure they get hits—radar or no radar."

Orazov winced, not just from the pain now, but from Zarazi's completely ridiculous order. "Where is Colonel Turabi?" he asked, ignoring the order.

"Colonel Turabi informed me that he wished to stay on patrol in the northeast in case the Russians try another assault," Zarazi replied. "He asked for more supplies, enough for perhaps another week, and then he asked for his task force to be relieved."

"You should recall Turabi immediately to help with defending this base," Orazov said tersely. "He is out in the desert safe and plinking off simple Russian probes, while we sit on this airfield and have our heads handed to us by the Russians!"

"I agreed with the colonel's reasoning that the Russians will very likely try another heliborne assault," Zarazi said. "Their air bombardment was not nearly as effective as I'm sure they anticipated. Turabi thinks they desperately need to open up another front."

Orazov wiped sweat from his forehead caused by the excruciating pain and suppressed a disgusted laugh. Easy for this Afghan desert rat to think the Russians' air assault was "not nearly as effective"—*he* was safe in a deep underground shelter while Orazov and his men were on the surface trying to defend their base and getting the hell blasted out of them. The only way the Russians had been ineffective was in not wiping them out of existence completely. "Is Turabi still deployed around Nishan?"

"I believe he has shifted his forces farther north and west, near Yagtyyol," Zarazi said. "Turabi surmised that the

Russians used the Chärjew pipeline to navigate to their in-filtration point and that they will not make the same mistake again—they'll stay far away from roads and pipelines."

"I have to give him credit. Colonel Turabi is a very clever and resourceful fighter."

"It takes more than being clever to win favor in the eyes of God, Major," Zarazi said. "The colonel is a capable fighter, but he needs to learn the relationship between being a good soldier and being a true servant of God. Fighting just for the sake of earthly goals is a waste of spirit and not a true calling at all."

"Oh, really?" Orazov said bitterly.

"You yourself are a true and loyal servant of God, Major—you know this very well," Zarazi said. "Fighting for other than the glory of God is the definition of evil."

Orazov took another puff, then painfully shifted himself in his chair so he could look at Zarazi out of the corner of his eye. Zarazi, as usual, was off in some transcendental fog. "Well, I think Turabi should be running out of fuel and water soon," Orazov said. "He'll be expecting a resupply mission today. I shall fly out and meet him. But first there is an important matter I must attend to."

"You will go out and see to the redeployment of our air defenses and then organize burial and rebuilding parties," Zarazi said. "We must be prepared for when the Russians strike again."

No response.

"Did you hear what I said, Major? Carry out my orders immediately."

Still no response.

Zarazi glanced back—and saw Orazov aiming a pistol directly at his head. "What in God's name is this, Major?" he barked, thunderstruck. "Put that weapon away immediately! Are you insane?"

"Not insane—just smart," Orazov said. "Smart enough to realize that you are no longer in command here."

"No longer in command? Of course I am in command here! This is my operation, my mission!"

"Not any longer," Orazov said. "From now on *I* am in charge."

Zarazi looked at Orazov, his eyes bulging in outrage. "How dare you point that weapon at me, Major," he breathed. "I am the leader here. You will obey my orders or you will be eliminated."

"You are no longer in control here, you old fool," Orazov said. "You are nothing but a religious fanatic who was fortunate enough to score a few meaningless victories against incompetent Turkmen soldiers. Your victories were just dumb luck. Now that the Russians are coming, you are nothing but a walking corpse. I was a fool to follow you. I think if I deliver you, Turabi, and a good number of your Taliban fighters to the Russians—alive or dead, it probably won't matter—they'll let me live. They may even make me an officer in their occupation army."

"I have been appointed by God to carry out His plan for a safe haven and training ground for all true believers!" Zarazi cried. "Do you think that God will look as favorably on you?"

"God doesn't give a shit if you or I believe in Him or not," Orazov said. "The plans have changed, and you are not included in my new plans."

"God will strike you down for blaspheming His name—"

"But *I* shall strike *you* down *now*," Orazov said, grinning as he pulled the trigger.

The entire back of Zarazi's head splattered on the door to Orazov's office, and the nearly headless corpse of the Taliban chief dropped to the ground like a puppet whose strings had suddenly been cut.

That job done, there was only one mission left to accomplish before getting the hell out of here and making contact with the Russians: eliminate Jalaluddin Turabi and his men. Until Zarazi's body was found, Orazov had plenty of authority to organize an attack mission. Once Zarazi was found dead, these quasi-Neanderthal Taliban fighters would search every square centimeter of the desert for him. But for now they would obey him, even to the point of executing an assault on their own patrol camp. Orazov had fooled Wakil Zarazi well enough that he was able to get almost as much authority as Turabi himself.

Finally, Jalaluddin Turabi was going to die.

TIGRESS MILITARY OPERATING AREA, FALLON NAVAL AIR STATION, NEVADA
That same time

"Kazoo, Devil flight up, base plus zero," the lead F/A-18 Hornet pilot reported to the E-2C Hawkeye radar aircraft. The pair of Hornets from VMFA-232 "Red Devils," Marine Air Group Twenty-four, Kaneohe Bay, Hawaii, had been on a predeployment workup at Fallon NAS in Nevada when they were given a great opportunity: chase some Air Force bombers around the training ranges. That was a deal no American fighter pilot would ever pass up.

"Roger, Devil flight," the air-control officer aboard the Hawkeye replied. At the same time he was electronically passing the latest target information to both Hornets' strike computers—the Hornets were still running radar-silent. One fast-moving target was to the southwest at about fifty miles, very low—less than a thousand feet above the high desert, trying to sneak past the Hornets by flying in fast between and parallel to the steep, rocky ridges that crisscrossed the Fallon ranges. By selecting the bogey with his target cursor, the lead Hornet pilot acknowledged the datalink and the vectors being received in the Hornets' Data Display Indicators. The two Hornets remained in combat-spread formation, wingtip to wingtip, separated by about a mile so they could watch each other's six.

It was definitely an unfair fight, especially with a Hawkeye in the mix, the Hornet pilots thought—the Air Force pukes didn't have a chance.

At the right moment the lead Hornet pilot pushed his nose over to accelerate, waited until the range to the target decreased to about thirty miles, then flicked on his APG-73 attack radar. Immediately afterward the pilot got the last datalinked target-deconfliction message: That's your bandit, cleared in hot. At the same time the pilot selected his AIM-120 AMRAAM radar-guided air-to-air missiles—making certain that the weapons themselves were SAFE—and watched as the fire-control system presented his missile-engagement envelopes and attack-solution vectors.

The target started a turn to the north—obviously his threat-warning receivers had picked up the Hornet's radar impulses and the crew had finally reacted. The turn was not very sharp. The bomber decreased altitude, now flying about four hundred feet off the deck. No doubt they're using terrain-following radar, the Hornet pilot surmised, but having all that granite right in front of their faces must still create big-time pucker factor. The bomber reversed direction—again it was a good healthy turn, but not a very aggressive one. Now the surrounding terrain made it difficult for the APG-73 to stay locked on, but after lining up again on the bandit and dialing in a little antenna-scan correction, the radar quickly reacquired, the target-indicator box locked on again, and an IN RANGE indication appeared on the heads-up display.

One last correction, just a slight one using a little rudder, and the flashing SHOOT indication appeared. Gotcha, fat boy, the Hornet pilot breathed. He checked one more time to be sure his master arm switch was SAFE—didn't want to fire the real thing at the good guys—then placed his finger on the pistol trigger. "Devil Zero-one, Fox—"

"Bandit! Bandit! Pop-up target, one o'clock, four miles!" the air-intercept officer on the Hawkeye radar plane shouted on the frequency. Another aircraft had appeared out of nowhere and was right in front of him.

"Devil Zero-two engaging! Hard left break and dive, Woolly!" the pilot of the second Hornet called out. The leader had absolutely no choice. Before he could pull the trigger, he was forced to break off the attack. As he turned, he hoped the newcomer would follow him, which should put him right in his wingman's gun sights. Where in hell did he come from?

But instead of turning hard right to pursue the leader, the bandit switched tactics—it rolled left, waited a few seconds, then turned right in a spectacular high-G climbing, twisting maneuver that placed the second Hornet right off his nose. There was no radio transmission. There didn't need to be. He could see a tiny dark shape off his right wingtip, low, with a bright blinking strobe light on it—the newcomer "shooting" at him. He was in front of the guy for only less than two seconds, but in the dogfighting game that was an eternity.

"Devil leader, Devil Zero-two got waxed," he radioed.

"No shit?" the leader replied incredulously. "What is it? The Air Farts didn't say anything about fighter escorts."

The second Hornet pilot tried to get a visual ID, but he couldn't see it. "It must be small as hell. I can't get a visual on it. I'm proceeding to the high CAP."

"Rog. Kazoo, bogey dope."

"Your bandit is at your two o'clock, twenty-two miles, low," the air-intercept officer reported. "Your tail is clear. Negative radar on any other bogeys."

The rest of the intercept was a piece of cake. Another lock-on, and this time he couldn't miss. The bomber made a few more steep turns during the attack, but again nothing overly aggressive. Maybe a student crew?

Both sides went back to opposite sides of the range and tried the engagement again, this time with the second F/A-18 Hornet in the lead. The strange little bandit didn't make another appearance, and the second Hornet claimed a kill just a few minutes later.

"Hey, Bobcat," the lead Hornet pilot radioed after the exercise concluded, "how about a photo op?"

"Sure," the bomber pilot replied. "You're cleared in to close formation." The Hawkeye air intercept officer gave the pilots a vector, and the two Hornets joined up on their quarry. It was an Air Force B-1 bomber, long and sleek, with its wings almost completely swept back along its fuselage.

"We're going to tuck in tight and get some close shots, Bobcat."

"Stand by," the pilot said. "We've got our little friend rejoining us. He's directly below us."

"Say again?" But moments later they could see what he was talking about: A tiny aircraft, resembling a fat surfboard, suddenly appeared out of nowhere. It rose until it was directly underneath the bomber. The bomber's bomb-bay doors opened, and a long basket thing appeared. The little aircraft scooted up inside the basket, which closed around it, and moments later it was gone—snatched up into the bomb bay. "That was *very* cool!" the lead Hornet pilot exclaimed. "Was that the thing that tagged my wingman?"

"Affirmative."

"Shit, I was shot down by a robot," the wingman said disgustedly. "That's gonna cost me big time at the bar."

"Stop by the Owl Club in Battle Mountain Friday nights at nine, and the first round's on the Bobcats," the pilot said. "Okay, Devils, you're cleared in."

"Devil flight moving in."

As surprised as the Marine Corps pilots were about seeing a drone being recovered by a B-1 bomber, that was nothing compared to their next discovery. The Hornets moved in close enough to get a picture of the bomber's pilots looking back at them . . .

Until they realized *there were no pilots visible in the bomber's cockpit!* "Uhhh . . . Bobcat, can you guys maybe move forward a little?"

"Move forward?"

"Yeah . . . so we can see your faces out the windscreen?"

"Sorry, Devils, but you're not going to see any faces through our windscreen," the voice responded, "because there is no one inside the cockpit."

"You're shitting me!" the Hornet pilot exclaimed. He inched closer. It was no lie—there was no one sitting in either pilot's seat. "Where's the damned crew?"

"Back at Battle Mountain," the voice replied. "You've been playing with two unmanned jets the whole time."

"You're flying a B-1 bomber—*from the ground?*"

"Yep. And I was just about to turn it over to my mission commander, go outside, and take a piss," the voice said. "Have a nice day."

What else they didn't know was, had this been an actual engagement, neither of the Marine Corps F/A-18 Hornets would ever have gotten a shot off at the B-1 bomber, because, orbiting in an adjacent range over 150 miles away, an AL-52 Dragon airborne-laser aircraft had been "shooting" at both F/A-18 Hornets during their simulated missile attacks.

Captain William "Wonka" Weathers, the wing munitions chief, sat in the jump seat between the aircraft commander and mission commander in the cockpit of the AL-52, watching in utter fascination. The mission commander, Major Frankie "Zipper" Tarantino, had locked up each Hornet at least a dozen times with the Dragon's adaptive-optics telescope that magnified the visual image in incredible detail. Tarantino was able to precisely place the crosshairs on any part of the Hornet, no matter how hard it maneuvered.

"What do you think, Wonka?" asked Colonel Nancy Cheshire, the Fifty-second Squadron's commander and the aircraft commander on today's mission.

"It's unbelievable," Weathers said. "Simply unbelievable. And how many times can you fire the laser?"

"About two hundred times," Tarantino said proudly, "depending on the targets we attack. Shooting through the atmosphere or hitting hard targets like tanks requires more power, which requires more fuel, which decreases the number of shots we can take. Check this out." He punched in commands, and the image on his supercockpit display changed. Now he was locked on to a pickup truck speeding across the desert. "I found this guy a few minutes ago, off-roading in the restricted Fallon bombing range. With a press of a button, I can update his position to the Navy military police who are out after him." He indicated another software button on his supercockpit display. "And if I pressed *that,* he'd be a smoking hole in the desert, even at this range. We can even punch a hole in a tank, but we'd have to be pretty close—maybe thirty or forty miles."

"Amazing. Do you still have the ground team locked up?"

"You bet." He hit another button, and the image shifted to a section of desert terrain, where two individuals could barely be seen on opposite ends of the display. Tarantino zoomed in to the one on the left and magnified the image. It was a commando in a Tin Man battle suit, carrying an electromagnetic rail gun. Seconds later the commando jet-jumped several dozen yards across a gully. Tarantino hit his radio button: "Fist Two, wave hello." The commando raised his right hand, and Tarantino was able to zoom in close enough to see his upraised middle finger. "Be nice, now—we've got brass on board."

"My God! We can see the guy giving us the finger from . . . what's the range?"

Tarantino checked his readouts. "One hundred forty-three point one-nine-three miles," he replied.

"And the laser . . . ?"

"I don't think the laser has enough power to hurt a guy in BERP battle armor at this range," Nancy said, "but I think we'd make him *very* uncomfortable *very* quickly."

At that moment they heard on the command frequency, "Bobcat Two-one, Control."

Nancy keyed the mike button: "Bobcat Two-one, go."

"Set condition Gold."

"Roger that," Cheshire replied. She switched radio frequencies. "All Bobcat and Fist units, set condition Gold. Acknowledge."

Weathers could see the Tin Man commando stop, look to the east, and jet-jump back in the direction of a waiting MV-32 Pave Dasher tilt-jet aircraft. One by one all the other players acknowledged the call and began heading toward designated recovery zones. Weathers could hardly sit still as Nancy Cheshire banked the AL-52 Dragon airborne-laser hard toward Battle Mountain, and Frankie

Tarantino cleared out of the range and got air-traffic-control clearance back to Battle Mountain.

As simply as that, the Air Battle Force made ready to go to war.

OVER THE EASTERN AZERBAIJANI REPUBLIC
That night

"Baku Control, SAM One-eight-zero, level at flight level three-niner-zero."

"Roger, SAM One-eight-zero," replied the ex-Soviet air-traffic-control center at Baku in the Azerbaijani Republic, which handled all flights going in and out of the former Soviet republics of Central Asia. It had been many, many years since he'd handled an American "SAM," or Special Air Mission—American diplomats did not come to this part of the world very often, especially since the new American president, Thomas Thorn, had entered office. "Be advised, sir, International Notice to Airmen Zulu-Three has been published regarding the airspace you are flight-planned to enter. Are you in receipt of this NOTAM?"

"Affirmative," responded the pilot of the American C-32A Special Air Mission aircraft. "We are an American diplomatic mission on official government business, and we have received permission from the Turkmen government to enter their airspace. Over."

"SAM One-eight-zero, I confirm you are in receipt of NOTAM Zulu-Three," the controller said. "Be advised, the NOTAM is nonspecific, sir. Even though your diplomatic credentials are verified, you are still in great danger if you proceed into the prohibited area as outlined in the NOTAM because of the state of the conflict in central Turkmenistan. I strongly advise you to reverse course."

"Thank you for the warning, Baku, but we will proceed on our flight-planned route," the pilot said.

"We cannot be held responsible for continued flight into the prohibited airspace, sir," the Baku controller warned. "I will continue to provide radar service, but I am not in contact with any of the Russian aircraft, and I cannot ensure safe separation from them. I have also observed considerable meaconing, interference, jamming, and intrusion on my radar displays and on all my air-traffic landline and wireless communications channels. I cannot be held responsible if communications are lost, for any reason. Again, I strongly advise you to turn back. Do you understand, sir?"

"I understand, Baku," the pilot responded. "Are you in contact with the Russian controllers or agencies who filed NOTAM Zulu-Three?"

"Negative, SAM One-eight-zero," the controller replied. "We are monitoring them on GUARD emergency frequency, but they have not responded to any of our calls."

"Roger, SAM One-eight-zero." The pilot turned to his first officer and asked, "So our closest emergency-divert base . . . ?"

"Baku, Azerbaijani Republic, almost directly under us," the first officer replied, punching up the Global Positioning System navigation information. "I'll give them a call right now." The first officer used the secondary radio to give the approach controllers at Baku notice that they were in the area. "We're checked in, but we do not have clearance to land. That will only be issued if we need it."

It was indeed a strange situation: International NOTAM Zulu-Three, issued by the Russian Federation, was one of the most strongly worded messages in years, warning all aircraft away from Turkmenistan's airspace and further saying that any aircraft flying within five hundred kilometers of the capital of Turkmenistan, Ashkhabad, would be fired upon without warning. But at the same time Turkmenistan was still allowing flights to cross into its airspace; the government of Turkmenistan was not restricting transit for any civil air carriers, even in and out of Mary, the scene of the heaviest fighting so far. Ashkhabad International Airport was still open, as were the civil airfields at Krasnovodsk, Nebit-Dag, and Chärjew.

The Turkmen government was doing all it could to make everything look like "business as usual," even though it definitely appeared as if the wheels were slowly but surely coming off this train. Despite all the reassurances, the Special Air Mission flight, carrying the former president of the United States and a U.S. State Department official, stayed as far away as possible from Turkmen airspace. It had enough range to fly all the way north to Moscow before turning south if necessary, but it settled for getting clearance through Turkish, Azerbaijani, and Kazakh airspace before heading directly for the Turkmen coast on the Caspian Sea.

The flight made a routine handoff from Turkish controllers at Erzurum to English-speaking Russian-sector controllers at Baku, which passed the flight off routinely as it made its way across the Caucasus Mountains and out over the Caspian Sea. The lights of thousands of oil wells and fishing boats on the Caspian made it look like a metropolis down below, contrasting sharply with the almost lightless landscape beyond as they approached the seemingly endless desert steppes of Central Asia. In just a few minutes they would be handed off to air-traffic controllers from their destination, Ashkhabad; in less than half an hour, they would begin the descent for landing.

"SAM One-eight-zero, contact Ashkhabad Control." The Baku controller read off a frequency—not the usual one in use by this sector, but reassigning and combining sectors and controllers was not unusual, especially at night, when fewer flights traveled in remote areas.

"Roger, SAM One-eight-zero, good night." The first officer switched frequencies, then radioed, "Ashkhabad Control, SAM One-eight-zero, with you at flight level three-nine-zero, six-zero kilometers east of Baku."

The reply was interrupted by frequent squeals and static—again not unusual for this area of the world and its antiquated radio systems. "Calling Ashkhabad Control, please repeat," the controller responded in broken but understandable English. Although English was the universal aviation language, it was not always well understood in some of the more remote areas of the planet, especially in the former Soviet republics of Central Asia. The SAM pilot repeated his report slowly, carefully. "Thank you, SAM One-eight-zero, at three-niner-zero," the controller responded through the static. "You are in receipt of NOTAM Zulu-Three, sir?"

"Yes we are," the pilot responded. "We accept responsibility in case there's a loss of communications for any reason."

"Very well, sir." They proceeded in silence for several minutes. Roughly halfway across the Caspian Sea, the C-32A crew heard a controller—it was hard to tell if it was the same one or not—say, "SAM One-eight-zero, turn right thirty degrees, fly direct Krasnovodsk, direct Ashkhabad. Expect descent in one-zero minutes."

"Direct Krasnovodsk, direct Ashkhabad, SAM One-eight-zero." The first officer called up the intersection on his flight-management system, and the big airliner banked right in response. Their original flight plan had them well north of the usual routing through this airspace. This vector and rerouting, the first officer saw, would place them squarely over Krasnovodsk, the Russian port city on the

Caspian Sea, and on a direct route to the capital, bypassing all the usual checkpoints and approach corridors.

Something was happening. They didn't know what, but things were starting to look a little haywire.

The new frequency was fairly quiet, just a few other planes on it, a Kazakhstan Airlines flight and a Gulf Air charter. The first officer could not hear any responses from the other flights, indicating that the controller was indeed talking and receiving on several different frequencies at one time.

Things seemed to be progressing smoothly. The captain called for the before-descent checklist and got up to step twelve when suddenly, through a rasp of static and loud, irritating pops, they heard, "SAM One-eight-zero, this is Ashkhabad Control on GUARD," in both English and Russian. "GUARD" was the international emergency frequency, which all aircraft were required to monitor at all times. "If you hear me, contact Ashkhabad Control on one-three-seven point six or UHF frequency two-three-four point niner-two. Acknowledge with an ident if you hear me. Over."

The first officer punched the IDENT button on his transponder—which would encircle their radar-data block with a bright, flashing identification box—then keyed his microphone: "Ashkhabad Control, SAM One-eight-zero, how do you read?"

"Loud and clear, sir, how about me?"

"Loud and clear as well. We just received a message on GUARD frequency to contact you on a different frequency. Did you give us a frequency change?"

"Negative. Remain this frequency, please."

"SAM One-eight-zero, wilco."

But the message on GUARD repeated, this time much more urgently and with a terrifying warning: "SAM One-eight-zero, warning, unidentified high-speed aircraft are approaching you at your seven o'clock, forty miles. Turn right sixty degrees immediately, vectors out over the Caspian to avoid the NOTAM Zulu-Three airspace. Please acknowledge on GUARD. Over."

"Ashkhabad Control, do you copy that radio transmission on GUARD channel?"

"Affirmative, SAM One-eight-zero. We are investigating. Remain on your present heading, direct Krasnovodsk, direct Ashkhabad. Disregard the instructions being broadcast on GUARD. If two-way communications are lost or disrupted, you are cleared to Ashkhabad International. After Krasnovodsk, descend and maintain flight level two-five-zero, then FMS VNAV profile at or above nine thousand feet at Syrdarja, cleared for the ILS runway two-seven approach. We will clear the airspace for you if communications are lost. Do you copy?" The first officer repeated the instructions.

The warnings on GUARD were getting more strident by the second. "Do you want me to shut that off?" the first officer asked the captain, placing his fingers on the GUARD switch.

The captain was about to say yes, but instead flipped his mike button to GUARD. "This is SAM One-eight-zero," the captain said. "Who the hell is this?"

"Thank God!" came the reply in excellent English. But the snapping and hissing on the frequency were growing louder—and it all sounded ominous, as if the frequency was being jammed or disrupted. "This is Colonel Okiljon Mirsafoyev. I am the facility chief of Ashkhabad Control. You may contact me on the listed frequencies in the International Flight Information Publications or via datalink to your embassy, but I must issue this warning to you in the clear. I don't know who's doing it, or how, or why, but you were handed off to an unlisted and completely incorrect frequency by an unknown person. I was notified by Baku Control minutes ago. I repeat, the controller you are speaking to is *not* Ashkhabad Control.

"Be advised, there are Russian radar planes and air-defense fighters in your vicinity. You need to turn right immediately and get away from the Turkmen frontier. . . . SAM One-eight-zero, one unidentified pop-up aircraft heading fast in your direction. Shut off all your exterior lights. Get out of there *now*."

The first officer's face looked as white as a ghost's. "What do we do?" he cried.

"We turn," the captain said, flipping on the switch for the SEAT BELT warning sign. "Shut off all the damn lights—cabin lights, too. Notify President Martindale and Deputy Secretary Hershel that we might be under attack." As if that's going to do any good, he thought grimly.

He banked hard right and started a descent. Seconds later the intercom beeped—he knew that his steep turn and sudden descent were going to unseat and maybe even hurt a lot of the VIPs, and they would be screaming to the flight attendants to find out what had happened—and, no doubt, to demand his head on a platter.

That was okay. He would be happy to take the heat as long as they survived this encounter. "Get on oxygen," he ordered the first officer. "Read me the emergency-descent and defensive-maneuvering procedures checklist."

"SAM Flight One-eight-zero," the first voice in broken English radioed on the bogus UHF frequency, "we show you in a left turn and in a steep descent. Is there a problem? Turn left direct Krasnovodsk as ordered."

"Don't answer him," the captain ordered. The first officer was fumbling to put on his quick-don oxygen mask, a procedure that usually took less than two seconds. He'd never seen any grown man so scared before—and hoped *he* didn't look that scared to him.

"Flight One-eight-zero, turn left immediately and level off. You are not cleared to descend yet." The captain only pushed harder, increasing the descent rate. "Flight One-eight-zero, acknowledge. Do you read me?"

"Turn off the transponder," the captain ordered. The first officer complied with shaking fingers. Only a "primary target," their radar skin-paint, would appear on the controller's radarscopes now.

All of the flight attendants' station intercoms were beeping; small articles were floating around in the negative Gs as they quickly descended. "What do we do?" the first officer bleated. "What's going on?"

"Ignore them. We're diverting to Baku. Call it up on the FMS and give me a heading."

Just then they heard, "Attention all aircraft, attention all aircraft, an air defense emergency has been declared. All aircraft are ordered to level off, decrease airspeed, and lower their landing gear immediately, or you will be considered a hostile enemy intruder. Repeat, level off, decrease airspeed, and lower your landing gear immediately. This is your final warning."

The voice was coming over the assigned UHF frequency—in English. It was the same voice who'd been calling himself the Ashkhabad air-traffic controller.

"Full countermeasures!" the captain ordered. The C-32A had a suite of decoys and first-generation electronic track-breakers to help defend the aircraft, but he knew they were strap-down, last-ditch gadgets only. The C-32 was unarmed and still virtually defenseless.

"SAM One-eight-zero, high-speed traffic at your seven o'clock, low, forty kilometers and closing fast."

The captain turned left twenty degrees, trying to keep the newcomer from getting a clear look at their engine exhausts—if he locked on to their hot exhausts, they wouldn't stand a chance. The sons of bitches . . . who the hell attacks unarmed aircraft?

"SAM One-eight-zero, target maneuvering, six o'clock, thirty kilometers and closing, almost at your altitude . . . SAM One-eight-zero, be advised, my radar is being jammed. Switching frequencies . . . Negative, negative, all frequencies showing heavy false target jamming. I am now painting multiple targets on my scope. I cannot provide further vectors. I cannot tell which is the real target. I am sorry, sir."

The captain squeezed the mike button: "Ashkhabad Control?"

"Go ahead, SAM One-eight-zero."

The captain looked at the first officer, gulped, then said, "Tell my wife I love her."

"Roger, Sam One-eight-zero," he heard through the growing static and squealing of the enemy's jammers. "I'll do it. God be with you."

The Russian Federation's MiG-29 Fulcrum fighter that had launched from Krasnovodsk Airfield several minutes earlier did so using light signals sent from a ramp supervisor's vehicle instead of receiving radio signals from the control tower. It made no radio broadcasts and did not use its air-traffic-control transponder or encrypted identification beacons. It did not even use any external lights. Because the fighter carried no external fuel tanks—unusual for any Russian interceptor—and only two R-73 heat-seeking air-to-air missiles, it climbed quickly into the cold night air, reaching fourteen thousand meters' altitude in less than three minutes.

The American aircraft was maneuvering, but it was a lumbering pig compared to the high-speed maneuverabil-

ity of the MiG-29, and the pilot was able to get a solid infrared target lock-on inside thirty kilometers' range—he
never activated his attack radar at all. The R-73s were
Russia's most advanced heat-seeking missiles: highly maneuverable, able to be aimed by a helmet-mounted sight
and launched from extremely high offset angles. They had
over four times the range and twice the warhead size of
any other heat-seeking missiles in the Russian arsenal.

The Russian pilot's orders were specific: Kill this aircraft without appearing to attack it. He knew that Baku
Radar Control would be tracking him and listening for
any hint of weapon or radar lock-on, so he had to do this
approach carefully. The R-73 was the perfect weapon for
the job.

As ordered, the MiG-29 pilot flew behind the American
aircraft, never pointing the fighter's nose directly at it,
never locking his attack radar on him or even turning it on.
Using his helmet-mounted sight, the MiG pilot locked the
R-73 missile's supercooled seeker head on target when
the American was over twenty-five kilometers distant and
far off to the left—the MiG-29 was actually flying *away*
from the American. Once he had a lock-on, he let the first
R-73 fly. The missile shot off its launch rail, flew straight
ahead for about a kilometer, then veered sharply to the left
and started its pursuit. The pilot let the next R-73 go seconds later, then turned to the east. The MiG pilot still had
never pointed his fighter's nose at the American, and seconds after launch the MiG was far astern of the American.
Normal air traffic routinely came closer than he had come
to his American quarry.

Because he had never used his attack radar and therefore didn't know the exact range to the target, the attack
computer couldn't give him a "time to die" countdown.
The MiG pilot started to count to himself, estimating perhaps twenty seconds maximum missile flight time for the

first missile. He pulled back the throttle and engaged the autopilot, then loosened his shoulder harness so he could look behind him. Even at well over thirty kilometers, he reckoned, he should be able to see the kill.

Sure enough, he saw a very bright flash of light off in the distance, followed by another seconds later. It was much quicker than twenty seconds, but he wasn't exactly sure of his counting.

Good hit.

The pilot turned to the north slightly so he could watch for any sign of an explosion. He expected to see another burst of fire, followed by a trail of fire as the target went down. Any second now . . .

SEVEN

OVER THE CASPIAN SEA
That same moment

Attack target one."

"*Attacking target one, stop attack,*" the computer responded. A moment later the laser-radar array on the AL-52 Dragon airborne-laser aircraft instantly measured the distance to the target, then electronically measured the size of the target and moved the laser's aimpoint to the aft one-third of the target, where the rocket motor was. Then a carbon-dioxide laser was fired through the main laser's optics at the missile, which measured and compensated for atmospheric distortion by predistorting the mirror in the Dragon's nose.

"*Laser ready,*" the attack computer reported moments later.

"Laser attack missile," Major Frankie Tarantino responded.

"*Laser attack, stop attack.*" Next the big plasma-pumped, solid-state laser came to life. Pellets of deuterium-tritium plasma fuel were ignited by a dozen low-power lasers, creating a sphere of superhot plasma—

atoms stripped of their electrons—exceeding the temperature of the sun itself. Confined, compressed, and then channeled by a magnetic field and by chambers made of walls of liquid lithium, the plasma energy was directed into a laser generator, which produced a laser beam over twice the power of any other airborne laser ever built. The laser beam was collimated, intensified through the laser tube running the length of the aircraft, reflected off the steerable/deformable mirror in the nose, and shot into space.

The AL-52's aircraft commander, Air Force Colonel Kelvin Carter, didn't see or hear a thing—no pulsing beam of light shooting off into space, no alien glow, no sci-fi warbling sound—and all he felt was a slight rumbling under his toes as the massive deformable mirror turret moved, smoothly tracking the targets far off in the distance. When he looked over at the supercockpit display on the mission commander's side of the instrument panel, all he saw was a spark of light, then detonation.

"Splash one Archer!" Zipper Tarantino exclaimed, patting the top of the glareshield of his beloved Dragon. He had just shot down a supersonic air-to-air missile fired from the Russian MiG-29 Fulcrum from over two hundred miles away in less than twelve seconds with two bursts of laser light. "Good Dragon."

"Good shooting, Zipper," Carter responded. Kelvin Carter, from Shreveport, Louisiana, had been one of the senior flight-test pilots at the High Technology Aerospace Weapons Center. Along with Patrick McLanahan and Nancy Cheshire, he knew more about the Megafortress series of bombers than anyone else, so he was the logical choice as the operations officer of the Fifty-second Attack Squadron at Battle Mountain Air Reserve Base, flying the incredible AL-52 Dragon.

As familiar as he was with the modified B-52 bombers

that he'd helped develop at Dreamland, Carter was still amazed by the weaponry at his command: a two-megawatt, plasma-pumped, solid-state laser, the most powerful non-land-based, directed-energy weapon in the world. Seconds earlier, as he'd sneaked a peek at Tarantino's wide-screen supercockpit display, he'd been looking at the telescopically enhanced image of a Russian air-to-air missile actually *in flight*. But almost as soon as the image had appeared on the screen, Tarantino had placed a set of crosshairs directly on the rear motor section of the missile—and then it was gone in a burst of fire.

The image then switched to the second missile and, with one command—"Attack target two"—Tarantino had initiated the attack sequence. Moments later the second AA-11 Archer air-to-air missile had disappeared in a ball of fire, well short of its prey: the U.S. Air Force C-32A VIP transport, carrying former president Kevin Martindale, Deputy Secretary of State Maureen Hershel, and their entourage.

Now the image in the full-color supercockpit display wasn't one of a Russian missile—instead it was the image of a real live Russian fighter pilot, clearly visible in extraordinary detail through the cockpit of his MiG-29 Fulcrum jet fighter. Zipper could see the straps on the pilot's oxygen mask, see the bulky helmet-mounted sight that controlled his air-to-air missiles, and even see that he was wearing a black turtleneck sweater under his flight suit.

"Hot damn!" Carter exclaimed. "You got the Russian pilot himself dead in your sights, Zipper. You're clear to engage." Tarantino then changed the laser's aimpoint to the MiG's left wing root, the spot where he knew an explosion would quickly and instantly send the fighter completely out of control. "Put the aimpoint back on the pilot," Carter grumbled.

"What?" Tarantino asked.

"I said put the crosshairs back on that sumbitch."

"Sir, it won't matter—"

"Son, that bastard is looking over his shoulder, probably back to where he fired his Archers," Carter said. "This bastard just shot at an unarmed, defenseless diplomatic aircraft. Fry his ass."

Tarantino rolled the trackball aiming device smoothly until the pilot's image was again centered on the supercockpit display, then locked it in. Carter followed the steering commands presented on his heads-up display; seconds later, they received a READY indication. Carter thought Tarantino might hesitate—but he didn't. The crosshairs appeared, he saw a blinking L in the upper center of the display . . .

And seconds later the MiG-29's cockpit canopy disintegrated. They watched in horrified fascination as the pilot's head was jerked backward and his helmet, skullcap, and oxygen mask were ripped off by the sudden wind blast. For a second the Russian was able to pull back up and began fighting for control of his fighter—when Carter and Tarantino saw the Russian's head, shoulders, and upper torso turn black, as if the pilot had instantly turned into a big lump of charcoal. Sections of his corpse started flying away in the slipstream, until moments later there was nothing left but unrecognizable pieces of his lower torso. Then the cockpit around the corpse burst into a bathtub of sparks and flame, milliseconds before a massive fireball erupted from behind the corpse and obliterated the image. When Tarantino zoomed out, all they could see were burning hunks of the MiG-29 fluttering through the sky.

"Jee . . . sus," Tarantino breathed.

"I'll bet he don't feel much like a bad-ass aerial assassin now, does he?" Carter said. He looked at Tarantino, who was not moving, just staring at the supercockpit display. "Son, don't you dare feel sorry for that rat bastard. Any man who can pull the trigger on an unarmed plane full of civilians deserves to get his ass cooked. And he sure as hell would've joyfully put two Archers into *us* if we let him get close enough."

"I know it, sir," Tarantino said. "But it doesn't make killing a man any easier."

"You're not an airman—and you're sure as *hell* not a man—if you agree to use your talent and skills to fly a mission to kill defenseless men and women," Carter said. "Be thankful you ridded the world of a mindless bloodsucker like that. Now, pat your Dragon on the head like you always do, say thank you, and let's find out how our folks are doing."

Tarantino still didn't move.

"Did you hear me, Zipper?"

To emphasize his point, Carter punched instructions into one of his multifunction displays. The beam-control telescope switched back to target number one: the C-32A VIP transport. The adaptive optics showed the plane in remarkable detail. Carter was even able to zoom in on the cockpit windscreens, showing both pilots working together, quick-don oxygen masks on, checklists out. The readouts still showed the plane in a descent, getting below Ashkhabad's radar. "See that, Zipper? Our guys are still alive and still flyin'. You did good, son. You're a defender, not a killer." He put his gloved hand out and clasped Tarantino's left shoulder, firmly but gently. "You gotta understand the difference, son. Otherwise you might as well not be wearin' that uniform."

He didn't think Tarantino heard him, thought the kid might be heading toward the deep end—until he saw the young officer reach up and pat the glareshield. "Good Dragon," he said in a strong, resilient voice. "Good Dragon."

"There you go, son," Carter said approvingly. Some guys never made it back to the world after scoring their first kill.

He knew that Frankie Tarantino would—eventually—be okay. "There you go."

NORTH OF THE CITY OF MARY
Daybreak that morning

Jalaluddin Turabi spooned the last of the rice into his mouth, pretending that its stale, bug-infested taste was really the savory juices from succulent lamb mixed with exotic Chinese spices. He knew he was the last man in his company to be fed, so that spoonful also marked the last of their rations. And he didn't need to pick up his canteen to know that their water had almost run out, too. Damn it all, where in hell was their resupply flight? He knew that Aman Orazov was an incompetent asshole, but certainly even *he* could muster enough brainpower to load a few helicopters with supplies and fly it out here.

Abdul Dendara, Turabi's first sergeant, stepped over a few moments later and began to speak, but Turabi held up a hand. "Let me guess: We just ran out of fuel for the power generator?"

"That ran out an hour ago, sir, remember?" Dendara replied. "We just ran out of water." He took Turabi's canteen and replaced it with another, which had about a liter of fluid in it. "You may want to pour it through your shirt first to filter it. It was the last drop from the metal emergency barrels we scrounged from Yagtyyol last night. I got out as much sand and rust as I could."

"Thank you. Any possibility of getting more water from the city?"

"Power is still shut down—we can't get water from the wells," Dendara replied. "Unless General Zarazi can get the power turned back on from Mary, we've taken every drop of water from that entire town." He paused, then added, "I can order a patrol to start going house to house, looking for water. . . ."

"I already said no, Abdul," Turabi said. "The people out here are suffering just as much as we are. If the homes are evacuated, you can take water from there—make sure every cistern, every shelf, every refrigerator, and even every toilet tank has been searched—but if the house is occupied, stay away from it. I'll personally execute any man who disobeys my order. Is that understood?"

"Yes, sir. I'll pass the word again."

"Do that," Turabi ordered. "Now, assuming our men hoarded half their normal daily ration of water, we should last—"

"Until tomorrow morning," Dendara responded. "Then we're out of war-fighting mode and fully into survival mode."

Turabi checked his watch, then nodded. "We won't wait until then. If we don't get supplies within four hours, we'll head back to Mary."

"Very good, sir," Dendara said.

When his first sergeant walked away, Turabi tried the radio. He knew he was ordered to maintain radio silence, but this was an emergency. Breaking off this scout patrol before discovering what the Russians might be up to was very dangerous. Abandoning it for the sake of a few hundred liters of water and diesel fuel from just a few kilometers away made even less sense. He keyed the mike: "Hawk to Condor. Come in." No answer. He tried several more times—nothing.

Turabi took the canteen and drank the last of its contents, grimacing as he swallowed what tasted like welding beads. Shit, he thought, I'll just as likely die of lead poisoning as I will from enemy action. He knew that hoarding water would do no good—in the desert, one rationed sweat, not water—but he knew also that desperate, scared men would save a liter or two of water on their persons.

He noticed Dendara come running a few moments later, and Turabi stepped quickly toward him. "What is it now, Abdul?"

"Just got word from one of our patrols that came back from Mary. The Russians attacked Mary last night," Dendara said. "Heavy bombers with cruise missiles and anti-radar missiles, all from standoff range."

"Oh, shit," Turabi said. "That's why we didn't get a re-supply chopper, and that's why the radio's been down. Any word on General Zarazi?"

"Nothing." Dendara looked worried, which was unusual for this veteran warrior. "What are we going to do, sir?"

"We go back to Mary at once and link up with the general," Turabi said immediately.

"But the Russians . . . don't you expect another attack?"

"It doesn't matter, Abdul. Wakil Zarazi is our leader. If he's alive, we'll follow his orders. If he's dead, we'll avenge him on every Russian we can get our hands on, and then I'll take command of the brigade."

"And then what, sir?"

Turabi hesitated, but only for a moment: "And then I'll lead the brigade home," he said.

"Home . . . ?"

"Home to Afghanistan, home to our families and our tribe," Turabi said. "This fight is Zarazi's fight, not mine. If Zarazi is alive, we are honor-bound to follow his orders. But if he is dead, once we have avenged his death, I take command—and in my eyes and in my heart, we have accomplished our mission, the one given to us by our tribal elders. We shall return home, turn over our equipment to the elders, and then reunite with our families."

"Then . . . then Zarazi's mission is . . . *false* . . . ?"

"Not false, at least not in his heart," Turabi said. "He

truly believes that he is carrying out God's wishes, and that is good enough for me and for all of us. Every Taliban leader must search his heart and make the right decision. My decision will be different from Wakil's, but that does not make either one false. Get going now. Organize the patrol, and let's head back to Mary."

"Hawk, this is Snake," one of the lookouts radioed just then. "Scouts report a chopper inbound from the south with slung cargo. Looks like a water tank."

Thank God, Turabi thought. "Acknowledged," he replied. They needed ammo and diesel to continue this flanking patrol, but they *absolutely* needed water first. One of the helicopters had survived, and they thought of using it to resupply this patrol. It was a surprisingly heads-up thing for Aman Orazov to do. "Make sure the air-defense squads are on their toes. Don't let anyone get complacent."

"Acknowledged."

Turabi looked out across the sands and saw Dendara shouting orders to his platoon commanders, telling them to maintain watch while the helicopter came in. Many times the enemy sneaked in while the men were preoccupied with their relief-supply helicopter.

But his orders were useless. Sure enough several dozen of the men—mostly Turkmen recruits, but a fair number of his Taliban tribesmen followed along as well—were running in the direction of the incoming helicopter, gesturing frantically for it to touch down. Some were waving canteens and buckets, and one man even waved his SA-14 shoulder-fired antiaircraft weapon. That fool was going to get disciplined, Turabi vowed—loudly, painfully, and publicly. He would see to it himself.

The supply helicopter was coming in fast and very, very high, at least five or six hundred meters in altitude. With Russians possibly in the area, he was taking an awfully big chance coming in so high. It was hard to see clearly, but it appeared that the load was on a very short sling, meaning that the pilot would have to hover closer to the ground to unsling his load—which would kick up plenty of sand and dust and make unslinging the water tank that much harder. Poor discipline, he decided. He would have to see to setting up a retraining course for his chopper pilots as soon as he got back to Mary.

The helicopter pilot was obviously confused by the onrushing soldiers—and no doubt by the idiot waving the shoulder-fired missile in the air. He swung sharply to the west, the slung load arcing dramatically to the right. Turabi was about to shout out an order to his men . . . when he took a close look at the underslung load. Several of his men, closer to the helicopter, stopped and pointed at the load in confusion as well. It was not a water tank, or a diesel-fuel bladder, or a supply net.

It was a bomb, an incendiary bomb, pointing downward, resembling a huge cylinder with a long fuse on its nose and stabilizing fins on the aft end. The pilot was not swerving to get away from the soldier with the SA-14 missile—he was swerving to toss the bomb toward Turabi's patrol while he turned away to get as far from the blast as he could. And, as he watched, the bomb fell away from the helicopter directly at his encampment.

"Take cover!" Turabi shouted, waving his arms downward. "Take cover! *Incoming!*"

"Get down!" he heard a voice shout. It was his first sergeant, Abdul Dendara. Turabi turned just in time to see the man plow into him at full force, pushing him into the trench Turabi used as a temporary command post. Dendara then leaped in right after him, covering Turabi's body with his own.

Turabi looked up and was about to order his first sergeant to get the hell off of him—just as a bright flash of light instantly turned the dawn into high noon in summertime. Seconds later he heard several loud pops, followed by an ear-shattering explosion. Turabi saw Dendara pulled backward as if caught in a powerful vacuum, seemingly sucked right back out of the trench.

And then Dendara's body was instantly turned to a cloud of ash as the sky—no, the very air—was transformed into a wall of white-hot fire.

Turabi rolled over onto his belly and buried his face in the sand as the ocean of fire raged barely two meters above him. He felt his clothing and skin turning to flame, and he covered the back of his head with his bare hands and screamed and pleaded for God to take him before he could feel himself burn to death. The searing heat crept up his legs, and he could do nothing else but slap and kick the fire out and try not to expose any more of his body to it. What a nightmarish way to die, he thought. At least poor Abdul got the privilege of dying instantly, not bit by bit like this. . . .

It was the powerful explosion itself that saved him. The furious blast and overpressure swept hundreds of kilos of sand down into the trench, extinguishing the spontaneous flames that burst out all over Turabi's body and threatened to broil him to death, creating a thin but effective layer of insulation over him.

He had no idea how long it was before he awoke. At first he thought he'd been buried alive, but he found he could easily move aside the sand and create enough space to take a deep breath. The sand felt very warm, almost hot, but it didn't seem to be burning him. He experimented with his limbs and neck, trying each body part carefully, and found himself in pain but able to move, with no apparent serious injuries. Turabi reached above himself and found that his hand had popped out of the sand. He struggled to his knees and then to all fours, brushing sand from his face, marveling that he was still alive and dreading what he might find above.

The first thing he found, praise be to Allah, was a squad of his fellow Taliban soldiers searching the area. They had managed to chase away the Russian attackers, Turabi thought happily. He looked over and saw Aman Orazov himself, standing on an armored vehicle, listening to a verbal report from one of the men. Yes, Orazov was an ass, but right now he was surely a welcome sight. Turabi thought it appeared to be about midmorning—he might have been unconscious for three or four hours. He brushed more sand out of his ears as he hunted for a foothold on the edge of the trench.

As he did, he heard Orazov say, "Excellent. Looks like our attack worked perfectly."

Turabi let go and immediately dropped back down into the trench. What in hell did he mean, "our" attack?

"Negative, sir," he heard another soldier say—another Turkmen turncoat, like Orazov. "There's no sign of any living thing here. One hundred percent casualties. Everything that was aboveground was incinerated. The fuel-air explosive worked exactly as planned."

It wasn't a Russian attack? It was Orazov? *Their own men had attacked them?* Impossible . . . !

No, not impossible. For Orazov it was *very* possible. It clearly meant that Wakil Zarazi was dead also. Orazov had obviously betrayed Zarazi and then undertook his first mission: to kill Turabi and the rest of his patrol. He probably intended to win favor back from his former Turkmen officers or the Russian army, once they'd completed their reoccupation.

Jalaluddin Turabi knew that his mission had now changed. Instead of capturing booty for his tribe back in Afghanistan, Turabi's new mission was simple: avenge Wakil Zarazi's death. He was sworn to do it. Orazov had to die, and by Turabi's own hand. Nothing else in life mattered. Zarazi might have been misguided, blinded by some invisible, mystical calling—but he was still the leader, and Turabi's new duty was to avenge him. Then he could lead the loyal survivors back home, tell the elders what had happened, and prepare to take command of the tribe—or face the wrath of the elders.

But he couldn't confront Orazov now. That would be suicidal. He had no choice but to play dead and hope they would go away.

Turabi slinked back into the sand, slowly, carefully nudging it aside, intent on burrowing back down and burying himself. Standard procedures would be to search the trenches for survivors or bodies—he hoped Orazov was lazy or stupid enough to merely look around, decide there were no survivors, and go back to Mary. Maybe, *maybe,* if he did so, Turabi could escape, make his way back to their stronghold in Chärjew, then assemble a fighting force, sneak back to Mary, and carry out his new mission—kill Orazov.

Turabi was about three-quarters of the way back under the sand when he heard the first dog bark. Shit, he thought, maybe that Turkmen pigfucker Orazov wasn't so stupid after all—he'd remembered to bring guard dogs with him. Turabi fairly dove into the sand, but it was too late. Seconds later two scrawny whelps jumped into the trench. One clamped his jaws onto Turabi's left hand, and the other took a bite on the back of his neck and right ear before grabbing his right sleeve. Soon men were leaping into the partially sand-filled trench, and Turabi was dragged over to Orazov's vehicle and thrown onto the blackened desert floor.

"Well, well, the colonel is still alive," Orazov said, jumping down from his armored vehicle. "What a pleasant surprise. We should search all the trenches for survivors."

Turabi was held suspended by his arms between two Turkmen soldiers. Several surviving Taliban soldiers from his detail saw Turabi and rushed over to him but were pushed aside by more Turkmen soldiers. "Brilliant idea, Orazov," Turabi muttered.

"Is that any way to talk to your rescuer?" Orazov asked.

At a nod from him, one of the Turkmen soldiers punched Turabi in the side of his head. The Taliban soldiers surrounding them shouted a warning and tried to rush to Turabi's aid but were again roughly shoved back. Orazov didn't seem to notice—he was too intent on seeing Turabi suffer some more.

He stepped closer to Turabi and pulled his head up by his hair. "You'll wish you had died in that fuel-air blast, Turabi, I guarantee it."

Turabi tried to spit in his face, but he no longer had any moisture in his mouth at all. "What has happened to Zarazi?" he asked.

"The same that will happen to you, Turabi: I'll put a bullet through your stupid head, watch your brains splatter on the wall behind you, and then I'll wrap you up in a carpet and have you buried in the desert," Orazov said.

"You'll die for that," Turabi croaked through dry, cracked lips. "I'll slice out your heart myself."

"You didn't believe in the old man's holy mission any more than I did, Turabi. You're just too blinded by that idiotic clan-loyalty nonsense to realize it," Orazov said. "Forget about your ridiculous blood oaths and feudal allegiances, Turabi. Spend your last moments on earth thinking about this entire useless mission of yours in Turkmenistan and how badly you wasted the last few weeks of your life, waging a war with an idiot like Zarazi who thought he was fighting for the greater glory of God. Spend the next moments looking at the faces of your loyal men—because they'll join you in hell in a few minutes, too." He jabbed a thumb in the direction of a giant trench dug in the desert, where men and vehicles were dumping the remains of dozens of horribly burned and mangled men. "Good-bye, Colonel. Give my regards to General Zarazi—in hell."

Unable to stand and only half conscious, Turabi was dragged off toward the mass grave. He heard shouting and then gunshots behind him, followed by laughter, some shouted words in Turkmen, some screams, more gunshots, and more laughter. His men were being slaughtered trying to save him. He especially heard Orazov's screeching, high-pitched laugh, more like a young girl's than a man's. "You will have plenty of company in hell, Colonel," Orazov shouted with glee. "Your men seem more than willing to sacrifice themselves trying to save you!"

Turabi shut his eyes to try to erase Orazov's bizarre little shrieking laugh out of his head, but it was impossible. If anything, the sound started to grow louder and louder, until Turabi thought his head would explode from the pressure.

And then, suddenly, the entire world around him *did* explode.

Orazov's armored vehicle disappeared in a burst of fire and smoke not twenty meters away. Turabi and his captors were tossed off their feet by the blast. An earthmover on the other side of the mass grave exploded seconds later, followed by a light tank parked about a hundred meters away.

It was then that Turabi recognized that screeching sound, what he'd thought was Orazov's laughter—it was the same sound he remembered hearing what seemed like eons ago, when their little band of Taliban fighters was attacked by American unmanned drones. But it couldn't be. The Americans were not involved in this. Could it be the Russians . . . ?

Turabi's captors ran off to find cover, leaving him by himself. Still dazed and hurt, he needed all his strength to drag himself by his elbows and knees toward the mound of sand surrounding the grave. It was the only cover he could—

"No!" he heard a voice shout behind him. "You will not get away so easily!" And suddenly Aman Orazov was sitting on Turabi's back, his hands under his chin, pulling backward and trying to break his neck, or his back, or both. "I promised I would finish you off, and I will!"

"Bastard!" Turabi shouted. Using the last of his strength, he bucked Orazov off his back. Struggling to his hands and knees, with pieces of burned metal and hot debris digging into his skin, Turabi withdrew his knife from its sheath.

But Orazov was on top of him again in an instant, and he quickly and easily took the knife away from Turabi. Exhausted, Turabi was powerless to stop Orazov from rolling him over on his back.

"This is the better way to die, I think—hand-to-hand, face-to-face, by your own blade." Orazov raised the knife. . . .

But it did not come down. Turabi looked up—and saw a figure in a dark gray outfit, a bug-eyed helmet, and what appeared to be small tubes running along his arms, legs, and torso. He held Orazov's upraised arm in his hand, and no matter how hard Orazov struggled, the stranger held his arm with ease.

With a shock Turabi realized he *recognized* the stranger. It was the same one he had encountered south of Kiyzl-arvat when he went out to investigate the drone crash.

"Prasteetye," the stranger said in Russian in an eerie, electronically synthesized voice. *"Ya eeshchyoo Jalaluddin Turabi."*

"Shto eta znachyeet?" Orazov shouted. "Who in hell are you?"

With Orazov distracted, Turabi was able to respond, "I am Turabi. Good to see you again, sir."

The stranger nodded, then flipped his wrist. Orazov screamed and flew back as if hit by a bull charging at full force, his right arm twisted unnaturally. Turabi unsteadily crawled across the scorched sand, picked up a rock, and started to crawl over to where Orazov was lying holding his arm. "What are you doing?" the stranger asked in Russian.

"I must kill this man, to avenge my mission leader."

"You are barely conscious, and he is like an injured animal," the armored stranger said. "Better leave him alone."

"I am honor-bound to avenge my leader's death."

"We have more important things to do."

"I cannot think about saving my own life while my leader lies murdered in a shallow grave in the desert, betrayed by that man, whom he trusted," Turabi said. "This I cannot stand."

"The fate of a nation may be in your hands, Turabi," the stranger said. "Why not go after him later? Or I will have him taken into custody, and you can deal with him later."

"That is not the law," Turabi replied. He was still crawling toward Orazov. The Turkmen soldier was now on his feet, muttering something. Orazov had slipped his broken arm inside his shirt to support it. Within seconds he had found the knife and held it before him, ready to defend himself or attack if presented the opportunity. He was warily eyeing the big stranger, wondering if he was going to intervene in their fight, but because the stranger was no longer even looking at him, Orazov decided he was going to let the Afghan and the Turkman fight it out.

"Nike, this is Taurus, I still show you at the objective

point," Colonel Hal Briggs radioed a few moments later via their secure satellite commlink. "What's the holdup?"

"We have a slight cultural dilemma to address here first, sir," Sergeant Major Chris Wohl replied.

"At the moment I don't care about cultural dilemmas— I want our target exfiled out of there *now,*" Briggs said. "We're on a tight timetable. Move out."

"Yes, sir." Wohl went over to Turabi, picked him up by his load-bearing harness, and said, "Sorry, sir, but you have to come with me, right now."

"No!" Turabi screamed. "Put me down!"

Orazov incorrectly interpreted Wohl's action as coming to his rescue. He shouted happily and charged, the knife raised high. Turabi tried to kick free, but he couldn't break Wohl's microhydraulically assisted grip.

"Oh, for Pete's sake," Wohl muttered. "Some bozos just don't know when to quit."

As he held Turabi aloft with his right hand, he grabbed the knife away from Orazov's right hand, then butted the Turkman with his left forearm. Dazed, Orazov dropped to the ground. Wohl dropped Turabi, who fell onto his knees, still weak from the fuel-air explosive attack—and then he dropped the knife right in front of Turabi.

"Finish him off, sir," Wohl said in electronically translated Russian. "And I'll have you know, sir, that if you let him kill you, my ass will be in a sling."

For a moment it looked as if Turabi would just kill the guy, and they could be off. But the Turkmen traitor fought like a bull, and he knew that Turabi was still weak. Turabi pounced on Orazov and was just a few inches from plunging the blade into the traitor's chest, but Orazov was able to grab his wrist and hold the blade away.

"You can't kill me, Turabi," Orazov said, laughing. He glanced at the armored stranger and smiled when he realized he wasn't going to make a move to help either side. "Die like a man in front of that outsider. Roll over on your back and drop the knife. I'll make it quick—just like I did Zarazi."

That was not the correct thing to say to a man bent on revenge. Turabi's eyes blazed, he let out a loud, animal-like howl, and then head-butted Orazov on his nose. Orazov's vision exploded into a field of stars—but then went instantly dark as Turabi thrust the knife into the Turkman's chest.

"Forgive me, Allah," Turabi said, reciting the prayer of absolution, "but allow me to be the instrument of vengeance for the faithful." He twisted the knife with his last remaining gram of strength, felt a fount of warm blood wash over his hand, then held the knife in Orazov's chest until the flow of blood ceased.

"Nike, what in hell is going on over there?" Briggs radioed. He could peek into Wohl's electronic visor via the satellite datalink built into the Tin Man battle armor and see what Wohl was seeing, and at the moment all he could see was Turabi lying on the bloody corpse. "Is that the target lying on that DB? What's he doing?"

"He's resolved that cultural dilemma I mentioned a moment ago, sir," Wohl replied. He grabbed Turabi by his LBE harness again as if he were a rag doll, then took the knife away from him. "We're on the move now, sir," he added, just before he jet-jumped away.

OFFICE OF THE PRESIDENT OF THE REPUBLIC OF TURKMENISTAN, ASHKHABAD

A short time later

"So the American aircraft disappeared off radar and has not been detected since?" Kurban Gurizev, the president of Turkmenistan, asked after reading the conclusions of the report from the air force general standing before him. Unlike most of the Turkmen around him, Gurizev was short, his eyes were blue, he had skin tanned from the harsh sun instead of being olive-complexioned. Although born in Turkmenistan and a resident there most of his life, he spoke in slow, choppy Turkmen, with a definite and clear Russian accent. "What in hell happened?"

"There was a great deal of electronic jamming and false-target propagation just prior to losing radar contact," the general elaborated. "Both Ashkhabad Control and Baku Control were affected. We were not able to ascertain if the aircraft hit the Caspian Sea or if—"

"My God, we are all dead men . . . *dead men!*" Gurizev breathed. "The Americans are going to come in and crush us! Who in hell did this?"

"Sir, the Russians had numerous air patrols all around the country. It was obviously one of their fighters that brought the American down," the general said. "All aircraft were warned repeatedly of the danger of flying into the area. The Americans ignored those warnings; the crew unexpectedly and illegally broke off normal air-to-ground communications and most likely began responding to false commands, and it made unusual and provocative maneuvers in violation of air-traffic-control orders. They were in the wrong."

"And it was attacked by a Russian MiG-29 when it—"

"We do not know that for certain, sir," the general said.

"The *facts* as we know them, sir, were that a Russian fighter patrol was in the area but never made any move toward the American aircraft; that the American aircraft broke off contact with air-traffic control for no reason and began making violent, unexplainable maneuvers; and that contact was lost with the plane. That's *all* we know."

"The Americans are going to bury us," Gurizev cried. "We might as well start digging our graves right away."

The telephone in the office rang. An aide picked it up, listened, then hit the "hold" button. "Mr. President, it's Thomas Thorn, the president of the United States. He wishes to speak with you."

The short, beefy president of Turkmenistan pulled a handkerchief from his coat pocket, dabbed his forehead and lips, took a nervous gulp of water, then picked up the telephone. "This is President Kurban Gurizev speaking," he said in broken English. "To whom am I speaking, please?"

"This is President Thomas Thorn calling from the White House, Mr. President," came the reply. "This is an emergency, sir. I must speak with you immediately."

"I assure you, I have been notified of this unfortunate accident, and all of my country's resources will be immediately mobilized to determine what has happened."

"Thank you, Mr. President," Thorn said. "But I can tell you precisely what happened."

"You can?" Gurizev asked, perplexed.

"We already know that our diplomatic mission was attacked by a Russian MiG-29," President Thorn said, as calmly as if he were talking about a nice glass of wine. "We know this because as we speak we have air-defense and reconnaissance aircraft flying over Turkmenistan, and one of our planes detected the attack on our diplomatic aircraft and destroyed the MiG-29."

Gurizev didn't understand everything Thorn said—but he did understand "MiG-29," and his blood ran cold. My God, he thought, just minutes after the attack, and the Americans knew about the MiG . . . ?

"President Gurizev, are you still there? Do you need another translation?"

"Yes . . . yes, I am here, Mr. Thorn . . . er, Mr. President," Gurizev stammered. "Ah . . . we have no information whatsoever that there was any attack."

"I see," Thorn said. "Nonetheless, we have incontrovertible proof that such an attack took place, and we shall soon release this data to the world. You may want to ask your military advisers if the MiG ever made it back to its base. I can tell you, sir, it did not. It was destroyed."

Gurizev jabbed a finger at another phone, and the air force general picked it up and called his headquarters. "This . . . this is most unusual, sir," Gurizev said. "We . . . we shall of course immediately investigate your information."

"Please do," Thorn said. "We regret the loss of life, but it was necessary to save the lives of former president Martindale, Deputy Secretary of State Hershel, and the others on that plane."

"How was the pilot killed, sir, if as you claim you have only reconnaissance and defensive aircraft over Turkmenistan?"

"I'd rather not reveal how at this time, Mr. President," Thorn said. "But it was an American warplane that shot the MiG down—after we observed him attacking our diplomatic mission with heat-seeking air-to-air missiles. We have even identified the missiles—they were AA-11 'Archer' missiles, what the Russians call the R-73M2, one of Russia's most advanced weapons."

Gurizev looked over at his air force chief of staff, and

when he saw the man's blank, confused expression, he had to carefully suppress a gasp. "Could you hold the line, please?"

"Of course, Mr. President."

Gurizev placed the call on hold with a shaking hand. "Get that son of a bitch Russian military liaison officer over here *now!*" The air force officer issued the order, listened, then peered at the phone. "What in hell is it now?"

"The operator cannot contact the Russian defense liaison's office. There is no answer."

"What?" The Turkmen chief of the general staff grabbed the phone away from the air force commander. He barked orders into the phone, but soon he, too, was dumbfounded. "No response from the Russian liaison, and now the direct line to my office is completely out. What in blazes is going on?"

"Could this be true?" Gurizev thundered. "The Russian fighter was shot down—*by an American combat aircraft?*"

"The MiG should have already returned to Krasnovodsk," the general said, checking his watch. "It would have run out of fuel long ago."

"Could it have carried the weapons Thorn described?"

"Of course, sir."

"Yop tvayu mat!" Gurizev swore loudly in Russian. He often forgot his adopted Turkmen language when he was nervous, excited, enraptured—or scared. "How in hell could the Americans know all this?"

"They must have sent stealth aircraft over our country to escort the American diplomatic aircraft," the chief of staff said as he stood with the phone to his ear. "We must assume that the Americans have more such aircraft overhead right this very minute."

"My God . . . this cannot be happening," Gurizev muttered. "This is unbelievable." He looked at the phone in his hand, then punched the blinking line button. "President Thorn, I apologize for placing you on hold. We are unable at this time to get independent confirmation of your assertions. We must be allowed to investigate this matter further."

"President Gurizev, you can't get through to your Russian liaison officer and your defense staff because the Russians have cut off all government communications going in or out of the capital," Thorn said. "We have detected several cargo planes landing at Krasnovodsk and Ashkhabad. Assuming each plane holds only one hundred soldiers plus their equipment, we estimate at least a battalion-size invasion force is marching against your position right now."

"*A Russian invasion force? Why?*"

"My guess is Russia intends to take over the government to prevent it from falling into the hands of the Taliban or any other foreign power," Thorn said. "You have only a few minutes to evacuate your offices—it may already be too late. Mr. President, if you need my help, ask. Give me permission to send military forces into your country, and I'll do everything I can to protect you."

This time Gurizev didn't bother putting the call on hold—he was too scared or confused to know what to do with his hands. "Where is Kasimov? Why is he not briefing me on the state of our air defenses or of Russia's intentions? I pay that bastard a lot of money to advise me—he had better get in here immediately!"

"He hasn't been heard from in several hours, sir," the chief of the general staff replied. "I'm trying every office—"

"President Gurizev . . ."

"*Kharasho,* Thorn!" Gurizev said. "All right, I agree. I

want your help. I don't know what the Russians want here. You have my permission to send in any forces you desire to protect myself and my staff. Just get us the hell out of here!"

"A few questions first," Thorn said. "Who ordered the attack on the Taliban forces outside Mary?"

"I did."

"And the commando insertion?"

"I received an execution order from President Sen'kov about nine hours before they were ambushed."

"Who ordered the attack on the deputy secretary of state's plane?" Thorn asked.

"I don't know," Gurizev said. "When the commandos were ambushed by the Taliban, Gryzlov issued a warning order to seal off our airspace and send in bombers to blast hell out of them."

"Did Sen'kov sign the execution order for the blockade and the air raid?"

"If he did, I never saw it," Gurizev said. "If he had, I certainly would have rescinded the authorization for the diplomatic visit."

"Why didn't you rescind the authorization after the Taliban's attack on Mary or when Sen'kov authorized commandos to be inserted near Mary?"

"Sen'kov wanted you to see what the Taliban had done," Gurizev said. "He wanted to prove *they* were the instigators, not us!"

"But then why seal off the airspace *after* the diplomatic flight left Bahrain?"

"I didn't know anything about the Taliban ambush outside Mary, about the air raid, or anything about the blockade, except for the warning order," Gurizev replied. "I asked for clarification of the order, but I haven't spoken to anyone in Moscow in days—and I haven't seen my Russian liaison officer either, the one who is supposed to keep me apprised of such actions!"

"You did not receive the execution order?"

"After the Taliban ambushed those commandos, I received no more communications from Moscow. *Sreka!* All I wanted was for the Russians to stop those Taliban insurgents."

"You'd better make your way out of there, Mr. President," Thorn said. "Take a cellular phone with you and dial this number now." Thorn gave him a coded number unlike any regular phone number.

Gurizev dialed it. "What do I do now?" he asked.

"You don't have to do anything. In a few moments we'll pick up the digital signal from your phone by satellite, and we'll be able to locate and track you as long as you're in range of a cell site," Thorn said. "We'll send in rescue forces as quickly as we can. Now, get out of there!"

Gurizev simply dropped the corded phone, pocketed his cellular phone, and shouted, "Did you get in contact with anyone yet? Can anyone tell us where the Russians are?"

"Something's wrong . . . now I can't get through to the defense-operations center," the chief of the general staff replied. "The line is completely blank." He waved the air force general to wait on the phone for him, then said to Gurizev, "Sir, I recommend you evacuate the capital. Your car should take you out of the city immediately. Once we're safe, we can decide where to go."

"Then let's get out of here!" Gurizev shouted. "Have my armored car waiting in the secure parking facility immediately!" He grabbed his briefcase and headed for the door, with his staffers and military advisers close behind.

Suddenly the door burst open, and a dozen Russian soldiers with assault rifles drawn burst into the president's office and roughly shoved everyone back into the room. Cowering against a wall, they were ordered to place their hands on their heads.

"What is this?" Gurizev shouted, hoping that his voice would soon stop shaking. Then, to everyone's surprise, Colonel General Boris Kasimov, the Russian liaison to the Turkmen general staff, walked in, holding an AK-74 compact assault rifle in his hands.

"There has been a change in leadership, Mr. President," Kasimov said in Turkmen. "I'm under orders from General Anatoliy Gryzlov, chief of the general staff of the Russian Federation's military forces. He has declared martial law, and he has ordered that I take over as leader of Turkmenistan during this national emergency."

"What in *hell* are you talking about?" Gurizev exploded. "Get that gun out of my face! I demand that you leave my office immediately."

"You have no need to make demands, Mr. President," Kasimov said. "All you have to do now is relinquish the last bit of your authority. Allow me to assist you." At that, General Kasimov braced the AK-74 against his right hip and fired a three-round burst into Gurizev. The president was dead before his eviscerated body hit the floor. "Now, is there anyone else who would like me to further explain the situation here?" Kasimov asked. Complete silence. "Very good." He motioned to his soldiers, and they took the Turkmen away at gunpoint.

Kasimov picked up the telephone. "President Thorn?" he asked in very good English.

"This is Thomas Thorn. Whom am I speaking to, please?"

"This is Colonel General Boris Kasimov of the Army of the Russian Federation. I am an adviser and liaison to the Turkmen government regarding national defense and manpower."

"Gdye Rookavadeeteel Gurizev?" Thorn asked in Russian.

"I have been asked to inform you that General Anatoliy

Gryzlov, chief of the general staff of the Russian Federation, has declared martial law in the Republic of Turkmenistan under the terms of the Treaty of Friendship, Cooperation, and Mutual Defense between the Russian Federation and Turkmenistan signed in 1991 and in accordance with the Treaty on Joint Citizenship signed in 1993, which also provides for Russian involvement in the defense of Turkmenistan," Kasimov said in English, ignoring Thorn's question. "General Gryzlov has directed that I assume the duties of president and commander in chief of the armed forces of Turkmenistan during the emergency."

"Mozhna mnye pagavareet's Rookavadeeteel Gurizev, Colonel General?"

"Unfortunately, the president is not being allowed to take calls, Mr. President—now or ever," Kasimov said matter-of-factly. "I must inform you, Mr. President, that the actions of your armed forces over Turkmenistan have been monitored and analyzed by Russian military forces, and they are the principal reason for the imposition of martial law."

"Ya nee paneemayoo, Colonel General."

"I would be happy to explain. The downing of our MiG-29 was a completely unprovoked and irrational act of murder. You have introduced deadly offensive warplanes without permission over sovereign Turkmen airspace. Since these are stealth aircraft, designed and employed to deliver weapons of mass destruction on a first-strike, preemptive basis, the presence of such aircraft over Turkmenistan represents a deliberate act of war between the United States and the Republic of Turkmenistan. Under the provisions of the treaties between the Russian Federation and Turkmenistan, the actions of the American military forces over Turkmenistan have left us no recourse but to declare a state of war between the United States and the Russian Federation."

"What are you saying?"

"The following regulations are to be imposed immediately," Kasimov went on, as if reciting a well-rehearsed script onstage. "American citizens who are not representatives of the U.S. government have twenty-four hours to leave Turkmenistan, or they may be detained at a location of our choosing without cause or explanation for an indefinite period of time. Any diplomatic or embassy personnel may stay but will be restricted to the embassy in Ashkhabad.

"Any uniformed Americans entering or already inside Turkmenistan without my express written permission shall from this moment forth be considered combatants and will be treated per the Geneva Conventions. Finally, any agents of the American government without proper credentials verified by the Russian government will be treated as hostile enemy provocateurs and will be imprisoned, tried by a military field tribunal, and, if found guilty of espionage, summarily executed. Do you understand all these things, Mr. President? I do not wish for there to be any misunderstandings between us."

"*Ya paneemayoo,* Colonel General," Thorn replied.

"In English, Mr. President—I would not want you to claim that you gave the wrong response because of your poor command of the Russian language."

"I understand, Colonel General," Thorn said in English. "Now, *you* had better understand this. Are you listening, Colonel General? I would not want you to claim you did not hear or understand my response to you. I shall provide you with a translator if you would like."

"Please proceed, Mr. President," Kasimov said with laughter in his voice. "I need no translator. And please speak in English. My command of English is much better than your Russian, I'm afraid."

"Very well. You may tell President Sen'kov and General

Gryzlov that the United States will use every tool at our disposal to protect and defend American interests anywhere in the world, including the Republic of Turkmenistan."

There was silence on the line for several minutes. Finally Kasimov asked, "Is that all, Mr. President?"

"That's all, Colonel General."

"Well, I will certainly pass along your dire warning to my superiors," Kasimov said, the humor still evident in his voice. "In the interest of safety, Mr. President, may I suggest that you inform me of the whereabouts of any American agents or combatants in Turkmenistan right now? If they agree to give up their weapons and go peacefully with my men, I promise to you that they will be released unharmed to your embassy in Ashkhabad within twenty-four hours. Is that agreeable to you, sir?"

"That is a very reasonable offer, Colonel General."

"Then you *do* have combatants inside Turkmenistan, sir?"

"We do."

Kasimov paused, obviously surprised to hear Thorn admit to all this. "Well, then, sir, I think we can quickly come to an agreement to protect and preserve these men's lives. Please advise me what forces you have in Turkmenistan, their approximate numbers, and their locations, and we shall attempt to make contact with them. If your military commanders can inform them that we have a deal to protect them, no harm should come to them."

"I don't know their exact designations, Colonel General," Thorn said. He paused for a moment, then said, "Could you hold the line for a moment, Colonel General?"

"I'm very busy, Mr. President. It can be only for a moment."

"Thank you."

What in hell was he doing?

A few moments later another voice came on the line: "Colonel General Kasimov?"

"Who is this?"

"My name is Major General Patrick McLanahan, United States Air Force," Patrick McLanahan replied. "I have been directed by the president of the United States to answer your questions regarding our forces in Turkmenistan."

"Is this some kind of joke, General?"

"I'm just following orders, sir."

"Very well. What ground forces do you have in Turkmenistan right now?"

"We have one Battle Force team on the ground now, outside Mary and in Chärjew."

"And the composition of this team?"

"Eight soldiers, plus a support team of twelve."

"Eight? I assume you mean eight squads, or perhaps eight companies . . . ?"

"No, sir. Eight men."

"One squad? Eight men?" Kasimov said warily. He thought that this McLanahan was joking with him now, but the man seemed perfectly at ease and forthcoming. Was this some kind of game? "Any other combatants in Turkmenistan, sir?"

"Yes, Colonel General."

"How many? Their description, please?"

"Stealth warplanes," McLanahan said casually. "All defensive in nature, but quite capable of supporting our forces on the ground."

"How many?"

"The number changes with the threat," McLanahan said. "The more troops you send in to Turkmenistan and the more targets we uncover during our reconnaissance, the more stealth aircraft we'll send."

"For what purpose, sir?" Kasimov asked. "What is your intention?"

"First of all, Colonel General, the Russian Federation just declared war on the United States," McLanahan said. "So we damned well will destroy any Russian aircraft, vehicle, or warship we encounter. For example, I'm looking right now at a squadron of eight Mi-28 attack helicopters parked outside a hangar at Krasnovodsk Airport. It appears they're being fueled and readied for a mission."

"We have no such helicopters at Krasnovodsk, sir."

"Ah . . . well, you certainly don't anymore, Colonel General—because they've just been destroyed," McLanahan said casually.

Kasimov motioned to an aide, who immediately lifted a radio to his lips. They did indeed have Mi-28s at Krasnovodsk, and they were indeed getting ready to deploy them, first to Ashkhabad to cover the occupation of the city, then to Mary to start hunting down the Taliban. "You find this humorous, General McLanahan?"

"It's certainly an unusual way to go to war, isn't it, Colonel General?" McLanahan responded. "Now I'm looking at an intelligence-gathering vessel several miles off the coast from Krasnovodsk in the Caspian Sea. My intelligence officers tell me that it is a Type 394B-class spy ship and that it was probably responsible for trying to spoof our diplomatic-mission aircraft into going off its flight plan, where your fighters would then have a reason to shoot it down. The ship has Cyrillic characters and the number five ninety-one on the side—yes, that checks, it's a Type 394B, the *Kavkaz,* if my information is correct."

"The *Kavkaz* is an unarmed communications vessel, sir, not a spy ship!"

"Your 'unarmed communications vessel' just fired two heat-seeking missiles at our stealth warplane, Colonel General," Patrick said. "And . . . it appears our aircraft was just hit . . . yes, we've just lost that aircraft."

"You don't seem too upset, General."

"I'm upset to lose any aircraft, sir, even an unmanned one."

"Unmanned . . . ?"

"Yes, General. Tell your sailors on the *Kavkaz* good shooting—and then tell them to prepare to abandon ship. Because I've just committed two more stealth aircraft to sink the *Kavkaz*."

Kasimov covered the mouthpiece of the telephone when he saw two of his aides grabbing the radio from each other, their eyes wide in surprise. "Well? What in hell is happening?"

"Krasnovodsk is under attack, sir!" one of his aides said. *"What?"*

"Several helicopters and transport planes were destroyed, and the command post, a power facility, and the radar site were heavily damaged. The air defenses all came under attack by precision-guided weapons and cluster bombs."

"Are you still there, Colonel General?" McLanahan asked over the phone.

"I demand to know what is going on here!" he cried.

"You declared war on the United States, Colonel General, and the United States is responding," McLanahan said. "May I make a suggestion? You should undeclare war on the United States—right away."

"Are you insane, General McLanahan? What kind of nonsense is this?"

"Colonel General, you tried to intimidate President Thorn by making this ridiculous declaration of war, thinking that the president was going to be cowed into not acting while you moved more troops and heavier weapons into Turkmenistan," Patrick said. "Well, it didn't work. The United States is already in Turkmenistan, and we have stealth warplanes orbiting your military installations in Ashkhabad and Krasnovodsk right now. Unless you call off this declaration of war, we will continue to locate and attack Russian military targets that we feel are a threat to U.S. forces and interests."

"I . . . I must report your demands to General Gryzlov and the general staff—"

"You've got sixty seconds to do so, Colonel General," McLanahan said, "before two of my stealth aircraft launch missiles at the *Kavkaz*. The next target will be your office in Ashkhabad. We are obviously not in your office at this time, but I would warn any staff members you have in your head-quarters building to evacuate within the next two minutes."

"What is it you want, General? What are your intentions?"

"The United States has no intentions, Colonel General," Patrick replied. "It is *Russia* who declared war on the United States, *Russia* who fired on the deputy secretary of state's aircraft, *Russia* who has assassinated President Gurizev of Turkmenistan, *Russia* who is threatening to imprison and execute Americans in Turkmenistan, and *Russia* who is invading Turkmenistan on a pretext of protecting it. Russia's intentions are clear: You want to take Turkmenistan, and you're willing to kill anyone who gets in your way."

"That is not true, sir! Russia wants only to protect the peace and sovereignty of an important ally and friend. It is the Taliban insurgents that threaten the peace! We have an obligation to—"

"Excuse me, Colonel General," Patrick interrupted, "but we just put four mini-Maverick missiles with thermium-nitrate warheads into the *Kavkaz*. Our aircraft will come around for another pass, and that should do it for the *Kavkaz*—it's already listing pretty well to starboard. You have ninety seconds before I put four missiles into Twenty-eight President Niyazov Avenue, southwest facade—that *is* the address of your headquarters in Ashkhabad, isn't it?"

General Kasimov banged the telephone receiver down with a half-furious, half-terrified, half-human cry. "What is going on with the *Kavkaz?*" he shouted.

"No contact with the ship as of yet, sir," an aide replied.

"This is a nightmare!" Kasimov shouted in complete frustration. "This cannot be happening!"

"Shall we order an evacuation of the headquarters building?"

"Yes, damn it, *get everyone out of—*"

Just then there were several bright flashes of light from outside, like flickers of lightning. Seconds later there were several loud, sharp explosions that rattled the windows and caused the lights to flicker. "Oh, my God!"

Kasimov's aides ran to a window. Kasimov didn't need to look for himself—their slumping shoulders told him everything. "Fires have broken out in the headquarters building!" someone shouted. "Shit . . . another one! Another explosion!" The rattling windows and reverberating explosions were like hammer blows on Kasimov's skull. *"We're under attack!"*

Kasimov picked up the telephone, but it was dead—and moments later all the lights went out in the office as well. "Get the damned power back on immediately! And then get me General Gryzlov in Moscow—*right now!*"

CHÄRJEW, REPUBLIC OF TURKMENISTAN
That night

"Peace be unto all true servants of God.

"My friends and neighbors of the Republic of Turkmenistan and any within the sound of my voice, my name is Jalaluddin Turabi. I am not Turkmen. I was born in

Afghanistan, raised as a true servant of God. I believe in the oneness of God; I believe that Mohammad is His true prophet; and I believe with all my heart in the Day of Judgment and the resurrection of the faithful in the arms of God.

"I am also Taliban. I know this immediately brands me and my people as fanatical, fire-breathing murderers. But I tell you this: We are what we are, and that is as our name says, 'seekers of the truth.' We do not know the truth; we do not profess the truth; we do not attempt to impose our knowledge or opinion of the truth on others.

"The knowledge that we have is passed along to us from a council of elders, chosen from each of a province's clans. This council of elders directs activities of each clan or groups of clans. These activities are organized into either *siyaehiyya*, or tasks, and jihads, or sacred missions. In my case I was appointed to undertake a jihad to secure weapons, equipment, and funds for the council. My friend, Wakil Mohammad Zarazi, was my leader. We trained together in Iran and Sudan as members of Hezbollah to employ military and commando-style weapons and tactics to fulfill our missions and to train others in those tactics.

"Our mission inside Afghanistan was not successful. We lost many men, but Wakil Zarazi survived a deadly assault, and he led us to the Turkmen frontier. He believed that his survival was an act of God, and he dedicated himself from that day forward to serve God by bringing together the faithful into a strong army that could resist all nonbelievers, no matter how rich or powerful they were.

"Wakil Zarazi did many evil, despicable things because he believed that God told him to do these things. For this I ask God for forgiveness, and I apologize to the people of Turkmenistan, because as his friend and soldier, I obeyed his orders and helped him do these things. He lost the way of the leader and warrior because he believed that was what God wanted him to do. When he put me in charge of his armies, I sought to follow the ways of a true warrior as well as a jihadi. I served my leader and God by remembering that a leader succeeds not by fear and intimidation but by strength and leadership.

"Wakil Zarazi is dead, assassinated by a man he trusted—a Turkmen soldier, Aman Orazov, who joined our ranks after the siege of Kizyl-arvat. He was one among thousands of Turkmen who joined our jihad, but he was the only one to betray its leader. As is our custom and responsibility after the assassination of a leader, I avenged Wakil Zarazi's death by killing Orazov with my own hands. I am now in command of Zarazi's army.

"I have been proud to serve this jihad, and I am proud of my soldiers. I am equally proud of your Turkmen brothers who joined our jihad. Although by Taliban law and custom I now decide how best to accomplish this jihad, I realize that I have a responsibility not only to my fellow clansmen and fighters from Afghanistan but to the Turkmen who joined Zarazi's jihad. The men from Turkmenistan fought with our army not because we paid them or offered adventure but because they believe as we do: that we can create a special place in the deserts of this country. Turkmenistan is wealthy beyond imagination, yet its people, the faithful, don't seem to be enjoying the benefit of living in this harsh, lonely place. With your help we can change this.

"The situation is this: Your president, Kurban Gurizev, has been brutally assassinated by Colonel General Boris Kasimov, the Russian liaison to the Turkmen government. Many Russian army regiments have already entered the capital. Yet the Russians do not as yet control Turkmenistan. The reason: The United States of America has intervened in this conflict and has sent air and ground forces to face the Russians.

"My brothers, I know you have no cause to love the

Americans, just as you may not love the Russians. Both nations have sought to take your substantial mineral wealth at far less than market price and at the same time conspire with unscrupulous bureaucrats in your government for payoffs in exchange for lucrative development contracts. But the Americans rescued me from certain death by the Russians and by Aman Orazov, and they are here, standing by and awaiting your word. Before he died, President Gurizev authorized their presence in Turkmenistan, although the Russian army is in charge, under the pretext of abiding by a mutual-defense treaty between Turkmenistan and the Russian Federation.

"You may choose not to believe my words, but I tell you, it is the truth: The Russians want nothing more than to crush the Taliban and deter any other Muslim groups from gaining a foothold in Turkmenistan. They mean to crush all Muslim participation in government and stamp out any thought or attempt at equity for the Muslim majority, as they do in Chechnya and other republics and provinces.

"I know you have no reason to believe me. I am an outsider. I attacked your towns and cities, fought your soldiers, and took your property. I also know that for many decades the Russians have protected Turkmenistan—first as conquerors and dictators in their empire, but later as neighbors and partners, although for mostly self-serving reasons. You may consider them your friends and defenders and consider me your enemy.

"But I will say this, and then leave you to consider my words. Wakil Zarazi entered your country several weeks ago with a band of exactly two hundred and seventy-one men in a caravan of battered old pickup trucks. Today Zarazi's army numbers over twenty-seven thousand. Zarazi's army may have begun with a handful of Taliban desert raiders from Afghanistan fleeing from a Western assault, but we have transformed into a fighting force composed of soldiers from all over Central Asia—but mostly men from Turkmenistan. I never realized it until now, but the army once led by Wakil Zarazi, the army I command today, is in reality a Turkmen army, not a Taliban or Afghan army—the first Turkmen army since Alexander the Second of imperial Russia not to be commanded by a Russian.

"So the choice is yours, my brothers and sisters of Turkmenistan and all of Central Asia. If you reject me, I will take what remains of my army and go home. If there is another among you who wishes to lead this army, have him step forward and present himself to me and the troops. But if you wish it, I will continue to battle for independence from Russia. You will know where to find me—as will the Russians.

"This battle will be one of two kinds: a battle for survival for myself and my men or a fight for freedom and independence against General Gryzlov and the Russian army. Make your wishes known to me—I will be listening. Thank you, and may God bless you and your families, and grant you peace."

DIEGO GARCIA, INDIAN OCEAN
That same time

The broadcast, played live on world news channels, ended, and the military and political analysts began discussing the speech.

"He did a good job," Rebecca Furness said. "But he's a fucking Taliban. They won't have him lead their troops. He'll be lucky to get out of the country alive."

She and Daren Mace had been listening to Turabi's

speech via satellite on Diego Garcia. They had already finished their first patrol period after arriving in-theater, a total of eighteen hours and three aerial refuelings—which did not include the sixteen hours and three aerial refuelings it had taken for the first flight of EB-1 bombers to·fly from Battle Mountain to Turkmenistan.

After refueling over the Arabian Sea just south of Pakistan, Rebecca Furness and her First Air Battle Force team flew at very high altitude over Pakistan, Afghanistan, and Turkmenistan, evading their surveillance and air-defense radars. They were able to stay on patrol over their assigned area in Turkmenistan for about three hours before having to depart and go back to the refueling track. Each crew flew three such patrols, a total of eighteen hours, before landing at Diego Garcia.

They had been on patrol all over the countryside, responding to surveillance and attack requests, but had not fired any weapons. The AL-52 Dragon airborne-laser aircraft were the primary air-defense aircraft, with the manned Vampires flying as backups. The manned Vampire bombers carrying three rotary launchers: the forward launcher carried sixteen AIM-120 Scorpion medium-range air-to-air radar-guided missiles, the middle launcher carrying ten AIM-154 Anaconda long-range hypersonic air-to-air missiles, and the aft launcher carrying eight AGM-165 Longhorn ground-attack missiles.

Each Air Battle team had two unmanned aircraft in its formation, each of which carried four StealthHawk unmanned combat air vehicles on a rotary launcher in the middle bomb bay. The forward bomb bay contained extra weapon clips for the StealthHawks, and the aft bomb bay carried a spare fuel tank that could be both used to refuel the UCAVs or used by the bomber itself in an emergency.

Each UCAV carried six AGM-211 mini-Maverick missiles with thermium-nitrate warheads.

Rearming and refueling the StealthHawks proved to be a simple engineering feat, accomplished with technology and equipment they already had at Battle Mountain. After retrieval each StealthHawk was locked on to the rotary launcher and rotated to the top of the Vampire's middle bomb bay, with the UCAV's own bomb bays open and facing upward. Six-round clips of mini-Mavericks were slid over from the forward bomb bay, lowered into the Stealth-Hawk's upturned weapons bay, and locked into place; at the same time a refueling line filled the UCAV's fuel tanks. The forward bomb bay held twenty-four weapon clips. If necessary a StealthHawk could be rearmed and relaunched less than five minutes after retrieval.

Typically the unmanned Vampire bombers would arrive over their patrol area, release their StealthHawks, return to the air-refueling track to refuel, return to the patrol area, retrieve the StealthHawks, refuel and rearm them if necessary, then repeat the process. As long as they had fuel and weapons, the process could be repeated indefinitely.

Now Rebecca and Daren were in their detachment headquarters on Diego Garcia on "crew rest"—which meant supervising their team's refueling and reloading, reviewing intelligence data, and planning their next patrol. They took catnaps when able, alternating attendance in meetings and inspections, then filling the other in as they went off in search of a quiet closet to take a nap. They still had six hours in which they hoped to be able to get some real rest, but that was probably going to be impossible.

"All Air Battle Force participants, this is Bravo. Stand by for an intelligence update," Brigadier General David Luger announced via the secure satellite datalink. "As of the top of the hour, satellite-reconnaissance and intelligence data indicates that the Russian air force is mobilizing an additional three bomber and fighter regiments. Along with the fighters at Saratov and the bombers at Engels, we're now seeing activity at Astrakhan and Volgograd. This makes a total of six bomber and five fighter regiments mobilized in the past six hours. All of these regiments are within normal unrefueled combat radius of the various aircraft involved. In other words, we believe with high probability that all of these regiments are being mobilized for action over Turkmenistan."

"That's not good news," Daren said. "Wonder what the boss is going to do?"

Rebecca looked over at Daren and smiled. "Well, I just want you to know, Daren, that the work you've done since you arrived here has been nothing short of amazing," she said. "I never thought we'd have this capability—that we'd be flying around up here while a couple B-1 bombers are cruising nearby with us *with no one on board*. It's a freakin' miracle."

"Thanks, Rebecca," Daren said. He reached over, took her hand, and gave it a squeeze. He then realized what he'd done and was expecting a rebuff, but he didn't get one. "It's been great working with you again—although this cockpit is sure as hell different from the last one we went to war in." He paused, looking at the satellite imagery and analysis data being presented on the supercockpit display in front of him. "Wonder what the general is going to do?"

"I don't see he has much choice. He's got to withdraw," Rebecca said. "Nine regiments—that's as many as a hundred and twenty aircraft, if the regiments are fully staffed. We're outnumbered twenty to one, and I don't think even the airborne laser or what few weapons we have in place can make up for that." She looked at Daren. "What do you think?"

"I think you're right," Daren said after a long pause. "It would be better if we had some help—a couple B-2

stealth-bomber squadrons and a few fighter wings for
starters. Otherwise, we can hold out just long enough to
get our guys out—if that long. The Russians have too
many planes too close to Turkmenistan. It's too easy for
them to surge numerically superior forces."

"So McLanahan has to pull back." She gave Daren a
wry smile and added, "That'll be a first. I don't even think
he knows how."

THE WHITE HOUSE, WASHINGTON, D.C.

That same time

"I'm sorry things have escalated to this point, Mr. President," Thomas Thorn said. He was seated in the Oval Office with Vice President Lester Busick, Secretary of
Defense Robert Goff, and Joint Chiefs of Staff chairman
General Richard Venti. "The United States does not want
a war with Russia or anyone else."

"Your military forces have destroyed dozens of aircraft,
heavily damaged a communications vessel on the high
seas, and killed seventeen men and women, sir, all in one
night," Russian president Valentin Sen'kov said. "If you
don't want war, President Thorn, you have a strange way
of showing it."

"I take it by your words, Mr. President, that you did not
actually declare war on the United States of America?"

"That's the most preposterous thing I've ever heard,
President Thorn," Sen'kov said. "No one in my govern-
ment has declared war, and certainly not with the United
States. Yes, I consider the Taliban a threat to peace in
Turkmenistan, but I have not declared war on them or any-
one else!"

"Then Colonel General Kasimov's declarations and

warnings were not authorized or sanctioned by the Russian government?"

"I don't even *know* a Colonel General Kasimov!" Sen'kov retorted. "Is this some kind of game, Mr. President?"

"We have e-mailed the Russian embassy in Washington with a digital recording and transcript of a conversation I had with Colonel General Kasimov, who said he was the Russian liaison to the Turkmen military general staff. He announced the imposition of martial law in Turkmenistan and said that, because of U.S. actions in Turkmenistan and by authority of treaties between Russia and Turkmenistan, a state of war existed between our countries."

"I . . . this is outrageous! This is nonsense!" Sen'kov exploded. "I authorized nothing of the kind! It must have been approved by General Gryzlov, my chief of the general staff."

"We are also monitoring a very large-scale buildup of tactical and strategic forces in Russia," Thorn went on, "that all appear to be getting ready for air assaults in Turkmenistan."

"I know that General Gryzlov issued a warning order directing mobilization and preparedness," Sen'kov admitted. "He has that authority. He was very concerned about the shoot-down of the MiG-29 over Turkmenistan—fearing it might have been from a secret attack by the Taliban—and these recent attacks in the Caspian Sea and Krasnovodsk only reinforced his fears. However, I have not authorized any attacks against any forces anywhere."

"So you issued no execution order for any attacks in Turkmenistan?"

"No, I did not," Sen'kov said. "I understand that General Gryzlov delivered a draft execution order to my office. It is sitting here right in front of me on my desk, still unsigned."

"So what does this mean?" Thorn asked. "Is General

Gryzlov acting on your orders, or is he provoking a war on his own?"

"I don't know if he has access to information I do not, or if he has misinterpreted a directive from my office," Sen'kov said. "In any case we will investigate immediately. But I assure you most emphatically, Mr. President: Russia is *not* at war with the United States."

"I believe you, Mr. President," Thorn replied. "But the world will soon see what we see: Russia getting ready to attack someone. We must have some kind of assurance that war is not imminent. The American Congress will certainly want a full explanation, and our military forces will press to go to a heightened state of alert. If that happens, we may not be able to control the escalation."

"Then I suggest a meeting, Mr. Thorn," Sen'kov said. "An emergency summit, in Reykjavik, Iceland, tomorrow morning. We shall issue a joint statement telling the world we are not at war; we shall both pledge to restore peace and democracy to Turkmenistan and work together to solve racial, cultural, religious, and ethnic conflicts all over the world."

"Agreed. I'll be there," Thorn replied.

"Very good, Mr. President. I look forward to seeing you in Iceland."

Thorn set the phone down and turned to Vice President Lester Busick. "Summit meeting between Sen'kov and me, tomorrow morning, in Reykjavik."

"Well, at least the bastard chose someplace more or less in between our two capitals," Busick said as he picked up his phone to start making arrangements. "The asshole probably denies the whole thing."

"I have a feeling he's as much in the dark as we are, Les."

"Real fucking great. That doesn't make me feel any better."

"What's the status of our folks in Uzbekistan and Turk-menistan, Robert?" Thorn asked.

"Everyone's standing by, sir," Secretary of State Robert Goff replied. "Secretary Hershel has been in contact with the Taliban leader, Jalaluddin Turabi, who told her he wants to see what the people of Turkmenistan say. Gur-izev is dead; we feel it's far too dangerous for any Ameri-can to go to the capital while the Russians control the city. I believe her mission is done."

"Same here," Busick said. "Let's get her the hell out of there."

"All right," Thorn said. "General Venti, have General McLanahan's aircraft escort Deputy Secretary of State Hershel's aircraft out of Uzbekistan and stay with it until it's safely back on friendly soil. Then have the rest of McLanahan's force evacuate to Diego Garcia. I want max-imum protection for the entire contingent. He's author-ized to use every aircraft he's got to see to it that Hershel and his ground forces are safely out of the region."

"Should McLanahan's teams stand by on Diego Garcia, in case they're needed again over Turkmenistan?"

Thorn thought about it for a moment, then replied, "No, General. As soon as Deputy Secretary Hershel is back on U.S. territory, bring them home. Be sure to pass along my thanks for a job well done."

"Yes, sir," Venti said. He picked up a telephone and be-gan issuing orders.

Secretary Goff was the only adviser not otherwise oc-cupied. "So what do you think this General Gryzlov is go-ing to do next?" he asked Thorn. "Is he a loose cannon, an opportunist, or just plain crazy?"

Thomas Thorn thought about the question for a mo-ment. "I think he's going to make his voice heard," he said. "He obviously has something to say, and he has the power and authority to force others to listen. We are definitely going to hear from him again—soon."

THE RESIDENCE OF THE PRESIDENT OF THE RUSSIAN FEDERATION, THE KREMLIN, MOSCOW
That evening

As soon as Valentin Sen'kov left his official residence at the Kremlin, his security and transportation network went into action. Three shell-game groups of three armored limousines departed the Kremlin, with Sen'kov's group in the middle, taking a different route than in times past. Each limousine flew the crest of the president of Russia, so it was impossible to tell which actually carried him.

In general, government flights, especially ones taken by the president, originated from Zhukovsky Airport southeast of Moscow, which was both a military airfield and a government research facility. Two of the shell-game groups headed toward Zhukovsky, each taking a different route. This time, however, the third team broke off from the others and headed northwest, to Sheremetyevo-1 Airport. Normally used for regional and Commonwealth flights, Sheremetyevo-1 was once Moscow's largest international airport—that honor now belonged to Sheremetyevo-2—so it could easily handle large international flights.

The president's motorcade drove into the airport through a side entrance and was picked up by airport security police and MVA Interior Ministry and OMON special-operations troops. It continued on at high speed to a secure ramp area, where a Tupolev-204 medium-range VIP transport was waiting. Sen'kov and his staff members quickly boarded via the main port-side forward airstair. There was no sendoff, no ceremony, no pomp and circumstance. The president of the Russian Federation was greeted by the captain and the chief of the aircraft's security staff, a female OMON officer, and shown quickly to his seat in the rear VIP cabin, along with several of his senior staff.

Once Sen'kov was seated in his plush high-backed seat and positioned for takeoff, he turned to his chief of staff. "General Gryzlov's location?" he asked.

"As of ten minutes ago—in official quarters," his aide replied, checking his notebook. "He made only four phone calls, all to staffers back at his office, routine calls. His computer and cellular phones have not been used. His staffers have made numerous calls, but all callers have been verified and their conversations monitored. Nothing out of the ordinary."

If he was planning a coup, Sen'kov thought, he was doing it very, very quietly indeed. "Is he aware of this trip?"

"If he is, sir, he has not contacted anyone that might be considered unusual or suspect," the aide said. "Minister of Defense Bukayev will contact General Gryzlov when he awakens in the morning and notify him that the president has departed for the summit meeting."

"Everyone else in the cabinet sticking to their schedules?"

"Yes, sir."

For the first time since he left the Kremlin, Valentin Sen'kov could relax. General Gryzlov was obviously too busy with his invasion plans to worry about planning a takeover of the government or of the president's last-minute travel plans. Although it was probably not completely wise to leave Moscow with this showdown brewing between him and Gryzlov, Sen'kov was confident that a meeting with Thomas Thorn would give him the look of a peacemaker and enhance Gryzlov's image as a dangerous and unpredictable berserker. If Thorn was smart and well briefed, he would treat Sen'kov as his equal; that would help keep the Duma—the Russian parliament—and the people on his side so he had a chance of weathering this crisis.

For the first time security forces showed the world that the president was on board the plane as vehicles with flashing lights escorted the Tu-204 to the runway for take-off. Sen'kov felt vulnerable and nervous—he wished the escorts would go away so the VIP transport had a better chance of blending in with all the other airliners. But the Tu-204 was a big plane, there were only three others like it in existence, and they were the only ones with the word RUSSIA painted in big red Cyrillic letters on the side, along with the president's crest on the tail. It made a big enough stir by itself, let alone surrounded by a dozen security vehicles. Before he knew it, though, the huge twin-fanjet transport was airborne, heading northwest on the great-circle route to Iceland.

Sen'kov was finally able to relax. He reclined his seat back, buzzed the galley, and ordered a glass of ice-cold vodka and some toast points and caviar, which were served him in just a few minutes. Sen'kov turned on his computer, checked his messages, and then called up the latest intelligence and cabinet staff briefings. Things actually seemed to be calming down. Even Gryzlov's airpower mobilizations were slowing a bit. Everyone's locations and activities appeared normal—no clandestine meetings, no evacuations, no runs on banks.

Gryzlov still had plenty of time to fuck things up, Sen'kov thought as he sipped his vodka, but right now the government seemed to be plodding along pretty much as usual. He could definitely feel the tension in the air, but perhaps the boiling point had not yet been reached. Iceland was a pretty good place to be right now.

Sen'kov loosened his tie, removed his shoes, turned on a Western satellite-news channel, and munched on caviar—farm-grown caviar, he hoped, not the crap they were still harvesting from the Caspian Sea. He checked the large computer flight-tracking screen on the bulkhead, which plotted out their position and showed their altitude, airspeed, world times, and estimated time en route. They were just over the Gulf of Finland, safely out of Russian airspace. He was tired, but he needed a little relief from the job before he thought about sleep. Sen'kov briefly considered inviting one of the female OMON security officers back to his private cabin for a little horseplay—she had definitely signaled some interest in some private pleasures, no doubt in exchange for some professional favors—but decided he needed the rest more than he needed—

At that moment the phone buzzed. Sen'kov looked at it strangely. His phone was set on "private" when he didn't wish to be disturbed, and if one of his aides had something very urgent, he would simply walk in and give it to him. Sen'kov ignored the buzzing, knowing that one of his aides or someone in the communications cabin would pick it up—but no one did. Irritated, he picked it up. *"Ko-moo,"* he said curtly.

"Mr. President, you didn't tell me you were departing the capital," General Anatoliy Gryzlov said.

Sen'kov's blood turned cold when he heard Gryzlov, especially using that ominous tone of voice. "What is it, General? Bukayev was going to notify you at dawn. I'm trying to get some rest."

"Try that OMON captain from the Thirty-first Rifles. She told me she was looking for a promotion and a transfer to Kaliningrad," Gryzlov said. "She'll give you anything you wish in exchange—*anything.* Believe me, I know. It was my recommendation that got her promoted to captain and a billet in the presidential security detail."

So Gryzlov *did* have extensive connections in OMON, Sen'kov thought—and he most certainly did in the MVD Interior Ministry as well. Oh, *shit . . .* "You called to tell me about one of your OMON sluts?"

"I called to tell you, Sen'kov, that you broke faith with me and with Russia by not signing that execution order, then blabbing about me to the Americans," Gryzlov said. "I don't appreciate being lied to and having my name smeared to a bunch of Americans."

"Your name is *dead,* Gryzlov!" Sen'kov thundered. He immediately buzzed the outer working area for his aides, then started typing a message on his computer, informing the MVD and OMON security officials to arrest Gryzlov. "I won't tolerate your insubordination any longer! You've threatened me for the last time. I hereby relieve you of duty, General. Have your deputy report to the Defense Ministry for instructions. You will be confined to quarters. If you submit your resignation and retirement request immediately, I won't press for a court-martial."

"How generous of you, Sen'kov," Gryzlov said. "But that won't be necessary. I will depart the general staff this morning—and I will confine myself to the Kremlin White House."

"What are you talking about?" There was no reply to his buzzer, and the e-mail wasn't being transmitted. He reached under his desk and hit the "panic button," which was supposed to send every security officer on board rushing into the cabin—but no one showed. He picked up the phone to the cockpit. It rang, but no one answered.

"It is simple, Sen'kov: You're out, and I'm in," Gryzlov said. "Oh, and I would recommend that you do not open the door to your VIP cabin."

"What did you do, Gryzlov?"

"Nothing too dramatic—just a simple slow failure of your plane's pressurization system," Gryzlov said. "Plus, I disabled the cabin altitude-warning lights and the oxygen-generating system. When the cockpit reached four to five thousand meters altitude, your flight crew should have experienced the first symptoms of hypoxia—oxygen starvation—declared an emergency, and donned their oxygen masks. The masks won't work, but they won't have realized that until too late. Everyone in the main cabin should have been unconscious from hypoxia by then, and a few minutes later the flight crew would have succumbed to oxygen starvation. Right about now your plane should be on autopilot, cruising over western Finland with everyone on board unconscious—except you. Remember, don't open your cabin door—your cabin is sealed pretty well against pressurization loss."

Sen'kov leaped to his feet and pounded on the cabin door, but no one answered. He checked the peephole—sure enough, the security guards were sound asleep. *This can't be happening!* he screamed to himself. This was a *nightmare!*

He looked out one of the portholes on the starboard side of the Tu-204 and was surprised to see a Russian air force MiG-29 in close formation with him. He waved, and the pilot waved back. Relieved, Sen'kov went back to his desk, punched another satellite channel, and waited to be connected.

"I have requested that all communications to your flight go through the president's office, Sen'kov," he heard Gryzlov say. "I'm here in your office with the members of the general staff, the deputy speaker of the Duma, and the cabinet. We are all very concerned about your safety, but I'm afraid there's not much anyone can do right now."

"You bastard, Gryzlov!" Sen'kov screamed. "You'll burn in hell for all eternity for this!"

"Not exactly, Sen'kov," Gryzlov said. "What will happen is that you will die when your plane either runs out of fuel or turbulence trips off the autopilot and you crash somewhere between Sweden and the Arctic Ocean. Unfortunately, the air will eventually leak out of your cabin as well, and you'll be unconscious, too, so you probably will not experience the thrill of hitting the tundra or the ocean at terminal velocity or feeling the wings rip off your plane—"

"You're a sick, twisted bastard, Gryzlov. How dare you just snuff out the lives of all these innocent men and women on board?"

"You have one chance to save them, and I'll tell you how you can do it, Mr. President," Gryzlov went on. "You must hold your breath, run to the cockpit, take control of the plane, and then descend below three thousand meters so you can breathe. You would have to descend at, let's see . . . seven thousand meters per minute to make it down in time. The way to do it: pull the power back to idle, lower the landing gear and flaps, lower the nose, and fly in a very steep banked turn. Then you can descend quickly without ripping the wings off. Remember, you'll have about twenty seconds after you let your breath go to do it—that's the average time of useful consciousness with your cabin altitude above eight thousand meters. For the sake of those fighter pilots who are trailing you, you must try it. If you crash, it will be a horrible and terribly tragic accident that will be witnessed by those brave fighter pilots that are feverishly trying to figure out some way to get you down safely. God, I hope they won't be scarred for life. Good luck, Mr. President."

"I suppose all of you were in on this from the beginning?" Sen'kov asked.

"Not right away, but by the time you told the Americans what my plan was, we all agreed that you could no longer lead this country forward," Gryzlov said. "You have been tainted by corruption and have been forced to accede to threats from the United States to survive. We cannot sit by and watch you flush our future down the toilet. Everyone in this room is in agreement. Everyone else—the vice president, the prime minister, the speaker of the Duma, and a few members of the cabinet—well, they cast their vote with their last living breath. Just as you are about to do.

"Now, you had better get going, Mr. President," Gryzlov said. "You'll probably have to equalize pressure between the cabins to open your door. Just flip the red-guarded switch inside the panel on the port side of the door. According to our calculations, if you manage to get control of the plane, you will still have plenty of fuel to make it back to St. Petersburg, or the fighter pilots will lead you to an alternate base in Sweden or Finland with a very long runway. You can still be the hero here, Sen'kov. Oh, and you'd better dress warmly—it's liable to be cold up front. Take several deep breaths before you open the cabin door. To disconnect the autopilot, simply turn the control wheel hard left or right—you'll have to overpower the computer, but you can do it. Pull the throttles back all the way, start a steep turn—forty-five degrees of bank should do—find the gear handle and lower it. You can do it, Mr. President."

"I'll see you in hell, Gryzlov," Sen'kov said. "To the rest of you—I hope you lie awake thinking about what you've done here tonight. The lives of every innocent man and woman on board this plane will be on your heads." He slammed the phone down.

Sen'kov was shaking so hard he could hardly don his overcoat, hat, and gloves. As he dressed, he took several deep breaths to flush the carbon dioxide out of his lungs—

after doing so he found he could hold his breath for about sixty seconds. He rehearsed the route he had to take several times in his head. After nearly passing out from hyperventilating, he found himself remarkably calm. This was possible, he thought. The smug bastard Gryzlov had given him everything he needed to know to do it.

The Russian president went to the door and tried it. Sure enough the higher pressure inside the VIP cabin was holding it closed. He located the pressure-relief switch in a panel behind the door, took several more deep breaths, held it, and flipped the switch. He heard a loud *whisssh!* and a thin fog immediately formed inside the VIP cabin. It was instantly thirty degrees colder. Oh, shit . . .

He flung open the door and started forward. The main cabin was like a freezer. Every man and woman inside had an oxygen mask on—and every one was soundly sleeping. How could anyone—even that sick, homicidal maniac Gryzlov—do such a thing to his *own people?*

It took him just ten seconds to reach the cockpit door—thankfully, it was not locked. The pilots, navigator, and flight engineer, all wearing quick-don oxygen masks, were unconscious. Sen'kov dragged the pilot out of his seat—and nearly jumped out of his skin when the pilot moaned; he'd forgotten that no one on board the plane was yet dead—sat down, and examined the controls and instruments. He recognized the artificial horizon and the altimeter—the metric one read eleven thousand six hundred meters—saw the red line on the airspeed indicator, and found the throttles and gear handle. He grasped the control wheel and tried to turn it, but the autopilot fought back. He turned harder, but it fought harder. He finally yanked it over with all his might. A red light marked MASTER CAUTION snapped on, and another red light marked AUTOPILOT DISCONNECT came on. Forty seconds to go.

He pulled the power to idle, grabbed the gear handle

and pulled it down. More red lights—he didn't try to identify them. He grabbed the control wheel and pushed the nose over. The airspeed needle immediately crept toward the red line. What had Gryzlov said? Put the plane in a steep bank to keep the wings from ripping off? He turned the wheel left to the first large mark, thirty degrees, and the airspeed stopped increasing but the vertical speed increased. He put in more bank angle, to the next large mark, sixty degrees. The airspeed was actually slowing, and the descent rate was pegged at five thousand meters per minute. "Great! I can do this!"

Then he realized he hadn't *thought* that last remark—he'd *said* it. He couldn't hold his breath any longer. The final clock was ticking now. He was surprised to find he could breathe normally—he thought he'd be gasping for air. Maybe he had more time than he thought.

Sen'kov increased the bank angle even more. Now the altimeter was *really* unwinding. The heading indicator was also spinning wildly, but he didn't care. The airspeed needle was very much lower than the red line—just what he wanted. He pushed the nose even lower. My God, it was *working!* That rat bastard Gryzlov really underestimated him! He saw with glee that one of the fighter jets escorting him was visible out the copilot's side window. Pretty damned fancy flying, he thought. He was in a very steep bank, but the fighter was right there with him as if they were welded together. The altimeter swung past eight thousand, then seven thousand, then six thousand meters, that fast—just a few more seconds and he would do it! Already he was feeling better—my God, he was going to make it!

There! Five thousand meters! He turned the control wheel to the right and was surprised to feel how easy it was to turn. The artificial horizon was spinning like a top that was about to fall off its pedestal. He could breathe! He'd done it! He'd saved everyone on board! Now he could get control of this thing, bring it home, and then exact his revenge on Gryzlov for trying to kill him. The copilot moaned loudly. Sen'kov prayed he would wake up. *"Copilot! Help me!"* Sen'kov screamed. "Wake up, damn you! *Wake up!"*

Four thousand meters . . . three thousand . . . Sen'kov pulled back on the control column. It came back easily enough—maybe too easily. The control column was loose and floppy in his hands. It was hard to stay upright in his seat. Although he felt as if he had things pretty well under control, the plane felt as if it was still spinning. The artificial horizon was flipping and flopping, blurring almost into a continual shade of gray—what was wrong with *that* thing now? Two thousand meters . . . Shit, how was he supposed to stop this thing from . . . ?

"I see. Very well. Instruct them to report their position to the Swedish radar controller, and then they may return to base." Gryzlov replaced the phone in its cradle, then turned to the men around him. "I regret to inform everyone that it appears that President Sen'kov's plane has crashed. The MiG-29 pilots escorting his plane saw him take the controls, then put the plane into a steep spinning dive. The bank got steeper and steeper until the plane entered a vertical spin, from which it was unrecoverable. The pilots observed the president's plane hit the ground through their night-vision goggles."

General Gryzlov took a briefcase from an officer and nodded. The officer removed a key and gave it to the general. "Because of the unexplained disappearance of the vice president, prime minister, and speaker of parliament, the normal order of progression has been interrupted, and I find it necessary to impose martial law in the Russian Federation.

"The first order of business is control of the special-weapons-unlock keys. As you can see, I now have the master special-weapons-unlock code key; Minister of Defense Bukayev still has the secondary key. The nuclear weapons of the Russian Federation are secure.

"We shall inform the people of the Russian Federation and the world of this tragic accident, the heroic efforts of President Sen'kov to save the lives of the crew, and of the smooth, peaceful transition of power. A search will begin immediately for the missing members of the executive and legislative branches. Until then I will assume responsibility for the central government as well as for the defense of our homeland."

Gryzlov stepped behind the president's desk, leaned over it with his knuckles pressed to the smooth top, and added, "Our first order of business: launch an immediate strategic and tactical bomber attack on the city of Chärjew in the Republic of Turkmenistan. I don't want one Taliban sympathizer or foreign interloper alive to threaten us again. We must recapture the oil and gas pipelines in that country and be sure they remain secure. Have ground-invasion forces standing by."

CHÄRJEW, REPUBLIC OF TURKMENISTAN
Less than two hours later

"We're outta here," Hal Briggs said. He had jet-jumped to where Chris Wohl was standing guard with his electromagnetic rail gun. "The folks in Uzbekistan are airborne. We'll rendezvous just before the Afghanistan-Turkmenistan border."

"Outstanding, sir," Chris Wohl responded. "I'd rather not stick around."

"Mount up, then," he said. He then turned to Jalaluddin Turabi, who was speaking with a large group of Central Asian soldiers. "We need to be airborne in just a few minutes, Turabi," he said. The computers in his battle armor translated his words into Russian for him. "What's the verdict?"

"The Turkmen representatives have decided to allow me to lead their armies," Turabi replied proudly. "We are getting ready even now to set up barricades and defenses around Chärjew."

"Well, you deserve it," Briggs said. "I never thought I'd say it, but you're a good man, Turabi. You're a good leader. The Turkmen made a wise choice."

"Thank you for saving my life and helping my fighters, Taurus," Turabi said, using Briggs's call sign while in his Tin Man battle armor. "I will be forever grateful."

"I'll be grateful to you if you'd lead this country out of the dark ages of fundamentalism and help them rebuild themselves," Briggs said. Turabi looked quizzically at him. "I wouldn't want this country to turn out like Afghanistan did under the Taliban."

"I don't know how it will turn out," Turabi said. "If the leaders of this country turn to the Taliban for help in rebuilding this country, I would be happy for that."

"If that happens, I hope we'll never meet again, Turabi, especially if you intend to keep on raiding United Nations convoys," Briggs warned him. "We might find ourselves on opposing sides—again."

"I will remember that, Taurus. But I am Taliban. I will follow my God and the leaders of my clan and try to be a loyal servant—to them, to my family, and my conscience."

"My advice to you: Serve yourself and your family first, and then listen to your chiefs. Their goals may not be the same as yours," Briggs said. "I wish you luck, Turabi—

because if you're ever in my sights, I won't hesitate to blow your shit away. Count on that." He turned and walked toward the waiting MV-32 Pave Dasher, loaded and with its engines spooling up, getting ready for takeoff.

Just then he heard, "Bandits, bandits, bandits. All Battle Force units, this is Bobcat One-three. Numerous bandits inbound, bearing two-niner-zero, one hundred ten miles bull's-eye, very low altitude, speed six hundred knots."

Briggs didn't hesitate. "Tin Men, dismount," he ordered. "Take defensive positions *now!* Everyone else, stay on board." He turned to Turabi and said, "You'd better get your men into shelters, Turabi. The Russians could strike at any moment."

Turabi ran off, waving for the others—Turkmen and Afghans alike—to head for underground shelters.

"We've been ordered to depart!" the pilot of the MV-32 radioed back. "They're still at least ten minutes away—we've got time to make it out."

"I said Tin Men, *dismount!*" Briggs repeated. "Bring your gear! Spread out to the northwest. Dasher, as soon as my men are out, you split. Get across the Uzbek border to Samarkand."

"Damn it, Briggs, we can *all* make it out!" the pilot argued. "Why in hell are you staying?"

"I said *get going!*" Briggs shouted. As soon as the eighth and last Tin Man was out of the tilt-jet aircraft, he jet-jumped to the northwest. The other Tin Men spread out with him, deploying about two miles apart so they could concentrate their firepower, cover as much territory as possible, and avoid being caught in one single-weapon attack. Each Tin Man commando carried an electromagnetic rail gun with plenty of tungsten-steel projectiles, plus a support bag with spare battery packs and spare parts for their battle armor and powered exoskeleton.

The MV-32 Pave Dasher lifted off in a blinding cloud of dust and sand and had just started rotating its engine nacelles from vertical lift to airplane mode . . . when the first Russian cruise missile hit. Several fuel-air explosions bracketed the MV-32 perfectly, creating a gigantic vise-like crushing machine that shattered the tilt-jet aircraft and its passengers and crew into several thousand pieces and slammed it all into the sand.

EIGHT

CHÄRJEW, REPUBLIC OF TURKMENISTAN
A few minutes later

T in Man, Tin Man, report," Briggs shouted into his
commlink. One by one his men reported in. Their
datalinked vital-sign information already showed
them all alive, but he really needed to hear their voices,
too—and he thought it was important for them to hear his.

Last to report in was Chris Wohl himself. "You okay,
Taurus?" he asked.

"Affirmative. But the folks at the airfield got creamed."
Actually, he thought "cremated" might be a better word.
"Everyone, check your gear, check your weapons, set up a
defensive perimeter, and get ready to move out. Top, I expect the Russians are going to move in with paratroopers
next. Figure out likely drop zones nearby and draw us up a
plan to move there."

"Roger."

"Base, this is Taurus. The airfield has been hit by multiple fuel-air explosions," Briggs radioed back to Battle
Mountain. "They came out of nowhere—probably cruise-

missile attacks. Dasher One is out—shit, Base, I can't even see the pieces."

"We copy, Taurus," Patrick McLanahan responded from his Battle Management Center in Battle Mountain. Damn it, he swore to himself, he should've *known* they'd lead off with a fuel-air cruise-missile attack—it's exactly what Gryzlov did in Chechnya and Mary. He should've had all the ground forces move away from Chärjew across the border and then exfiltrate them. "The first wave of Russian bombers is turning northbound—I think they're done for now. We're picking up multiple waves of aircraft still inbound. Could be more bombers launching cruise missiles."

"The fuel-air things won't hurt us unless they drop one right on our heads," Briggs said. "We're far enough away from the airport now."

"Can you find some shelter, Taurus?"

"We're probably safer out here in the open, rather than heading back toward the airfield," Briggs replied.

"Copy that. Any suggestions?"

"I think the Russians are going to turn this entire area into a moonscape, and then they're going to start dropping invasion troops in," Briggs said. "We can spread out to likely drop zones and see if we can tag a few of their drop planes. But if they get a sizable force on the ground, we're done for the day. We can't hold off a massive infantry assault for very long with the weapons we have."

"What about Turabi and his army?"

"They've scattered," Briggs said. "Assuming they survived the Russians' air assault, I think they'll be hightailing it back home."

"All right. Take a look at the topo maps and come up with some guesses as to where they'll insert troops, then deploy to those areas and wait," Patrick said. "We'll watch the satellite and radar imagery and let you know what happens. We have an Air Force special-ops group standing by in Samarkand to evacuate you if necessary. Keep an eye on escape routes into Uzbekistan. If things go to shit any more, you may have to get out of there."

"Believe me, we're watchin' north all the time," Briggs said. The Uzbek border was just fifteen miles from their position, across the Amu Darya River. "Okay, we'll redeploy and stand by for instructions." Then, to Sergeant Major Wohl, "Top!"

"Sir?"

"Do you have that plan ready to move to likely drop zones?" Briggs asked. "I want to bag us some Russian drop planes."

"Already got it laid out for you, sir." Briggs saw the flashing information icon in his electronic visor and selected it. He saw a chart of the Chärjew area, with lines drawn to the northern quadrants, showing the movement and positioning of Briggs and his seven-man Tin Man commando team. Briggs was surprised to see that Wohl had suggested that Briggs himself be deployed to the southeast, to the spot farthest away—three miles away, on the other side of the airfield. "Uh, Sergeant Major—you put *me* on the southeast side? Why don't you just suggest I deploy to Los Angeles or something?"

"Pardon me, sir," Wohl growled. There was no question, even through the satellite datalink, that Wohl was pissed off. "Are you questioning my deployment strategy?" He sounded as if the very thought of Briggs's doing that was too unbelievable to even imagine.

"I'm not questioning your strategy, Top, just the choice of men in each position."

"You are referring to where I positioned you in particular, sir?"

"Damn straight I am. I'm the farthest away from the action! Why?"

"As I understand it, sir, you have just two options: You can accept the results of my years of expertise in planning such assaults, or you can reject my recommendations and plan your own."

"Answer the question, Sergeant Major."

"Yes, sir. First, you are the team leader, and you should not be stuck in the middle of the most likely focus point of the assault. Second, you are the oldest member of the team with the exception of myself—but your relative inexperience cancels out your age advantage."

"That's bullshit, Top—"

"Let me finish, sir. Third, I'm not convinced that the Russians' main axis of attack will be from the north. I think they'd anticipate we'd set up the bulk of our forces to the north. I think there's a very good possibility that they'll try to set up a major flanking force to the southeast, then try a pincer move to either pin us down or push us across the border—or both. If they try that, I want you set up down there to alert us. Now, are there any *more* questions you have about my plan?"

"No, Sergeant Major, there aren't," Briggs replied. He still didn't like being stuck the farthest away, but at least Wohl had some pretty good reasons for doing it. Besides, Briggs thought, Wohl was right: The Russians might just pull a sneaky end-around and try to pin the Tin Men in between two forces. "Good job. Deploy the team per your recommendations."

"Yes, sir. Thank you, sir." He said "thank you" as if he really meant to say "fuck you," but he did it in a nice way. Briggs knew that Wohl liked to be questioned about his plans and tactics, just to show that he knew much more than the officers he worked for knew. "Red Team, check your weapons and gear, lock and load, clear your jump paths, then move out."

One by one the Tin Men started jet-jumping toward their planned positions. Hal Briggs couldn't help it—he stood and watched as his men flew out of their places of concealment, their weapons at port arms and their equipment bags slung across their backs, with a not-quite-upright stance. They flew about thirty feet in the air, trading altitude for distance. At the apogee of their flight, they transitioned to a feetfirst fall, still at port arms. A second hiss of compressed air signaled when they were about to hit the ground as they used a shorter, less powerful burst of air to arrest their fall. They really didn't need to stop their fall with their powered exoskeletons, which could dampen out the shock of the fall very well, but unless there were enemy soldiers nearby, they were instructed to use compressed air to slow their descent rate to avoid overstressing the exoskeletons. Each man flew about one hundred feet. Chris Wohl, the biggest man on the team, flew a bit less; Hal Briggs, the smallest man, usually flew the farthest.

If it weren't so serious, Hal thought as he watched them jet-jump away, it would be comical. They almost looked like big gray fleas jumping across the desert. But they were going off to fight a vastly superior force that was undoubtedly coming to smash them. If they were successful, lots of Russians would die; if they were not, they would be captured and certainly taken to Russia for interrogation.

If they were smart, they'd be running north, to the relative safety of Uzbekistan.

"Are you having a senior moment, sir?" Chris Wohl radioed half angrily, half sarcastically. "Or do you feel like questioning my deployment plan again before you get your ass in gear?"

"Bite me, Sergeant Major," Briggs said, the pride evident in his electronic voice. "I'm good to go."

BATTLE MANAGEMENT CENTER, BATTLE MOUNTAIN AIR RESERVE BASE, NEVADA
A short time later

"Sir, I think you should reconsider."

Secretary of Defense Robert Goff shook his head. He was on the secure videoconference link with Patrick in the Battle Management Center, his image on one of the monitors at Patrick's station. "It's not going to happen, Patrick," Goff said. "The president is pretty firm on this: He wants Maureen Hershel and President Martindale out of there and protected, your forces packed up and headed back to Battle Mountain, and that's it. I'm sorry about your men aboard that tilt-jet aircraft, but the president doesn't want any other action in Turkmenistan. If your men have the capability to get out of the area safely and make it into Uzbekistan, we have men and aircraft standing by to get you to Samarkand, and then we can airlift you home. It's only—what, fifteen, twenty miles to get across the border? You guys should be able to do that in a few minutes, the way you move."

"Sir, the Russians just bombed our position with fuel-air explosives," Patrick argued. "We're watching several more formations of jets, probably more heavy bombers followed by medium bombers, already inbound—"

"You told me that already, General," Goff interrupted irritably.

"It's only a matter of time before the Russians send in a ground-invasion force," Patrick said. "They can take Chärjew with ease once they've flattened everything else."

"That's not our problem."

"The Turkmen have voted to accept Jalaluddin Turabi as their armed-forces commander," Patrick said. "He can organize the Turkmen army to hold off the Russian invasion— *if* we help them."

"General . . ."

"If we don't help them, sir, they'll destroy Chärjew just like they wiped out Vedeno in Chechnya and Mary in Turkmenistan," Patrick went on angrily. "Gryzlov will just keep launching bombers and sending in troops until he's taken the entire country."

"General, that's *enough*," Goff snapped. "The president has ordered you out of there."

"But, sir . . ."

"Are you not hearing me, General? Don't you get it? There's no government in Turkmenistan anymore, Patrick—that's been taken over by the Russians! Their army was led either by Russians or Taliban fighters—and now the Russians have executed their president. It won't help your argument for the president, the Congress, or the American people to learn that the Taliban are now in charge of their military."

Patrick fell silent. He knew there was no use in arguing any longer.

"Get your guys out of there, and do everything you need to do to protect Hershel's return."

"Yes, sir," Patrick replied.

"Again, sorry about your tilt-jet crew, Patrick. The president and I will send our condolences to the families."

"Thank you, sir." Goff terminated the connection. Patrick threw his headset on his console desk and leaned back in frustration.

"Hal has redeployed his guys around Chärjew, waiting on the Russian airborne. He does not have permission to open fire yet," David Luger, seated in the vice commander's seat next to Patrick, said after a few moments' silence. "It's too hot to send in any special-ops guys there, if you're thinking about an exfiltration, but they can hop on out of there pretty easily. Once they're north of the Amu Darya River, they're fairly safe—it's a clear shot to the Uzbek border."

Patrick was silent for several more long moments. He then pressed some buttons on his keyboard, calling up status reports on all of the men and women, aircraft, satellites, and weapons under his command. Several minutes later he put his headset back on. "Rebecca? Daren?"

"Go ahead, sir," Rebecca Furness responded. "We're both up."

"I hope you two have had your crew rest."

"Oh, shit—I don't like the sound of that," Rebecca responded.

"I'm in!" Daren Mace shouted happily. "What do you want destroyed, sir, and when?"

MILITARY COMMAND CENTER, SIVKOVO, RUSSIAN FEDERATION
Two hours later

"Eta lehchi chim dva paltsa abassat," Colonel General Yuri Kudrin, division commander of the Second Bombardirovchnyi Aviatsionnaya Diviziya (Heavy Bomber Division), Engels Air Base, radioed with a laugh in his voice. "It was easier than pissing on two fingers, sir."

Kudrin was the commander of the organization that held operational control of the Russian Federation's heavy-bomber and support regiments west of the Ural Mountains: Tu-160 and Tu-22M bomber regiments and an Ilyushin-78 air-refueling regiment at Engels Air Base; one Tu-22M bomber regiment at Belaja Air Base near Kirov; one Tu-22M and one Tu-95 "Bear" bomber regiment at Razan Air Base southeast of Moscow; and one Tu-95 bomber regiment at Mozdok Air Base in Chechnya. He had planned this raid on Chärjew in record time, launched a large bomber force with minimal preparation and brief-ings, and had been wildly successful. Now he was ramp-ing up his entire division at Engels, preparing to surge his bomber forces full speed to destroy any opposition in Turkmenistan.

"No fighters up there?" General Anatoliy Gryzlov asked. He was speaking with Kudrin via secure satellite link from the command center in the underground fortress at Sivkovo, southwest of Moscow, built only recently to replace the command center at Domededovo, which had been destroyed in a clash between Russian and Lithuanian bombers several years earlier. "Not even surveillance radar?"

"Not a squeak, sir," Kudrin replied. "All of the sorties are back, and not one of them was highlighted—not even search radars. The only radars up at all were from units controlled by our ground forces in Mary."

"Did the fighters keep up with you?"

"We had no problem with our fighter escorts," Kudrin replied. "We took one squadron from the One-eighty-sixth Fighter Regiment at Astrakhan all the way to the launch point, but they were bored waiting for something to happen."

"Any trouble from Baku radar?"

"We were never within their airspace, sir. We stayed out over western Kazakhstan and west of the Aral Sea, then a straight shot across Turkmenistan to Chärjew. No radar coverage in that area at all. We didn't need electronic jammers."

"What support do you need for the follow-on attacks, General?"

"Only one: more fighter protection for Engels Air Base, sir," Kudrin said. "I'd like at least another air-defense reg-iment in the area, preferably using the civil airfield at

Saratov. Engels is definitely full now: The second strike team will be over Chärjew in about two hours, and I've got a third team ready to launch in fifteen minutes, just before the first strike team lands at Engels. We've got over one hundred heavy bombers flying out of here now every ten hours."

"All of your bombers are launching out of Engels?" Gryzlov asked. "Isn't that risky? If the Americans attack, won't that disrupt all your attack plans?"

"The Tu-22Ms already require one prestrike and one poststrike refueling launching out of Engels, sir," Kudrin replied. "If they launched out of Ryazan or Belaya, we'd need to give them an extra prestrike refueling. Coordinating all those launch and rendezvous times became too time-consuming and cumbersome. Engels has plenty of fuel and weapons—all they needed were the airframes."

"General, I didn't put you in charge so you could cut corners and make life less time-consuming and cumbersome for yourself," Gryzlov said. He didn't want to sound too angry—Kudrin was one of his most experienced air force commanders—but this plan didn't sound right at all. He had a very bad feeling about this. "If you need more tankers and more mission planners, ask for them. I don't want to overload Engels's resources, and I sure as hell don't want all our bombers knocked out by one attack on one base."

"Yes, sir." Gryzlov heard a frantic passing and rustling of papers, then, "In that case, I'd like to gain the tankers and fighters from the Eight-fortieth Fighter Regiment at Lipeck and the Ninetieth Fighter Regiment at Morozovsk," Kudrin went on. "I'll deploy the Eight-fortieth to Morozovsk, and we can set up another air-refueling anchor near Volgograd for the Tu-22Ms coming from Belaya and Ryazan. The fighters can use the refueling anchor as well."

"Now you're saying what I want to hear, General," Gryzlov said. Kudrin worried too much about the wrong things sometimes—but usually all he needed was a little push in the right direction and he was back in step. "Your request for those units is approved—you'll have authorization to deploy those regiments immediately. You're doing good work out there. Let me know if you need anything else." There was no reply, just the clicking and beeping of digital static. Oh, well, Gryzlov thought, Kudrin wasn't much of a chitchatter. . . .

SOUTH OF ENGELS AIR BASE, RUSSIAN FEDERATION
That same time

Kudrin had hung up the phone in a hurry because, at that moment, he received the first warning that his base was under air attack.

"Search radar, SA-10, twelve o'clock, forty miles," Daren Mace reported. "Coming quickly into detection range. Let's step it on down, Rebecca."

Rebecca pressed the command button on the control stick of her EB-1C Vampire bomber and spoke: "Terflew clearance plane one hundred feet." The Terflew, or Terrain Following, system commanded the autopilot to fly lower until the aircraft maintained at just one hundred feet aboveground—less than a wingspan's distance away. "Clearance plane set. How are we doing?"

"Shit, that SA-10 is going to nail us," Daren said. The terrain in this area was completely and utterly flat, with only a slight rise north of the Volga River. Daren hit his command button. "Launch two TALDs."

"Launch two TALDs, stop launch," the computer responded. Seconds later two devices resembling large, fat

lawn darts ejected from a bomb bay in the Vampire's tail and began gliding away. The TALDs, or Tactical Air Launched Decoys, were small gliders with electronic emitters on board that, when activated, appeared as gigantic, slow-moving aircraft on an enemy's radarscope.

"Still tracking us," Daren said. "It's got us and the TALDs together. Our trackbreakers can't shake it."

"Hang on," Rebecca said. "Terflew off." She jammed the throttles to full afterburner and hauled back on the stick. The Vampire bomber shot skyward at fifteen thousand feet per minute.

"That's good . . . that's all we need." They were passing five thousand feet—way too high with an SA-10 in the area. "Rebecca, let's get our nose down, we're *too high!*"

"Warning, SA-10 height-finder, twelve o'clock, twenty-five miles," the threat computer reported in a silky female voice. Seconds later: *"Warning, missile launch, SA-10 . . . warning, missile launch, SA-10!"* The computer announced four more missile launches—an entire SA-10 launcher unit had just opened fire on them.

"Break right!" Daren shouted. Rebecca threw the Vampire bomber into a hard right turn. "Full countermeasures!"

"Countermeasures active," the computer responded. From canisters in the tail, a bullet-shaped device unreeled itself at the end of an armored fiber-optic cable. The ALE-50 towed decoy was an external antenna for the Vampire's jammers, designed to move the source of the bomber's jammers away from the aircraft itself in case an enemy's antiaircraft weapons could home in on the jamming.

The first SA-10 missile went right for one of the TALDs and scored a direct hit. The other three SA-10 missiles guided right for the Vampire bomber. The defensive computer system released two more TALDs, and one SA-10 guided on it—it was too inviting a target to ignore. Flying at three times the speed of sound, the last two SA-10s were only seconds away from impact. . . .

"Break left!" Daren shouted. Rebecca instantly reversed her turn, flying toward the oncoming SA-10 missiles. But because of the turn, the towed decoy slowed down and moved sideways, making itself an even larger target. Both SA-10s guided on this big fat target, one hitting the towed decoy and the other detonating as it hit the debris field of its brother.

"Give me a right one-eighty and let's get away from here," Daren said. He unreeled a second towed-decoy array as Rebecca turned south. "SA-10 radar still tracking, six o'clock, twenty-three miles." The modern Russian SA-10 antiaircraft system could control as many as twelve four-missile launcher vehicles and engage up to six targets simultaneously with two missiles per target—they were definitely still not out of the woods. "Base, did you take a picture yet?"

"Got it coming in now," David Luger responded from Battle Mountain Air Reserve Base. "The NIRTSats just downloaded the images. Stand by." Days earlier Patrick McLanahan had ordered a constellation of NIRTSats—Need It Right This Second Satellites—inserted into a low earth orbit, designed to cover the region between Engels in Moscow—the largest bomber base in Russia and the origin of the air attacks against both Chechnya and Mary in Turkmenistan—and the Arabian Sea. Sixteen NIRTSats were launched four at a time from a rocket carried aloft by a modified DC-10 aircraft and inserted into their orbits. The TV-size satellites contained high-resolution synthetic-aperture radar sensors that could see and identify objects as small as an automobile from eighty miles in space. Sixteen satellites meant that one satellite passed over the area every three minutes.

The problem was, the images were high-resolution

radar images—they saw everything that could reflect radar energy, including decoys and other targets that looked like threats, and threats could easily be concealed inside buildings or even simple shelters. The only way to draw the decoys out to plot their position was to give them something to shoot at. The cruise missiles carried by the Vampires—FlightHawks, StealthHawks, and Wolverines—were too small and stealthy to fool a strategic surface-to-air missile battery. They needed the real thing.

The SAR images were downloaded to Battle Mountain's BATMAN Center and displayed on the large screens. The computers picked the most likely targets and quickly displayed them. "There it is," Luger said. The image he was looking at definitely showed a standard brigade-level SA-10 engagement battery: a command-launcher vehicle, its four missile tubes already erect; two more simplified launcher vehicles, separated by about two miles from one another, only one of which had its tubes raised to launch position; a radar vehicle; a towed, mast-mounted radar for detecting low-flying aircraft and cruise missiles; and several service vehicles, including trailers with extra missiles and cranes to lift the reloads onto the transporter-erector-launcher vehicles. Other SAR images showed the front-level command vehicle, about six miles away, which coordinated the activities of several SA-10 engagement brigades.

"Nice to see you guys," Luger said. He rolled a set of crosshairs onto the command-launcher vehicle and pressed a button. The geographic coordinates of the vehicle were instantly transmitted via satellite to the Vampire bomber and loaded into the attack computer. He repeated the process with the rest of both the SA-10 brigade and the front-level vehicles in order of priority. "I got all my pictures, guys. I'm ready anytime."

"Set three hundred clearance plane," Daren said. When

they climbed to the proper altitude, he said, "Here they go." Daren uploaded the target coordinates to the weapons in the aft bomb bay. The bay held a rotary launcher with eight AGM-165 Longhorn Maverick missiles. The two-thousand-pound Longhorn missile had a two-hundred-pound thermium-nitrate warhead, a two-stage solid-rocket motor that gave it a range of almost sixty nautical miles, and an imaging-infrared guidance sensor. Once he'd programmed the target coordinates, Daren ordered, "Attack commit Longhorn SA-10 brigade."

"Attack commit Longhorn, stop attack," the computer responded. After a short pause the aft bomb doors opened, and one by one the Longhorn missiles were shoved into space. After they'd fallen about sixty feet, their rocket motors ignited and the missiles shot ahead, then arced over and above the Vampire bomber and headed back for the SA-10 missile site.

Thirty seconds before impact the Longhorn missiles began transmitting imaging-infrared images via satellite to both the Vampire bomber and to the Battle Management Center back in Battle Mountain. David Luger recognized the very same SA-10 brigade photographed by the NIRTSats just minutes earlier. The Longhorn's crosshairs were only a small distance off the command-launcher vehicle. He used a trackball to move them back on target, then locked them on. "Got target one," Luger announced.

"I got targets two and three," Daren said. He was looking at the infrared images being transmitted from the second and third Longhorns in a window on his supercockpit display. Again the crosshairs needed only slight adjustments to bring them dead on target, and he locked them on. Daren then switched to the first Longhorn, and he was able to watch as the Longhorn missile got closer and closer to the command-launcher vehicle, destroying it moments later. "Good hit on target one! Yeah, baby!" he crowed. Targets two and three were destroyed shortly thereafter, and the SA-10 threat from that site was gone. There were other SA-10 batteries in the area, and Luger loaded their coordinates as well, but they were far enough away at the moment to be a threat. They needed the Longhorn missiles to knock down any threats closer to their target complex.

Daren selected a waypoint on his supercockpit display. "SA-10s are down. We're heading in, guys. Center up, Rebecca. Clearance plane two thousand." She made a hard right turn toward Engels Air Base. With the surface-to-air-missile threats reduced, they could afford to climb a bit higher to stay away from any optically guided antiaircraft artillery sites that might pop up in front of them.

Now that the SA-10 site had been destroyed by Longhorn missiles, the road was clear for an attack on the base itself. From then on, the Vampire bomber was little more than a manned missile-launching truck. David Luger had already identified two large antiaircraft artillery sites near both ends of the base's long runway, and Daren fired a Longhorn missile at each of them and destroyed it moments later. One Longhorn took out the base's surveillance-radar antenna, and the last two missiles were sent into the middle of the petroleum-storage facility, setting the entire complex of storage tanks afire.

But the main target was still alive—Engels's huge inventory of bombers, poised to strike Turkmenistan again.

The center bomb bay contained a rotary launcher with eight AGM-177 Wolverine cruise missiles. The turbojet-powered cruise missiles had three internal bomb bays that could hold a total of three hundred pounds of ordnance, plus a fourth high-explosive warhead section. The Wolverines had been preprogrammed with their own "mission" to fly, so it was just a matter of flying within twenty miles of Engels Air Base, opening the center bomb bay, and letting them go. They were not as fast or as pinpoint-accurate as the Longhorn missiles, but they were perfectly suited for this mission.

One by one the Wolverine missiles flew over Engels's twelve-thousand-foot-long runway, northern taxiway, and the mass aircraft-parking ramp, about two thousand feet aboveground. As the missiles cruised in, they dropped small canisters on parachutes. Called the CBU-97R Sensor Fuzed Weapon, or SFW, each canister had a small radar sensor in the nose that detected targets below, and it would steer itself and rotate its business end at its targets according to images picked up by the tiny radar. At a computed point in its fall to earth, the SFW canister detonated. Ten copper disks instantly melted and fired from the front of the canister, aimed toward the detected targets below. The white-hot blobs of molten copper could pierce steel up to three-quarters of an inch thick. But as the copper slugs pierced the outer armor they cooled, preventing them from blowing out the opposite end. The result: Each blob of molten copper became thousands of red-hot BB-size pellets that ricocheted around inside at the speed of sound, creating an instantaneous but deadly meat-grinder effect.

On Engels's runway, taxiways, and aircraft-parking ramp, the result was devastating. Each SFW canister could hit as many as ten targets—aircraft, vehicles of all sizes, or buildings. Each bomb bay on the Wolverine cruise missiles held nine SFW canisters. The Wolverine would eject one SFW canister every few seconds as it cruised across the airfield, emptying one bomb bay per pass. Then it would orbit away from the base, turn around, fly down the runway or taxiway from a different direction, and drop another bomb bay–ful of SFWs.

The timing of the attack was perfect: The ramp and taxiways were choked with thirty-two Tu-22M Backfire and Tu-160 Blackjack bombers preparing for takeoff.

For the next twenty minutes, the eight Wolverine cruise missiles assaulted the base, staggering their attacks so that they deconflicted each other and so that the SFWs would not attack the same target. The results were spectacular and horrifying at the same time: When a Wolverine missile made a pass, the ground below it would suddenly erupt into a carpet of stars as the SFW did its deadly work, followed by explosions and a burst of flame; then the effect was repeated a few dozen yards away as the next SFW detonated. The Wolverines' orbits changed slightly each time so there was no risk of a missile's being targeted by ground fire or of its attacking targets that had already been struck. When the Wolverine's three bomb bays were empty, the missile itself plunged into a final fixed target, detonating its internal high-explosive warhead on support buildings and hangars near the runway, power substations, communications buildings, nearby bridges, and weapon-storage areas.

While the Wolverines did their damage, Rebecca Furness and Daren Mace had their own job to do—get their Vampire bomber out of Russia alive.

Daren activated the Vampire bomber's LADAR, or laser radar, arrays, which instantly "drew" a high-resolution picture of the world around the bomber in all directions for a hundred miles. Each LADAR "snapshot" took only two seconds but produced an image that was of nearly photographic quality—accurate enough to measure objects, compare their dimensions with an internal catalog, and identify them within moments.

"LADAR picked up a flight of four MiG-29s, five o'clock, thirty-three miles, our altitude," Daren reported. "Second flight of two MiG-25s at nine o'clock, high, forty-seven miles, coming in at Mach two." The Vampire bomber automatically turned slightly right to present a thinner profile to the MiG-29s and to point its hot exhausts away from the MiGs as well in case they attempted a shot with a long-range heat-seeking missile.

"Come and get us, kids," Rebecca said. She hit the voice-command button. "Best speed power profile."

"Best speed power," the computer responded. The computer immediately set full military power and started a steep climb. The higher it flew and the faster it reached a higher altitude, the greater its average speed would be.

"MiG-29 radar lock-on, twenty-five miles," Daren said. He hit his voice-command button. "Attack commit MiG-29s."

"Attack commit MiG-29, stop attack," the computer responded. It immediately turned farther right, almost going head-to-head with the MiGs, then opened its forward bomb-bay doors and ejected four AIM-120 Scorpion air-to-air missiles. The missiles dropped several yards below the Vampire, then ignited their solid-rocket motors, shot ahead, picked up the datalinked steering information from the Vampire, and began the chase. As soon as the missiles were away, the attack computer turned the bomber to the left and back on course.

The Scorpion missiles followed the steering signals until about ten seconds from impact, then activated their own onboard radars. The Russian MiG-29 pilots never realized they had been fired on until that moment, and their survival depended on their reaction. In combat-spread formation, each pilot had a specific direction to evade and enough room to do it. All he had to do was execute, without more than a moment's hesitation.

The pilots that survived were the ones who reacted immediately when the threat warning blared—dropped chaff and flares and turned to their evasion heading as fast as they possibly could. Once the Scorpion missile switched to its own internal terminal guidance radar, it was easily spoofed—akin to walking along normally at first, then walking while wearing blinders. The Scorpion's radar locked on to the biggest, brightest, and slowest-moving radar reflector within its narrow field of vision—which for two of the four MiG-29s happened to be the cloud of the radar-reflecting tinsel called chaff they left in their wake. But the other two MiG pilots were more worried about losing sight of their leaders or screwing up their formation work than about saving themselves, and the Scorpion missiles clobbered them easily.

Daren flashed on the LADAR once again after the Scorpions' missile-flight time ran out. "Two Fulcrums down," he reported. "Man, we sure—"

"Warning, missile launch MiG-25 AA-10, eight o'clock, high!" the threat computer reported.

Rebecca immediately threw the Vampire bomber into a tight left turn. At the same time Daren ordered, "Attack commit AA-10 and MiG-25!"

"Attack commit AA-10 and MiG-25, stop attack," the computer responded. As soon as the bomber rolled almost wings-level, the attack computer opened the forward bomb doors and launched four AIM-120 Scorpion missiles. The first two were aimed at the large radar-guided AA-10 air-to-air missiles fired by the MiG-25 "Foxbats." The Foxbats immediately peeled away after launching their missiles. Like the Scorpion missile, the Russian AA-10 missile had its own radar and locked on to the EB-1 Vampire when less than ten seconds from impact. Heading nose-to-nose with the oncoming AA-10, Rebecca started a series of vertical jinks, trying to get the Russian missiles to overcorrect and blow past the Vampire.

Successfully attacking an air-to-air missile with another air-to-air missile was a long shot—and in this case completely ineffective. Both Scorpions harmlessly detonated well away from the faster Russian missiles.

The first AA-10 missile flew just a few yards under the Vampire and hit the towed array as it homed in on the jamming signals from the array. The second AA-10 looked like it might miss as well, passing over the Vampire by a scant few feet, but it steered itself on target at the last moment and detonated right between the fuselage and the trailing edge of the right wing.

"Crap, we lost the number-four engine, and number three looks like it has a compressor stall," Rebecca shouted. But the power-plant computers had already reacted: They had shut down the destroyed engine, brought the power on the number-three engine back to idle, then trimmed out the adverse yaw in the bomber by adjusting its adaptive skin. The computer also shut down the affected hydraulic, pneumatic, fuel, and electrical systems. Seconds later it automatically attempted a restart. "Damn it, number three's not restarting. I think the computer's going to shut it down in a sec—" Just then the FIRE NUMBER 3 warning light winked on, then off as the computer shut down the engine and cut off fuel. "There it goes."

"Looks like a flight-control fault on the right. We're losing both the number two and the emergency hydraulic systems," Daren reported. "Weapon computers reset . . . bomb-door malfunction . . . looks like no more Scorpions today."

"Base, this is Bobcat."

"We see you, Rebecca," David Luger said from Battle Mountain. "Continue your left turn to heading two-niner-five. Your bogeys will be at your twelve o'clock, sixteen miles, same altitude, two MiG-29s. We're trying to analyze the malfunction in the number-three engine. If we can find it, we'll attempt a restart from here."

"You got some help up here for us, Base?" Rebecca asked excitedly. At that instant, they saw a spectacular flash of light directly in front of them, followed by a spiral of fire that spun down into the darkness below. "Never mind, I see it." An unmanned Vampire bomber orbiting over Kazakhstan's airspace miles southeast of Engels Air Base had fired ultra-long-range AIM-154 Anaconda air-to-air hypersonic missiles at the MiG-29s from over 130 miles away. The missiles had been fired at maximum range *almost two minutes earlier* and were just now finding their targets.

But at that extreme range, even with a sophisticated laser-radar attack system and ultraprecise guidance systems, the weapons were not perfect. The Anaconda missiles fired from the unmanned air-defense Vampire missed the fourth MiG-29 and one of the MiG-25 Foxbats bearing down on the stricken Vampire bomber—and moments later the MiG-29 opened fire from short range with two AA-11 air-to-air missiles. The AA-11 missile was Russia's most maneuverable and most reliable antiaircraft missile—but it didn't need to be to hit Rebecca and Daren's EB-1C Vampire bomber. One missile detonated just aft of the number-one and -two engines; the other missile punched away most of the Vampire's vertical stabilizer.

The warning and caution panel was lit up like a keno board. Rebecca now had both hands on the control stick, trying to keep her Vampire under control.

"You got it, Rebecca?" Daren shouted.

"Shit . . . damn it . . ." She never answered, but she didn't need to—Daren could tell that she'd lost control. "I am *not* going to lose this plane . . . !"

"Time to jump out, Rebecca," Daren said, managing to reach over and touch her hand. "It's over. You did a good job—*we* did a good job." She continued to fight the controls, but it was no use. The attitude indicator began to spin; the spin was verified by the rapidly unwinding altimeter and the pegged vertical-velocity indicator. Even the flight-control computer offered no suggestions. Rebecca's Vampire was indeed dead. "Let's get out of here."

Rebecca swore, then gave the controls one more try. She saw the altimeter go below two thousand feet aboveground—and she couldn't even tell which way was up anymore. "Get out!" she shouted. "Get the hell out."

Daren nodded, straightened up in his seat, put his hands on his armrests.

He stood, and pushed his chair back. Rebecca followed right behind him. They squeezed past the technician at the console right behind the aircraft commander's seat and looked at the flight-path depiction on his computer screen. The Vampire had just hit the vast floodplain of the northern Caspian Sea coast. "Impact," the technician said. "Couple miles north of Lake Aralsor in Kazakhstan. You flew almost seventy miles with virtually no flight-control system and just two engines, and she still took three Russian missiles before she finally went down. That area is pretty marshy, and the plane was in an almost vertical spiraling dive—it may have buried itself a hundred feet into the mud."

Rebecca studied the monitor, checking to see if the plane had gone down in an uninhabited area. As far as she could tell, it had. She opened up a bottle of water, took a deep swig, and passed it to Daren. "Crap—I hate losing a plane," she said. "Even if it is a *robot* plane."

Daren gave her a kiss on the cheek, then opened the door to the portable virtual-cockpit control cab. The small warehouse in which the VC had been set up on the tropical island of Diego Garcia was supposed to be air-conditioned, but the heat and humidity they felt as he opened the door were still oppressive. To them, though, after the past five hours in the VC, it felt glorious. Right beside them was a second VC, which another crew was using to control the unmanned air-defense EB-1C Vampire.

"Just remember, Rebecca," Daren said, smiling as he took her hand and stepped out of the cab, "any landing you can walk away from is a good one."

"Shut up, Daren," she said. She smiled back, realized he was still holding her hand—and she gave his a squeeze. "Just take me to my room, get me a drink, get this flight suit off, then take me to bed."

"Don't we have to debrief our mission or something?"

She rolled her eyes in exasperation, pulled him to her, and gave him a kiss. "You have your orders, mister," she said with an inviting smile. "Carry them out."

"Yes, *ma'am*," he said.

OUTSIDE OF CHÄRJEW, REPUBLIC OF TURKMENISTAN
That same time

"Contact, two troop choppers inbound," Hal Briggs reported. "I've got three more attack helicopters coming in farther south."

"We've got a total of six troop and four attack helicopters inbound from the northwest," Chris Wohl said. "The troop helicopters are outside the range of my weapon. They look like they're unloading."

"Three attack helicopters to the southwest," another of his commandos reported. "Looks like they came right over the city. They . . . they're firing, Red Team, attack helicopters opening fire with antitank missiles. Incoming, incoming."

Hal Briggs steadied the electromagnetic rail gun using

his powered exoskeleton, centered the helicopter in his electronic sights, and was about to squeeze the trigger when all three attack helicopters opened fire on his position. He immediately jet-jumped away seconds before a half dozen AT-16 laser-guided antitank missiles hit at exactly the spot where he'd been hiding a second ago. "Looks like they got some longer-range missiles on those choppers—they fired from almost six miles away," Hal said. He studied his electronic tactical display—almost every one of his men had to dodge missiles launched at them. Whatever sensors the Russian attack helicopter gunners were using, they were extremely effective.

Hal immediately jet-jumped toward where he thought the troop helicopters had touched down. He found the group of two transport helicopters, one Mi-6 and one Mi-8, just as they were lifting off after offloading their troops. Hal raised his rail gun and was about to fire on the larger Mi-6 when the earth erupted just a few feet in front of him. One of the Russian Mi-24 attack helicopters had found him and had opened fire with an antitank missile, narrowly missing him. The rail gun was blasted out of his hands, and he flew thirty feet through the air from the force of the missile explosion.

Hal was able to get to his feet. The rail gun was gone. When he looked up, he heard it—the unmistakable sound of the heavy Mi-24 Hind attack helicopter bearing down on him. His suit registered a laser beam hitting him. He was being targeted with a laser-aiming device from the Hind. Less than two miles away—it couldn't miss now. . . .

Suddenly two small missiles streaked through the sky and hit the Hind helicopter from either side. The big chopper's engines exploded, and it plummeted to the ground, cartwheeling for over a mile before the wreck of burning, twisting metal finally came to a stop.

"Ho there, my friend!" he heard a voice shout in Russian. *"Byt v glubokay zhopi,* eh, Comrade Robot?" It was Jalaluddin Turabi. He was holding an SA-14 manportable antiaircraft-missile launcher. He handed the expended weapon to an aide and took back his AK-74 assault rifle. "Fancy meeting you here!"

"What are you doing here, Turabi?"

"We were busy retreating, getting out of Chärjew before the Russians dropped a nuclear bomb on us next," Turabi said. "But then we ran into your little party here, and we thought we'd crash it. You don't mind, do you?" He retrieved his portable radio and a map and issued orders in Pashtun. Moments later the desert around where the Russian soldiers had just alighted was obscured by mortar and grenade blasts. Several more shoulder-fired missiles flew through the sky, knocking down Russian helicopters.

"I think this would be a good time to get out of here, my friend," Turabi said. "My men are scattered pretty thin. We can't hold the Russians off for long."

Just then Hal heard a beeping sound in his helmet. He shifted his electronic visor to mapping mode—and what he saw made him smile inside his battle armor. "Not quite yet, Turabi," he said. As Turabi watched in puzzlement, Briggs simply stopped and stared at the Russian exfiltration spot, then turned and stared for a moment at another Mi-24 attack helicopter, about five miles away. "Where else have your men made contact, Turabi?" he asked.

"They are everywhere," the Afghan replied. "They are coming from all directions. They—"

At that moment the Hind helicopter that was turning and lining up for an attack run exploded in a ball of fire. Seconds later the ground where the Russian soldiers were advancing on them disappeared under dozens and dozens of small but powerful explosions.

"We are under attack!" Turabi shouted.

"Not quite," Briggs said. He pointed skyward. Turabi looked—just as a small, dark StealthHawk unmanned aircraft passed overhead. "Our little buddies are back." As they watched the StealthHawk fly away, it launched an AGM-211 mini-Maverick missile on another Hind, shooting it out of the sky.

"Well, I never thought I'd be happy to see those devil birds again," Turabi said. "I don't suppose they could inform us as to where our friends the Russians are now?"

"They can indeed," Briggs said. He took Turabi's chart and a grease pencil and, using the electronic map projected onto his visor, drew the locations of all the known Russian airborne troops on the ground in the area. "Need some help with them, Turabi?" Briggs asked.

"If you would be so kind as to take care of the attack helicopters with your devil birds up there," Turabi said after he reported the Russians' positions to his men deployed around Chärjew, "my men can take care of the infantrymen." He extended his hand and smiled broadly, his teeth gleaming white against his dark, burned skin. "I believe that makes us even now, doesn't it, Comrade Robot?"

Hal Briggs couldn't help but smile inside his battle armor. "Yes, we're even, Turabi—I mean, *Colonel* Turabi."

"I am happy enough just being Turabi, thank you," he said. "Now, if you don't mind, we have a city to defend. If you would kindly exit my battlefield by the most expeditious route, my army and I will get to work."

"Sure thing—*General* Turabi," Briggs said. The Taliban fighter smiled, nodded, and hurried off to lead his men into battle once again.

EPILOGUE

We have your aircraft, we have your air raid on Engels Air Base on tape, and we have footage of your drones and bombers attacking our base," General Anatoliy Gryzlov shouted into the phone. "This is a complete outrage! An unprovoked sneak attack on a Russian military installation by two American strategic bombers! It is an act of war! We have your dead crew members as positive proof that you attacked our country in a sinister act of aggression!"

"You have our crew members?" President Thomas Thorn asked. He had to stifle a smile.

"Their crumpled bodies were found not far from the crash site," Gryzlov said. "Their pictures will be on the front page of every newspaper and magazine on earth if you do not halt this aggression and immediately recall all your forces!"

"As I told you, General, I have already recalled our forces," Thorn said. "My forces were deployed to Turkmenistan only to protect our deputy secretary of defense's flight as it departed the region. We had permission and full authority from President Gurizev to enter Turkmenistan."

"Gurizev was a liar and a traitor to his people," Gryzlov said. "If he hadn't allowed those murderous Taliban forces to roam around inside his country so freely, none of this would've happened. They were certainly in collusion. Soon they would have stolen those American oil and gas pipelines and wells from you, but by then it would have been too late to stop them."

"The Taliban commander has just been commissioned by the new Turkmen president as commander of the army," Thorn pointed out. "He's being called a hero for repelling those Russian troops from Chärjew."

"He'll have to pay dearly for that," Gryzlov said. "I don't care if the Turkmen parliament or so-called interim president authorized or sanctioned his attacks after the fact. It was an act of cold-blooded murder."

"It seems to be a legal resolution to me, General, voted on and signed into law by the interim president."

"That new president was not elected by the people," Gryzlov said, "and a state of martial law is still in effect."

"But the Turkmen parliament meeting in Uzbekistan has voted in a new interim president," Thorn said. "Surely the Russian military authorities will recognize the new government and allow the president and legislators back into the country safely?"

"You're getting off the point of my call, Thorn—namely, the air attack on my military base!" Gryzlov interjected. "The death toll will certainly reach two hundred, and the damage will easily exceed one billion dollars. You will issue an apology to me, to the men and women of Engels, to the people of Russia, and to the world. You will pay reparations to alleviate the suffering of the families who lost loved ones in that dastardly attack and to rebuild what you have destroyed. You will *pay,* or, by God, Thorn, I will see your country burn hotter than the fires of hell. Do you understand my meaning, Thorn?

What is your answer? Will you apologize? Will you pay reparations? Or does a state of war exist between our two countries?"

"Stand by, General." Thomas Thorn put the call on hold, then looked at the others in the Oval Office with him: Vice President Busick, Secretary of Defense Goff, Chairman of the Joint Chiefs Venti, Deputy Secretary of State Hershel, General Patrick McLanahan, and former president Kevin Martindale. They had all been silently reacting to Gryzlov's tirade with scowls, astounded expressions, and shaking heads. Everyone was amazed that the president managed to keep his cool so easily while talking to this homicidal maniac.

"Tell him to go fuck himself, Mr. President," Busick said. Everyone else seemed to agree, some by encouraging expressions, others by nodding heads. "He's a damned nobody—he can't tell the president of the United States what to do."

Thorn looked to his friend and chief foreign-affairs adviser, Robert Goff. "He's nothing more than a two-bit military strongman, Thomas," the secretary of defense said. "Eventually the Russian parliament and the people will rise up and toss his ass off—it's just a matter of time. The United States needs to lead the resistance against him, or he'll turn into another Stalin."

Thorn turned to McLanahan and Martindale. Both wore stony expressions. Martindale jabbed a finger at Thorn and said, "You're the leader of the free world, Thorn, whether you like it or not. *Be* the leader of the free world, for Christ's sake."

Thorn remained expressionless. He looked at McLanahan impassively—Patrick thought he detected a bit of resentment or maybe betrayal in the president's face. The president pushed the line button. "General Gryzlov?"

"What is your answer, Thorn?"

"My answer is this: The United States will pay reparations," Thomas Thorn said. Busick, Martindale, and even his good friend Robert Goff wore absolutely stunned, then disgusted expressions.

Even Anatoliy Gryzlov sounded surprised. "Well . . . I'm glad to see you show some common sense, Thorn," he said.

"The United States will pay a sum to the government of the Russian Federation equal to what the Russian Federation pays to the United Nations to rehabilitate and rebuild the government and infrastructure of Turkmenistan," Thorn said. "In case any hostilities break out between Russia and the United States, the money is cut off forever."

"What? Russia *pay* the United Nations to rebuild Turkmenistan?" Gryzlov retorted. "What kind of deal is that? That pissant country was about to be taken over by Taliban desert rats—we *saved* it from ending up like Afghanistan or Pakistan! We've already invested trillions in that country. We're not going to invest one more ruble into it! Is this what you mean by taking responsibility for your actions, Thorn?"

"I hope you'll reconsider, General," Thorn said. "The United States will pledge twenty million dollars to help rebuild Turkmenistan, in the hopes that Russia will match that gift, and we shall also pledge the same amount for the families of the victims of our attack.

"As far as an apology goes—yes, I will apologize to the people of the Russian Federation and the world," Thorn went on. "In my apology, which will be broadcast live around the world, I will explain why we conducted the attack on your bomber base: I will explain about how your Russian liaison officer murdered President Gurizev; how Russia firebombed Mary, as it did Chechnya, to kill Muslims—"

"That is a lie!" Gryzlov shouted.

"—and I will tell how you sent a Russian fighter plane to shoot down an American diplomatic mission, and how you sent a massive armada to bomb a small city in Turkmenistan into submission so you could invade it with hundreds of airborne commandos," Thorn continued. "I will explain why we chose Engels Air Base as our target— because Russia was massing over one hundred supersonic long-range bombers there to continue pounding Turkmenistan into the sand so you could walk in and take over."

"You call that an apology, Thorn?" Gryzlov retorted.

"I call it the truth, General," Thorn said. "I'm willing to admit to the truth—the question is, are you?"

"This matter is not settled between us, Thorn," Gryzlov said in English after several long moments of shouting and epithets in Russian. "You will not be permitted to wantonly attack a Russian military base like that—a Russian *bomber* base. In case you don't know, I was a bomber commander—your striking that target was like striking at my own children." There was a slight pause, then, "May I speak with Major General Patrick McLanahan, please?"

The president turned toward Patrick, switched on the speakerphone, then said, "Go ahead, General. General McLanahan can hear you."

All eyes were on Patrick. "What is it, General?" Patrick asked.

"I know it was you who planned that strike on Engels Air Base, McLanahan," Gryzlov said. "You spoke with General Kasimov and told him precisely which Russian targets in Turkmenistan were going to be struck and when—you could know all that only if you were in direct command of those attacks as well. This is the same McLanahan who participated in the air attacks against Russian forces in the Balkans and near Zhukovsky Flight

Test Center recently. This is also the same McLanahan who participated in attacks against Russian military forces in Lithuania and, I presume, even participated in the attack against the Kavaznya laser ballistic-missile defense site in Siberia some years ago. I am sure that, with a little analysis, we can probably trace your involvement in many other significant covert military actions by the United States over the years—China, Taiwan, Iran."

The surprised expressions turned into shocked expressions. Most of those in the room knew a little about a few of Patrick McLanahan's military adventures—but *no one,* not even former president Kevin Martindale, knew that Patrick had participated in almost *every* major wide-scale conflict throughout the world over the past fifteen years.

"We could go on and on about your past, General," Gryzlov said. "In Russia you would be a national hero, perhaps even president. Why in your own country you are nothing more than an insignificant Air Force officer with no real responsibilities or authority is a mystery to me, but it matters not.

"I am here to tell you here and now, General Patrick McLanahan, that we are enemies, you and I," Gryzlov went on with an amused but ominous sneer in his voice. "You have used your bomber forces masterfully over the years, and you may have a technological edge. But you are weak because of weak commanders like Thomas Thorn. As long as you are led by men such as him, you will be powerless to stop me when I move against you. I will see to it that you are destroyed, General. Your friends, your bases, your crews, your aircraft—even your precious son, Bradley—will all be destroyed before finally you, too, will be destroyed. You will be destroyed because you mindlessly follow weaker men, thinking it is your duty to obey their orders. It will destroy you and all those around you that you love."

"Listen, you son of a bitch, if your own officers and people don't get you first, we sure as hell will!" Vice President Busick shouted. "You're nothing but a two-bit generalissimo."

"It will be my bombers against your bombers, General McLanahan," Gryzlov went on, ignoring Busick. "The battle will be on my terms, on my home court. You cannot choose where and when the battle will take place, because you are too weak to do so, and you are weak because you follow weak leaders. So gather your planes and drones and missiles together like a child in his playpen, General, and get ready for the showdown."

"Bring it on, General Gryzlov," Patrick said, but the line had already gone dead.

For several long moments everyone in the Oval Office was stunned into silence. They had never heard someone openly and so brazenly threatened like that before during an official government phone call. Finally Vice President Busick said, "Mr. President, I'd like to discuss this idea of paying reparations to the Russians—"

"The attack on Engels Air Base was not approved," the president said. "General McLanahan may have misinterpreted directives from Secretary Goff, but I don't think so. I believe that the attack on Engels was deliberate and calculated. Whatever the final outcome, the mission was not sanctioned. We have a moral obligation to repay the Russians for the damage."

"*Like hell,* Mr. President!" Busick shouted. "We don't owe them *squat!* They started this whole thing—we just helped finish it. The general may have jumped the gun a little, but he did exactly what he thought was needed to be done to protect our guys out there."

"General, is that the way you see it?" Thorn asked.

Patrick looked at Thorn, then at Martindale, and finally back to Thomas Thorn. "No, sir—there was no misunderstanding," he replied. Both Martindale and Busick closed their eyes in frustration, and even Robert Goff shook his head sadly. "I was ordered by Secretary of Defense Goff directly to get my forces out of Turkmenistan after Deputy Secretary of State Hershel's flight was safe. My ground forces were only fifteen miles from the Uzbek border—they could have been picked up easily, before or after the attack on Chärjew. Instead I kept my ground forces in place and planned an air attack on Engels."

"Because you *knew* that Gryzlov was going to launch more attacks on you."

"Yes, sir, but mostly because I wanted to hurt Gryzlov," Patrick admitted. "I wanted to defeat his bombers on the ground. I wanted to strike into the heart of Gryzlov's bomber force. I had the weapons and the opportunity, so I took it."

Thorn looked at each of his advisers in turn, then said angrily, "That's why we're paying reparations to the Russians, folks. America might be accused of being a bully every now and then, but when we screw up like that, we should at least have the guts to admit to it and pay for our mistake." He and everyone in the room fell silent. "That will be all, everyone."

Kevin Martindale stepped up to Thomas Thorn, looked him in the eye, shook his head, and said derisively, "You're going to be a pushover next fall, Mr. President." He turned to Patrick and said, so everyone including Thorn could hear him, "Don't let him get to you, Patrick. Gryzlov is right—but it doesn't mean it has to stay that way. Keep on fighting the way you know how to fight."

Finally it was just Thorn and McLanahan left in the Oval Office. Thorn looked at the two-star general. "You're dismissed, too, General," he said. Patrick looked as if he was about to say something, but Thorn held up a hand. "Don't say anything, General—I know you won't mean it anyway. Just get out. Go home and give your son a hug. Take him to the beach. I'll decide what to do with you later."

Patrick left the White House and made his way to the West Wing gate. As he waited to be let out, he heard a car horn beep behind him. Maureen Hershel rolled down her window in the backseat of her limousine. "Give you a lift somewhere, General?" she asked.

Patrick looked at her, then stood and looked back toward the Oval Office—and was surprised to see Thorn looking back at him through the window, the phone to his ear but still watching him intently. Patrick took a deep breath, confused and, yes, a little uncertain.

"C'mon, General," Maureen said. "I could use a drink right about now—and you look like you could use one too."

Patrick McLanahan stood at attention and saluted the Oval Office. The president saluted back, then returned his attention to his phone call. Patrick dropped his salute with a snap, smiled, and nodded. "I'd love to, Maureen," he said. "I'd love to. Let's go."

SHADOW COMMAND

By

DALE BROWN

Available in hardcover
June 2008
From William Morrow
An Imprint of HarperCollins *Publishers*

ARMSTRONG SPACE STATION
February 2009

"Okay, suckers, c'mon and poke your head out—just a little bit," Captain Hunter "Boomer" Noble muttered. "Don't be afraid—this won't hurt a bit." This was day two of their new patrol, and so far they had squat to show for it except for a persistent headache from watching the sensor monitors for hours at a stretch.

"Hang in there, sir," Air Force Master Sergeant Valerie "Seeker" Lukas said gaily. "You're anticipating, and that negative energy only *keeps* their heads down."

"It's not negative energy, Seeker, whatever *that* is," Boomer said, rubbing his eyes. "It's that TV picture—it's killing me." Hunter rubbed his eyes. They were staring at a wide-screen high-definition image of a suburban section of the southeast side of Tehran, in what used to be called the Islamic Republic of Iran but was now referred to by many in the world as the Democratic Republic of Persia. The image, shot from a telescopic electro-optical camera mounted aboard a U.S. Air Force RQ-4 Global Hawk unmanned reconnaissance aircraft orbiting at sixty thousand feet above the city, was fairly steady, but every shake no matter how occasional felt like another pinch of sand thrown intro Boomer's eyes.

The two were not sitting at a console in a normal terrestrial combat control center, but in the main battle management module of Armstrong Space Station, positioned two hundred and seventy-five miles above Earth in a forty-seven degree inclination easterly orbit. Noble and Lukas were among four additional personnel brought aboard to run the U.S. Air Force's Air Battle Force monitoring and command mission over the Democratic Republic of Persia. Although Boomer was a space veteran, with several dozen orbital flights and even a spacewalk to his credit, floating in zero-G staring at a monitor was not what he joined the Air Force for. "How much longer are we on station?"

"Just five more hours, sir," Lukas said, smiling and shaking her head in mock disbelief when Noble groaned at her reply. Seeker was an eighteen-year U.S. Air Force veteran, but she still looked barely older than she did the day she enlisted in January 1991 when Operation Desert Storm kicked off, and she loved her profession just as much now as she did back then. The images of laser- and TV-guided bombs flying through windows and down ventilator shafts fascinated and excited her, and she started basic training two days after graduating from high school. She joined every high-tech optronic sensor school and course she could find, quickly becoming an all-around expert at remote sensing and targeting systems. "Besides the powerplant, environmental, and electronic systems, the most important systems in strategic reconnaissance are patience and an iron butt."

"I'd rather be out there flying myself," Boomer said petulantly, readjusting himself yet again on his attachment spot on the bulkhead in front of the large monitor. He was a little taller than the average American astronaut that most of the instruments on the space station were obviously designed for, so he found almost everything on the station just enough of the wrong size, height or orientation to irk him. Although the twenty-five-year-old test pilot, engineer, and astronaut was a space veteran, with dozens of orbital missions and even a few spacewalks to his credit, most of his time in space had been spent strapped into a nice secure spaceplane seat at the controls, not floating around in zero-G. "All this remote-control stuff is for the birds."

"You calling me a 'bird,' sir?" she asked with mock disapproval.

"I'm not calling anyone anything, Master Sergeant—I'm giving this particular procedure my own personal opinion," Boomer said. He motioned to the screen. "The picture is really good, but it's the radar aiming thingy that's driving me nuts."

"That's the SAR aiming reticle, sir," Seeker said. "It's slaved to the synthetic aperture radar and highlights any large vehicle or device that appears in the sensor field of view that matches our search parameters. If we didn't have it, we'd have to manually scan every vehicle in the city—*that* would really drive you nuts."

"I know what it is, Master Sergeant," Boomer said. "But can't you make it stop darting and flitting and shaking around the screen so much?" The monitor showed a rectangular box that appeared and disappeared frequently in the scene. When it appeared, the box surrounded a vehicle, adjusted its size to match the vehicle, and then if it matched the pre-programmed size parameters a tone would sound and the camera would zoom in so the humans could see what the computers had found. But it would only stay focused on one vehicle for five seconds before starting the wide-area scan again, so Boomer and Seeker had to almost constantly watch the screen and be prepared to hit the HOLD button to study the image before the computer jumped out again. "It's giving me a damned headache."

"I think it's incredible it's doing what it's doing, sir," Seeker said, "and I'm more than willing to put up with a few jiggles if it helps us spot a . . ." And at that moment the computer locked onto another vehicle, which had just appeared atop a parking structure beside a cluster of apartment buildings. Seeker slapped the HOLD button a second later. "Hey, we got one!" she shouted. "It's a Katyusha . . . no, I think it's a Ra'ad rocket! We got them setting up a Ra'ad!"

"You're mine, suckers," Boomer said, instantly forgetting all about his purported headache. He glanced at the monitor, but he was already busy making sure the target coordinates obtained by the Global Hawk were being uploaded properly. The live image was incredibly detailed. They watched as four men carried a large rocket, resembling a large artillery shell with fins, out of the parking garage to the back of a Toyota pickup truck—it must've been very heavy, because it appeared they were having difficulty carrying it. The pickup had a large steel skeletal pedestal mounted in the pickup frame, with a circular cradle atop it. The men rested the rocket on the back of the truck, then two of them hopped up and they began struggling to lift the rocket up to the launcher.

"Don't drop it, boys," Seeker said. "You wouldn't want to spoil our fun, would you?" She turned to Boomer. "How much longer, sir?"

"Target coordinates uploaded," Boomer said. "Counting down now. How long do we have?"

"Once they get it up into the launcher, it could be fired in less than a minute."

Boomer glanced up and watched the monitor. Several children ran up to the truck to watch the terrorists at work—at first they were shooed away, but after a few moments they were allowed to get a closer look. "Looks like 'Career Day' is on in Tehran," he said gloomily.

"Get out of there, kids," Seeker murmured. "It's not safe for you there."

"Not because of us," Boomer said coldly. He hit a transmitter button on his console. "Ripper to Genesis."

"I'm right here, Boomer," responded Lieutenant-General Patrick McLanahan, "standing" on the bulkhead behind Boomer and looking over his shoulder. The twenty-one year Air Force veteran and three-star general was the commanding officer at Elliott Air Force Base, Groom Lake, Nevada, the home of the High Technology Aerospace Weapons Center, or HAWC. HAWC developed the XR-A9 Black Stallion spaceplane, along with countless other air weapons and aircraft, but it was leaders like Patrick McLanahan that saw the capabilities and possibilities of those experimental devices and brought them to bear in crisis situations where America or her allies would otherwise suffer tremendous losses or even defeat. Short, husky but not large, with disarming blue eyes and a quick smile, Patrick McLanahan did not at all resemble the hard-charging, determined, audacious globe-crossing aerial bombardment expert and master tactician portrayed by his reputation. Like Boomer and Seeker, McLanahan was becoming a veteran astronaut—this was his third trip to Armstrong Space Station in as many months.

"We've got a good one, sir," Boomer said, nodding at his monitor. "Not a little homemade Qassam or Katyusha this time, either." Boomer studied the young three-star Air Force general's image carefully, noticing his eyes flicking back and forth across his monitor—not just looking at the rocket, Boomer thought, but at the kids clustered around the makeshift terror weapon launcher. "The master sergeant thinks it's a Ra'ad rocket."

Patrick appeared as if he hadn't heard him, but a few moments later nodded excitedly. "I agree, Seeker," he said. "A Hezbollah weapon, based on a Russian battalion-level battlefield attack missile. Two-hundred-pound warhead, simple but usually effective barometric fuze, airburst with a backup impact detonation, killing radius a hundred yards or more, usually loaded up with glass, ball bearings, and pieces of metal along with high explosives to increase the injury toll. A real terror weapon." He shook his head. "But there are too many civilians around. Our ROE says no non-combatant casualties and minimal collateral damage. Pick a different target, Boomer, one with fewer bystanders. There will be plenty of opportunities . . ."

"We don't see many Ra'ad rockets, sir," Seeker said. "That's not a homemade rocket—that's a military-grade short-range ballistic attack missile."

"I know, Master Sergeant, but our orders are specific and . . ." At that moment the insurgents shooed the children away again, more forcefully this time, as another insurgent fitted ignition wires to the tail end of the rocket in final preparation for launch. "*Now,*" Patrick snapped. "Take it down."

"Yes, sir," Boomer said enthusiastically. He issued commands on his computer, checked the computer's responses, then nodded. "Here we go . . . missile counting down . . . doors coming open . . . ready . . . ready . . . now, missile away."

He checked a countdown timer. "Don't anyone blink, 'cuz this won't take long."

Over the Caspian Sea two hundred and twenty miles north of Tehran, an unmanned EB-1D Vampire bomber opened its combined forward and center bomb bay doors and released a single large missile. The D-model Vampire was a modified U.S. Air Force's B-1B strategic bomber, converted by the High Technology Aerospace Weapons Center to a long-range unmanned flying battleship. It was capable of autonomously flying itself from takeoff to final parking with an inflight-reprogrammable flight plan, or could be flown by satellite remote control like a large multi-million dollar video game from a laptop computer located almost anywhere.

The missile the Vampire had just released was an even more sophisticated weapon developed by the engineers at HAWC. Its unclassified designator was the XAGM-279A SkyStreak, but anyone who knew anything about this missile—and there were only a handful of persons on the entire planet who did—called it the "Streaker." It resembled a cross between a bullet and a manta ray, with a pointed carbon-carbon nosecap and bullet-shaped forebody splaying out into a thin, flat fuselage and pointed tail section. After stabilizing itself in the atmosphere, four solid-fuel rocket motors ignited, pushing the weapon to well past Mach 3 and one hundred thousand feet of altitude in just a few seconds.

Within eight seconds the motors had burned out and a wide, flat oval air intake popped open underneath the missile. Supersonic air was ingested and compressed by the shape of the now-empty rocket motor casings, mixed with jet fuel, and ignited by high-energy pulses of laser energy. The resultant energy propelled the missile to over ten times the speed of sound in just a few more seconds, and the missile ate up the distance between its launch point and its target in no time, climbing to two hundred thousand feet as it raced downrange. The missile burned all of its jet fuel in just a few seconds, and it quickly decelerated and began descending back through the atmosphere. Once the outside skin temperature was within safe limits, the bullet-shaped forebody detached from the spent propulsion section, which automatically blew itself to bits moments later.

Small stabilizer finds popped out of the forebody, and it became a supersonic re-entry vehicle, guiding itself to its target with its onboard navigation computer refined by Global Positioning Satellite signals. Fifteen seconds to impact, the protective nosecap detached, revealing a combination millimeter-wave radar and imaging infrared scanner, and the warhead began uploading video signals via satellite to Boomer and Seeker back in Dreamland. The steering cue in the video image was several yards off, but Seeker used a trackball and rolled the steering rectangle back on the pickup truck, which sent steering correction signals to the warhead.

The video image from the warhead was sharp and clear all the way to impact. Patrick had a brief glimpse of a young man, no more than fifteen or sixteen years old, wearing a mask and carrying an AK-47 assault rifle that looked almost as big as he was, who looked right up at the incoming weapon milliseconds before the image vanished. Patrick knew that the warhead was programmed to explode a tenth of a second before impact, splitting the warhead apart into thousands of small hypervelocity fragments, increasing the killing radius of the weapon out to about forty to fifty yards.

"Direct hit!" Boomer shouted happily. He looked at the control monitor and slapped his hands together. "Total time from detection to impact: forty-eight point nine seconds. Less than a friggin' minute!"

"It's more like a Maverick missile—or a sniper's bullet—only fired from *over two hundred miles* away!" Seeker exclaimed. She had switched back to the Global Hawk's image of the target area and zoomed in to take a close look at the

Streaker warhead's impact spot. "Pretty good urban weapon effects, sir, exactly what you were hoping for. A really good-sized hole, about fifteen to twenty feet in diameter—looks like the center punched through the concrete parking garage roof into the floor below—but no damage to the nearby buildings that I can see except for a few broken windows. Even a two hundred and fifty pound Small Diameter Bomb might have caved in the sides of the building facing the blast."

"With no explosive warhead on the Streaker, there's nothing there to create any collateral damage," Boomer said. "We put just enough shaped explosive charges in the warhead to break it apart milliseconds before impact, and that was both to increase the weapon effect slightly as well as to destroy as much of the evidence as we could. All they should find are tiny pieces of . . ."

"Oh . . . my . . . God," Seeker breathed. She had zoomed out to survey a little more of the surrounding area. There were clusters of people, perhaps two dozen or so, just outside the apartment complex area lying on the sidewalk and street, with others attending to them, waving frantically for help. "What in hell happened here? Where did those people come from, and why are they lying on the ground like that? Are they from inside the apartment complex . . . ?"

"The Streaker must've set off the Ra'ad rocket's warhead," Boomer said. They all carefully studied the image as Seeker took manual control of the camera and zoomed in. "But what's going on? Those people over there weren't anywhere near the blast, but they're staggering around like they were hit. Was it shrapnel from the Ra'ad warhead? The Streaker doesn't have an explosive payload—it's all kinetic energy. Is the Persian army moving in? What's going . . . ?"

"A chemical weapon cloud," Patrick said.

"*What* . . . ?"

"It looks like some sort of chemical weapon cloud, spreading out from the target area," Patrick said. He pointed to the monitor. "Not more than thirty feet away. Here's a little bit of the cloud . . . see, it's not rising like a cloud from an explosion or from heat, but traveling horizontally, blown around by air currents." He looked closer. "Not twitching . . . it's hard to tell, but it looks like he's rubbing his eyes and face and is having trouble breathing. I'll bet it's a blister agent . . . lewisite or phosgene. Mustard agents would take longer to incapacitate someone, even in high concentrations . . . look, now someone collapsing across the street. Jesus, the warhead must've had several liters of CW in it."

"My God," Seeker gasped. "I've been operating remote sensors for almost twenty years, and I've never seen anyone die from a chemical weapon attack."

"I have a feeling the powers-that-be aren't going to like this," Patrick said.

"Should we recall the Vampire, sir?"

"Hell no," Patrick said. "We still have three more Streakers on board, and another Vampire loaded and waiting to go at Mosul. Keep on scanning for more insurgents. Congratulations, Boomer. The SkyStreak worked perfectly. Nail a few more insurgents for us."